MW00613751

CHASING GOLDIE

HOLLY ROBERDS

CHASING GOLDIE

HOLLY ROBERDS

CONTENTS

BOOKS BY HOLLY ROBERDS

VEGAS IMMORTALS

Death and the Last Vampire

Book 1 - Bitten by Death

Book 2 - Kissed by Death

Book 3 - Seduced by Death

The Beast & the Badass

Book 1 - Breaking the Beast

Book 2 - Claiming the Beast

DEMON KNIGHTS

Book 1 - One Savage Knight

Book 2 - One Bad Knight

LOST GIRLS SERIES

Book 1 - Tasting Red

Book 2 - Chasing Goldie

Book 3 - Igniting Cinder

THE FIVE ORDERS

Book 0.5 – The Knight Watcher

Book 1 - Prophecy Girl

Book 2 - Soulless Son

Book 3 - Tear in the World

Book 4 – Into Darkness

Book 4.5 - Touch of Hell

Book 5 - End Game

* For recommended reading order, visit www.hollyroberds.com

Dedicated to the plus sized baddies who know their worth...and who would also enjoy being railed by bear shifter.

CHAPTER I

SWEARING OFF THE D

GOLDIE

"I am beautiful. I am capable. And I am swearing off men—mage, fae, and human alike," I announce.

"If you can actually do that," Cinder retorts in her usual deadpan tone. I shoot a quick glare over my shoulder at my friend.

Everyone's a freaking critic.

The warm hues of the early morning slide past the windows of the car as our little trio drives in the direction of my new destiny. Driving from Boston into the suburbs, the trees multiply, explosions of greenery that signal summer is in full swing.

"Really? No men, at all?" Red's light gray eyes flicker with skeptical mirth, even as they stay fixed on the road. "Not even the ones that look like princes but turn out to be warty, nasty toads?" Her voice is raspy. I'd kill for that seductive huskiness. The red of her sweatshirt matches the brilliant crimson of her hair that earned her the nickname.

"I mean it, this time," I stress. "No more being blinded

by good hair and flattery." Frustration and vulnerability seep into my voice. "It's not like I want to date all these losers. But every time I meet someone new, all I see is potential." A wistful sigh escapes me.

A *pop* accompanies the round lollipop exiting Cinder's mouth. "You do tend to see the best in people. Even when they have red flags exploding out their butt from the get-go."

I adjust the top of my bubblegum pink top before nervously twirling a blonde curl to keep it bouncy. Though we are not speaking his name, I know they both are expecting me to get back together with Lawrence.

We've been on and off again for the last six months, and when we're off, I am like a serial dating machine until Lawrence comes sniffing around again. But I'm not going to fall for it again.

Lawrence has been 'voluntarily unemployed' since I've known him, always complaining bitterly about how he's too smart for a nine-to-five job.

Initially, I'd been drawn to his dreams about starting his own business. He painted big, beautiful pictures of his future with his words.

His castles in the air match mine. I have big dreams of err. . . having big dreams.

Like with men, I tend to bounce around with ideas of what's going to fulfill my ultimate destiny. I jumped majors at Boston University four times. I went from the department of microbiology of Fae beings, to Magic historical studies, before broadening to business then architecture. That doesn't even include my dabbling in cosmetology, a yoga teacher training, or the countless applications I've sent to reality TV dating shows.

Whenever I get swept up in the rush of excitement over

either a guy, or a new business venture, it always wears off almost as soon as it starts.

I decided to take the semester off so I could sort out exactly what the faefucks I was doing before wasting my hard-earned bar tips on more college credits I may not even use.

Lawrence's barbs from last week came hurling at me from my subconscious. "You are vapid, flaky, and you bend yourself to be liked by everyone just to make up for the fact you look like a fat, slutty Barbie doll."

Spears of pain shoot through my stomach, jabs that hit on the bullseye of my own insecurities.

My hands fist into the fabric of my pants. I am *not* going to get sick in Red's car.

It's not the first time I'd heard such insults. They'd long ago burrowed under my skin, becoming a part of me until I didn't know if I'd learned to live with burrs sticking into my soul or if I'd made friends with the prickly demons.

With a sniff, I adjust my top and curls again. At least he got the Barbie part right. I remind myself she could do *anything* while rocking pink. I was the edgier version with tattoos and pleather, but maybe I could also be a doctor, an astronaut, and a dog walker at the same time.

Or something far more magical, my subconscious whispers. I wave the thought away, trying to ground myself in the here and now instead of getting swept up in possibilities.

In the time I dated Lawrence, I hadn't witnessed him make a single damn thing other than smoke weed and wax poetic about how he isn't appreciated in a traditional business world.

Then last week we ran into one of his old bosses, and it turned out his unemployment wasn't voluntary at all. In minutes, the run-in turned into a red-faced screaming match between the two where it all spilled out onto the sidewalk. Turns out Lawrence was canned for being an "entitled douchebag."

In the aftermath, I stroked Lawrence's ego, trying to get him back on his feet. He could achieve all his dreams if he took the first step, and I'd be right there to help him.

Next thing I know, I'm the bad guy.

Lawrence exploded that he would have started his business already if it weren't for my neediness.

Apparently, asking to see him more than once a week, show up on time to anything, or not flirt with other women was 'needy.'

Though I think fifty to sixty percent of his verbal assault was fueled by the fact his boss met me for two seconds and went on about how I deserve better, and to give him a call so he could take me out to dinner as soon as I took out the trash.

My tattered self-esteem managed to cling to that interaction, and the Barbie comparison. That, and I managed to avoid sliding into a potentially dangerous pit of despair courtesy of a girls' night with Cinder and Red after we got off shift from the Poison Apple. They plied me with a new cocktail they made in my honor, 'The Golden Ratio,' then took me out dancing until dawn. No one can be sad with a curated buzz while dancing to Taylor Swift's "We are Never Getting Back Together." I suspect Cinder or Red had a little chat with the DJ.

I'm opening a new chapter and in doing that, I can face up to my own part in the toxic relationship. "It should have been a tipoff when Lawrence went on in the beginning about how my extra weight didn't bother him at all. It was always him, never me, who brought it up. And in hindsight,

I can see he was basically jerking himself off for being so high minded to date who he ultimately thought was a fat girl."

What an absolute trash-wad.

A low growl comes from the backseat. Cinder's narrow, violet eyes flash with barely restrained violence.

But still, after so many failed relationship attempts, I'm starting to suspect that I'm the problem.

I must have said it out loud because Red jumps right in.

"It's *not* you. You are beautiful and awesome and an absolute fucking gem. It's just that you seem to have a knack for attracting the wrong kind of guys."

The unladylike snort that comes out of Cinder's nose would rival a bulldog with a severe cold. "He's an inexcusable scum who should be de-sacced with a melon baller."

I shudder. That's a bit vivid for me.

Throwing her long fiery locks back over a slim shoulder, Red frowns. "That and you tend to get a bit. . . "

"Obsessed?" I fill in.

"You haven't found the right fit yet, and it throws you off balance," Red says diplomatically.

"Fuck these guys," Cinder adds in a voice as monotone as ever. "And definitely butt-fuck Lawrence right off a cliff into a pit of ogres and spikes. You don't need them. After all, as of today, you are going to be way too busy to date anyway."

She really isn't wrong, which sends twin spirals of fear and excitement careening through me.

The car comes to a stop, reminding me of the purpose of our little road trip.

For the first time, I'm not chasing an opportunity. This time it landed right in my lap.

In the shape of an unexpected inheritance from my estranged aunt.

Red and Cinder exit the car, but I hold back a moment. Flipping down the mirror, I pull out my lipstick.

Sliding the bright pink across my lips, I gift myself the affirmations I need. "You are capable. You are enough. And you don't need a man." I finish by sending myself a kiss in the mirror.

Hope is a pearlescent bubble, threatening to burst in my chest.

Something *clicks* inside me. It's a quiet but firm feeling, and I know everything is about to change.

Maybe, just maybe, this time I'll get it right.

CHAPTER 2
THIS HOUSE IS JUST RIGHT...FOR A HOMELESS MAN

GOLDIE

Under the blissful shade of the New England trees, I remove my hot pink sunglasses to better take in the view, I breathe, "It's even more perfect than I remember."

"I don't think perfect is the right word here, Goldie," Red says next to me, skepticism evident in her voice. Red, a creature of comfort when away from work, opts for her usual Boston University sweatshirt and jean shorts. Though she is already peeling off her top layer and tying it around her waist. The morning is fast moving into the muggy heat of an oppressive New England summer.

I, on the other hand, chose to dress for the occasion. Or how I imagine one dresses when receiving a sizable inheritance.

In the sweltering heat, my outfit is a bit overkill. Moisture beads at my forehead and between my breasts. I'm wearing black pleather shorts and a pink tank top, paired with a lighter pink suit jacket. I'm already sweating profusely under the jacket, causing it to stick unpleasantly to my arms. I glued rhinestones onto my fuchsia heels to match my sunglasses.

The things I do to step into my Boss Bitch self. It's an important ritual that usually includes my hair curler, and pop music up at full blast. It may be overkill, but I feel armored up.

My getup would make Elle Woods proud. Fuck Lawrence. I looked 'illegally' hot.

An indecipherable grunt escapes Cinder. An oversized black metal band shirt dips past her shorts, making her look like she's not wearing any.

Cinder looks as out of place as a black skull amidst a pile of pastel stuffed animals. The fresh air rushes by us, making her high onyx pigtails sway on either side of her sharp cut bangs.

The three of us stand before the nine thousand square foot, sage green Victorian house I just inherited. Sure, the paint is half peeled away, a lot of the wood looks rotted out, and sure, there is a distinct musty smell emanating from it though we haven't even set foot inside, but I'm going to do what I always do. I choose to LOVE it.

"Come on, it just requires a little vision," I insist with a broad grin.

The front left banister on the porch chooses that exact moment to wail a loud, deathly creak as it falls away from the rest of the structure. It smashes into the wild, overgrown mass of bushes below. The shaking limbs cause three mice to dart out from under it with surprised squeals, before they veer around to burrow under the porch.

My stomach twists in a knot, shooting up into my throat.

Err, at least they aren't spiders. If I name them, they won't freak me out so much. Peanuts, Tuffy, and Robert Hunnington the Third.

There. Already better.

"How did your aunt pass away?" Cinder asks.

"Scuba diving accident in the Poconos."

"Damn," Red whistles. "I'm sorry Goldie."

I shrug. "Thanks, but at least she went doing something exciting and fun. I remember her saying if she had to go, she hoped it was in the middle of one of her grand adventures. Her biggest fear was getting sick and being trapped at home. So I guess she kind of got her wish." And I got a massive neglected Victorian.

Red throws her pale arm around my shoulders. "Well, if anyone can see the bright side of this crumbling wreck, it is definitely you."

"Seconded. It's very...private," Cinder says, taking in the surrounding woods. Then she notices the sizable cabin just down the hill from my new house. "Well, almost."

The large deck spans out from the back of the house, and the Victorian looks right down on it.

I shrug. "It will be nice. Someone to borrow a cup of sugar from. It's going to be completely different from the city."

I'm less than twenty minutes from downtown. Close enough to commute to the bar where we work, but far enough away to be alone and figure my shit out. It's perfect. Out here I will be able to focus and key in on what I really want without any distractions.

"Hey," Red nudges me. "I totally dish out the sugar. And the good coffee grounds, on a regular basis, Ms. Suddenly Forgets The Free Pass And Extra Key She Has."

I giggle and wrap an arm around my friend's waist,

pulling her bony body in against my cushy curves. "I could never forget what a good neighbor you were. I'm keeping that key by the way," I say, giving her a serious look.

"Well, you'll have to give our apartment key back because I need it for the new roommate," Cinder says.

A trill of anxiety goes through me. Cinder claims it's fine that I'm moving out, but I can't help feeling like I'm leaving her in the lurch. Is she secretly holding in feelings of resentment or relief over my moving out?

I shake a hand at my side, trying to get rid of the paranoia and insecurity.

"Can we see the inside?" Red asks.

"I'm dying to see the inside," Cinder says in complete monotone. Anyone else might think she's being sarcastic, but I know her well enough to know she really is excited.

"Duh," I respond, suddenly back to near bursting with excitement.

I lead them up the soft wood stairs to the front door.

I'm already obsessed with the old skeleton key I slide into the lock. It feels like magic. And I always wanted to be a mage. This might be the closest I get to it, though every day I hold my breath, waiting for magic powers to manifest.

After eating 'special' cookies, it's very possible I could develop powers any day.

Red's grandma is world famous, being one of the few level five mages in existence. She made those cookies to help her granddaughter unlock her potential. She wasn't aware that Red was passing the tin of cookies around to Cinder and me.

While Red immediately launched into her power, Cinder and I are left in suspense, waiting to see if we manifest powers too.

So far, zilch.

Cause magic = cool.

But inheriting a big beautiful old house from an aunt I hadn't seen since I was fourteen is pretty dramatic too.

As soon as we enter the house, the three of us burst into coughing fits.

The smell fills my mouth and nose with choking toxicity, making my eyes water.

I jog to the front sitting room and open the windows to air the place out. Once a breeze makes the room semi-breathable, I take it all in.

A thick layer of dust covers the vintage furniture, a chandelier dips down from the ceiling, barely hanging by a wire, and it's possible an animal might have curled up and died somewhere in here, judging by the stench.

"Sweet witchtits," Red exclaims, covering her mouth to keep more dust particles from choking her. "When was the last time your aunt was here?"

"Not since her last marriage. He was number seven, or was it eight?" I can't remember. A tremor of fear races through me, but I shove it down. That won't happen to me. I'm not like my aunt.

"Eight?" Cinder's brows rise.

"I never met any of her men. She wasn't home often, always jet setting somewhere. I mainly got postcards with a picture from whatever cruise or trip she was on with her latest husband. At first it seemed exciting and glamorous," I admit. "But as I got older, and she hit her fourth or fifth husband, I started to realize things probably weren't all roses."

Only because my mom told me that. Whenever I was envious of my aunt, mom would jump in to point out that my aunt wasn't exactly stable. I still couldn't help but be envious of how admired, how worshipped she was by these men. Her life was exciting and so full of fun. Or it felt that way the summer I spent with her in this house.

She might be flighty, but everyone couldn't help but fall in love with her.

But now I understand the reality of her situation. So many attempts at love, even more failure and heartbreak. She never found her person, was never safe to fully love. Never fully loved in return.

My chest twists painfully, recognizing how my storyline paralleled hers eerily close. Falling in love constantly with places, ideas, and men, but none of them sticking.

Lawrence's words return, pummeling the valves of my heart like a punching bag.

Vapid. Flaky.

I suck in a lungful of stale air and try not to feel the bruises form.

Granted, I hadn't married any of my beaus, but that wasn't for a lack of trying. Some of the guys fed me pillow talk about envisioning me in a white dress, or holding their baby one day, but when it came to any real commitment, they crumbled like pecan sandies.

If I got any more desperate or hit a certain age, I also might start collecting husbands and heartbreak like a hoarder.

Fear has me in a chokehold while my numerous broken hearts fight in my chest with jagged edges. Faelords, why does nothing work out for me?

Why can't I find the thing I love? Why can't I find a man to love?

And if I did, would they even love me back?

I swallow hard over my constricted throat, trying to calm myself.

But I've sworn off men, so I won't end up like her, I assure myself.

Still, the fear hugs my skin like sticky molasses. All the expectations, disappointments and possibilities threaten to overwhelm me, pressing on me like a weighted blanket.

Come on, Goldie, let's live in the moment. We are standing at the literal threshold of opportunity.

I'm here with my friends who love and support me. Life is good.

"I think I can flip this place for some good money," I say in a hushed, reverent tone. "Or maybe even turn it into a Bed and Breakfast. It will just take some sweat, equity, and a hella lot of coats of paint."

"You hate sweating," Cinder points out, as she toys with the dirty, plum-colored curtains in the front room.

It's then I notice an absence of air conditioning units. Oh faefucks. I do hate sweating.

Running my fingers on the staircase banister, I leave a clear, clean trail behind. My tips are instantly blackened by the grime.

"Now you've done it," Red says with a small smile. "Now we'll have to clean the rest." She disappears down the hall, toward the kitchen.

"If you think I'm scrubbing these floors, you're out of your damn mind." Cinder shakes her head.

I reach out and give her arm a squeeze. "I would never. I'm only asking you to come over for mimosas once the place is spiffed up." I pause, cocking my head in thought. "Or maybe drink mimosas while watching me work, to keep me company."

Cinder nods solemnly. "I can do that." Then she eyes a neglected broom in the corner, covered in cobwebs. She grabs it, wiping it off with her hands. "I suppose for you, I can sweep." She points a finger at me in warning. "Only one, maybe two rooms."

Before she can say another word, I grab her for a hug and squeeze her tighter than is necessary as a trill of anxiety goes through me. "I promise I'll be the best ex-roommate ever."

I can't shake the fear that my moving out could cause the dynamics to change overnight. I try to tell myself my friend isn't so changeable, but I still can't get rid of the icky little anxiety.

Cinder drops the broom to hug me back. "We'll always be friends, you know that, right?" she says quietly, giving me an extra squeeze. "Even if I don't wake up to one of your baked goods or need you to do my makeup and hair for work."

"Of course," I say, even as something twists in my chest.

I nod, forcing a smile though a bitter memory flashes in my mind—a group of girls whispering, their eyes fixed on me, their laughter sharp and piercing. The fear of being cast out, still haunts me, making moments of reassurance like this both precious and necessary.

Something at the back of my mind calculates how I can be an even better friend to Cinder after moving out, so she doesn't change her mind about that. Periodically showing up with her favorite green tea mochi might just do the trick.

Refocusing on the house, I pause. My heart pounds against my ribs.

What if I fail. . . again? What if everyone was right about me?

I take a deep breath, steeling my resolve. *No. I've worked too hard to give up now. I can do this.*

This place could really be something, and I don't intend to waste the chance.

Potential. This place is nothing but potential.

"Hey girls," Red calls out from the kitchen in an overly nasal voice, like she is plugging her nose. "I found out what died in here."

Okay, potential and a body or two. Nothing I can't handle.

CHAPTER 3
MY BROTHER, THE SLUT

TED

When the leggy, disheveled brunette walks into my kitchen wearing nothing but a man's shirt that nearly hits her knees, I'm not surprised. Pissed as hell, but not surprised.

Her scent slips up my nose before sliding down the back of my throat and spreading onto my tongue. It's an overpowering concoction of cashmere wood, plum, and—*ugh*—sex with my brother.

The downside of having a supernaturally strong sense as a werebear. Smells instantly turn into taste. One of the numerous reasons why I like to live out in the forest is the clean scents.

I continue to sip my coffee and read the paper, my hip resting against the sink, acting like I can't see her.

Unfortunately, she doesn't take the hint.

"Hello, hi there, you must be JJ's brother." The girl who could have stepped right out of a Bollywood film waves a hand to get my attention with a falsely bashful smile. Pointing at the cup in my hand, she asks, "Know where I can get some of that?"

I can't help the heavy sigh from escaping me. "Cabinet over the coffee pot," I say in a gruff voice.

"Thanks." She smiles, tiptoeing past my hand carved table, and clatters around for several moments before she clears her throat.

For faefucks sake.

I set down my paper and roll up the sleeves on my plaid shirt, trying to pretend I don't notice her.

She does it again. I still don't turn around.

Finally, she asks, "Do you have any cream and sugar? Or maybe some sugar-free vanilla syrup?"

Tell her to get out. Tell her she shouldn't be in your house because you like it nice and quiet. Because you are intensely private and hate people so much as looking in the direction of your property, much less being inside your house.

"Cream is in the fridge," I answer in a disgruntled rumble instead.

I may be resentful as hell, but I can't bring myself to be completely rude.

And then horror of horrors, the girl pulls out a chair and sits down next to me.

Why me? What the fuck did I do to deserve this? I grind my teeth as anger and disappointment sit heavy in my gut.

"So where is JJ?" The girl's voice is high pitched with youthful glee. Realistically, she's only a couple years younger than me, but I feel old as shit sitting next to her. Luxurious brown hair falls over her shoulders, her skin glows from the vigorous workout I heard last night. She cozies my black stone mug up to her face, while glancing around with a secret smile, as if my brother might pop out from one of the cabinets at any moment, just to surprise her.

Fucking kill me now.

"He's gone," I say even as I turn my attention back to the paper.

"Gone, where?" Her voice still has that chirpy giddiness.

"Back into Boston, where he lives and works," I explain.

Her perfect, thick brows bunch in confusion. "I don't understand. I thought this was his house."

Godsdamn, I need a mouth guard to keep up with all this teeth grinding.

"Nope," I clarify, bracing myself for what's coming next. "My brother lives in the city. This is my house. He only stays over when he goes to the bars and..."

Her face falls.

Shit. I never get this part right. No matter how many times I've had to deliver the news, I never know the right thing to say to the poor girls my brother finds and bring to my house after a night out in Boston.

While he could easily take them back to his place, he chooses to taxi the twenty minutes to my house that's tucked away in a nice private wooded area.

Except my brother keeps turning my fortress of solitude into a depressing fucking brothel.

JJ complains that if he takes girls back to his place, they don't leave. And as he works from home for his very important tech job, he can't afford the distraction or the hassle of getting them out of the house.

What an absolute prick.

When my brothers finally moved out, I thought I'd finally get some time to myself while still staying close enough to enjoy the bond of our pack. But I wasn't sure if I spent more time cleaning up after their messes now than before they left.

Tears well in the pretty girl's eyes as she looks away, realizing she's been blown off.

How does he do it? Seriously, how?

Some of the girls walk away none the worse for the wear, but why did most of them act like they'd found their soulmate in just one night? Either Freddy truly was as slick as salmon oil, or he was a god in the bedroom.

The urge to vomit presses up into my throat. It was bad enough that I had to hear it. I don't need to visualize as well.

I set the paper down and sigh again, but it's softer this time.

"Do you need me to call you a ride?"

Some of the girls admit to me they can't afford to get back to the city, so I foot the bill. I'm not psyched about it, but no girl will end up stranded on my watch. Especially not in my house.

Turns out I can be selfish and selfless at the same time.

She plasters on an indifferent smile despite watery eyes and flushed cheeks. "No, thank you." She starts to leave the table, but I sense her hesitance as she glances at her coffee mug.

"Take your time with the coffee. I'll be on the back porch if you need anything."

Yet again, I pick up my mug and newspapers, stepping out of the kitchen and onto the expansive deck I built two years ago, right after my brothers moved out. I'd practically raised them in this house, but the minute they left, I started making it my own. Except I made the mistake of leaving their bedrooms as is.

Maybe if I refurbished those spaces with spikes sticking out of walls and floors, they'd think twice about visiting.

It wouldn't be hard. For witchtitting sake, I'm a contractor with my own business. It would take me a mere weekend to transform their rooms.

Damn pack bond. Despite my desire for distance, we need each other. Weres need their pack to survive, literally. Too much time apart and something inside us begins to disintegrate and we waste away. Though right now, death by separation sounds like absolute bliss.

I breathe in the pollen and heavy spring scents. There's something even sweeter in the air than usual. It sends pleasurable tingles of heat spiraling through me.

Birds chirp happily from the feeder I always keep full in a tree nearby. Plants and flowers I got at the beginning of the month cover the railings. My bare feet pad along the sun-warmed wooden boards as I lower myself into one of the handmade Adirondack chairs. The sturdy yet comfortable oak chairs are positioned so I can fully enjoy the beauty of the massive New England trees.

Some of the tension melts away from my body as I bask in the rare spring sunshine. My face turns to soak it up while I can. The afternoon will likely bring pouring rain again.

Out here is where I find my peace, my solitude, my—

"Hi there, new neighbor," a feminine voice calls from a distance

My eyes snap open.

Instantly my sight zeros in across the way, up the hill, to my neighbor's dilapidated Victorian house. A busty, voluptuous blonde adorned in hot pinks and black is waving at me from the front porch.

New neighbor?

My fingers clench around the ceramic handle. The 'something sweeter' in the air is five yards away and it bypasses my nose and slaps my tongue with the jolt of a sugar rush.

Oh no. Oh faefucks no.

She waves again, more earnest this time.

Like I could miss her in a pink outfit that burns my corneas even from a distance. On that depressing, crumbling porch, she looks as out of place as a hyper puppy wanting to play fetch in a graveyard.

Or maybe I just feel like I'm suddenly at a funeral. One that commemorates the death of my peace and quiet.

Holding my breath to keep from inhaling more of this newcomer, I consider staying out here or going back inside and facing the teary-eyed, and now-likely pissed off woman inside.

They tend to start at heartbreak but quickly graduate to anger. And wonder of wonders, I get to be the one nearby to take it out on.

"My name is Goldie," the girl calls out again, her voice a musical lilt.

A beat passes, then I get to my feet, turn on my heel and go back inside, my mood turning incredibly foul. Even from a distance, I catch her arm falter from my periphery.

Don't worry Ted, she won't last.

Astrid lives up there and she may go off traveling the world, but she always comes back. Usually, every seven months before traipsing off again. Just don't let this renter, or tenant, or whoever the hell this sugary sweet blonde chick think we are going to start any of that neighborly shit.

CHAPTER 4
WELCOME TO THE POISON APPLE

GOLDIE

As the bar picks up, we run around, making drinks and shaking our hips to the music pounding through the club.

When the clock strikes midnight, the emcee appears in a vibrant burst of blue powder on stage by the massive lantern lit tree. The crowd hushes as they turn their attention in that direction.

In a cobalt blue top hat and coattails, with no shirt underneath to show off his muscular chest—Geanie enters bodybuilding competitions in his spare time, but here he is our emcee and self-proclaimed ringmaster.

The swirling whirlwind of magical sparkles and vivacious colors isn't real magic, they are all illusions for humans, by humans, as Rap puts it.

The room dims, and a spotlight focuses on Geanie, casting elongated shadows that playfully tease the anticipation of the crowd.

"Good evening, ladies and gentlemen, sprites and spriggans!" His voice booms, suddenly the live pulsating heart-beat of the Poison Apple Bar itself. "Welcome to the most enchanted spot this side of Fairyland, where dreams meld with reality and the night blooms with bewitching allure. And where I can guarantee you ain't never had a friend like me."

The lights dim down as Geanie lays on his side, head propped on one hand as he croons into his mic. "Here at the Poison Apple, we welcome all wandering souls, all those who have run away from home to escape the mundane."

Like every night, Geanie has the audience in the palm of his hand as he seduces each and every patron. He picks a man and makes intense eye contact as he goes on. "Here is a place where you can unleash the desires hidden in the crevices of your heart, where you can do whatever the fuck you want, a playground where every dream finds a voice, every yearning finds a home."

Then Geanie jumps to his feet without using his hands, the spotlight growing bright as dance music swells. "So step right up, folks! Allow our Lost Girls to weave their magic, to mix you a poison that titillates your titties, a concoction that caresses your cock." The crowd laughs even as they lean closer to our charismatic emcee.

With a fluid agility he flips in an audacious somersault off the stage, landing perfectly on his nimble feet, a testa-ment to the acrobatic prowess that earned him the job. He strides toward the bar where we are. "But first, let us meet the original lost souls who ran away from home."

A graceful flourish of his hands beckons a cloud of sparkling gold dust that materializes enchantingly over the bar, setting the stage for the entrancing spectacle to come.

Next, the emcee waves his hand towards another pulsating portal. " First up, we have the fiery maiden from the forest, a vision in crimson and burgundy. With a flick of her wrist, she can summon flames of passion in the coldest of hearts." Red climbs the short set of stairs behind the bar to get up into the spotlight. She strides forward, a mischievous smirk on her face, her hands gracefully maneuvering an array of fiery bottles. "Get ready to be entranced, for Red will mix you a mocha martini that will make you wanna slap your grandma and say godsdamn!"

Twirling effervescently, the emcee directs the crowd's attention to Cinder, who steps up next to Red. Her violet eyes flicker, casting a secret smile that sends the crowd into a frenzy of cheers. Expertly flipping a glass, she catches it effortlessly, her charisma undeniable.

"Behold, our exotic enchantress, who journeyed here from the vibrant lands of the east, leaving behind any semblance of inhibitions. Cinder is the mistress of the midnight moon, creating concoctions so potent, you might just leave with one less shoe!"

Red pours a dash of liquor into the outstretched glass, Cinder knocks it back with a seamless grace.

"Last but not least..."

The spotlight shifts, bathing the bar in an entrancing golden hue, calling me forward. A flutter of anticipation dances in my stomach as I ascend to the pinnacle of the bar, joining Cinder and Red, who dance and work the crowd.

"... please welcome our sweet golden girl who traded cornfields for skyscrapers, found her spice in the big city lights, and transformed from a sugary maiden to a sassy sun-kissed vixen!" Geanie's voice vibrates with a tantalizing tease that prickles my skin with exhilaration.

"Her signature drink? The Golden Ratio. Where the portions of this sassy sunny blonde are always just right.

It's a blend that will wrap you in a golden embrace that seduces your inner romantic."

With a whirl of excitement bubbling within me, I take center stage. The crowd's energy electrifies the air, fueling me up. With a twinkle in my eye and a smile that promises adventures in golden lands, I grasp a cocktail shaker in one hand and a bottle of liquor in the other.

Then, in a display of grace and fiery spirit, I start my dazzling performance. With impeccable precision, I spin the bottle high in the air, its golden contents reflecting the mesmerizing lights of the bar, casting fleeting golden rays that dance with the shadows. As the bottle descends, I catch it behind my back without missing a beat, pouring a golden stream into the shaker with a flourish that draws gasps and applause.

Geanie tugs at his collar, popping it up as he does an impression of Marlon Brando, bringing things to a close. "So let loose, let go, and let the Lost Girls take you on a journey of hedonistic delight, where every potion is a ticket to a realm where all your wildest fantasies come to life!"

With a final, sweeping gesture, he signals the lights to return to their original soft glow. The music fades into the typical dance music, the normal buzz of the bar resumes, and we get back behind the bar to please the people with booze.

Snow is my shadow for the night. It doesn't require her to do much more than watch me work to get comfortable with the flow of things.

"Have you noticed how every guy in this bar can't take

their eyes off you?" she finally asks. She really leaned into the role of 'shadow,' so at times I forgot she was there.

"It's the three of us," I say, shrugging it off. "A lot of people come here to hang with the Lost Girls."

Still, I can't help but notice she's right.

Snow goes on with her questions when there is a lull; Cinder on the other side of her. "Do you guys get hit on a lot here?"

Cinder and I exchange smiles. Rap doesn't want us to scare her off, but Snow needs to know what she is getting herself into.

"All the witchtitting time, but it usually is with the intent to score free drinks from us," Cinder answers.

Something sours in my heart. I pull out a glass and shovel ice into it. Filling my glass with water before taking several large gulps, I am determined to stay hydrated. "I don't recommend taking the flirtation past this bar."

One of Snow's eyebrows raises at the venom in my voice.

Cinder pulls out a rag and wipes her already clean countertop. "Don't mind her. She's bitter because she's sworn off men." Then her lips twist. "Though they seem to sense it and are coming after her harder than ever before."

It's true.

In fact, the moment I swore off men, they seemed to come at me like a gang of sexy cannonballs, testing my resolve.

"How about women?" Snow shoots back. Then she tenses as her eyes widen, as if she can't believe she just said that. I bark out a laugh and Cinder giggles. A rare but wonderful tinkling sound. Snow's shoulders lower a fraction as she realizes she's still safe.

What happened to her, I wonder? Something that forces her to measure every word before committing to one.

It pulls on something deep inside me. A part of me that understands having to measure all of my actions and words until I've made myself as small as possible. And when I wasn't small enough, because—faelords—I've never actually been so. . . I wished I could disappear altogether.

I plan to coax it out of Snow. Sweetly, persistently, in a way she won't even know she's given up clutching her trauma, so I could help ease the pressure on it just a fraction.

Cocking my head to the side, I pretend to think about it. "Touche, I guess I didn't say that. Females are fair game." My smile doesn't reach my eyes at my own joke though. I've always done far better with men than I have with women.

You have good female friends now, Goldie. Everything has worked out.

Cinder scoffs. "Pfft, like you could give up the sausage."

I nod gravely. "It's true, Snow, I'm an absolute carnivore. But as of now," I raise my glass in a cheers. "I am committing to meat substitutes from here on out."

Snow's nose crinkles as she gives me a half-smirk. "Is that like a veiled commitment to dildos only?"

Cinder's snickers explode into a full-on laugh as she rests her head against her arm on the bar.

I gravely nod at Snow. "Yes. I am only seeking the one true sex toy to rule them all. And when I find it, I will marry it."

Snow's lips stretch into a devious grin, showing off her straight teeth. "Dibs on maid of honor."

An invisible pressure lays against my skin. Automatically, my gaze lift up to meet a pair of smoldering brown eyes. They are already trained on me, despite the fact the brown-skinned smoke show is standing with four friends. They are talking, but he doesn't even pretend to listen. I have his full attention.

He asked me out as soon as he stepped up to the bar earlier. He seemed almost as surprised as I was by his date proposal, but then a strange hunger crept into his eye.

I'd been so thrown off; it was easier than I expected to turn him down. He shook his head, as if trying to clear his head, then ordered a drink. I had Cinder take over, not trusting myself enough to stand in front of him and say no a second time.

His gaze darkens with something tempting and intense, and my breathing turns shallow.

Then the girl next to him, slides her arm through his, pulling him closer to her side. The girl in an orange dress with heavily made-up eyes stares at me with icy menace.

I avert my gaze, as the cold of her glare hits me in the chest and drips into my stomach. I'm not sure if he's hooking up with her, or if she just wishes he was, but I can clearly see she is claiming her territory.

He asked *me* out, yet the pressure of guilt expands in my gut.

Another guy steps up to the bar. "Were you working last night?" The ginger haired guy has a sweet look about him, dimples in his cheeks and soft green eyes. I immediately peg him as the kind to bring a girl breakfast in bed. He wouldn't be intimidated by my love for pink and would be a great father.

"I sure was," I confirm, leaning my hands against the bar top, pushing my breasts up and together. His gaze drops, and a sense of feminine satisfaction snakes through me.

It's a dangerous game, this dance between attraction and power. A dance I've known since I was too young.

I drop my hands and roll my shoulders back.

Dammit, Goldie, stop trying to reel them in. We are off the sauce. On a sausage break. Going vegan. Being strong and independent.

My food related celibacy metaphors only half help. Still, I wonder if his tall lankiness translates into a matching length in his pants—

I groan, trying to ignore the rising heat in my body. My inner muscles clench, feeling empty and achy. Now I've sworn off men and sex, but now it's all I can think about. All I see.

I roll back into my mantra. I am capable. I am enough. And I don't need a man.

"No, I would have remembered a stunning girl like you." His smile quirks up on one side, and his eyes turn glassy, focusing on me with more intensity.

"You ordered a witches brew and three rounds of fireball for you and your friends," I say, easily rattling off his drink order in a flat tone. I remember people. I learned a while ago that people love to be noticed and remembered. We all want to be seen, so I see as many people as possible.

"Wow." He leans an arm on the counter and comes so close I can smell his earthy cologne. "How did I not remember a stunning beauty like you? Let me buy *you* a drink."

His gaze is nearly scorching my skin now, and I can't decide if I'm flattered or unnerved. I shoot a look at Snow who is watching closely, making me self-conscious.

"How about we stick with the norm, and I get *you* a drink, seeing as I'm at work?" This is the seventh offer I've had for a drink in the last two hours. While it's normal for people to get drunk, happy, and want the bartender to join in with their festivities, this is an aggressive pace.

He leans in and reaches across until his fingers touch mine. Eyes fluttering shut, his body shudders before he meets my gaze again. "If I don't get to buy you a drink, beautiful, I think I might die."

The laugh that escapes me is more a nervous titter. That's. . . a lot.

Part of me loves it, the rest of me is completely thrown. Seriously, did someone send a memo out to all the men to test my resolve? I feel like someone must be nearby filming me to watch me squirm.

"Goldie, we are out of olives," Red says, butting in, while forcibly grabbing my shoulders and pushing me off to the side. "How can I help ya out?" she asks the ginger haired guy, forcing his attention on her.

It's a total ploy to give me an exit. She and Cinder have been bailing me out all night. I'm starting to feel shitty about the workload they are taking on in my stead. I'll need to bake them something to make up for this bizarro night.

"Should I come with you?" Snow asks quietly, but I need a moment to myself.

Strange. I love being in the throng of people. But all this attention feels. . . off.

"No, it's okay. I'll be right back." I turn to head to the back storage room.

Why is the universe so cruel and ironic to keep throwing interested dudes at me when I don't want the attention? It feels like an unwelcome spotlight, resurrecting the ghosts of days I thought were long behind me.

As I walk toward the backroom, eyeballs cover me like cling wrap. Some are slathering me with sexually charged interest, but a number hold the same spite as the girl in the orange dress. It's not just men who've noticed me, the women in the bar have noticed the men noticing me.

Say that five times fast.

"I am beautiful, I am capable, I am enough, I don't need a man," I mutter under my breath. I clung to mantras I crafted in those lonely high school years, a shield against the hurtful whispers and the judging eyes.

Strangely enough, I wish the men tonight would treat me more like my dickwad neighbor. I instantly feel an itch under my skin again at the thought that he doesn't like me.

But it's only because he doesn't know me, I reason.

My focus shifts from the intense amount of male attention I'm getting, to my game plan to be the best neighbor that dude ever had. Before long, he'll be on my doorstep asking for a cup of sugar just to bask in my awesomeness. I'll do what I've taught myself to do years ago.

Kill him with kindness.

CHAPTER 5
BEARS HATE FUN

TED

I didn't order anything, but I expect a package is what will be on my front step when I'm summoned by the doorbell Sunday morning.

Maybe one of my asshat brothers sent something to my house again, planning to pick it up later, like I'm some kind of personal postal depot for them.

But I find something far worse. A curvy, blonde woman wearing black yoga pants adorned with rhinestones, and a pink shirt that dips down on one side, revealing the tan, moisturized skin of her shoulder.

For the second time, the smell of her turns to taste, melting along my tongue like sugar. I instantly hold my breath, trying to keep the deliciousness at bay.

She has to tilt her neck back to look up at me. I've got over half a foot on her. Honey brown eyes meet mine from under long, curled lashes as her bright pink lips curve in a smile. She smells like honey. Honey and something lightly floral, with just a hint of strawberries.

There is an inherently seductive quality to her face, though I'm not observant enough to know if it's due to her high cheekbones, the slant of her eyes, or because of her full lips. But I do recognize she capitalizes on all three traits with makeup, turning up the volume on her sexy.

For a moment, her pupils dilate as if she is fully taking me in. For a werebear, I'm big. To a human I seem like a giant. It's not long before she covers up her initial reaction.

"Hi, I'm your new neighbor, Goldie. I thought I'd come over and officially introduce myself," she chirps.

Fuck, fuck, fuck.

My hand clenches on the door, as I turn to stone.

"What happened to Astrid?" I ask in a flat tone. Dammit. The question forces me to inhale more of this girl's scent. I suppress a groan at how smooth it tastes.

My crankiness jacks up another notch.

Lines crinkle at the corners of her eyes as her lips twist in displeasure before she resumes her glowing smile. "Astrid was my aunt. She passed away." The mirth drains from her eyes and is replaced with a sadness. "She left me the house in her will."

The right thing to say is 'sorry for your loss,' but a whirlwind of questions flood my brain with sizzling heat.

Is she really going to try to be Ms. Cheerful neighbor, coming over and annoying me anytime she feels like it? She was already here with a passel of girls before. Is she going to keep doing that? Inviting people out here? Am I going to lose the privacy to shift or walk around naked on my property as I please? Dear faelords, what's going to happen when my brothers catch sight of this pink frothy cream puff on my porch? My heart pounds out of my chest as panic eats away at every other thought.

"How long are you going to stay?" is what finally ends

up coming out of my mouth in a low rumble. My chest feels like someone is steamrolling over it.

A line forms between her furrowed brows. She doesn't like my question.

"A long time?" She says with a shrug, and I can't tell if it's a statement or a question. But if she is looking for my approval of her staying, she won't get it.

Then my eyes drop to what she's holding. She clutches a glass dish. On it is a pink frosted cake in the shape of a heart, decorated with strawberries.

Her expression brightens as she lifts it up. "It's a cake. Strawberries and cream. I mean usually it's customary for the neighbors to greet the newcomer with baked goods," she says, her gaze flicking away as obvious resentment seeps through. "But I figure you must be busy doing..." Her voice falters as she tries to look past me into my house, but I'm blocking the way."...whatever it is that you do?"

It's a prompt, and she expects me to answer.

I can't decide what smells better. This brash blonde girl, or the cake. My mouth waters, but that's the only part of me that wants any part of this. The fact that she is beautiful and ballsy doesn't affect me at all.

"Astrid and I didn't really talk," I say, hoping she'll get the message. Hot buzzing still runs rampant through my head and spreads through my body.

And what is the scent embedded in her skin? Underneath the sugar and honey. It's unlike anything I've ever encountered.

But I'm not the curious sort. Instead, I try holding my breath to keep from getting another whiff.

The beast inside me is getting antsy. I feel caged and it makes me want to tear right out of my own skin. Literally.

"That sounds like her," Goldie says with a light, tinkling

laugh. "She was always too busy getting married or traveling around the world making new friends." She cranes her neck to look around me, clearly hoping I'll invite her in. "Would you like me to set the cake in your kitchen?"

I step in closer, my body further blocking the door and forcing her head to tilt back even more.

Oh fuck. I hate that this close, her scent is even stronger —a physical caress against my body. I'll need to shower after this to get her off me.

"I don't like cake."

Still not taking a step back, her expression flattens. "You don't like cake?" she repeats, her tone dripping with skepticism. "Everyone likes cake," she counters.

"Not me," I insist. The mixture of strawberry cake and this girl's deliciousness is flooding me, sparking a hunger in my stomach and. . . lower. Damn animal instincts.

"Well, how about a pie?" she says slowly. "I could bake you a pie."

I shake my head. "I hate pie."

Her grip tightens on the glass dish. "Cupcakes?"

"No."

Her eyes narrow, sparks practically spitting from them. "Cookies? You hate those too?"

I nod.

"How about fun? Do you hate fun?" She cocks her head to the side, her voice assuming a biting tone.

Something inside me rears up and takes note of her sass.

"Definitely," I confirm.

"Well, that makes six things I know about you other than your name," she says, still glaring at me like she wishes she could stab me with red hot pokers.

"What?" I ask, my brows knitting.

She holds the cake with one hand to count off fingers with her other hand. "You hate cake, pies, cupcakes, cookies, fun, and are a complete ass. If you tell me your name, I'll know seven things about you."

Smart ass.

It almost, *almost* makes me want to break into a smile. But the threat she poses to my peace and quiet is far more pressing, and it's currently pressing me into being an ass to effectively drive her away.

Goldie curls the cake closer into her body, as if she realizes I don't deserve her amazing gift and I'd have to beg on my knees for it now.

"The seventh thing about me is that I like to be left alone. How's that?"

Somewhere inside, I cringe at how harsh that sounds. But then I think again about my brothers catching a whiff of this delectable girl on my doorstep and immediately harden up. I need her far from here. For all our sakes.

Goldie's mouth forms a small 'O' as if she can't believe I actually said that. When she recovers, her jaw clenches and as sweet as a dagger coated in pink sugar, her words emerge through clenched teeth. "I'll be sure to write that one down too. Thanks for sharing."

Before she can say another word, I step back and shut the door in her face.

A strangled cry of outrage comes from the other side. I vigorously rub at my forehead and the fast-forming headache, trying not to feel so guilty over how I just acted, even as it gnaws at me.

It's going to be fine, I assure myself. You did anything but roll out the welcome mat and that cream puff clearly won't last in that massive, crumbling old Victorian. She'll be gone before you know it. And you can deal with the regular shit shows that visit your house without piling on.

Letting out a sigh, I turn and decide to avoid my back deck for the rest of the day, so I don't risk another sighting of her. Because having scented her now, there's no way I won't be able to sense this Goldie chick with every nerve ending of my body.

Dammit.

My mouth waters again. I should have taken the cake.

CHAPTER 6
A SNOWY LOST GIRL

GOLDIE

"**W**hat an absolute ass," I rage for the tenth time since my shift started, as I haul another rack of dishes to the washer. I'm flush with anger, but at least at work there is air conditioning. I spent the day dripping in sweat, as I took my first whack at cleaning up that monstrous house.

"Are you sure he saw you?" Red asks for the second time, where she is polishing a wine glass.

Cinder is busy pouring a craft beer for Lysander, her attractive male friend who sits at the bar. For the past month, we've let him hang out at the Poison Apple before we open as we all patiently wait for Cinder or Lysander to make a move on each other. The pale, slender University student impassively listens, the image of art nouveau cool in his skinny jeans, horn-rimmed glasses, and sporting a beanie despite the summer heat. They met in a painting course and bonded over their love of gothic art and hatred of their professor.

Cinder already heard me complain about my dick neighbor even as we cleaned up the house as best we could, before moving in my large trunk's worth of clothes.

Red and Cinder are the absolute best friends in the whole freaking world, and I promised them they could have as many staycations as they wanted at my bed and breakfast.

If they were okay sharing the same air as my jerk next-door neighbor.

"He definitely saw me," I confirm. "He looked right at me, so I called my name out to him. Then he stood up and walked back inside, like I was some kind of disease he was afraid of catching."

Something sour churns in my stomach at the slight. He's an absolute ass, and *absolutely* made me feel like trash. How dare he?

No one gets to make me feel bad for being friendly. Not anymore. Not since I moved halfway across the country to get away from that. No way I'm going to move in next door to someone who thinks ripping down others joy is acceptable.

More than that, I hate that I don't know his name so I can curse him. Of our group, I'm known as the interrogator. So not getting a proper response gives me an itch I can't scratch.

I blame my extra orneriness on the fact I must have sweat four bucketloads and ruined my cute outfit. At the moment, I can't spend any money on air conditioning units if I stand a chance at turning around even a fraction of the Victorian mansion.

But how dare my neighbor tarnish the beauty of my

new dream with his rudeness on day one? I do *not* need this right now. My jerk-wad quota is all filled up from Lawrence. He's already turned about face and is blowing up my phone with alternating texts of contrition and irritation that I haven't fallen back at his feet. My tolerance for any more of that bullshit is nonexistent.

"I didn't see him," Red says, pausing her polishing. "Is he some old angry dude who moved out to the forest to keep kids from stepping on his lawn?"

I shake my head. "I didn't get a good look at him other than he was big, with dark hair and a beard, young-ish? But he was far away, and it's hard to tell with guys who cover up with facial hair. I do know he wore plaid, like a sinister brawny man. His sleeves were rolled up, like he was ready to chop up someone's joy for the day." And mine had been on the block for him to cleave.

My anger only made me sweat more profusely. Grabbing a napkin, I blot my forehead not wanting to mess up my makeup. Gah, now that's turned on, I can't turn it off. I may need to go hide in the walk-in fridge to cool off both literally and figuratively.

The Lost Girls—aka Red, Cinder, and I—have a reputation to uphold at the Poison Apple. It is one of drink-slinging badassery and glamour.

After moving, we went back to Red's place where we showered, primped and curled before slapping on our respective outfits. Red's taut stomach is exposed between the low-slung leather pants and a crop top. It accentuates her sleeve of tattoos and navel ring. I opted for a tight, pink halter dress that puts all the focus on my generous cleavage. It's so much easier to feel good when you know you look good. Or in my case, like hot pink fire that could decimate any man who should look upon me.

I suddenly wish my neighbor would walk in so he could get a bit singed.

"New Englanders are not known for their overabundance of friendliness," Lysander points out before sipping on his craft beer the color of dark chocolate.

I wave a hand dismissively. "That's a myth. If you are nice to people anywhere, they are nice back. It's just people in the Northeast are *aggressively* nice," I point a finger and shake it. "Like—hey, you look lost, you better let me give you directions before I rush off to my very important next appointment and you're welcome." My south Boston accent is abysmal, but I feel I made my point. "But this guy is something else."

"Do you need me to kill him?" a growly voice asks from across the bar. Long silver hair falls into the sharp, predatory eyes of Brexley Moon, Red's fiancé. He is also known in some circles as the Big Bad Wolf, a notorious assassin and werewolf. He gave it up for his bride to be, moving fully into private security, but I have zero doubt his offer is idle.

While Red locked down a werewolf who could understand and accept her half mage, half werewolf heritage, sudden rages, and lusty episodes, I got what felt like a big brother.

And a whole lot of envy for their explosively passionate love affair rolled into what seems like domestic bliss.

"Can I let you know?" I ask Brexley with a sigh.

"Murder is a fireable offense," Rap, aka Rapunzel, our boss at the Poison Apple says evenly from her stool next to Brexley, without looking up from her laptop. With her banana blonde and rainbow mohawk, tattered designer clothes, and resting bitch face, most people find her intimidating.

She may be a hard ass but she's fair. And she has a soft

spot for us Lost Girls who need a place to find our grounding and make some good money while we're in college. If it weren't for her, I would have never made it in this city. She always makes sure we have time for our studies, and a safe place to work. But apparently, she draws the line at murder.

Rap did, however, bend the line of the Poison Apple being a humans-only bar, seeing as Red is a full-blown level five mage and Brexley is a fae creature.

"If *I* do the killing, Goldie can't take the blame." Brexley's eyes flash an amber glow. Despite his grumbly voice, there is a congested thickness to his words. Turns out he's allergic to Red's house rabbits, Bangs and Bombs. But I know he'd rather die via stuffy nose than make Red give up her fur babies.

"Oh! Or maybe I can request the hit on Goldie's behalf," Red pipes up excitedly. "Seeing as tonight's my last night working the Poison Apple, so I can't be fired."

Cinder loudly groans as if she's in physical pain as she rejoins us. "Don't remind us."

Cinder's strappy black top and dark purple lipstick complete her goth aesthetic. And she winged her narrow Asian eyes with a stiletto-sharp liner. I watched her hold up an actual knife against the corner of her eye as a guide for a sharper line. Faelords, I love the shit out of her.

"How dare you leave us to live your dreams to go work as an accountant," I add, hopping on the blame train.

Red shrugs with a lop-sided smile. "It's your fault for encouraging me to go after my dreams. Now I get to intern at a firm before I even graduate, and I can pay the rest of my way through college."

Not that she needed to with her insanely rich and famous grandma.

43

Still, I respect Red's tenacity in building a life on her own terms. She's always wanted a human life and she's getting it.

Granted, I may have initially strong-armed Red into joining our ranks at the Poison Apple, but I wasn't sorry for a second. Once a shy, insecure girl, she rocked her boots and red leather bustier like a dominatrix who owns everyone in the room.

No one would guess looking at her that she's now one of the few level five mages on Earth, like her grandma.

Not that I want Red's power. She can literally devour and destroy anyone's magic. It's a power the mage council has never seen before.

After Red used it in self-defense against some blood-thirsty mages, she was forced to agree to never use her power again.

What fun is it having powers if you can't use them?

But seeing as I also ate one of those magic cookies, along with Cinder, I was hoping to unlock some kind of awesome magic powers of my own. Unlike Red's heritage though, the two of us are one hundred percent human, so it might not happen.

Red was half mage already, but her grandma explained the recipe was meant to unlock genetic code, so if there are any dormant mage abilities in us, we might find ourselves with some unusual talents. But that was months ago and so far Cinder and I had seen zero, zippo, and zilch on the magic powers front.

"Hey," Brexley interjects, wrapping a hand around his beer, "I helped you achieve your dreams, too, little Red. All those tireless hours I put in helping you study." Then he shoots Red a wolfish grin packed with heat.

Red's cheeks flush into a color that matches her hair. "Yeah, you helped me... study."

My eyes bounce between the two of them, then avert when I realize there is some sexual subtext going on.

"Flirt on your own time," Rap says in a deadpan tone, eyes still glued to the keyboard.

"I thought you paid us to flirt," Cinder points out with a sly side smile.

"I do, but don't tell the new girl that or you might scare her away," Rap says, finally looking up. Her emerald eyes flashing in warning.

"Oh," I cry out, clapping my hands when a familiar head of white hair bobs through the room, heading our way. "She's here."

Barely an inch over five feet, the diminutive girl flashes me an uncertain smile that almost looks like she's baring her teeth. Her white hair contrasts yet complements her cool, twilight skin. Her icy blue eyes are large, round, and doe-like. Her lips are set in a permanent sultry pout. There is something dangerous and dark that licks around the corners of her that makes me want to squeeze her tight.

"Everyone, meet Snow," I announce, waving my hands in her direction like Vanna White.

"Hi, Snow," comes the chorus.

She ducks her head, hair falling in front of her face.

If I didn't know better, I would have pegged her as a nymph. But nymphs tend to stay amongst their own fae-kind and tend to be about six inches tall. Still, there is something so unearthly about my new friend. Though she assures me she's human, I'm sure there is more to her than even she realizes.

Red casts me a knowing look. I know exactly what she's thinking. Snow lacks confidence, grounding, all the things

Red was missing before she came here. We've found another Lost Girl.

Rap's laptop shuts with an audible click. "Nice to finally meet you. I'm Rap. Goldie's told me a lot about you. Why don't we have a chat in my office and see if this is a good fit, eh?"

Cinder, Red, and I exchange glances. We already recognize one of our own. Snow is *definitely* a Lost Girl. She dutifully follows Rap to the back, where I've no doubt she'll be hired on the spot.

Turns out I'm a pro at setting other people up with their destinies but shit at it for myself. I'm happy to do it though. Getting people connected and passing along opportunities truly makes me happy.

"Where did you find this one?" Cinder asks with a fond smile.

I try to suppress my grin and fail. Grabbing a wet cloth, I begin to clean the bar top. "Met her at the Book and Bean."

"My favorite coffee shop," Red gasps as she clutches at her heart, eyes going round and her mouth going slack. The girl has a serious addiction to mochas, but we haven't called for an intervention... yet.

I dump the rag back into the disinfectant bucket. "She was hoarding the free honey packets like they were going to be breakfast, lunch, and dinner for the next couple of days. Turns out she moved here a month ago, and still hasn't gotten used to the city while she figures her life out. She was a bit evasive about whether she'd come from a bad relationship or a bad home life, but I'll get it out of her eventually."

"Of course, you will," Cinder says, shaking her head with that sly smile again. "You collect people like someone would collect shells they find on a beach."

"I do not," I protest, grabbing a glass from the stack that Red is still polishing to help. "I just love people. Is that so bad?"

"And they love you," Red says.

My smile falters. While it's true, I love people as a whole which is why I love living in the city, I don't know so much about what she says. Lawrence's words start to play in my brain like a broken record.

"You are vapid, flaky, and you bend yourself to be liked by everyone just to make up for the fact you look like a fat, slutty Barbie doll."

I resist the urge to smack the side of my head to make it stop.

My grip tightens on the glass as a chorus of similar insults start to rise behind Lawrence's. My attention snaps to my hand and I loosen my grip before I shatter glass. I set it down and leave Red to it. I already restocked the bar; I can afford to relax for a minute, take a breath, maybe five.

"Speaking of love, how is the swearing off men thing going?" Red asks.

Brexley perks up at that. "Oh?"

I practically dive for the glasses again, resuming the polishing. If I have to spit on them myself to make sure they need extra attention, I'll do it. "It's fine. It's great. Best decision I've ever made."

"It's only been twelve hours," Cinder points out.

"And I haven't fallen in love a single time," I announce, tilting my chin up.

"Hey, the bouncer let me in before you all open, I think I left my cellphone here last night. Can someone help me out?" a decidedly attractive male voice calls out from the other side of the bar.

I don't know what it is that makes me *decide* his voice is

attractive, but when I look up I see the tall, dark and hand-some man waiting there matches his voice.

My heart skips a couple beats. I trace the line of lips, determining he has the potential to be an excellent kisser, that our kids would be adorable, and his mom would love me.

Before I know it, I'm floating in his direction.

Cinder steps in the way.

"How many?" she mutters.

"How many what?" I ask in a distracted tone; my head is in a dizzy fog as my heart beats like three girls skipping through a jump rope.

"How many kids did you just imagine having with that cute guy?"

That snaps me out of it. It's then I notice Red and Brexley are also watching me.

"What?" I scoff. I huff. I scoff again. "None. I was just going to close him out."

"How many?" Cinder presses.

"Three. Two boys and a girl," I admit. I don't tell her about the dog.

With a sharp, knowing nod, she pats my arm and takes off to close the guy out.

I sigh and slump against the bar.

"Twelve hours down, hundreds to go," Red says with a crooked smile, giving me two thumbs up. Brexley frowns at her before snapping to and offering me two thumbs up in solidarity.

"Girls," a sharp voice gets our attention. Rap strides out from the back room. Snow is on her heels, looking wary, but she rolls her shoulders back as if readying herself. "Ready to concoct delicious potions for all the poor unfortunate souls of Boston tonight?"

Cinder and I straighten and salute her like she's our captain. Snow's gaze bounces between us before doing the same. Rap's eyes narrow. We honestly can't tell if our boss loves or hates the gesture, but she doesn't tell us to stop.

With a curt nod, Rap's soft-looking mohawk dips with the movement. How does that thing stay up without an obscene amount of hair gel? I asked her once. She gave me a secret smile and said, "Magic."

"Then let's make magic," Rap says and nods to one of our bouncers to open the doors to the Poison Apple.

CHAPTER 7

THE NFH AND JEDI POWERS

GOLDIE

"He refused my cake," I screech over the phone, wiping sweat off my forehead with the back of my hand as I attack a stubborn stain on the wall..

"Maybe he was having a bad day, honey," Mom counters from states away. We are cleaning in tandem, while chatting, to make the work easier. My scrubbing intensifies with my frustration.

"Wouldn't a cake help with that? A kind gesture from a stranger?" I switch hands, my muscles straining from the effort. This freaking stain is like the men I've met—unwilling to change.

Which is why I have to be the one to get stronger and better.

"Hmm." I can almost see Mom's brows knit and her biting her lip in thought.

"Listen, I get it," I go on. "Everyone is going through their own shi—stuff. But he was an unmitigated jerk."

Even if he does have swoon-worthy blue eyes, sexy dark curls, and the broadest shoulders I've ever seen in my life, it doesn't exempt him. I bet some girls swoon over the way his lower lip pouts out from his trimmed beard when he is scowling with that icy stare. Some girls love impossibly tall, muscled mountain men, and the scent of fresh soap, pine trees, and warm masculinity.

Hot tingles start to twirl in my bloodstream at the memory of him first towering over me, making my belly flip and flop like a fish out of water.

I am *not* that girl. I like blondes, who smile, wear designer cologne, and act like gentlemen toward me. Or for a while anyway, before they devolve into slimy jerks.

It's not hard to imagine girls falling over themselves for my neighbor from hell in grade school. I bet it fed his massive ego from a young age, until he became unimpressed with the entire world. People that jaded should live alone in the woods, where they can't bother anyone.

Oh, right.

Well, I learned my lesson. No more cakes for the NFH— ie the neighbor from hell.

Or maybe. . .

My brain starts to double down on a plan to win him over.

I'm allowed to hate NFH, but he won't be able to resist my charm. Despite his gruff exterior, I saw the hungry look on his face when he spotted the cake. Oh, he wanted it all right.

"Do you need me to come out there and tear into him for being mean to my little girl?" Despite the firmness of my mom's voice, I know it's an empty threat. She is terrified of flying and doesn't have time to make the drive to Boston from the Midwest.

My twelve-year-old brother is also out for summer break. Between his baseball camps and the volunteer work my parents do, it would be hard for her to drop everything for me.

It had been my choice to move to a big city far away from my loving parents and the safety of what I knew. But I couldn't ignore the hot burning at the pit of my stomach that swelled and swelled until I thought I would explode. I came to the conclusion it had to do with fulfilling my potential. I was meant for bigger things than Iowa had to offer.

But this was the tradeoff. My stalwart champions are halfway across the country.

My heart squeezes painfully. I miss them so much. I miss my mom's warm hugs, my dad's corny jokes, and playing video games with Noah. Our age gap allows us to get along better than most siblings.

"No, you don't need to come out here," I say, pausing my work to lean against a broom, a heavy sigh escaping me.

She doesn't fight me on it.

"Well, I'm really glad you have such good friends like Cinder and Red out there to support you. Are they helping you with the house?" Her voice took on a hesitant tone. It's as if she knows how much of an undertaking it is to clean out this pigsty of a house.

"This is my thing, so I'm doing my best not to drag them into it," I say, determined. Swiping a gloved hand across my forehead, I feel the trail of grime I leave behind. Ugh, I should have cleaned the bathrooms first. I plan on going straight from here to work tonight. All I need is a shower to get clean and reset.

"I'm going to flip this house and make a crushing profit and start flipping houses for profit."

Silence on the other end. Cold dread snakes in my tummy.

"Mom?"

"Baby, you know I support whatever you want to do. But maybe you should just try this and see how it turns out before..."

"Before what?" Impatience tinges my words, which I instantly hate. Mom is a saint and doesn't deserve it. I tap my fingers impatiently on my leg then give voice to the words I know she is thinking. "Before I make my entire personality about this and then crash and burn if it doesn't go well."

I have a tendency to get a bit obsessive. And then if it doesn't go well, I get despondent and dramatic when I don't achieve what it is I think I want.

"Goldie baby, I just want you to stay open to possibilities. When you get fixated on things, you tend to..."

Lose my ever loving mind?

"...lose sight of what's really important."

"Is that my girl on the phone?" a familiar male voice says in the background.

A smile splits my face as there comes a shuffling sound before my dad is on the phone. "Hey baby, how ya doing?"

Talking to my parents gives me a glimpse of a healthy relationship—something I haven't found yet, but I'm not in a hurry. Right now, it's about me and my journey to independence.

"I'm good," I chirp. "Just cleaning up."

"Now you know how your mother feels, cleaning up after your aunt all these years." His chuckle is cut short by what sounds like a smack on his chest.

"Hank," my mom scolds.

"Whoops, I'm in trouble, gotta go," he says before my mom comes back on the line. I hear the distinctive sound of a kiss between them. My shoulders slump as I sigh. Why can't I find someone to measure up to my parents?

No wonder I can't find a good guy. The bar is sky high, and Boston is crawling with sports-addicted, fuck boys who treat commitment like a disease they can't afford to catch.

Though lately, anyone would think I was some kind of Boston-boy catnip.

Straightening, I remind myself that I don't need any man. I'm beautiful, I'm capable, and I'm enough.

"Well, I've got to go pick up Noah from the bus stop, but let's tandem talk and clean tomorrow too," mom suggests. "You blessed thing, you helped me get through cleaning all the bathrooms, but I have a mountain of laundry I'm saving for our chat tomorrow."

"Sounds like a plan," I say with a smile. We give our love and hang up.

Something about being on the phone while cleaning makes it so much easier. I go from task to task without thinking about it. It's like blackout cleaning. When I hang up, I look back and see how much I've done, but I only remember spending time with my mom.

It especially helps when the summer heat is pressing down on me, trying to murder me one degree at a time. I'm positively sopping with sweat, and it's hard to breathe.

Maybe I should ask Rap to take on more shifts so I can afford some A/C units? But then I'd have precious little time to invest into this beautiful monstrosity.

I take in the absolute wreck that is *my* house. Spider-webs have taken over the vaulted ceilings—I'll need a ladder for those. After a bit of scrubbing, I discovered the tile floors are actually a light pink color when I thought they were brown. The only way I'm going to cut through the grime is by getting on my hands and knees with steel wool, peroxide, and baking soda.

This house is like my life: messy, a bit broken, but full of possibility. And both have suffered a lot of neglect.

Oh. And we are both hot as hell.

"We're still standing, baby," I say out loud to the house. Maybe if I talk to it, I can befriend it and it will work with me instead of against me.

Perhaps my powers will manifest, and I'll find I possess some kind of awesome telekinesis that I can use to clean this place with the snap of my fingers.

Spotting the old vacuum in the corner, I found it in a closet and it sucks well enough. Narrowing my eyes, I focus, willing the machine to turn on and start moving around.

Nothing.

I squint harder and hold out a hand like Darth Vader even more intent.

The vacuum remains immobile.

Dropping my arm, I scowl. *Witchtits*. That would have been fantastic.

The task is daunting, but I've faced disappointment and heartbreak before. Each room I clean, every stain I remove, will be a testament to my strength, my resilience. I'm not waiting for some man to come and rescue me—I'm rescuing myself, one scrubbed tile at a time.

Then a cheerful thought occurs to me. Maybe my powers will manifest as death rays I can shoot from my eyes at my jerk neighbor.

And if that doesn't work, I've already got a plan B for the NFH in the works.

CHAPTER 8
THE GINGERBREAD FROM HELL

TED

My breath hitches as I step onto my porch and my toes instantly squish into something soft and gooey. Lifting my barefoot with pink gunk stuck to my it, a growl of irritation rumbles through me as my nostrils flare. The sticky frosting fills the space between my toes and if I put my foot down anywhere else on the front porch, I'll step in it again.

Cake—pink heart cakes with strawberries crowd around my door, a menacing army of confections.

They are identical to the first cake I rejected from my neighbor.

Disgusted, anger rises in me like heat from burning embers. Everywhere I step, I'm reminded of *her*. This is Goldie's fifth, or is it sixth, attempt to be the 'best neighbor ever?'

Day by day, she's been subtly altering the world around my cabin. Like the birdhouse she installed right on the divide of our property lines. Every morning is now filled with melodious distractions. Anyone else would find it enchanting, but it reminds me how close she is.

I learned to ignore the knock at the door when she is on my steps. Even through the walls of my cabin I can smell her, taste her unique sweetness. It makes my mouth water and my blood pressure rise.

Inevitably, there will be something left on my porch—a basket of peaches I know came from one of the trees on her property, a pink ribbon tied in a bow around the handle with a note wishing me a good day and how glad she is that we are neighbors.

I left them on the porch where the squirrels and hot sun could ravage them.

Then came the clippings of fragrant lavender and wildflowers, again, tied up in a pink bow.

Those too, I left on the porch where they dried up in the heat until they were crumbling bouquets.

A pink envelope appeared in my mailbox with a handwritten invitation to come by the Poison Apple—the bar she works at—for a drink on her. The paper crumpled in my fist before I dropped it in the waste bin. But then the bright color mocked me from the corner of the room, so I had to take the whole thing out to the recycling in the garage.

I have never hated a color so intensely in my life like I hate the color pink. I can't even see it on a billboard without feeling my blood boil and white-hot tingles sweep through me, conjuring the image of my neighbor's brilliant smile.

But the more I resist her friendly advances, the more persistent she gets.

Just as I reach down to move one of the many cakes meant to intimidate me into friendship, someone pops out of the bushes.

Nothing could have prepared me for the sight before me.

At the base of the steps, stands an adult woman dressed head-to-toe as a gingerbread cookie. Glittery gumdrop buttons twinkle under the afternoon sun, and her icing-lined smile stretches too wide, almost grotesquely so. It's like one of those ludicrous nightmares where logic takes a back seat, only, I'm wide awake.

Before I can utter a word, her shrill voice begins to blast a modified version of Rick Astley's, "Never Gonna Give You Up."

'Never gonna stop the cheer,
Always gonna be right here,
Gonna make you love this neighborly tune!
Never gonna fail to try,
Never gonna be that shy,
Always here to brighten up your day's gloom.'

Horror roots me in place. It was the most atrocious butchering of a song I've ever heard. Every cell in my body bristles with shock and growing rage.

The undeniable and delicious aroma wafting from the strawberry cakes as well as the basket of gingerbread cookies she holds adds to the dissonance of the moment.

Only one person could be this evil, despicable, and saccharine sweet all at the same time.

The frothy pink cream puff of doom.

My restraint is stretched too thin, and I feel a change boiling within me. Animal growls, guttural and fierce, rip their way out from my throat. My skin prickles, fur begins to sprout as my bones creak, trying to shift.

It takes every ounce of willpower not to go berserk before breaking the messenger into two pieces before flinging them onto Goldie's property.

The singing cookie's eyes widen in terror. She bolts, abandoning her song mid-verse. Her basket of cookies tumbles, scattering the treats across the lawn as she runs away, screaming. I'm left grappling with the raging beast within, pulling at the reins of control.

With a supreme effort, I grab the impulse to shift and reel it back in until the emerging fur recedes and the menacing growl dies in my throat. I never lost control of my animal before.

I take a deep breath, the scent of gingerbread lingering as a taunting reminder. A car screeches out of the driveway, kicking up gravel in the singer's wake.

Fae creatures don't typically live in human cities, and I usually have no problem keeping a low profile and blending in. But my neighbor is making it supremely witchtitting impossible to keep my head down.

And now this? A barrage of pink heart cakes holding me hostage at my own door while someone *sings* at me?

My jaw clenches so tight, my teeth threaten to crack.

Goldie is clearly psychotic, and this ends now.

Not bothering to avoid the confections, I stomp through them, head around my house and walk up the hill to the Victorian mansion.

The door rattles under my fist.

I don't stop knocking until it opens. The sight of her throws my anger completely off tilt as I swallow hard, feeling my heart pound into my ribs with earth shaking force. Goldie stands before me, barefoot in an oversized shirt and cut-off jean shorts that show off her generous thighs. Surprisingly her nails are painted a glossy black. I would have guessed she'd go with pink since it comprises everything else she wears.

Her wheat and sun-streaked hair is up in a messy bun

and dirt is smeared across her face, like she's been rooting around a dirty basement.

I try to hold my breath as best I can as her scent shoots straight down to my tongue again, teasing and tingling every taste bud I have.

Pink lips slide up either side of her face. "Good morning," she chirps.

There is a menace behind her greeting, and I know to my bones she is as evil as she is adorable. With that smile and pep, she could get away with murder then be let off with no charges and a ride home.

But I'm not fooled. She's the devil incarnate.

"This has to stop."

"What has to stop?" she asks, batting her lashes at me.

My stomach flips over backwards several times.

Fuck. Why does she have such a visceral effect on me? And what the faehell is that unique scent under all her sweetness?

"Oh, did you get the present I left on your doorstep?" she continues. Those big brown eyes track down my body until they connect with the dirty pink remnants stuck to my feet. An eyebrow raises.

"You're psychotic," I growl. "And I told you, I like to be left alone."

Goldie rolls her eyes. "I don't see why you need to make things so unpleasant. If you got to know me, you'd see I'm a great person to have around."

"You aren't listening, I don't want you—"

Goldie jerks at a crash from inside the house. Adrenaline shoots through me, and my hackles start to rise.

"What was that?" I ask, already pushing her aside with an arm, walking straight into the house. I try to ignore how soft and warm her body is against my forearm, or the jumble of nerves that wriggle in my chest at the contact.

"Not again," she grumbles, moving my arm away so she can walk ahead of me. Senses on full alert, I follow her into the living room. Despite the crumbling mess of the exterior, the front room smells of lemon cleaner.

I note the sage green cream wallpaper catches and holds the warm light from the sparkling clean bay window. Two red and white plaid wingback chairs are set on either side of the stone fireplace that has been scrubbed until it gleams. A bookcase crammed with books is set invitingly off to the side, most of them thrillers and romance books with broken spines.

Apart from the sweltering heat of the house that made it feel like being inside an oven, the room begs to be sat in and enjoyed for a weekend of coffee and relaxation. A pang goes through me that I can't identify.

Pushing that aside, I stay on Goldie's heels as she goes to a massive picture that lay face down on the ground clearly having fallen from the wall where long stickers flap half off it.

"Witchtits," she curses, trying to pry her fingers underneath to lift it.

I can only handle five seconds of her struggle before I push her aside, again ignoring the feeling her soft warmth inspires in me. Picking up the heavy piece with ease, I find it's actually a mirror set in an ornate carved frame.

"Did you try to put this on the wall with stickers?" I ask, incredulous.

Her already full lower lip pouts out further. "I don't want to ruin the wallpaper with nails."

"This not only needs proper mounting with nails or

screws, but it will also need anchors, so it doesn't tear down the drywall," I say, setting the piece against the wall.

Around the corner is a breakfast nook, where I find a table covered in various tools. They are old and rusty, but there is a lot here.

"What are you doing?" she protests as I dig into a half molded cardboard box full of screws, and wonder of wonders, find some mounts. Then I pull out an ancient power drill and its set of rusted bits.

"Putting this up properly so it doesn't fall on you and crush you to death."

Goldie sets her hands on her hips and huffs out an agitated breath as if uncomfortable with my presence. "I thought you came over to kill me. Why would you—"

Her words are drowned out by the high pitch screech of the drill. Every time she tries to speak, the drill interrupts her as I make holes in the wall before hammering in the mounts then working the screws in. I suppress a smile every time she's silenced by the overpowering electric screams. In under ten minutes, I have the mirror back up and placed perfectly.

An itch gathers under my skin when I see a project I want to sink my teeth into. Goldie has made progress with this place, and clearly has an eye for design. With my help, this house would be flipped in no time.

Hell no. I do not want to help her. I do not want her to stay. Hopefully, this place grinds her down with problems until she gives up and sells.

Part of me doesn't believe what I'm thinking.

Goldie steps forward, her fingers brushing lightly against the back of my hand. An unexpected shiver races up my spine, and I involuntarily pull back. The sudden distance between us feels simultaneously too great and not far enough.

"I could've done that myself," she declares, though the uncertainty in her eyes betrays her.

"Seems to me you've got your hands full," I comment, referencing the grime on her face and her tousled appearance.

She huffs, her cheeks puffing out in defiance. "Contrary to how even the men have been treating me at work all week, I don't need a man. I don't need you waltzing in here and acting like a knight-in-shining-armor."

What men? A snake of something hot and angry writhes inside me as I think of other men doting on her. I shove the thoughts and the sensation down, refocusing on why I came over in the first place.

"And I don't need a neighbor bombing my porch with cakes, or to be interrupted by singing cookies. This makes us even."

She rolls her eyes, exasperated. "Why can't we just be friendly neighbors?"

The idea of being friends with this woman is repulsive to me. She's pushy, perky, and an absolute pain in my ass.

Speaking of her ass, I don't want that tempting rear anywhere near my place where my brothers pop in and out at random. The thought of her even being in the same room as my brothers is enough to make my blood boil. Their eyes would strip her like vultures circling an animal. They wouldn't be able to stop themselves from wanting to know how it felt to run their hands along her soft, sun-kissed skin. They'd want to fill their hands with those full thighs and generous ass and kiss those pink lips until that ridiculous color is smeared all over their faces. The temptation to fill their hands with her invitingly generous breasts while planting feverish kisses up her neck would be unbearable. Their sole goal would be to see how her face screws up in pleasure and to find out what makes her eyes turn glassy and her jaw slack as they work her over.

I pull in a shaky breath, girding myself against the horrible, unappealing manner my brothers would treat this cream puff. Heat coils and sinks below my belt, causing an unprecedented stiffness.

Must be the weather.

"I came out here for solitude. You've got everyone else in the world to be friendly with."

Goldie pauses, taking a deep breath before her eyes harden. "Fine. If you want your solitude, you'll have it. But don't you dare think I'm going to apologize for trying to be a decent neighbor."

I take a step back, my body tense. "Alright, truce. No more surprise gifts, and I won't barge in to fix things."

"Deal." Her voice is like steel as she thrusts out a hand.

As our palms meet, a spark shoots between us, zinging up my arm and exploding in my chest. Something kicks me square in the stomach. I jerk back, rubbing that same hand down the side of my jeans. Her pupils widen, her lips parting slightly, as if she's trying to make sense of the unexpected sensation too.

Maybe it was just a static charge.

A glance down and I grimace. I've tracked dirt and pink frosting onto the hardwood.

"Sorry," I mutter, gesturing to the mess. "For the floor."

She follows my gaze, then looks back at me, her expression softening a fraction. "A little dirt and frosting never hurt anyone."

Feeling the odd pull to remain, but knowing I should go, I turn to leave. "I better head out."

"Yeah," she agrees, her voice soft and distant. "Things to do."

I exit, throwing a final glance her way. She stands there, a contemplative furrow in her brows, the palpable energy between us still lingering in the air.

But it's done. We won't talk, interact, or have anything to do with each other from this point on.

My gut clenches and my muscles tighten with a strange restlessness.

This is exactly what I wanted.

So why do I feel like I just made the worst mistake of my life?

CHAPTER 9

PORRIDGE AND ADULT NAPPERS

GOLDIE

The wind howls eerily against the windows and the creaking floorboards beneath my feet serve as a constant reminder of my new surroundings. Everything groans, as if the house may collapse under my feet.

"Steady old girl," I whisper lovingly to the house, running my hand down the door jamb as I pad into the kitchen. Or am I saying it to myself?

All through my shift at the Poison Apple, the attention from the guys grew more intense, like it had over the past week. Their increasing infatuation felt off. It was as if every compliment and lingering look became more exaggerated, more suffocating. Maybe I'm overthinking, but it's all beginning to make me uncomfortable. It's as if the more they act like they want me, the more fake it all seems.

Which keeps turning my brain back to my interaction with the NFH this morning. Presumably, our *last* interaction.

Or rather Ted. I know his name from when I slipped the invite to the Poison Apple into his mailbox and caught sight of the letters. It wasn't intentional. When I pulled his bills out and sifted through them—that was intentional. But I still maintain the NFH moniker fits him better.

I can't stop thinking of the thick cloud of tension that practically vibrates between us, especially when he came crashing over to my front door today. Or the way his presence heats up my blood and brings all my nerve endings to attention. The way he helped with the mirror then disappeared into his cold indifference, left my head spinning.

It's three AM, but I'm starving, having not had a chance to grab a shift meal or snack. I meander to my rickety dining table with a chipped bowl of oatmeal. Again.

When I'd been going through everything that first day with Red and Cinder, I stumbled upon an unexpected find. A massive barrel of oats next to a dusty saddle in the detached garage. The best I can surmise is that my aunt either once owned a horse or planned on getting one. Another wasted or lost dream my aunt left behind.

Spooning a bland bite of porridge into my mouth, I wonder if the NFH contributed to my relations not sticking around. Maybe Aunt Astrid had to go on all those trips, leaving this house to rot, because *he* made living out here so unbearable.

Or maybe I'm just cranky from the thick heat smothering me, making it so my skin feels suffocated. Or maybe it's the way this meal is going down.

For several days straight I've been making oatmeal for every meal because it's an obvious way to save money. Thank the fae for shift meals and a barrel of oats, because I don't have to spend any money on groceries. It all goes back into the house. Though I did splurge a bit to put the NFH on his toes with singing telegrams and cake.

The porridge goes down like bland, thick sludge, and lands like a heavy stone in my gut.

I just need to pretend I'm some adorable orphan on the precipice of a great destiny like Oliver Twist.

Who knows? Maybe I've stumbled onto the greatest diet of all time! A month of this and I'll drop twenty, thirty, or maybe fifty pounds. They'll call it Goldie's Porridge Solution. I could get infomercials and sell programs that change everyone's lives.

My mom's warning that I tend to obsess and get carried away interrupts my fantasies of being interviewed by Oprah.

Okay, I can admit I get obsessive. And the only thing I've been more obsessed about than this house is my neighbor. Admittedly, it started as a genuine attempt to win him over, but it devolved into blatant attempts to yank his chain. I itch to do it again, even now.

But then there he was at my doorstep. Angry, shoulders heaving, as he bared down on me. Electricity raced through my veins. I'd forgotten how tall and broad he was. Even in his anger, the blue-black curls that fell over his forehead softened his rugged features, making him more alluring. Again, in that strong mountain man kind of way that suggested he might pin me against the wall and swat my behind.

And then a spark sizzled in my lower belly, signaling that I really didn't hate that idea as much as I should.

My heart had raced as I stared up at him, feeling alive in a way I hadn't in so long. Was it anger? And since when did anger cause me such a rush of desire that made my knees weak? I could feel the heat radiating off him and the way he towered over me made me feel small and vulnerable. But the full force of his scowl directed straight at me devastated me in a way I couldn't explain. Like I was the center of his whole universe and nothing else mattered.

These are the thoughts of a crazy person.

At least, I know it.

For faefucks sake, I have to pretend I didn't rifle through his mail to learn his name. It still bothers me he wouldn't just introduce himself like a normal person.

But again, he's so different from how the men at the bar who wax poetic about me and vie for my attention. There is something so real and intense about the NFH that I can't shake.

But it's all over. We called a truce, and there's no reason to see him again. Not that I want to. Not that he deserves another second of my time.

I set the empty bowl into the sink with a hollow clang of ceramic. Gods this house is way too big for one person.

By the time I find my way to bed, I'm completely drained. The bedding is cold, the room filled with the weight of the day. The whispers of the old house seem to echo my confusion. Why does someone so distant elicit such intense emotions? Why, when surrounded by admirers, am I so consumed by the one person who seems indifferent?

But blissful sleep takes a while to come when I can't stop thinking about my neighbor's cold eyes and confusing demeanor.

At some point between worrying I'll never fall asleep and if this entire endeavor is an absolute failure before I've started, I drift off.

It's only when a warm arm encircles me do I start to

wake again. It takes a full minute before I realize that I went to sleep alone.

This bed is too soft. Why is the mattress sagging underneath me? I move my leg but it doesn't find the edge of the bed like usual. The mattress keeps going.

I blink my eyes a couple times, coming to the slow and horrifying realization that this isn't my bed, and there is a man snuggled up to my side. A chill runs down my spine. My breathing becomes erratic, each inhalation shaky and tinged with the taste of fear.

Early dawn peeks through shiny silver window treatments. Deep purple silk sheets surround me, and they stink of cologne and sex. My hand covers my mouth and nose to dampen the powerful punch.

My heart feels like it's about to explode from my chest. I mentally scramble, trying to piece together the puzzle. Was I drugged? Abducted? Assaulted? Everything feels fine in my coochie realm, but does that really mean anything? Though my pajamas remain untouched, cold dread continues its death grip on me.

Even as I extract myself from under a lanky male arm I don't recognize, every worst-case scenario races through my mind, each more terrifying than the last.

Regardless of how it happened, I need to get the hell out of here. The man on the bed is long and lanky with a full head of long dark hair. I can't see his face, but I don't think I recognize him. The bed is massive, if broken and saggy, to accommodate a frame that is probably just under seven feet. I'd remember a giant of my acquaintance.

The only guy similar in size to this behemoth is my NFH, but I can tell at a glance this isn't my neighbor. Not enough broad shoulder, or barely restrained anger.

I slink out from the rank, sex-soaked bed. I can't see the

man's face and can only tell he has dark hair and snores like a chainsaw.

I take a step and the wood betrays me, its loud creak a death knell in the tense silence. I hold my breath, praying he remains asleep. The pounding in my chest feels deafening in the stillness.

Don't wake up, don't wake up.

His sudden movement nearly sends me into cardiac arrest. But then he grabs a pillow and draws it into his body before falling back into a rhythm of steady snores. I let out a shaky breath I hadn't realized I'd been holding.

My breath comes out shaky; the stress making my muscles lock up. Every step toward the door feels like a lifetime. The very air feels thick, heavy, like trying to move through molasses. My trembling hand reaches for the doorknob, its cold metal the only real thing grounding me.

I turn the golden knob and slowly ease it open, trying to prevent any sudden loud creaking that might wake my potential kidnapper. With the softest click, I close the door behind me, feeling a little better to have a barrier between me and the random guy.

Do they have another name for a kidnapper who doesn't take kids but full grown adults? Adult—napper? For some reason it bothers me in this moment that I don't have a word that fits the situation even as I pad down a wooden hallway watching every step trying to keep from being heard or seen.

The staircase creaks loudly, sending cold shoots of panic up through my legs before spearing into my brain. With a quick glance out the window I find myself I'm in a forested area similar to the one I live in. Maybe I'm not too far from home?

If only I had my phone. I could call 911 or my friends.

The house is decorated in a masculine mountain man kind of way from the wood-paneled walls to the plaid furniture. The smell of pine and coffee fill the air, but I don't take the time to enjoy the pleasant mixture as my nostrils are full of my own fear.

And that fear intensifies when I begin to suspect who's house I'm in.

Oh gods no.

CHAPTER 10

A CREAM PUFF RUINS BREAKFAST

TED

The stack of flapjacks and bacon pieces steam on my plate. I made too much, a habit I never bothered to break since my brothers still drop in so frequently.

I'm about to take the first sip of my coffee when a loud creak met my ears. A sweet feminine scent reaches my nose. A woman is coming down the stairs with measured steps. One who is trying to be sneaky but failing.

Godsdammit. Not again.

Setting the mug back down on the table without tasting the dark roast, I consider pulling out the whiskey.

It's not even eight AM. Let's hold off, shall we?

I'm half between deciding if I should flee out to the balcony or stand my ground in the kitchen—it is my house after all—when the woman's scent intensifies.

Ripe strawberries, thick sweet amber honey, and a hint of light spring florals spreads along my tongue.

My stomach drops the same time my hearts shoots up, lodging itself in my throat

Before that plump, silky tan leg steps into view. I know *exactly* who is in my house.

My voluptuous neighbor steps into my foyer, in full view of the kitchen. The girls my brother usually brings home love to wear his shirts, and swim in the length of fabric. But she wears an absolutely touchable, silken, pink and white striped sleep set.

Goldie's blonde curls are tousled from the roll she likely just had in JJ's bed. She tip-toes forward, drawing my attention to her bare feet. For faefuck's sake, even her toes are sexy.

And holy witchtits, is that a tattoo peeking out from under her shorts on her upper thigh?

She licks her already glistening lips and I wonder if my brother even enjoyed kissing those soft petals, or if that ungrateful swine treated her like any other of his conquests.

JJ's smell clings to her. Acid coats my esophagus, so I push the steaming mug of coffee away from me. My stomach churns with something that erases my hunger entirely. Something that I'd never known to be possible.

In a split second, my peaceful morning routine is ruined. I don't want to eat my hot breakfast and take my coffee to the deck to soak in the sunshine on my face. There's only the overwhelming urge to slam open the liquor cabinet and pour a full glass of whiskey and march straight back to my bedroom with it, put on a fishing show and stay there the rest of the day with the curtains drawn. That or give into something far more feral deep inside me that desperately wants to be let loose.

When Goldie's gaze lands on me, her lids fly wide.

Maybe JJ told her this was his house like he's told all the other girls. I bet she believes him even though she's only seen me here the last couple weeks. The only one she's been torturing.

"So when I wouldn't show you the house, you decided to find another way in?" The dry words pop out of my mouth before I even think.

"I—" Her mouth flaps open and shut, and there is this wild look in her eyes. And why wouldn't there be? I'm being rude. *Again.*

Goldie's eyes widen as she seems to take in the surroundings. Surroundings I never intended on letting her see. Not because I'm ashamed of my house. In fact, I'm quite proud of my home. It's cozy and rustic with upgrades I added myself, like automatic shades and Moroccan tile I installed in the bathrooms.

But seeing her in my personal haven is now burned into my brain. I don't need this.

I push up from the table, abandoning the coffee and my hot breakfast. "Well don't think this means there is an open door policy now. That you can just come in here any time you feel like it."

The scent of her wraps around me, creating all kinds of confusing, painful feelings for me to soak in. I need to get out of here, so I grab my keys from the table and head to the garage at the back of the house, and away from her. I don't particularly need anything from the hardware store, but I'm sure I'll find something once I get there.

Pausing with my hand on the knob, I shut my eyes and sigh.

You are better than this.

Am I?

Try to be.

I turn to look at her though I can't force myself to wipe off the dark scowl from my face. Especially when I see her arms wrapped around her body, knees turned in toward each other, as if she is trying to bodily protect herself. From my rudeness no doubt.

"Feel free to have breakfast and some coffee before you let yourself out. I won't be back until much later."

At least, I made an effort. I whip the door open before slamming it behind me. It's only much later, some time between browsing the hardware store's side yard of broken appliances for a project, that I wonder why she was wearing a pajama set.

Normally, the girls end up swimming in one of my brother's shirts. They wear it like they've already decided they are his girlfriend and their one night has made it official. Or because it is a better alternative than their tight party dresses.

Did this mean she came over deliberately in her nightwear? How did they meet? At the club? In my backyard, before he lured her over.

A horrible thought occurs to me and my fingers grip so tightly around the washing machine lid I've opened that the metal dents under them.

Is this not a casual hookup? Does he have plans on seeing her long term? Not that I'd ever seen him bring the same girl over more than twice, but why wouldn't he?

The cream puff is a lovely little knockout who is friendly as all get out and makes cakes in the shape of hearts. Not to mention she's an absolutely irresistible smart ass.

This is exactly what I feared would happen.

My heart plunges into my ice-cold stomach then springs back up into my throat, vibrating with panic before repeating the action three more times.

Would he visit more so he could be near her? Would the honey-eyed girl sit across from me at my breakfast table while she fawns over my brother in front of me in that same silky pajama set?

I slam the washer lid down so hard the metal caves in on the top now too.

"Hey Jim," I call out in a hoarse tone. "I'll pay you a hundred for this one." After a quick scan around the yard, I add, "I'll take whatever else you got too for that matter."

"Whoa," Jim says in his old creaky voice. "Slow season at the job right now?"

"No, not really," I mutter. But he doesn't hear me as he starts to ring up all the crap I'll haul away later to try and fix. I only hope by the time I've tuned up all this junk, I've also straightened out the knots filling up my chest. But some part of me doubts it.

CHAPTER II
CRACKING UNDER THE PRESSURE

GOLDIE

S ome girls keep things inside until they can figure stuff out and then they present a dilemma or issue to others.

I am *not* that girl.

As soon as I get home from the NFH's house, I call Cinder and tell her everything. As I speak to her, I walk into my kitchen and find all the lights were on. I could swear I turned off all the lights before I went to bed. Maybe I flipped them on in my sleep? A shiver of unease races up and down my spine.

Some other smaller items have moved around, like a ladle, a book, and one of my makeup compacts. Or maybe I'm making it up.

When I get to work later, Cinder pulls me aside to go over it all again. We are in the small locker room where we keep our stuff during shifts. There are two mirrored vanities as well, in case we need to do our makeup or change. It's small and functional but Rap agreed to let me paint all the lockers bubblegum pink to add some hominess to it. After the fiftieth time I asked.

My heart aches for Red to be here too, but when she's not being put through the wringer with schoolwork, she's at her new job. But I know she and Brexley have promised to come over and help me out with the house soon. Telling her can wait.

Tense energy vibrates through me, yearning for some kind of release or outlet. Cinder rubs her hands--covered by fingerless gloves--up and down my arms to calm me, and admittedly it helps a fraction.

I'm already dressed for work in a black leather dress and black boots to match my smoky makeup and jewelry. My dress is short enough to show off half the garter tattoo on my upper right thigh. Cinder has three times the tattoos I have, but I love when the lines of my clothing accentuate the floral tattoos on various parts of my body and the Libra scales on my inner forearm.

Cinder's hair is up in a high bun, offset by the sharp cut of her thick curtain of bangs. Her top is an edgy mishmash of chains and fishnet, and she wears baggy cargo pants that droop low.

"Did you decide to call the police?" she asks.

"And tell them what? I woke up in a stranger's bed in my neighbor's house and then my neighbor thought I broke in to see his house because he views a couple friendly gestures as me stalking him? They'd arrest me before I even finished explaining."

My neighbor's reaction had completely thrown me for a loop when he offered me breakfast before practically fleeing his own home to get away from me. Granted, the insanely delicious smelling food made my stomach rumble with desperate hunger pains. But there was no way I was sticking around.

If not for that, I absolutely would have called the cops. But the whole thing was wrong, and I couldn't make sense of it. When I thought I caught a flash of hurt in Ted's eyes, I knew I really had lost my grounding.

Cinder rubs my arms more vigorously. "We can't just let this go. You are sure nothing happened to you?"

I nod. "Pajamas and panties intact. I just don't understand why that mystery guy would come into my house, drug me and carry me over to his bedroom. That's the best explanation I have, but it also doesn't make any sense. The only other explanation is. . . " I stumble on the words, not wanting to say it out loud.

The arm rubbing stops. "What?" Cinder prods.

"Maybe subconsciously I wanted to see inside my neighbor's house so much that I sleep-walked over there and broke in." I wanted more than to see inside the house. I wanted to burrow deeper under Ted's skin. Now my subconscious took control and worked to fulfill those whims.

I should want to run for the hills to get away from him. Instead, he made a truce I immediately hated. I had more nefarious plans in mind for my thundercloud of a neighbor. Maybe donate to a charity in his name, buy him a puppy, or get an article written into one of his absurd newspapers about how wonderful he is (who the hell reads an actual newspaper anymore anyway?). All until he realizes he is a monster, and I am the sweetest girl there ever was.

Cinder's brows knit together, skin tightening around her mouth. "We lived together for four years, Golds. I've never known you to sleepwalk."

"I know, I know." I rub my hands over my face while

staying careful not to mess up my makeup. "But maybe the stress of this whole situation is getting to me."

It's true. Swearing off love, taking on an insane amount of debt, worrying I'll turn into my flaky aunt, and dealing with a gruff unfriendly neighbor has built up to a pressure I fear I'll crack under. Or rather the pressure the male patrons are putting on me has my bones groaning from the weight. Not to mention the way women have been looking at me. The whispers have been getting louder, less careful.

Slut.

Whore.

Who does she think she is?

She's too fat to be that pretty.

I do my best to retreat into my mantras to protect myself from the onslaught, but the comments I hear are so much worse than I want to admit. Men have started to flirt with me in front of their significant others. It's not something I condone, or even want, yet I'm the 'whore.'

Bile coats my throat and my stomach churns as invisible clamps squeeze on either side of my temples.

If sleepwalking is a side effect, I would be grateful that's all I suffer.

The breaking and entering thing I'm not such a fan of. Waking up in bed with strange men and no recollection of how I got there. That could be a problem.

As if sensing I'm awash in anxiety, Cinder pulls me in for a full body hug now. I sigh and lean into her slight but strong frame. Before me, Cinder didn't like anyone touching her for any amount of time. It has a lot to do with her upbringing and the step-family from hell. But I admittedly pushed past her barriers. I never take for granted that I'm now one of the few people Cinder is comfortable enough to be touched by. My hold on her tightens as something in my chest swells, making tears prickle at the back of my eyes.

I blink them away before they even form.

"Hey guys, do you know where—" Snow's words die off when she pops her head into the locker room and sees us embracing. "Oh, sorry. I'll ask later." Her shirt is cut up to reveal a blue glitter covered shoulder and her skirt is short. Cinder must have lent her some fishnet and combat boots because I instantly recognize them.

"It's okay," I assure Snow, breaking away from Cinder. "We're coming. Thanks for prepping the bar to open."

Snow nods. "I can try to cover for longer if you guys need more time."

I shake my head, though my voice is thick with emotion. "No, no, I'm good. Thank you, though."

"Okay, well if you need anything please let me know."

A lot of people say that just because it's the thing to say, but from Snow I feel she sincerely means it.

As soon as the door closes behind her, I ask Cinder. "Is Lysander coming by tonight?"

Pink tinges her cheeks as her violet eyes dart away. "Probably."

We've talked way too much about my problems. I need to focus on Cinder and her life so she knows I care.

"If he's not salty about our heated argument the other night. Inspired by one of Professor Stick Up My Ass's lectures, we ended up debating whether it's morally right for private collectors to hoard important works of art in their homes. Did you know a private collector has Napoleon's tiny shriveled up dick locked away in a closet?"

"And that's. . . bad?"

"Yeah, art is supposed to be a shared experience other-wise it loses all meaning. But Lysander said some bullshit I immediately translated into hoarding art like that makes the piece far more valuable and precious." Cinder snorts dismissively.

"Right, well I was more wondering if there was anything *new* with him? Any *developments*?" My words are loaded with innuendo. As much as I care about how art is curated. . . wait, I don't.

She adjusts her fishnet stockings. "Last week we did end up fooling around one night after watching one of those crappy art films on campus."

My jaw drops. "And you didn't tell me immediately? Was it good? Who started it? I need to know everything." Even as I delve into Cinder's life, fear presses into my mind. She doesn't trust me. I bet she told Snow first. I'm more problems than I'm worth.

"You know me," she shrugs one shoulder. "I have to process things for a long time before speaking about them. I started it. He's a good kisser, though nobody got to finish, if you know what I mean. I was left with a severe case of blue tubes." Her bow lips flatten as she sighs. "But nothing has happened since then. "Snow says Lysander seems like the kind of guy to process things slowly and independently, like me. She thinks he'll be back after a little space, but to look out for subtle signs."

"I like Snow. I think she's the perfect addition to the lost girls. And hopefully she's a semi-decent roommate?" My voice chirps up hopefully, trying not to focus on how I missed the girl talk. It doesn't mean anything.

Insecurity has slowly but surely ballooned inside me in a way I haven't felt for years and I can hear it in my own voice. At least, Cinder and Snow don't seem to resent all the male attention I've been getting. Everything is fine, I try to convince myself.

If I have to replace myself, I have to make sure it's the best damn replacement. Nothing but the best for my Cinder baby. Even if that means she and Snow end up better friends without me.

Even as I think it, something stabs my heart.

Nodding, Cinder confirms. "She is very nice."

"Nice? That tells me nothing," I pout. The need to know everything almost overwhelms me.

Cinder laughs, turning to the vanity and uncapping a black lipstick. It glides across her small but perfect cupid's bow lips. "She doesn't leave wet towels on the ground, if that's what you're asking."

"Hey." I cross my arms over my chest. "I am very busy and important. I don't always have time to clean up." It's true, I was notoriously the messy roommate. And here I was trying to tidy up a shit show of an old house. I wonder if this constitutes as irony. "But seriously, I think Snow has had it rough and really needs our support, so we better get our asses out there before Rap chews us out."

Cinder gives me that half smirk, a knowing shine in her eyes as if she sees all. "You can't help but see the best in everyone, don't you?"

"Whoa," I hold my hands up. "That's not true. Remember how I grilled Brexley to the nth degree? I had to make sure he was good enough for our Red."

Cinder rolls her eyes, still smiling as she holds the door open for me to enter the bar. "Please, you were always going to be besties with the Big Bad Wolf. Everyone can't help but love you."

My smile is weak. I used to strive to get into everyone's good graces, but the polarized attention I've been getting is wearing away at me.

One person more than others has a more prominent

effect. "If that were the case, my neighbor wouldn't be such a raging douche to me." Ugh, why does it bother me so much? I could chip the ice off his blue eyes when he looks at me. It stabs deep squishy vulnerable parts at my core, and I hate it. I don't deserve the way he treats me, and I should leave it alone. I should chalk it up to him being miserable, but part of me still wants to go over and break his door down and demand why he doesn't like me?

Because I sleepwalk and broke into his house. Or maybe it was the singing telegram...

"Do you really not know who the guy in the bed was?" Cinder asks as we near the counter.

I shake my head. "If not an evil adult-napper, then maybe big and grumpy's lover?"

Cinder hops on the bar top and slides across the clean, glossy surface. In a couple hours it will be sticky, wet, and covered in fingerprints. "Want me to go over to his place and find out?"

My height and size don't allow for me to pull off what she did, not gracefully anyway. So I catwalk around the bar and assume my spot. My confidence bolsters with every step. This is the Lost Girl's house and I own this space. I feel more like myself with each moment we get closer to opening. "Faelords, no, please don't."

It's then the bar opens and patrons stream in.

That's when the shit show begins.

CHAPTER 12

MEN ARE A NIGHTMARE

GOLDIE

I'm busy organizing the liqueurs when a suffocatingly sweet aroma suddenly envelops me. It's so cloying that I have to stop myself from coughing. As I straighten up, a tall man with disheveled blonde hair comes into focus, an ornate, antique perfume bottle in his hand.

"I thought you might like this," he says, leaning in too close for comfort, his voice dripping with an unsettling sweetness. He spritzes the air around us generously, coating me in the scent. "It's called 'Goldie's Elixir'. Made it just for you."

While part of me is touched by his effort, the reality of being trapped in a cloud of this invasive scent overwhelms any trace of flattery. I'm trapped in this invasive aroma; it's on my clothes, in my hair. It feels violating. His gesture feels grotesquely intimate, yet he's a stranger. Still, I offer him a weak smile, my mouth dry, trying to hide my discomfort.

A few female patrons, witnessing the bizarre exchange,

whisper amongst themselves. A hot rush of embarrassment paints my cheeks.

Their glances my way are a mix of pity and disdain. One with a snide tone loud enough for me to hear remarks, "Some people will do anything for attention."

Cinder swoops in. "Hey, this bar has its own signature scent. It's called 'Respecting Personal Boundaries'." Her deadpan expression turns to a threatening glower. "You should try it."

His face flushes, as she chases him off. I take a moment to catch my breath—i.e. cough my lungs out.

The bearded man sitting at the bar witnessing the whole show, quietly nurses his same drink. Our eyes meet occasionally, and he always offers a small smile. My gut begins to churn nervously when he slides a small velvet box across the counter.

Opening it, I'm met with the unsettling sight of a braided lock of hair, light and dark. "A token," he murmurs, his gaze intense. "Our hair intertwined. Forever."

Pure horror snakes through me with slithery scales that wrap around my neck.

Two women at the bar watch, and I clearly hear one say, "What do you think she let him do to her to get that kind of devotion?"

"Probably use the back door," the other one laughs meanly.

My mouth goes dry, but I force a polite smile for the bearded man. "Where... did you get this?" I manage to ask through clenched teeth, though I'm already dreading the answer.

"I cut off a piece when you weren't looking," he replies with a sparkle in his eye. As if he's the most clever boy on the school yard.

Every instinct screams to run away. Keeping my voice steady, I excuse myself. Within minutes, Rap directs the bouncers to quietly escort the man out of the bar.

Midway through the night, the atmosphere shifts dramatically. The lights dip, casting long shadows across the room, drawing an anticipatory hush over the crowd. As the familiar chords of an 80s ballad play, a sudden tightness grips my chest, a premonition of something profoundly embarrassing.

A man in a glaringly bright, glittering suit appears on stage. His eyes are locked on me. The obnoxious gleam of a boombox held high over his head signals the start of what can only be described as a spectacle. My pulse quickens, dread rising like bile in my throat, as he begins his serenade.

My stomach drops, twisting into tight knots. His voice, off-key and overly passionate, belts out ridiculous verses, with forced rhymes all centered around my name. With each new line, blood rushes to my face, the searing heat of unwanted attention singeing my skin. The laughter and whispers around me sound amplifies, a cacophony of judgment.

But what's worse are the women at the bar. Their voices, dripping with contempt, cut through the awkward giggles and chatter. "Slut, slut, slut!" they chant, their eyes gleaming with cruel satisfaction. My heart feels like it's being squeezed, each chant a vise tightening around it.

I'm paralyzed, trapped in this spotlight of mockery and judgment. The weight of all those eyes on me feels like chains, heavy and restricting. An icy sweat breaks on the nape of my neck, my palms clammy, and I have to suppress the urge to run, to hide, to escape this nightmare.

Then, as if this spectacle wasn't harrowing enough,

our emcee, Geanie, makes his dramatic move. With the spotlight following his every move, he tries to wrestle the mic away, leading to a chaotic, slapstick battle. It's a whirlwind of flying glitter, swiping hands, and exaggerated tumbles, each moment only increasing my profound mortification.

The situation crescendos into utter chaos until the bouncers finally step in. But the damage is done. I'm left raw and exposed, the weight of the night pressing down on me, the echoes of laughter and jeers ringing in my ears.

But then something far worse happens. The face making its way through the crowd has my nerves on edge, like teeth on tinfoil. It's my ex-boyfriend, Lawrence.

High cheekbones and androgynous good looks. His blond hair is slicked back with gel, and the sleeves are rolled up on his light pink button-down shirt. His slacks probably cost more than an entire month's rent at the apartment Cinder and I shared. Daddy's money. He's not particularly tall, but he has a compact frame from working out.

"Hey, baby girl," he croons, hands in his pockets.

Lawrence has been hanging around the bar again. The messages about getting back together have stopped and I know he thinks he can get into my good graces again by physical proximity.

I am capable.

I am enough.

And I don't need a man.

My mantra gives me strength. My system seems tired of this back and forth cycle of passion and abuse. And does he seem smaller? Not quite as manly as before? Maybe he should try to grow a beard? The guy can't even cook.

I only give him a quick nod as I suddenly busy myself,

rearranging liquor bottles. The feeling of being trapped closes in on me.

I know he will perch at my side of the bar for the rest of the night and try to engage me in conversation. He'll find a way to talk about all the girls slipping into his DMs to see if he wants to hang out. As if it will make me jealous.

He leans in further, his voice dripping with faux concern. "You used to love chatting with me, remember? Has work been treating you well, Goldie?"

Inside, a pressurized distress builds, a part of me itching to retort, to assert my newfound boundaries. But the ever-present need to be liked, to avoid conflict, bubbles to the surface, urging a kinder, gentler response.

Forcing a smile, I find myself nodding, my voice betraying a hint of the old Goldie as I reply, "Work's fine, Lawrence. Just busy as usual." I feel a piece of my resolve crumble, a small victory for him.

"Goldie," his voice softens. "I know you don't believe me, but I've changed. I can't live without you. I'm starving for the way you've supported me, the way you look at me like I matter." He lowers his voice so no one else can hear. "The way you suck dick. It's all I can think about, baby girl."

My face flushes at the memory. How many second chances have I given Lawrence? Too many according to Cinder and Red. But I don't expect someone to be perfect, I just need them to try.

An inner turmoil stirs within me, a maddening concoction of attraction and apprehension. I have always had this weakness, this inability to shut people out completely, always giving them a chance, one too many perhaps. It's Lawrence's relentless pursuit that chips away at my resolve, piece by piece.

My grip loosens as memories of our better days

together flood back. The shared laughter, the private jokes, the chemistry that was undeniable. Most of the time I knew exactly how to make him feel good. . . as he said.

"Don't worry baby girl, I'll prove I'm not going anywhere," Lawrence sets an arm on the bar. Then he leans in. "Can I get a Forbidden Fruit cocktail?" The name rolls off his tongue suggestively.

"Sure." I keep my gaze downcast as I mix his drink.

The invisible weight of someone's eyes pressing into me draws my attention across the room. Rap studies me intently, a question in her eyes.

Do we need to remove him?

My boss keeps close tabs on us and goes above and beyond when it comes to protecting us from patrons who mean to harass us.

Inwardly, I sigh. Lawrence is an unwelcome addition to the fan club that already is my section, but the truth is I need his extravagant tips. Without me around to pay his bills, Lawrence must have run back to daddy for money. And it's going to fund the appliances in my kitchen.

That's what I tell myself anyway.

It's then that Lysander strolls in and sits at the other end of the bar, giving me a polite nod. A genuine smile breaks out on my face as I wave. Cinder deserves happiness and I'm happy to be here and part of the continuation of events.

Something wriggles in my tummy, telling me I should give Rap the go ahead to boot Lawrence too. I squash down my reaction to my ex, envisioning the dishwasher that is going to be life changing.

I shake my head at her. Not tonight.

CHAPTER 13
BREAKING BEAR

GOLDIE

Though I'm bone tired, something tells me to wake up. I blink rapidly, until I focus on the black ceiling fan.

Except my room doesn't have a ceiling fan, and this bed is too hard.

I bolt upright, my butt digging painfully into the stiff mattress. Who the hell could ever sleep on this thing? Posters of busty, nearly naked mage models are tacked to the dark blue walls. Papers and car magazines clutter up the desk in the corner. The scent of stale body odor seems imprinted on the sheets, making my nose wrinkle. The whole place reminds me of a thirteen-year-old boy's room.

Launching out of bed, I wring my hands. "What. The. Fuck?" Chasing after my breath like it's a runaway train, white-hot heat prickles my forehead as anxiety closes around me like a vise.

At least this time, no one is in the bed. I don't think my heart could handle that a second time. Where the hell am I this time? I rush to the window and see familiar trees and catch a glimpse of my crumbling Victorian through them.

My hands cover my face and groan. I did it again. I'm in my neighbor's house *again*.

A flash of hot irritation rips through me. For a moment, I consider wiggling my generous ass out the window. But even if I could fit, it's on the second floor and I don't fancy falling that far.

Which means I'm going to have to sneak out the front. Again.

Kill me now.

I squeeze my eyes shut and try to activate any latent magic powers that want to show up and rescue me. I would be happy to transform into a bird, turn invisible, or teleport the hell out of here. All my muscles clench as I focus hard.

Opening my eyes, I'm met with the same sexy poster of a mage girl who starred on Magic Beach Watch.

Witchtits.

Sucking a breath and building my confidence, I slowly turn the handle on the door.

I'm on the same landing as last time but a few doors down from the other room. I pause to listen for any movement, but don't hear anything. Giving a sniff, I try to detect the smell of bacon and coffee. Any sign that grumpy neighbor is up and about. Nothing. Nothing but the fresh scent of pine and lemon cleaner.

Gulping hard, I begin down the stairs. I carefully check the kitchen for anyone before fully walking into view this time. It's empty, thank the faelords.

Sweat breaks out on my entire body as confusion and the stress of sneaking around gets to me. I hate this. I hate this so very much.

My rattled nerves calm when I successfully make it out

the front door. I turn around and take the time to slowly and quietly close it. Only when it's fully shut do I exhale a breath I'd been holding so long it's gone stale in my lungs.

I spin on my heel, and find myself face to face with a massive brown grizzly bear.

My scream is locked in my throat, and all I can manage is a faint squeak as fright courses through my veins and seizes my muscles. Time stops and an icy terror takes over my body until I can feel every beat of my thundering heart.

I am absolutely going to die and any second, I will feel the jaws of a predator around my head.

Except the bear doesn't pounce. In fact, he doesn't even move. I know he sees me because we are a foot away and he is staring directly into my eyes.

Oh faelords, am I not supposed to make eye contact? Do I play dead? Why did I spend all my time watching reality mage programs instead of studying wildlife documentaries, so I know what to do right now?

The bear huffs, his breath hotly sweeps over me. The longer he doesn't move, the more deeply I look into his dark eyes. There is something about them that strikes me. As if there is an intelligence there, and it makes me feel like he is. . . judging me?

With another huff of what I can only describe as disgust, the bear lumbers off and away into the woods. I don't move until he's completely gone.

After a couple more terrifying minutes, I make to run for my house. Hopefully he isn't waiting in the trees, hoping I'd give him chase. I don't bother to turn and look or listen if anything is after me, until I've leaped up the front steps and slam the door shut behind me. My heart jaggedly slams into my ribs as I struggle to get control of my breathing.

Not only did I somehow sleepwalk into my neighbor's house again, but I was almost eaten by a bear.

Marching up the steps to my bedroom, the uneasiness rocks my insides. Opening the door, I'm surprised to see I've been really busy in my sleep this time. My underwear is on display. It's as if I pulled out the laciest and sluttiest red silk, black lace, and pink crotchless pieces I own and set them out.

My fingers trace over the scratchy red lace of a crotchless one piece I got for Valentine's Day one year but never got to use. What a weird fucking thing for me to do. Some of these pieces were buried at the back/bottoms of my drawers.

Weirder than breaking into strange men's beds?

Maybe this is all a sign I need to bail. Pack up my bags and get the faefucks out of this house and beg Cinder and Snow to make room for me in the tiny apartment I came from.

My mind races in a hundred different directions. I need to calm myself.

"I am beautiful. I am capable. I am enough." I repeat the mantra until my heart rate slows.

And then I make a plan. I say it out loud to solidify it. "Step one, see a doctor about the sleepwalking. Step two, learn about bears. Step three, do *not* give up, Goldie."

CHAPTER 14
GET OFF MY (HER) LAWN

TED

"So it's serious," are the first words out of my mouth when my brother picks up the phone.

"Is what serious?" JJ asks, his tone conveying his usual jovial, relaxed demeanor. As if he doesn't have a care in the world. The only reason he doesn't is because of me. I should have been harder on him. But I did the best I could after our parents passed.

"With my neighbor. You've had her over twice now." My teeth ground against each other.

Running into her this morning had been less than pleasant. I'd been coming back from my morning walk when I found her sneaking out of my house, again. Again, I couldn't account for the way my heart sunk in my stomach. Naturally, she'd been terrified of me, and it occurred to me that I should have been walking around in my bear form the moment she moved in. It might have scared her off from my place and my dumbass brother.

But now that it was serious, I couldn't do that. I loosened my jaw with a loud pop.

"I don't know what you're talking about, but is she hot?" JJ laughs lightly.

I grip the wrench in my hand so hard my knuckles turn white. After I returned to my human form, showered and dressed, I retreated to my garage with my small army of broken appliances and projects.

JJ usually isn't one to deflect, but maybe he realizes he's crossed a line this time and is covering up.

"Two nights ago. You crashed at my house, and a woman came out of your room. The blonde cream puff. She's my neighbor. She snuck out again this morning."

"Are you okay, big bro?" he asks, his voice taunting. "Has the isolation pushed you to create delusions about beautiful women breaking into your house?"

Anger rips through me hot and fierce. If he doesn't even have the decency to confess that he's been getting intimate with the most irritating girl I've ever met, I might have to murder him. Does she think he's in love with her too, and he's just using her because she is close by?

Two rock hands squeeze around my heart as I think the two of them might be so serious he can't admit it yet. She deserves better than this runaround bullshit. She shouldn't be hidden. JJ needs to nut up and own that he is sleeping with my beautiful, overly-friendly neighbor who makes every nerve ending tingle when I see her.

"Stop being an asshat," I growl into the phone. "If you are messing around with my neighbor, tell me."

"I'd love to tell you that. But two nights ago, I sadly taxied back to your place alone. When I got up, not even you were in the house. And then last night, I had to stay here and work late. Massive software update to work on. No time for fun shenanigans, but you bet your big fuzzy ass I'm going to celebrate my face off once we get this update launched."

JJ works at a tech firm, one of the rare achievements in his life I can nod at with some semblance of pride. And while I usually want to pop his head off the rest of the time, right now I'm left in confusion. This lie is too specific and simple. Not to mention, he usually doesn't bother lying at all. He's an ask for forgiveness after the fact kind of guy.

"But when the time to party comes," he goes on, "Why don't you invite this blonde cream puff you speak of, over. I'd love to meet her."

I hang up. I'm getting nowhere with my brother. Per usual.

It's time I get my big snout out of his damn business and focus on my own. Which means turning to the place where I always find my grounding. Good, honest, work.

A LOT of days I end up working from home, doing paperwork and coordinating jobs for my employees. But after talking to my dumbass brother, I decide to head out to the construction sites to check in on my guys' progress. I built my contracting business from the ground up, determined to get in and transform wood, metal, and more to make houses into homes for people. A quick bounce from there got me into the restaurant industry. I got my own business license and started hiring guys I got friendly with at the hardware store.

Right now, we are tasked with gutting three houses for renovations, and building out a new industrial, health-conscious coffee shop. I was more than willing to roll up my sleeves, grab a chisel, and start removing the old tile with one of my guys, working side by side in peace for several hours. Losing myself in the work, my mind calms. I'm no longer plagued by visions of the blonde goddess next door rolling in the sack with my brother.

It's past six when I turn off to the long, winding street to my place. My AC valiantly fights off the blazing summer sun cooking my car. Thinking of the steak I'm going to grill after I take a shower, I find my attention on the car behind me.

It's unusual for any car to be on this road, as it is a bit of a hidden turn off and not many people live here. The driver is doing his best impression of an enema. He's so close in his silver Audi, that I can determine his eye color is green. An uneasy feeling twists in my gut the closer to the cul-de-sac with my and Astrid's... or Goldie's house.

I deliberately slow down a little more, and chuckle when his hands wave wildly in frustration as if to ask what that fuck I think I'm doing.

Suck it buddy, this is a residential area.

When I turn to the right to pull into my driveway and he takes a left toward Astrid's—or Goldie's—house, the uneasiness balloons into a sour unsettledness. I don't like this. I can't explain why, but I don't.

My garage is full of all the projects I'm currently tinkering with, so I park off to the side of my house. As I step out of my truck, I have a perfect view of Goldie on her porch. A pink kerchief is tied around her hair as she stands on a ladder, cleaning the front windows.

The guy practically leaps out of his car, as she steps down. Even from here, I can sense the tension in her body.

My hand curls around my keys, the metal teeth biting into my skin.

Go inside, Ted. It's none of your business.

The guy is emphatically waving his hands at her, and though I can't hear them, I note how she crosses her arms across her chest. It's a defensive pose, and she doesn't step down from the porch—almost like she is trying to bar the entrance from this guy.

Ted, she is JJ's problem. If that. Go inside.

He puts one foot on the bottom step as if to climb them and she takes a step back.

Before I know it, I've covered half the distance to her house, shoving my keys in my back pocket.

"Hey, what the hell is wrong with you?" I yell out when he takes another step up. I stay several yards away, not wanting to get much closer to Goldie's intoxicating smell. It turns my brain fuzzy and heats my blood.

Both of their heads swivel toward me. Goldie's eyes are rounded, making her look like a doe caught in a headlight. The ginger haired guy's mouth twists in displeasure, unhappy with the interruption.

"You can't drive like that in a neighborhood like this," I say, putting my attention on the man. "Sometimes kids play out here."

He rolls his eyes, but steps off the stairs. Something slight unclenches in me. As if I appreciate him getting off my territory.

But this isn't my territory. I shouldn't feel this way.

"I wouldn't hit any kids," the tall ginger shoots back as if I'm the dumbest person in the world for uttering such a thing.

I glance at Goldie who looks between us like she isn't sure which of us to be more wary of. Her arms are still crossed over her breasts. Her face and arms are generously smudged with dirt and grime. She's absurdly appealing, dirty like this. And then thoughts of showering off that voluptuous body assail my mind.

Pushing those thoughts away, I focus on the idiot again.

"I also don't appreciate you trying to climb in my trunk to visit your friend here," I say, waving at Goldie.

"Friend?" he scoffs. Then he turns to look at her, a glaze coming over his eyes. "We're more than that." His voice trails off as if he has receded into some kind of fantasy world and Goldie is at the center of it.

Is she screwing around on JJ? Not that I should care. He's never been known to be committed or faithful. Still, a spike stabs me right in the chest.

"How did you find out where I live?" Goldie asks, her arms dropping to her sides as she takes a step forward. Her posture has gone from protective to defensive.

He laughs. "We live in the age of information, baby. It's not hard to get anyone's details these days. And I knew you'd feel special when I came here for you. Seeing you at the Poison Apple, isn't enough."

Every alarm bell blares in my body. I am not fucking moving from this spot until this guy gets gone.

She shakes her head and runs a hand over her face, smearing more dirt on her forehead. Fuck, why do I like the way she looks dirty so much?

"You shouldn't have come here. I have a boyfriend."

It's like watching a log being split in his chest. The gleam in his eye dulls, shoulders curving forward as if he's taken a physical blow.

I knew she was seeing JJ, but hearing her say that also feels like a donkey kicking me in the chest.

His eyes darken as he turns toward me. "Is this him?"

The laugh that escapes Goldie comes out as a surprised bark. "Uh, no, definitely not."

"Likewise, sweetheart," I shoot back. Turning to the crestfallen guy, I say, "I may not be her beau, but I know him. And you don't want to be here when he gets back."

A slight exaggeration on my part. Okay, a huge exaggeration. JJ is conflict averse and has no problem shoving his hands in his pockets and walking away from a potential scuffle with anyone. He'd rather buy the guy drinks and chat over a mutual conquest than get in a territory war over a female. Oddly enough, that has worked pretty well for him.

When the red-haired guy doesn't move, I stalk forward, not bothering to keep my distance.

The guy's head swivels between Goldie and me as he rubs his forehead as if confused by something.

I round his car and open the driver's side door. "Here, allow me," I sneer.

He shuffles over as if weights are tied to his shoes, but he doesn't protest. I'm half surprised. I expected him to get in my face and try to throw a swing with the energy pulsating off him.

When he finally gets in, I say, still holding the door, "And don't drive like a douche as you see yourself out of my neighborhood." With that, I slam the door shut. Then I walk over between his car and Goldie, crossing my arms, making it clear I plan to stand right here until he leaves.

He pauses, so I shine my eyes at him. Goldie is behind me and can't see the supernatural glow I'm broadcasting at this guy like a danger beacon.

The big ginger shakes his head as if trying to clear it, then starts the engine and pulls away.

It's not until the dust settles in his wake that I drop my arms. I turn to Goldie who is staring at me like she is trying to figure out a puzzle.

"Did you just help me again, Tedford?" she finally asks. "Tedford?"

She bites her lower lips as her eyes dart away a moment.

It's only natural she knows my name if she's seeing JJ. But I don't care for the bastardization of it. Per usual, she's under my skin and scraping against my nerves.

I let out a huff. "I helped myself. It's bad enough you are here, but having asshats gather out here to kiss your feet is worse."

Her nose wrinkles as her chin tightens. "Great, wonderful. I'll do my best not to bother you from all the way over here." The words come out clipped with fury. "But I'd like to point out you broke the truce and walked an awfully far way to put your nose in my business."

"This neighborhood is my business," I shoot back, knowing I'm in the wrong even as I say it.

Her hands clench into fists as she practically vibrates. "Well, I am *not* your business. And I'll make sure to tell everyone at work tonight that no one is allowed to visit your little sanctuary. That way there will be no reason for you to come onto *my* property."

"What if I bring you a pink frosted cake with strawberries on it?" My sardonic tone is as harsh as it is taunting.

Her face turns blood red. The storm door slams behind her with a loud rattle, before the front door crashes shut after that.

As I make my way back home, guilt tingles hotly at the front of my forehead.

I'm trying to make sure we stay on our respective sides of the emotional fence, but do I really need to be such an ass? My neighbor brings out the absolute worst in me.

Sure, I can be crotchety. But it's usually in a neutral,

quiet kind of way. I act like a fucking animal around the cream puff and I hate it.

Dangerously close under the surface of my cake taunt was a very serious part of me. If I made an adorable, sugary confection like she had and showed up on her door, would she forgive me? Let me in? Let me kiss those plush lips and grip her ample hips—no. This is all wrong. I would never do any of that. It's wrong for all the reasons.

Instead of starting up my grill for the steak waiting in the fridge, I start up the shower and get under the hot spray. I want to wash away everything I've said to her. Splaying my hands on the cool tile, I drop my head completely under the intense spray. Shutting my eyes tight against the raucous thoughts swirling in my mind, intermixing with sour emotions, I completely lose any grounding I found earlier in the day.

Something swells in my chest as something firms in my mind. Sometimes my mind makes itself up before I've even recognized the thought that has formed. And when that happens, I have no choice but to follow through on whatever inane or ill-advised plan I have.

In no time, I'm dressed in a tee shirt and jeans, and back on Goldie's porch. Evening is setting in fast, turning the sky half midnight blue and half blazing orange. My senses are clear from the shower and I suck in a big breath of fresh mountain air before my knuckles rap against her door.

No answer.

I note that her car that's usually parked out front is missing, and all the lights are off.

I'll make sure to tell everyone at work tonight that no one is allowed to visit your little sanctuary.

Goldie must have left for work already, at the Poison Apple.

I've never been, but I knew of it before she even slipped those coupons into my mailbox.

This can wait until tomorrow, Ted. Sleep on it. Talk to her tomorrow.

Even as I tell myself that, I know I've lost the fight. When I have something I'm compelled to say or do, it must be done right then or I won't rest.

Which means, I'm taking a trip into the city.

I scrub a hand over my face. Every single part of me perks up at the idea of standing in front of the soft-looking blonde with the flashing honey eyes.

Which is exactly why I also dread it.

CHAPTER 15
OFF THE RESERVATION
TED

TED

The bars I go to are pubs, watering holes I take my guys to after a hard day's work. The few times I ventured into Boston's bars were not for pleasure and were usually some of the worst days of my life.

But here I am, waiting in line for half an hour to get to the big ornate doors of the Poison Apple. I'm surrounded by sparkly mini dresses, expensive shoes, and heavy cologne that's clogs up my nose and throat.

I'm grateful I thought to put on one of my nice silver button-up shirts with my jeans, though I'm still wildly out of place.

Shoving my hands in my pockets, I feel like an old grandpa next to these kids though I'm not much older. But I've been working since I was sixteen and never went out and partied. I skipped college in favor of working construction to support me and my brothers after our parents died. From there I built a successful business that allows me to pick my own hours and work with who I want.

This world of frivolous glitz, glam, and hookups is the one my neighbor rules. No wonder JJ's so attracted to her. It's his world too.

Just as I'm about to duck out of line and abandon this whole idea, the bouncer ushers me into the Poison Apple.

If I thought the people in line were glamorous, it's nothing compared to the scene that greets me inside.

A two-story display of liquors rises up behind the bar at the center of the room. Warm light spills through each bottle, casting a romantic glow on the beautiful people mingling with one another. Off to one side is a packed dance floor, surrounded by counter height bar tables with standing room only. The other side of the room has tufted burgundy couches laid out for conversational lounging.

My hands slip out of my jeans and my lips part as I soak in the feature at the center of the lounge area. A massive live tree wrapped in lights drips down over the luxury seating. I can smell the fresh dirt from here. Turning my gaze upward, I find the ceiling is mostly glass which must allow for the tree to drink in rays from the sun during the daylight hours.

Sweat pops out on my brow, and my heart beats too fast. If I felt out of place before, now I am completely blown out of my element. While I can appreciate the structural designs that make a place so grand, I am fast losing my nerve.

Then I spot her. A blur of bright bubblegum pink and black leather. Soft blonde curls are pulled up into a messy updo with fallen tendrils that caress her bare tan shoulders. Long gone is the grime from her cleaning.

My brows knit as my pants suddenly tighten. The dress she is wearing should be illegal. It leaves her upper body exposed, showing off her glistening warm skin and dipping down to showcase her ample cleavage.

Head snapping to the side, I flex my jaw, fighting my building hard on.

What are you doing? She is your brother's hookup. Don't be a scuz bag.

Inhaling sharply through my nose, I make my way toward the bar. My fists clench at my sides as a red haze clouds my vision when I find a passel of men gathered at the bar, clearly vying for her attention.

It's a mass of popped collars and greedy eyes drinking her in. There are two bouquets of flowers and even more boxes of truffles on the counter, left before her like an offering to a goddess.

A strange buzzing sensation licks against my skin the closer I get to the crowd.

Goldie smiles pleasantly as they all chat her up, but I notice something they don't seem to. There are lines of strain pulling at the corners of those luminescent eyes.

Standing behind her fan club, I clear my throat.

She's shaking a drink up when the clacking ice halts abruptly, her eyes flying wide as they fasten on me. Her petal pink lips part in surprise.

As if sensing a shift in the energy, the men turn to see who has captured Goldie's attention. Hot glares dig into me, but I brush them off as if they are nothing.

"Can I talk to you?" I ask.

Goldie pops the top of the mixer and pours out three martinis, her brows furrow as if considering my proposal.

"Do you need me to escort him out?" one of the men ask her.

"I'd be happy to do it," another eagerly jumps in.

Her eyes dart between them as she bites on her lower lip. They are making her nervous, but they don't notice.

The longer I stand there, the strange buzz against my skin lessens ever so slightly. Is it her effect on me? Or have all these guys been rubbing socks on carpet?

"I only need a minute," I explain, as if that will help. "Promise."

Goldie gives me a curt nod. "I'll be right back boys." She sets the three pink martinis on a tray off to the side. Almost instantly, a girl with cool black skin and pure white hair steps up to grab it. Her striking blue eyes widen as she takes me in.

Feeling more unsure than before, I stuff my hands back in my pockets.

"Can you cover me a minute, Snow?" Goldie asks.

Snow nods with a soft smile. "Of course. I'll just drop these drinks off then come take your spot."

With that Goldie saunters around the bar and breezes by me. Feeling the glare of a thousand daggers, I turn my back on the salty gentlemen she's abandoned and follow.

Goldie only gets a few steps before a much shorter man steps in the way. His blonde hair is slicked back, he wears a pink button up shirt and a watch that costs more than my car.

If it weren't for JJ this is probably Goldie's ideal type.

"Where are you going, baby girl? Is this guy bothering you?" he asks, sending a warning look over her shoulder at me.

I stare back at him with a flat expression. His compact muscles looks like they've been curated in a gym. But I'm almost a foot taller, and I'm a were, but he doesn't know that. I'm not technically allowed here in a human's only bar, but I figured it would be acceptable for a five-minute chat.

"No, I'm alright Lawrence. I'll be back out in a couple minutes," Goldie says in a pleasant voice, but like the lines around her eyes, I can tell it's strained.

After a long moment, he steps to the side. But not before he grabs her hand and gives it a squeeze. "Every minute you're away is torture, baby girl."

My eyebrows shoot up at that. No wonder she was pissed I didn't fall backwards over her heart-shaped cake. She's used to being treated like a rare jewel everywhere she goes.

Not that she doesn't shine and sparkle like one, but I've seen my own brother's core rot from being spoiled by the same kind of treatment.

Maybe that's what makes them perfect for each other. They are both charismatic and spoiled.

Something in my chest sinks to my stomach.

Goldie extracts her hand before resuming her journey to the back. I staunchly ignore Lawrence's glare and follow.

Goldie leads me past the restrooms into a room marked employee's only. It's small with bubblegum pink lockers.

Hmm. Wonder who's responsible for the decorating here?

As soon as the door clicks shut behind me, Goldie whirls around, heat blazing in her eyes.

"What are you doing here?" Her arms cross over her chest.

My mouth goes dry as I realize how close we are in the small space. That honey scent with light floral and fruity hints engulfs me and makes it even harder to control certain body parts.

No. I refuse to be that kind of bastard. I'm here to speak my peace.

But words erupt from me like a volcano. "You were so desperate to see inside my house, you slept with my brother?"

Goldie steps back, a hand covering that infuriating, enticing neckline. "Your brother? Your house?"

I pinch the bridge of my nose. This wasn't the plan, but it exploded out of me. The derailed train barrels forward. "Oh faelords, did he tell you it was his house? Because your *boyfriend* lives here, downtown. He only visits my cabin when he's... entertaining."

Good job, Ted. Way to be delicate about it.

Her jaw unhinges as she stares at me like I'm some kind of crazy person before those golden eyes flash with anger. "How dare you? First you rebuff a lovely cake I made myself, then next you barge in at my workplace and accuse me of sleeping with your brother?"

Holding up my hands, I get control of myself enough to talk in a more even tone. "I get it. JJ knows all the right things to say, unlike me. If you insist on carrying on with him, with whatever it is you both are doing, I just want to make something clear. I can't have you coming over any damn time you want. I need a certain amount of peace and quiet. Carrying on your affair with JJ at my house is one thing, but it doesn't mean there's an open door policy. I don't want to see you every morning, slipping JJ the tongue across the table from me."

Oh witchtits, that thought actually makes me sick to my stomach.

A strange squawk escapes her throat. Goldie shakes and her brows furrow, as if I'd said something deeply perturbing.

Why the fuck does her open, shocked expression make me want to dip down and kiss her?

But I am not scum. Despite my brusque nature, I really am saying all this to protect her. "I know this may seem entirely out of line, but I need to warn you about your boyfriend. He may be my brother, but you deserve the truth. If you think he's serious about you, you're wrong. My brother is a revolving door of women. Seeing as you are my neighbor, I don't want you to get the wrong idea."

There. That was what I came to tell her. Ever since she dropped that JJ's her boyfriend, I couldn't in good conscience let her think that without some more context. I should have written it down, so I didn't go off on so many tangents, but when I stand in front of this girl, I lose all damn sense.

Goldie swallows hard several times, emitting strange groans before she seems to get control of her voice again. "I am *not* sleeping with your brother."

"You said he was your boyfriend," I point out.

Her arms flap in exasperation. "I lied to get that guy out of my hair. I wasn't actually referring to anyone."

JJ's not her boyfriend. She's not sleeping with him.

My brain can't compute fast enough before she continues.

"In fact, I should be pressing charges against him and you and your brother."

"What?" Unfortunately, my brain is all too ready to reach horrible conclusions about the things JJ has done. He's not Eli, but after all the shit I've pulled my youngest brother out of it, nothing surprises me anymore. And not in a good way.

I step into her space. "What did he do to you?" The growl that rumbles from my chest is pure bear.

So help me faelords, if he hurt this woman I will rip his dumb face right off.

Goldie tilts her head up to see into my face, some of those flaxen curls sliding off the back of her shoulders. It must be the heat in here. When did it become a blazing temperature in this tiny space?

Fuck, I want to kiss her.

"I... don't know," she says hesitantly. Then her gaze drops to my mouth as if she is also considering the taste and texture, like I'm doing to her. Shaking her head slightly, she puts her hands on my chest and pushes me back a step. The feel of her skin scorches through my shirt.

"I mean. I hope he hasn't done anything," she swallows hard two more times, her hands still on me. The heat from her touch shoots straight down my body.

She's not making any sense. For fucks sake I'm about to give her mouth to mouth to help wet those lips if she can't get her words out right.

Thankfully she removes her touch from me when she covers her face with her hands. "By the way, are you related to giants? What is he, seven foot?"

Just about, but I don't get a chance to answer. Her eyes dart away as if she is having a hard time meeting my gaze.

"Don't freak out because I already have a doctor's appointment about this. It's super embarrassing and I swear I'm not doing it on purpose. Believe me, I have no intention of being in your house, but I think I've been sleep-walking and breaking in."

I blink once. Then twice.

"What?"

Covering her chest with her arms again, she looks anywhere but at me. "The last couple nights, I've fallen asleep in my bed, only to wake up in your house. The first time, I found myself in a massive broken-down bed that smelled like sex." Her nose wrinkles. "With a guy I didn't know, I'm guessing that would be your ho-bag brother?"

I don't bother to correct her. JJ is a self-proclaimed slut and he likes it that way.

Her fingers fly up to pull on a tendril of hair, seeming to grow more agitated by the minute. "The next night I went to sleep again in *my* bed but woke up on a small, hard rock of a mattress, alone thankfully, but I was in your house again. The only explanation, other than you guys have been drugging me and kidnapping me to your house, is that I've been sleepwalking. So I'm going to see a doctor about it."

Of everything I was expecting, that didn't even come close to being on the list. Something between a dry laugh and a wheeze escapes me. "You are not sleepwalking into my house."

Goldie's arms drop to her sides, shoulder straightening. "So you are confessing to kidnapping me nightly, Tedford?"

I'd balk at the nickname if the other suggestion weren't so heinous. "What? No." I take a step back. "I mean you couldn't be sleepwalking to my house. I keep the house locked up tight. Even my dumbass brother knows to keep it that way when he drops by. So unless you have lock picking skills when you are in REM, that doesn't explain how you are breaking into my place."

"I'm not breaking in," she screeches, flapping her arms out. "I'm probably just stressed."

"Oh yeah, it's so hard being you with men drooling over you, at your beck and call every night." Anger rises up into my chest like an expanding hot air balloon. Or is that jealousy?

Part of me knows I need to slow this down. Do I really believe she's sleepwalking? Is she still trying to cover up being with JJ? If so, why is he denying it too? Why would either of them bother to lie?

But my brain is zooming past all that and focusing on all the male attention she gets and how it must tickle her to no end. She's the male JJ. Looking for a fun time and getting it anytime she wants.

Something wiggles at my logic. Why would I care if she's like that? She can do whatever and whoever she wants.

But part of my pride smarts. How many other doorsteps has she shown up on with a pink, heart-shaped cake and sprigs of lavender? Nobody could resist her charm, and she clearly reaps the benefits everywhere she goes. I knew better than to think it was some special gesture for me, but way way way deep down, some part of me wanted it to be.

No one had ever brought me a cake. The last person was my mom and she would buy them for my birthday.

All I got was my brothers' troubles dumped on my doorstep. I couldn't afford to accept any of those heart-shaped confections, or I might want more. I couldn't afford to want more. She was better spreading her cheer around to other people.

But the idea of those fuckheads out there treating her like some carnival ride has my hands balling into fists.

Goldie pokes me in the chest. "Hey, your Tedliness, I didn't ask for that. It's not my fault the second I swear off men, they come at me in droves." The corners of her lips pull down as she frowns deeply.

Something twists uncomfortably in my chest. It's not just because she is warping my name into weird abominations. I don't like that look on her. I prefer her smiling or sassy.

I point a finger at the door. "You are telling me, you

don't love those idiots bowing and scrapping before you?" The raging heat of jealousy and anger twist faster around each other in a spectacular spiral.

Goldie wrings her hands, her frown deepening. "I mean, I appreciate the tips since I'm fixing up my aunt's house, but no, this is a lot, even for me. I've never had so many gifts or been asked out on so many dates in one week." She shoots a nervous glance at the door, and I'm fucking done in.

"Listen—" she rushes on. "It's not your problem. Like I said, I'm seeing a doctor tomorrow, so hopefully she'll give me meds or something, so I stop. I swear, I don't want to see inside your house—"

The idea snaps shut in my head before I barely knew it formed. The thing about me is once I make up my mind, there is no other option.

She turns to go, but I grab her arm. Faelords, touching her is unreal. It sends heat and electricity rioting through me every time.

"Make a deal with me. Promise not to see JJ, and I can help you with your problem."

Goldie rolls her eyes. "I don't want to fuck your brother, Tedson."

"Stay away from my other brother too," I add.

Goldie is practically vibrating now, cheeks flushed bright red. She steps in closer, holding up her hands. "Oh there's *another* brother? How could I possibly resist?" the words drip with sarcasm. "Please let me come roll around in your ratchet-ass beds with your giant-sized relatives. Oooh. How can I help myself?" An index finger with broken pink polish stabs into my sternum as she narrows her eyes. "You don't need to worry, Ted-ileena, I will strap myself to the bed tonight to make sure I don't end up anywhere near you again. I don't want anything to do with your brothers or you. You are insufferable, and rude, and—"

My hands cover hers to stop that finger from poking me again.

"And I can help you with the fan club," I say in a calmer voice, my resolve turning to steel no matter how ridiculous. I don't let go of her hand, noting how soft it is in mine. Her fingers flex and her eyes round.

Then she jerks away, and I release her.

"I don't need your help. I need a good night's sleep in the same bed." Her words are sharp as she turns to stalk away.

I catch her hand a second time, pull her closer, almost drawing her body up against mine. Her eyes widen as she tilts her head back to look at me. I feel her shallow pants across my face, and the tiny tastebuds on my tongue are all up and erect, trying to absorb as much of her scent/taste that I can. Knowing she isn't seeing JJ eases the guilt I have at starting to stiffen under the belt yet again.

"Promise me." The words come out in a low rumble as my gaze drops to her lips.

Her eyes search my face and before they soften. A tongue licks them almost reflexively, and I wish it was me tasting her mouth.

"I promise," she says in a quiet voice, eyes searching mine as if trying to comprehend something.

Letting go of her and stepping away may be the hardest thing I've ever done, but somehow I manage.

The door opens and a goth Asian girl with violet eyes enters. The one I'd seen behind the bar. "You okay Goldie? We need you up front." Her smoky eyes narrow as she regards me. It's either a warning or a threat being directed at me. But she doesn't need to worry.

Goldie clears her throat with some effort. "Uh yeah." And then she practically runs out to the bar. I follow behind, nodding politely at the goth girl.

These guys are giving her a problem? I plan to stick around and make sure they don't.

I'm a bear off the reservation, sticking his nose where it doesn't belong.

Faelords help anyone who tries to get in my way.

CHAPTER 16
AN INDECENT PROPOSAL

GOLDIE

I'd been gone less than ten minutes, but I came back to a restless crowd.

"Baby, I missed you." Alan—or was it Jimi who said it?

There'd been so many new regulars I couldn't even keep them straight, and remembering names and faces is one of my strong suits.

Slipping back behind the bar, I shoot Alan/Jimi a smile I don't really mean.

A month ago, I would have been over the moon to get this kind of attention. I would have mentally picked out my wedding dress and named our kids. Within days I would have asked him to clear a drawer for me at his place.

But these last few weeks have felt...wrong. There's an intensity in his eye, a gleam that has me on edge. I've seen it in every man lately.

All except my big, burly and presumptuous neighbor. He still glares and judges.

I was wrong about his eyes being ice. They were never cold. Up close, his eyes are stormy twin seas. They crash into me, dragging me down, drowning me with their pressure and intensity. They smash into me, stealing the breath from my lungs until I am caught in his monsoon. It's so hard to keep from moving closer into the pull of his innate gravity.

Sleeping with his brother. Ha!

It's so laughable. I pull Cinder off to the side while I let Snow field my section. Those hungry faces crane over her to watch me.

"Turns out my neighbor still thinks I'm going to fuck his brothers. Can you believe it?" I ask Cinder with an incredulous scoff.

Lysander, who is in earshot, just tips back his beer, minding his own business a little too well.

Cinder doesn't even blink.

I've known this girl long enough to understand every subtle twitch or non-twitch she makes.

"Whoa, that's rude. I'm hurt." I cover my chest, trying to soothe my bruised heart.

Cinder shrugs a shoulder. "It's not crazy for you to end up in some guys' bed, smitten before you know his last name."

The truth hurts.

My jaw drops. "You can't say that to my face."

Cinder wraps her arm around my shoulders. "I'm the *only* one who can say that to your face. Because I love you and don't judge."

"You totally judge," I whine.

Cinder rotates me around, giving my bicep a squeeze. "Only when you keep doing the same thing over and over that ends up with you disappointed. I think this break from dating is good for you."

"You deserve way better anyway," Lysander adds from the peanut gallery. Even in his encouragement, Lysander doesn't smile. I've never even seen him crack a small one. If he ever did, I'm sure the cool police would come and repossess his skinny jeans and beanie.

Cinder goes on. "I'm really proud of how you've kept to it the last couple weeks, focusing on yourself and the house instead. Especially with all the... opportunity."

I follow Cinder's gaze to the three guys who immediately wave at me.

Yeesh.

Then there is Ted. He steps up to the bar. He's a hulking figure next to them. This is not his scene, so why is he still here?

I make my way over to him. "You don't need to stay."

"I have a written invitation that says I'm due a free drink," he rumbles calmly.

I heave a heavy sigh though my heart kicks up in tempo. "What can I get you?"

"An ice tea, please."

Oh great, he's a teetotaler too. Is he here judging that I work in a bar?

My brain works overtime to point out every little thing that is wrong with him. I need it. I need to put some mental distance between us, after feeling the heat and hardness of his chest, the roughness of his hands, after being drilled into my unerring focus.

His Tedliness is staring at me again, with those stormy eyes. My gaze turns downward to the cache of clean glasses, my heart beating triple time. I refuse to get caught in his vortex. REFUSE.

Sliding his drink across the bar, I'm careful to make sure our fingers don't meet before scurrying off to take more drink orders, intent to ignore him the rest of the night. I had invited him here, so this should feel like a victory. But that was before I broke into his house, before he accused me of sleeping with his brother...

"I can help you with them."

What the hell does that even mean? Whatever he's planning, I don't like it. There are gears turning in his head. Big, stupid ones, but they are turning nonetheless.

My thoughts are interrupted by a particularly intoxicated member of my fan club who yells over the bar at me. "Goldie, everyone is always talking about who the hottest Lost Girl is, and before I would have said that hot redhead with no boobs, but now I don't even know how I could have thought that."

Heat floods my cheeks and forehead with uncomfortable prickles. It feels like someone ran a garden rake over my nerves.

Oh good, someone who thinks they can get me by not only comparing me to my friends but dissing them in the process. He laughs boisterously as someone else high-fives him.

Before I can bum rush him off my turf, Ted lays a hand on his shoulder and guides him out. He engages the guy in a conversation I can only catch a few words of, something about last night's hockey game. My eyes flit to the guy's hat with black and yellow logo of the team. The guy takes the bait, and Ted successfully redirects his attention away from me.

It's not even five minutes when another patron becomes noticeably loud as he comments on how I have the best rack of anyone in the whole city. Nauseating sensations crawl across my body as the group leers at me.

Ted appears at his side, casually mentioning the new craft beer on tap and effectively steering the conversation away from me or my friend's rack. Once again, he subtly defuses a potential problem, his calm demeanor and distracting tactics working their magic.

Though I'm constantly moments away from punching the next jackass right in the face, Ted keeps getting their eyes off me which lessens their fervor and crudeness.

As the evening progresses, I become more aware of his interventions, each one done with finesse and subtlety and on the whole, all of them start to chill out, their attention wandering away from me for once.

Even though I would never admit it out loud, there is something comforting about Ted's presence and the way he's decided to keep his promise. And it makes me wonder just a little bit more about the complex man that is Tedly bear.

Why do I feel better with him nearby? Somehow, safer?

The longer he hangs around, it's as if some kind of intense pressure has broken. The many pressing eyes suddenly find other places to look. Some of the men wander off, ones who've been glued to my section of the bar for days.

What in the holy hell? It's like Ted's broken some strange spell.

Maybe he's a repellent to them as he is to me.

And while he was an ass per usual outside my house this evening, I can't deny that he came to my rescue. Even if he didn't realize it, or it wasn't his intention. But having one of the patrons track me down to my home is a major red flag and every single girl's nightmare when she lives alone in a secluded forest. I left for work early to give myself time to pick up some pepper spray and a baseball bat I could leave by the front door.

Suddenly, Rap is at my side. There is a sharp edge about her. "Is he with you?" Her eyes drill holes into Ted's head as he continues to drink his tea and survey the place with an appreciative look in his eye.

"No," I burst out. Then I sigh. "Well, kind of. He's my neighbor."

Her brows lift for a moment. "The NFH?" Then her eyes narrow to slits as she keeps Ted in her sights. "How well do you know him?" For some reason that seems like a loaded question, like she's referring to something specific.

The words catch in my throat. Not at all. Hardly.

Well, enough to know how to yank his chain ten ways from Sunday and that he's helpful when he wants to be. That he smells like pine and something far more sensual that makes me tingle from my girly parts to my toes.

What comes out of my mouth is a strangled squeak.

"Right," she says, still without turning to me. "I think I'm going to have a word with him."

Rap rounds the bar, commanding every particle of air around her as she approaches Ted. He turns to her before she reaches him. Between the music and the dull roar of the crowd, I can't hear what they are saying, but both wear serious expressions. She tilts her head to the side and Ted gets up, leaving his drink behind. He trails after her to her office.

Something squeezes around my heart. I weirdly feel like I somehow got him in trouble and now he has to go to the principal's office.

Adjusting my bun of hair, I try to brush off the feeling. I didn't do anything. I mean I technically invited him, but he didn't have to come. And he certainly didn't need to stay. But why does Rap care so much about him being here? Specifically, him?

Is it because I've carried on about my neighbor from hell for weeks and she thinks he's a threat? A wave of shame washes over me. He's not really that bad. I wouldn't leave him alone when he asked.

A couple minutes after Ted and Rap leave, I feel a strange buzz around my body. One by one, the men start to sidle up to my part of the bar again, that hungry look back in their eye.

Good. I don't care. I can handle this.

I am capable. I am enough. And I don't need Ted's help.

Even as I internally repeat my mantra, I feel vulnerable and naked without him nearby.

I turn around and start to do some mid-shift restocking, leaving the drink orders to Snow and Cinder. It's not long before Snow comes to me, a little breathless and flushed.

"I held them off as long as I could, but they are requesting you like they'll die if you don't get over there and pour their next drink." She wipes some of the sweat off her brow. "You got one hell of a fan club, Goldie."

"Yeah," I mutter. "Pretty soon, they'll get matching jackets."

"As long as they're pink," Cinder says as she sweeps by to grab a bottle of vodka.

"Real helpful," I call after her.

Nerves racing with a jitteriness I can't account for; I thank Snow then head back.

There are six of them now, shifting anxiously, hungry gleams intensifying in their eyes the closer I get. Lawrence sits on the far side, and while his constant presence weirds me out, he isn't often in my face.

Pasting on a smile as I near the group of rabid jackals, I try to access my cheerful self. This is *my* house, and no one can ruin work for me. It's my happy place.

One of the men, Greg, makes to come around behind the bar. "Goldie, why don't you teach me how to make a drink," Greg's slurred speech carries an overtly flirtatious undertone.

My hackles rise. While I'm a touchy-feely gal who doesn't mind getting up close and personal, I loathe anyone who crosses that boundary behind the bar. It is a presumptuous move and instantly makes me feel claustrophobic. Cinder is there, getting him to step back across that invisible line.

Another one of the men gets my attention. "Goldie, I got this for you." He's good-looking with middle eastern features, a thick black beard, and wears a white polo that complements his well moisturized bronze skin. David? Gods, there are way too many in my fan club now.

While he's attractive, all the attention tonight has soured my mood.

Also, where is Ted? What is Rap doing with him and why is it taking so long?

The strange buzzing sensation of my skin jacks up to an uncomfortable level. Is my stress manifesting in even more fun new ways than just sleepwalking?

David slides a jewelry box over the bar.

"What the fuck is that?" one of the other guys asks.

What the fuck, indeed.

"Uh, thanks but I just take tips. You should save that for the next girl you date."

"I bought it for you," he utters in a low voice, with lidded eyes that should be reserved for the bedroom. "Just open it," he urges.

My skin prickles under so much attention. Again, I irrationally wish Ted was here.

"I can't," I insist. "But I'm happy to pour you a drink." I smile with a shrug. Low level alarm bells won't stop ringing in my head.

"It's okay," David goes on. "It's better I do it anyway." The box snaps open to reveal a massive sparkling pear-shaped pink diamond atop a ring. It's an engagement ring.

Oh fuck me up a rollercoaster. My stomach drops and panic explodes in my brain.

The bar around us stills.

"I know we only met last night, but Goldie you are the one. I can't stop thinking about you. I can't breathe without you. Please say yes and put air back in my lungs."

CHAPTER 17
THE TEDINATOR

GOLDIE

My head swivels first to Cinder and then Snow. They are wearing an identical gobsmacked expression, frozen where they stand.

This is a joke, right? I'm waiting for someone to explain the punch line, but it doesn't come.

Something far worse happens.

"You sonofabitch," Alan/Jimi says before throwing a punch. David's head snaps to the side, blood spraying from his mouth, droplets colliding with my chest.

All hell breaks loose as the six guys wail on each other with fists. Screams rise in the bar as the rest of the patrons either back up or crowd in to see what's going on.

Lysander is the only one who doesn't, continuing to sip on his beer as he takes in the spectacle, before shooting me an inscrutable look. As if he is trying to figure out some riddle.

What the witchtits kind of alternate reality have I fallen into?

Thankfully our bouncers plunge into the fray, actively pulling the guys apart, but it's three against ten. Glass shatters from somewhere nearby and the crowd shuffles to and fro. Angry yells drown each other out.

That's when Rap shows up. She doesn't waste a second launching into the middle, yanking arms from sockets and pushing guys back and away from another.

Cinder hops over the bar and jumps in to help her out.

My feet are frozen to the spot. This is because of me. They are fighting because of me.

Because some dude who came here for the first-time last night proposed to me with a big pink rock and the others didn't like it.

I can't. I literally, physically, emotionally just can't right now.

I'm gripped by two large, rough hands. Tilting my head, I find myself looking up into my neighbor's intense cerulean eyes, a fierce expression on his face. "Let's get you out of here."

I numbly allow myself to be directed out and around the brawl, Ted putting his body between me and the fray. The buzzing of my skin lessens with him around me, but it doesn't go away. In fact, it feels like the whole room is full of the strange energy licking at my skin.

We only get a couple steps before Lawrence shows up at my side. When did he get here? "Goldie, you should come with me. I'll keep you safe." He is earnest as his cold fingers tug at my arm, sending a sickening tendril roiling around my gut. My ex hasn't proposed or thrown a punch in my honor, but it definitely doesn't feel right to go with him.

"I've got her," Ted says, his hand tightening on my shoulder. I'm not sure which is more territorial—his tone or the way he is gripping me.

Oh faelords, is he also afflicted with whatever is affecting the mass of fighting males?

I push both of them off as I snap out of my daze.

"I'm fine. I can take care of myself."

I don't need a man.

I am capable.

I am enough.

And I am about to go down like a sack of bricks—is my last thought as one of the guys spots me and charges right at me with arms outstretched.

There's a crazed, wild look about him, like he is going to wrap me in rope and throw me in his basement while calling me things like 'my pet' as he strokes my hair and tells me to put the lotion on my skin.

Oh witchtits, he's not slowing down.

Ted takes a step forward, his meaty fist crashing into the guy's cheek. The way his face ripples under the blow is almost comical as his eyes roll back before he drops like a sack of apples.

My feet lose the ground as I'm hefted over a broad shoulder. I squirm as a hard bulky muscle digs into my gut.

"What the hell, Tedford," I yell even as he pushes his way through the throng of onlookers.

He even has the decency to reach up with his other hand to pull my dress down so I'm not flashing anyone. Bouncing with his every step, I watch the distance between me, and a frowning Lawrence expand. He doesn't follow, but there is a strange gleam in his eye.

Maybe he thinks the Tedinator is my boyfriend.

I'm angry and grateful at the same time, which sends my temperature spiking and confusing feelings spiraling through me.

Or maybe Ted is also under whatever weird spell has captured everyone else.

Is he going to throw me in his basement too? Pull the weird possessive male act on me with over-the-top flattery and gifts?

We emerge from the Poison Apple into a hot, sticky night.

He walks a ways down the street before my feet connect with the ground. I meet Ted's stormy gaze.

"What the hell kind of power do you have over those guys?" he asks. "You'd think they were drug addicts and you were their only fix."

Okay, no over the top flattery. In fact, his tone was all accusation. Again.

At least I don't have to worry about conjuring visions of a white dress and little kids with this big bully.

"I didn't do anything," I stomp my foot on the ground, but frustration still radiates through me.

"Of course, you did. Why—why do you have to be—?" With a growl, he rakes a hand through his hair, looking anywhere but at me now.

"What?" I put my hands on my hips, wondering how he'll turn things on me this time. "Why do I have to be so what?"

"So godsdamn likeable? Why do you have to make everyone fall in love with you? It's... irritating."

My heart flip flops in my chest at his words. Does that mean he likes me? But I irritate him? "That doesn't even make any sense."

"Goldie," someone calls out. David stumbles out of the bar, blood dripping from his nose. His white shirt is stained with blood too, though I couldn't say if it's his. He holds the jewelry box out in my direction. "I need your answer. Don't break my heart, my queen, my precious peach."

Panic shoots through me like an icy spike.

Before I can think through what I'm about to do, I throw my arms around Ted's neck and haul him down. My lips crash into his. It was meant to send a signal to David that I was taken. Then maybe he'd fuck off.

But I'm instantly pulled away from the drama I'm trying to avoid and swept into Ted's vortex. The taste of him—the feel of, oh faelords—it is shocking to my system. He doesn't hesitate for a second, parting his lips and sweeping his tongue across my mouth, arms closing around me.

The night is drenched with a sweltering heat, but I don't mind being crushed against his hot, hard body. Pine and his unique masculine intermix, surrounding me, making my knees weak until parts of me turn liquid. That liquid rushes south with shocking speed, turning me light-headed. But it's okay because he is holding me to him, making me feel safer than I have in a long time.

Suddenly I *need*. I'm hot and wanty, and ready to grind against this fucking oak tree of a man. And judging by his reaction to my kiss, he'd let me.

Uptight, brusque, rude Ted kisses me with a passionate wantonness I would have never expected in a thousand years. Like whatever dam holding him back crumbled and he's on the verge of doing every possessive male act to me.

Ted tilts his head the other way, gaining deeper entrance to my mouth. Usually, I don't care for facial hair, but his well-kept beard is equal measures of soft and delicious friction against my skin. His chest crushes against mine. The tips of my breasts are hard against him and I've no doubt he can feel it.

"Goldie..."

The kiss breaks, and I can't even focus on the person who choked out my name. I'm too busy meeting Ted's shocked gaze. He looks stunned, aroused, and maybe a little angry.

Is he pissed I kissed him, or that I stopped?

With a great deal of effort, I force myself to face David. I wipe the corners of my mouth. "David, I can't marry you. This is my boyfriend." I awkwardly pat Ted's chest as if to prove my point.

I'm looking right at David, but every last molecule in my body is focused on Ted, screaming at me to kiss him again. Faehell, I've never experienced anything that intense in my life. The need to mount him still gnaws hungrily at me.

Part of me is also worried Ted's going to refute my claim that he is my boyfriend in front of David.

*This girl? *cue laugh of disbelief* She's just my annoying neighbor. I wouldn't date her if she was the last girl on earth.*

David looks back and forth between us, as if trying to do the math and coming up with unbelievable figures. He takes a couple steps toward us, but his body deflates.

My heart pounds against my ribs in violent beats.

Then Ted grabs my hip and drags me against his side. "You heard the lady, get lost."

David's hand bearing the ring box curls protectively against his chest, before he slinks away. He shakes his head as if trying to get rid of something in his brain, and he doesn't look back.

More people begin to stream out of the club. The brawl is broken up and people are being ejected en masse. Ted releases my hip only to grab my hand. He drags me down the street before stopping at a familiar looking blue truck. He opens the passenger door for me.

I hesitate.

"Just until the street clears of your fan club," he explains.

Swallowing over the lump in my throat, I nod and get in.

What the hell happened to 'I don't need a man,' Goldie? That I am enough?

The first sign of trouble and I glom onto the one person who can't stand me, even though he accused me of sleeping with his brother.

Ted shuts the door after me before climbing into the driver's side. His intoxicating scent is even more intense in here. Hot tingles still rush through me, so I focus on how clean the cab of his truck is. I would have expected it to be full of dirty tools and fast-food wrappers, but it's damn near impeccable.

"I'm sorry," I blurt out. "I didn't mean to say you were my boyfriend. I panicked."

Ted's eyes are trained unerringly on the people on the street, making me feel like I'm talking to myself.

"I knew you were trouble the second I saw you," he mutters, not even looking at me.

I bristle at that. My spine stiffens. "Hey Tedinator, I didn't cause any of this. I didn't show up on *their* doorstep with a pink cake. This just started." My hands flail uselessly. "And it's been happening the last couple weeks."

Two dark pools turn on me under knitted brows. "Tedinator?"

"Well yeah, you punched that guy out like a freaking murder machine."

Turning back to the wheel, something about the set of

his shoulders makes me think he's uncomfortable. "I don't care for violence, but sometimes it's necessary." There is something there, buried in his words like a secret.

Maybe it's the reason why he is so damned rude and inconsiderate?

He did just let you kiss him and tell that guy he was your boyfriend. He did distract the maddening crowd before whisking you away from any danger.

I hadn't given much thought to why he's so hellbent on being left alone, but I'm starting to suspect there is a reason for it. Why haven't I considered that before?

Because I've been obsessed with screwing with him, and working on a house that I'm learning may be an impossible flip.

I study Ted while he's not focused on me. The streetlight filters into the car, casting a glow on his black hair. Observing his profile, I realize his blue eyes are lined in long, dark lashes.

He's intense and serious. And until just now, I thought it was the worst part of him. But the way he watches the streets, as if scanning for any danger, I wonder if he'd had to be on watch like this before. And it was also for my sake. He could have left me on the street, but he dragged me in here. He wouldn't voluntarily let me into his house, I had to practically shake his name out of him, and now I felt safer sitting in the seat next to him than I'd felt in a while.

"You're confusing."

Ted's eyebrows climb up his forehead as he meets my scrutiny. "I am?"

"Yes. I thought you hated me but—" I trail off, still not sure what to make of him.

He turns away before I can catch the expression on his

face. Fingers flex and wrap around the steering wheel, as if he is trying to ground himself.

"You don't know anything about me, cream puff."

Cream puff? "Is that some kind of crack at my weight?"

He rears back, looking at me like I grew a second head. "What? No."

"Then why are you comparing me to food?" Self-consciousness snakes through me. I've worked my ass off to build my confidence and I hate that he can undermine that with a couple words. Why do I care what this jackass thinks?

"Never mind," he mutters.

"What did Rap talk to you about?" I hadn't forgotten she pulled him into her office. The way she studied Ted, with probing intensity, I got the feeling she could see something I didn't. I should get to know what my boss and neighbor talked about.

His lips tighten.

"Fine, don't tell me," I grumble.

Once the street is cleared, I say, "I'm going back in."

"I'll come with you." He grabs the car handle.

"No," I exclaim. "You've done enough." He really has. I didn't ask for his help, but he gave it. Between the bizarre chain of events and how much I like his helpful, steady presence, I feel shaken.

"Seriously, I need to go talk to my boss and sort things out."

Ted leans closer, his eyes dropping to my lips, and the air escapes my lungs. I turn still as stone, though every fiber of my being strains forward, wanting to meet him halfway.

"I couldn't let you do that, not knowing what these idiots might try with you."

"What do you care?" I ask breathlessly. My lips tingle,

as a desperation to connect them with his again presses up against my skin from the inside. His beard excited my nerve endings, and they dance in anticipation of feeling that friction again.

The heat of his body radiates into mine. The desire to close the distance is so strong I bite down on my lower lip to keep myself from giving in. Those deep blue eyes catch the movement, and a low growl emanates from his chest.

Does he mean to intimidate me? And why does that sound send hot liquid coursing to my center with a needy throb? My hand tightens around the door handle as I work to keep still.

I realize then that he still hasn't answered my question. Why does he care what happens to me? Yesterday we agreed to leave each other alone.

Ted watches me. No. He *drinks* me in. My skin feels tight and I can feel a flush racing up my neck. An unknown emotion tugs at my heart, making it throb in my chest as if beating out a message only I can hear.

The air between us is heavy with tension and every breath I take is shallow—I'm almost afraid to draw too much of his scent into my lungs. I don't know why I feel almost in physical pain being this close to Ted. Or why it's hard to breathe. I desperately want something, but I don't know what.

My inner muscles clench around emptiness that leaves me feeling hollow and frenzied.

The car door slams behind me as I flee his truck. I don't turn around, but I can tell he doesn't follow. I swallow mouthfuls of the night air but still can't draw a full breath.

What is happening? My life is off the rails, and I don't know how it happened or how to get it under control again.

I am capable.

I am enough.

I don't need a man.

Though my brain counters that I may want one. One big, beefy, scowly, chivalrous bear of a man.

And that doesn't settle well at all.

CHAPTER 18
A REAL WET DREAM

GOLDIE

That night, I fall asleep in my bed and wake up in the same place. Glory Hallelujah!

Though I spend the night tumbling through dreams of stormy ocean eyes and lips I want to explore. I cling to broad shoulders and let a bearded face trail blazing hot kisses down my neck until I'm a puddle of need.

When I wake, I'm horny as hell and grumpy as sin.

Thankfully, I have the day off from work, so I don't have to worry about crazed men proposing to me. Rap pulled me into her office when I went back in after the fight and suggested I take a couple days off, or maybe the week.

I begged her to let me work my normal hours. I need the money and promised to find a way to thwart the fan club of asshats. Rap seemed skeptical but didn't fight me.

I have no idea how I'll actually accomplish that, but I have other things to focus on right now.

The day is spent scrubbing the grime laden windows

that should in all reality be replaced, and eating porridge that makes my gut churn.

My doctor's visit is not only unhelpful, it makes me more frustrated than when I went in. If I am sleepwalking the only things I can do is try to go to sleep at the same time every night and try to limit stress.

Limit stress?

I am living off a barrel of old oats because I'm pouring every last penny into getting my aunt's old house back into livable shape. I'm breaking my back and my nails cleaning the grime out of the baseboards to the ceiling corners of a rundown mansion. Every day I'm melting to death in a hot house I can't afford to get air conditioning for. I'm getting unexpected proposals, causing fights, and my neighbor thinks I'm a nosey slut trying to sleep with his brothers though he's the one haunting my dreams.

I am officially exhausted. Especially because I have to keep from rubbernecking to see what my maybe-not-so-terrible neighbor is up to. His truck is gone, and I don't see him all day. I tell myself I don't care, but I only get hornier, sweatier, and angrier.

At the end of the day, I am mindful as I prepare to get into bed.

I *do not* plan on ending up in Ted's house again.

Popping in my earbuds, I queue up not one but two sleep meditations while huffing lavender oil until I'm the most relaxed person on the face of the earth.

Everyone wishes they were as relaxed as me.

As I drift into dreamland, my chill mode morphs into something with heat and tension. Strong hands roam my body, as a pair of serious lips slide up my neck, causing shivers to rack my body and my hips to buck with need.

I'm dreaming again of intense cerulean eyes that come with a scowl I can't get off my mind.

My fingers run through soft, thick hair I can grab onto as insistent, hungry lips kiss a trail down south, licking and nipping at my sensitive skin. One of those calloused hands travels down my body, tracing my hip before sliding between my legs, cupping my center. I bite back a moan even as my hips jerk up into his touch.

At the same time a hot, sinful mouth closes around my nipple through my silk pajamas. A finger presses against my cleft, causing wetness to rush and meet him there. The muscles of my inner wall clench, making me feel achy and needy. I want my clothes gone.

A growl rumbles through the tip of my breast before the finger pushes even harder, fighting my pajama bottoms.

Oh faelords, swearing off men has made my dreams crazy hot. And if I can't get in real life, I can get my rocks off in dreamland. Works for me.

I reach and grasp until my hand closes around some-thing long, hot, and hard. I grab a cock through a pair of boxers, but that's doesn't stop me from giving it a long, slow stroke. Oh sweet witchtits, I want that in me. I want that in me so bad, a mewl of desperation escapes me.

Don't wake up. Whatever you do, don't wake up.

Another growl vibrates against my skin, before my bottoms and panties are ripped down my legs. My hands do the same, pushing down fabric so I can wrap my fingers around velvet covered steel. Holy fuck, it's so big, I can't even get my fingers all the way around it. I swallow hard as the tips of my breasts tighten almost painfully.

Any second, I'm going to wake up so horny and unsatis-fied, I'm sure I'll burst into tears.

He's kissing me again, drawing me against the length of

his hard body. I'm drowning, drowning in desire and need. I'm a girl who needs touch, affection, sex. I've never been ashamed of that, but I've been denying those parts of myself, making them all the more wild for gratification.

When the tip of his cock nudges my slick lower lips, reality penetrates the moment just before he does.

My eyes blink open as the air crystallizes around me. I'm awake, but the dream man doesn't fade away. In fact, I meet a pair of blinking, bleary blue eyes as if he is also bringing me into focus.

I am definitely not in my bed.

And Ted is definitely not a dream.

I am in my neighbor's bed, with a very naked Ted, and I can tell by the line between his eyebrows he's not sure how or when I got there either.

Unlike his brother's atrocious mattresses, this bed is just right. Or do I only think that because Ted's dick is partially in me and it feels so fucking good, I could cry.

A strangled groan of frustration comes out of my throat. All of that lavender sniffing, for nothing. I broke into his place again, and this time. . .

The reality of his rigid prick still at my entrance has not abated. Still, I don't move away. My body is so thirsty for more, I can't force myself to move. And there it is—his lips turn down into that scowl.

I open my mouth, eager to explain I didn't mean to climb into his bed. That it's an accident and I'm so sorry, before running from the room like my heels are on fire. But I can't. All the words get stuck in my throat while the animal side of me wants more.

"You need to leave," Ted says in a sleep-roughened voice. Faelords, why does his rejection sound so absurdly sexy?

The humiliation starts to creep up from my chest to my neck, but before it fully engulfs my head—drowning me—he continues, "Or so help me blondie, I'm going to do such dirty bad things to you, you won't be able to walk for a week."

Wait—what?

As if my body has a mind of its own, my hips rock against him, pushing that tip in half an inch as I groan. I need more. If I don't get it, I'm positive I'm going to die.

"Aw fuck," he hisses, fingers digging into my hips. Eyes squeezing shut, his head tilts back as if it's taking every ounce of his control not to move.

It's up to me to get us out of this.

Even as I think it, my hips roll, and he sinks a little further in.

Ted's head drops to my shoulder, his chest heaving against mine. "Cream puff, you are killing me."

"I need more," I murmur against his ear, surprised at the sultry sound of my voice. My fingers dig into his arms, feeling the muscles move as he clenches his teeth.

"No," he growls. "You don't."

"You don't really want me to leave," I argue. He doesn't answer. Every muscle in his body is strung tight, as if he's trying to keep it together by force alone. "You do want me to leave," I say.

Of course, he does. He hates me. I hate him.

I just also want him to push that massive dick inside me.

Faelords, I'm an absolute idiot.

"I don't want to take advantage of you," he grits out.

The laugh dies before it even reaches my throat. Is he serious right now?

The tingles running down my spine drop-kick all

149

sensible thought, leaving a crushing need to be fucked by this seriously sexy man. My mouth goes dry as I take in his exposed broad chest with a dusting of dark hair. I normally gravitate toward hairless men, but something about his overt masculinity is so undeniably appealing.

I'm done waiting. I align my hips with his and drive them forward, sinking him all the way in. My entire body trembles with pleasure as he fills me up and our groans echo off the walls of his bedroom.

Oh faefucks, he is so damn big. He stretches me past my comfort until I'm wriggling and squirming under the intense, painful pressure. But oh witchtits, it's also so fucking good.

I claw at his skin, seeking purchase. Ted stills inside me, giving me time to adjust. When I open my eyes, panting heavily, his dark brows are furrowed. He studies me as if worried about hurting me. Despite the lovely air-conditioned room, his skin glistens with sweat, and I notice a slight tremor in his arms as he holds himself over me.

I considered him a heartless ice-cold beast, but right now I can see him on the edge of losing control and damn if it isn't the most intoxicating thing I've ever witnessed.

The next thing I know, we're moving together. His thrusts are slow and powerful. Every inch of him is hard as steel yet he moves with an endless patience that belies his gruff exterior. Every time he hits the hilt of me, I make a new, unusual sound that's either a gasp or a squeak. The edge of his lips twitch as if he's fighting a smile.

My body reacts without thought or care. I'm lost in the delicious sensations of the friction as he thrusts into me, desperate and needy. Every moan and shudder of pleasure that passes between us only heightens our passion, and I let out a low whimper as his hands find my hips and he pounds deeper.

Then Ted rolls us over, so I'm sitting on his lap. Ted is handing over the reins to me, but a wave of self-consciousness washes over me. I don't imagine I look good from this angle, and the sheets are puddled on his thick thighs leaving me exposed and cold. At least I still have my pajama top on, which makes me feel a little better. I try to swallow down the thoughts crowding in and start to ride him.

I sense myself slipping away from the present moment. Suddenly, I revert to how I usually am in bed with my partners—an actress playing a part. The pleasure I was engulfed by drains from my body as I rock back and forth on his cock, moaning louder and more dramatically, like a porn star. I flip my head back and squeeze my own breast through my top, trying to make it look good for him.

When I get this way, my head crowded with thoughts, I know it's unlikely I'm going to come, so it's best I give him as good a time as I can.

Ted grips my hips, stopping me abruptly. "What are you doing?"

Confused, I open my eyes. My breath catches in my throat as his gaze penetrates right through me like a laser beam and he asks in a rough voice that strips me naked, leaving me vulnerable and unsure of myself.

"What does it look like I'm doing?" a nervous laugh escapes me.

Ted's eyes narrow as he studies me with that smothering intensity.

I'm about to get off him, when he rolls us over then grabs my wrists to hold them over my head in one hand. "I don't know what dumbass fuckboys you've been with, or how many of them let you fake it for their benefit, but that *will not* be happening in this bed, do you understand?" On the words 'will not' he thrust his hips, driving his dick into me deep before sliding back slow, drawing a genuine moan out of me. Pleasure ignites with hot sparks again, but I doubt it will last. The fire in me has cooled too much.

He continues. "In this bed, you are going to take as fucking long as you want or need until you come so hard your legs shake and you've creamed all over my dick. Got it blondie?"

His almost harsh demand is punctuated by another rough thrust of his cock that gets a squeak out of me. This time one side of his lips quirk up in a smug almost-smile. This is the closest I've seen him to smiling. The sight of it instantly infuriates me. Some part of me is still at war with the man next door. Worse, I also crave to see that half smile every day.

Despite the fact, he's seen directly through me as if I were a pane of glass, heat and anger flare in me. How dare he think he knows me?

Even though he does.

"I wasn't faking it," I lie, tilting my chin up in defiance, even as he holds me down.

His half smile turns dark and sensuous. "You are so busy trying to get everyone to like and approve of you, do you even know what *you* like, blondie?"

The protest dies in my throat when he slams back into me, filling me up to the point of pain, while his hip bone grinds against my needy clit. The impact scattered the intrusive thoughts from my brain.

"That's my good girl," he croons. "I knew you liked it rough before you did."

His what? Holy fuck, who is this guy? Really?

Though I'm not entirely sure he's wrong. And he sure as hell has the equipment and skill to make it rough.

"You fuck like you fight, hard and dirty. I bet no one can give it to you as good as they get from you." His hips slam into mine again, and fire swallows me up. How did I go from 60 to 0 then to 1000 so fast?

I mindlessly moan and beg for more under him. But he's never shown me mercy before, and I doubt he will now. And I kind of fucking love that.

"You want to know what makes it good for me?" he rasps into my ear, his body covering but not crushing me. The way he grinds against me, hipbone right on my clit is killing me. "Making you cum. The idea of watching you scream and twist and beg me to fuck you harder as you ride out an orgasm so intense you black out, makes me want to fucking blow my load."

I'm mesmerized by his dirty words, the way he is pounding pleasure into me, overwhelming me is unlike anything I've experienced before.

He plunges his hands into my hair and holds my head in place so that our lips barely touch as he moves inside me. His thrusts become more aggressive, almost punishing, but that only serves to make me want more and more of him.

He's not my type at all—a rugged manly man who doesn't rely on pretty words to butter me up—but yet here we are, two enemies fucking like there's no tomorrow, like all the tension between us has been reduced to this one moment in time where neither of us can deny how intensely attracted we are to each other.

For once we aren't fighting each other, we are working together and it's far more powerful and heady than any heckling irritation I could inflict on him.

With each movement, something inside me tightens

and unravels all at once until I'm moaning into his shoulder and clawing at his back with desperate need for release.

"That's it, cream puff, I want you to shake and melt all over this dick. Do it for me, blondie."

Ted's husky words and the visual they send me, of him watching me writhe and buck under him, begs me to give in to him.

"Please," I sob out, relishing the way he increases his pace. My body is a live wire, the coil on the inside of my wrists where he's holding my hands, the one between my thighs where he's rubbing against me until I'm sure I'm going to burst into flames. "Please... I'm almost..."

"You want it—you can have it, blondie. Give it to me. Give me that perfect pussy." His words are rough and raw and I want to give him whatever he wants though that's not necessary. He's going to take it from me. He keeps going, each word winding me up until I fear my back will break.

"That's my good girl. You are so fucking gorgeous, coming apart on my dick. I can feel it," his voice is a low seductive growl against my ear. "Let go," he commands in a gravelly tone. "You're so fucking close. I can feel you shaking."

He bites my bottom lip, yanking it out with a popping sound before shoving me over the edge. The orgasm tears through me like a hurricane, lighting me up from the inside out, and I shout into his neck. I come so hard that I literally see stars, then they morph into hundreds of shooting, glorious colors bursting behind my closed eyelids. I shake and shudder until I'm completely spent.

"That's my good girl," he breathes, before he slams his hungry lips against mine.

Again, who in the actual hell is this guy?

The thought runs through my brain before melting into the abyss with the rest of my senses. I grip the hard planes of his chest and hold on, losing myself to him.

Ted leans down, pausing his brutal strokes, he kisses me so tenderly my heart cracks. Fingers glide along my jawline as he tastes me. The way his lips slide across mine with such reverence, it's as if he is worshipping me. There is a terrifying sincerity to it that causes my heart to pound harder and faster than ever.

He pulls out of me, a petulant whine of protest escapes me as I feel cold and empty. Up on his knees, Ted's calloused hand pumps his rock-hard dick once, then twice before a powerful eruption of cum collides with my thigh. He bellows a guttural roar of pleasure that rattles the windows.

I'm fucking entranced by the vision of him succumbing to orgasm. Passion vibrates around him almost visibly. I can't breathe. I can't think. I just soak in his sexy masculine form, trying to burn it into my brain.

When the cloudy daze clears from his eyes, he blinks down at me with an inscrutable look.

My stomach clenches as tension fills the air. I already know what's coming. He reaches over and grabs some tissue from his bedside table, wiping the mess off my thigh, avoiding my gaze now.

He slips out of the bed, pulling his underwear back on. I'm quick to pull up the covers over my exposed legs.

Then he says those damning words that ruin everything. "I'm sorry."

Everything in me drops as if I'd been kicked out of a plane.

CHAPTER 19
DICKED DOWN AND HYSTERICAL

GOLDIE

I reach down and around my legs to locate my panties and pajama bottoms. I'm far too aware of the cold, wet silk fabric sticking to my chest from where Ted's mouth had been.

When the babbling starts, I can't stop. "I'm sorry. I swear I did my best. I even talked to a doctor and tried to take their advice, useless though it was." Now I'm more stressed than ever.

Which means I'll likely walk right into his bed again.

This is a nightmare.

"Calm down," Ted says, still in that rough voice.

I can't calm down. I woke up in a stranger's bed AGAIN. Except this time, we fucked.

That's crazy. I don't even LIKE him.

I dive under the covers, struggling to pull up my panties and shorts. His sheets are the softest things I've ever felt. Faelords, why does it smell so good in his bed? Unlike the other bedrooms, this one is clean—a surprising quality for a mountain man like him. The scent of cedar and pine fills my nose—subtle, but distinctly masculine, reminding me of the great outdoors.

And sex. It smells like our sex, which up until two minutes ago was completely intoxicating.

I'm an idiot. He told me to leave, and I didn't. Even after I swore off men. Even though I hate Ted.

Well not hate anymore, but strongly dislike.

I huff out more words, unable to stop the stream of consciousness from spilling out. "She said it could be my diet. I've been living on oatmeal for weeks, so it could be that. Or the stress of men at my work treating me like something gold-dipped prize. Or the housework is getting to me. Maybe if I could afford some air conditioning units, I'd sleep better. I'm melting to death every damn day. My gods do you even know how big that house is? Fixing it is going to break my body or my bank. I'm not sure which first."

Something at the back of my mind was telling me to shut up, but it was such an unusual instinct it came out as a quiet whisper, easily smashed back down as I let my neurosis fly. He fucked the sense out of me.

Emerging from under the covers, my hair flies around me in a static mess. "And I am *not* trying to break in. Believe me. You *have* to believe me," I beg.

Ted stands there in only a pair of boxers with sexy tousled hair, studying me like I'm either some kind of psycho, or maybe a puzzle he's trying to figure out.

Thoughts tumble through my brain and while a lot of them are panicked, the other half is taking in Ted's form. There is still an imprint of his hot, muscular form pressed against mine. Thick tree trunk thighs and his burly arms and chest affect me more than I care to admit. There is some natural and honest about his form, as if he spends all his time as a lumberjack. I'd know. I watch enough videos online.

And now I know how it feels against mine. My fingers tunneled through the black hair dusting his chest. And those scowling lips, my god, why do they fit mine so fucking well? They worked my lips and skin in ways I wouldn't think a man of his kind to be capable. My thighs clench together. Regardless of how I feel about him, my body has very strong opinions about his presence.

What is wrong with me? I shouldn't still be ogling my mean neighbor after he regrets my being in his bed.

Even if he is occasionally helpful, nice, and makes me come like a freight train. Frustration swells so suddenly it presses against my ribs uncomfortably.

Against my will, tears well in my eyes, blurring my vision.

His expression softens as he reaches out with a hand. "Please don't cry. I believe you," he says finally.

I shake my head adamantly even as tears spill over my eyelid. "I'm not crying."

"*I'm sorry,*" is what he said, but he didn't finish after that. Honestly, I don't need him too.

I'm sorry I fucked you. I'm sorry we did what we did. I'm sorry you may think this is more than it is.

I don't know what he is sorry for, but it doesn't matter. Any one of them still means this was a mistake he regrets.

It shouldn't affect me so much, it's just that I'm still in his bed, and I don't like sleepwalking.

Ted takes a few steps toward me. I pull the comforter up over my chest, clutching it to me.

"I'm sorry. I should have used a condom, but I don't

have any because I'm not. . . " his hands open and then close. "I didn't expect this."

And I didn't expect *that* to be what he was sorry for.

I pull the comforter even closer. Oh for faefucks sake, I'm an idiot and didn't even think about that. I transitioned from dreamland and rolled right into pound town and there wasn't enough of a gap to afford that sliver of reality. Thank the faelords one of us possesses a bit of sense, accounting for why he pulled out.

"I don't have anything. . . I mean to say I haven't been with uh. . . "

It's strange to see Ted so flustered, tripping over his words.

"I'm clean too," I say quietly. I get checked regularly. I've always been safe about it. Until now that is.

Ted's shoulders roll back, and he straightens, seeming to find his confidence again. "Here is what's going to happen," he says, taking charge. "I'm going to go downstairs, and you are going to take a minute to yourself. Come down when you feel ready and then we'll discuss this."

His tone magically helps the tears dry right up and steadies my emotions. But I can't let him know he has such an effect on me. "You're bossy, you know that, Tedster?"

Neither of us mention how much I loved that five minutes ago when he pounded into me.

His lips twitch. Was that almost a smile? Couldn't be. I'm hallucinating.

"Downstairs, when you're ready." Ted grabs a folded shirt from atop his dresser, shrugging it on as he walks out and closes the door behind him.

It's only after it's shut that I suck in a deep breath and let it out.

He wants to talk about this? He's not going to boot me

out of his house as fast as humanly possible? Is he drunk? On drugs? Or maybe orgasms put him in an amenable state of mind?

And holy fuckola, what an orgasm.

I fall back into the pile of plush pillows and cover my face not sure if I should be deliberately trying to recall the size and feel of him. He fit juuuust right.

What is wrong with me? Men throw themselves at my feet nightly, and I want the one guy who thinks I'm a special kind of pest sent solely to torture him.

Wait, I don't want him.

I'm not addicted and desperate for more.

I'd wear a pure white, ballgown with a sweetheart neckline and. . .

FUCK!

But that kiss last night, allowing me to tell that guy Ted was my boyfriend—gah, why did that stick to me like glue? The way he kissed me, so painfully sweet, just before he came. The way he called me out for faking it then giving me the most insane all-consuming pleasure of my life.

I have to get out of my head, so I focus on the surroundings.

To my left, a large window offers an impressive view of the lush green mountainside. The morning sunlight streams in, casting an inviting glow on the polished wooden floor. I'm in a hefty king-sized bed with a rugged, hand-carved wooden headboard that screams Ted.

I cover myself up with a plain comforter in a rich, earthy brown hue. I'm already mourning the loss of the plump pillows. On either side of the bed, matching nightstands hold small lamps with warm, amber shades.

To my right, a tall bookshelf reaches almost to the ceiling, filled not only with books but also fascinating bits and pieces: an old compass, a pair of binoculars, some vintage camping gear. Each item hints at the man Ted is—adventurous, practical, a man of the wild.

"That's my good girl."

Okay, I thought I knew him, but now I'm thinking I don't.

Across the room, a large oak dresser stands imposingly, its surface uncluttered save for a few essentials—a worn leather wallet, a silver pocket watch, a small bowl holding what appears to be assorted river rocks. Above it, a simple mirror with a rustic wooden frame reflects the room back at me.

As feminine as I am, with my love for all things pink and dainty, I can't help but feel the appeal of this room. It's warm, comfortable, and imbued with a charm that can only be Ted's—something authentically rugged, yet thoughtful. For a moment, I stand there, taking it all in, appreciating the unexpected allure of Ted's world.

But it's not my world. My heart cracks in ten different directions.

My friends are right. I fall too fast. I get way too obsessed and it's not healthy. I'm an absolute idiot and it's so much worse that he knows it.

Knowing I can't hide up here forever, I slip out from the way too comfortable bed and head downstairs. It's so weird how I know exactly where I'm going in this house, considering I've never consciously entered.

Maybe I can slip out the front door and avoid him all together.

I'm halfway down the stairs when a smell so delicious grips me and practically shakes me.

Bacon and coffee. Oh faelords, it's been so long since I've had anything but porridge. After the sex and stress bomb that exploded in my stomach, I'm absolutely starving.

Another step and I come into view of the kitchen to find Ted turning pieces of sizzling bacon. He looks up as if he sensed me the moment I left his room. He points at me and then the chair at his kitchen table.

"You, sit."

CHAPTER 20
MY OTHER IDIOT BROTHER

TED

I watch her cross her arms defensively, her brows furrowed. "Bossy much, Tedipedia? I don't have to do what you say." Despite Goldie's words, she stays put, her gaze rooted to mine.

What I did, eats at me. Not only because it was the best sex of my fucking life, but because I can't help but feel I took advantage of her.

Sure, she pushed me in the rest of the way into a heaven beyond my wildest dreams, but I know she hadn't meant to wake up in my bed with my dick partially in her.

Idiot I am, I didn't even think to find a contraceptive. Not that I have any. It's been two years since I had a sexual partner, and it only lasted a couple weeks.

And then the way I let go, talking to her in such a filthy way. . . I mean sure, it's how I operate, or it is with her. But I've been so mean to her. I shouldn't have said all that to her, even if it did make her shake and scream. It should have been sweet and doting, but I couldn't help but challenge her, push her past her limits.

Oh witchtits, I want to make her do it again though.

But she shouldn't even be here. I should have kicked her out for the same reason I made her promise to stay away from my brothers.

How the fuck does she have me confused, guilty, all while rolling in ecstasy? Like how my heart keeps skipping beats seeing her seated at the kitchen ready for me to feed her after what we did.

I lift the skillet off the gas stove top, reducing the gap between us. "You're damn right, blondie. You are going to sit down and eat the breakfast I'm making for you, instead of eating whatever slop you think is saving you money. And we are going to talk this out, or there will be consequences."

I'm close enough now to see her pupils dilate, her breath hitching. The proximity sends a jolt of warmth through me, my gaze hard on hers.

I have to keep focused or other things will grow hard.

A visible shudder runs through her, a blush creeping up her cheeks, and she swallows hard. "Consequences?" she asks, her voice barely audible. I feel a smirk pulling at the corner of my mouth.

Oh cream puff, I rather think you would enjoy them.

Ignoring the question, I reach behind me to pull out a chair for her, my expression unchanging. "Coffee or tea?" I manage to grind out, my tone on the rougher side.

She glares back, attempting to outmatch my stern look. "Coffee." Her voice is determined.

Her reluctance is evident even as she finally takes a seat. I pour her a mug of coffee and slide it across to her along with cream and sugar.

She reacts with a defiant huff. I can tell she doesn't appreciate the assumption, but I also know she likes her coffee sweet.

In response, she dumps in cream and sugar with a look that dares me to comment. I hold my tongue.

When I serve her breakfast, her eyes light up at the sight of hot pancakes, eggs, bacon, and a bowl of fruit.

The sound she makes as she bites into the pancake is more satisfying than I thought it'd be. She seems to find solace in the food, her demeanor shifting with each bite.

As she's halfway through, I realize I've lost myself observing her, my own breakfast is untouched.

"What?" Goldie suddenly straightens, looking defensive and oddly adorable.

A part of me fights the urge to tease her further, but I can't resist. "You like my food."

"I like food," she corrects me quickly. The way she brushes off my comment only makes me want to dig deeper, but for now, I let her enjoy her breakfast. She woke up, about to be violated by me. I'm not a monster, though I seriously considered giving into a dark, selfish side of me.

Pushing that aside before my body takes over again, I focus.

I set my coffee down. "Blondie, you couldn't have gotten in here last night. Not without breaking a window or something. I checked, and this place is as locked up as it was last night."

She continues to chew, but her face draws into a deep frown. "It *has* to be sleepwalking. Nothing else makes sense. Unless you are kidnapping and then gaslighting me about it." Goldie narrows her eyes at me in blatant suspicion.

I hold up my hands. "Again. I am doing no such thing."

"Damn," she sighs. Then she looks at me from under

her dark eyelashes, hair still a tangled mess. "I did not mean to—in bed, I mean. I was asleep and thought I was dreaming about—" She stops abruptly when I think she's about to elaborate on the dream. "And I woke up and then it was you and we were—"

I clear my throat loudly to stop her from adding to the discomfort. "Yeah, me too." Although I don't share the detail that I was dreaming specifically about a certain blonde cream puff sitting a foot away from me and happened to wake up to the real thing.

Fuck, the way she felt under my hands, my mouth.

I swear I touched heaven when my dick dipped into her sweet pussy and she looked up at me with glassy eyes and pink lips, puffy from my kisses.

For faefucks sake Ted, don't start thinking about it again or you are going to pop a boner and be stuck sitting at this table for hours, unable to get up.

A jangling comes from the direction of the front door before it cracks open. Both Goldie and I jump to our feet.

We look at each other with twin expressions of surprise and guilt. Like we've been caught doing something we shouldn't.

A familiar shaved head pops in.

My heart clenches so hard it could be the beginning of a heart attack. *Oh witchtits. Not now.*

Eli doesn't show up unless shit has gone sideways, and as he fully steps in the house, I easily see the black eye that's turned a good part of his temple and brow an ugly purple. I scrub a hand down my face.

Eli freezes when he realizes he's not alone. His gaze bounces back and forth between me and Goldie, as if trying to do the math. The kid first failed every math class he ever had before skating out of high school with a minimal passing grade.

Goldie nervously tugs at her nightshirt, and I sense her discomfort.

"Uh hey, big bro," Eli says.

I *really* don't want to introduce them.

So I don't.

Turning to Goldie, I say, "You need to leave."

Her body stiffens. I know my tone has turned cold, but it's not her. There's no time to explain. Hell, I never plan on explaining. I just need her out of here now, so I can deal with the fresh hell my youngest brother has brought to my doorstep.

"Thanks for the hospitality, Teddykins." She practically bares her teeth at me.

Oh, cream puff. If I could show you the kind of hospitality I wanted, you wouldn't be leaving, or even walking right now. As it is she does seem to be walking a bit gingerly, as if tender in some parts.

She breezes by Eli who smiles at her with an albeit confused expression. It's only when she opens the door do I notice she's not wearing any shoes.

For faefuck's sake, did she leave the last two times without shoes as well?

Pointing a warning finger at Eli, I say, "Sit. I'll be right back."

The smile slips off his face as he shuffles to the kitchen. At least there is food to keep him occupied.

It takes no time at all to catch up to Goldie. She's taken two steps off the porch when I call out to her.

"Wait a second, blondie."

She doesn't turn around, in fact, she walks faster. It

takes no time at all to catch up before I sweep her off her feet and begin to walk across the forest floor to her place.

"What in the witchtits do you think you are doing?" she demands, cradled in my arms. Her hands reflexively grab my neck. Oh, I like that *way* too much.

Sinking into her sweet, tight heat had been heaven, and faelords help me, I want to do it again. And again, and again. But this isn't the time.

Per usual my brothers are fucking things up.

"You don't have any shoes on," I say gruffly, not meeting her eye.

"Put me down. You are going to drop me, I'm too big to be—"

I catch the panic in her wide eyes. Pausing my stride, I face her. She doesn't know I'm a were and that picking her up poses no problem for me.

"I will not drop you." I pack the words with as much intensity as I can. Something about my delivery has her mouth snapping shut. She believes me. Afterall, I'm halfway to her house and I'm not losing my grip or even a little out of breath. Not like when she wrapped those pretty fingers around my—

"Good girl," I say as I continue toward her house. A flush turns her cheeks pink. Focusing past the enjoyment of having her hands grip my shoulders, I secretly rail against being able to have a normal morning with the aggravating, gorgeous girl of my dreams.

I set her on the welcome mat to her place. The porch needs some serious sanding and some new boards in places.

When she whips her front door open, I realize it wasn't even locked. *For crying out loud.*

Though I guess if she really is sleepwalking, she must be unlocking it to walk to my house.

I still can't believe she's breaking in. Because of Eli, I have extra security and locks on my house.

The sound of a revving engine and gravel flying pulls my attention away from Goldie.

A black SUV drives up between our properties before coming to a screeching halt.

Oh, faefucks on a waterslide.

"Go inside, blondie," I order, stepping off the porch.

"What?" Goldie asks, but I'm already striding toward the cars. Three men get out of the vehicle.

Two of them are thugs wearing tight sports tees. One of them has muscles on top of his muscles and a greenish tint to his scaly skin—a dracanoid. He's fae, like me. Usually, fae stick to their own kind and keep away from the human world, but with only a couple drops of dragon blood, this guy likely didn't have many places to go. And the dracanoid has ended up collecting debts for a low-life thug.

He's the epitome of what I worry will happen to my brothers.

Then again, that would at least mean Eli was gainfully employed...

A third man steps out from the SUV, white snakeskin boots crunching on the gravel. The powerful scent of shoe oil and musky cologne combines into a disgusting patina in my mouth. Dressed in all black, the sleeves of his button down rolled up. An expensive diamond clip is clamped to a turquoise tie. The trees reflect in his aviator sunglasses, making him look even more important and impressive somehow.

Against the smell of earth, pine and wildflowers, a sickening scent spreads over my tongue. Expensive brown liquor, old cigars, and the tanginess of other people's fear.

He's the leader

"This is private property," I growl, positioning between them and my cabin.

The thin-faced man removes his glasses, revealing cold, cruel eyes. In a south Boston accent dripping with insincere cordiality, he says, "We're looking for your brother. We have reason to believe he's here." His eyes flit over to where Eli's beat-up Jeep is parked next to my truck.

I sigh. "How much?"

The thin-faced scumbag toys with his sunglasses a moment, a smirk pulling at his lips. "Ten grand."

"For fucks sake," I curse, running a hand through my hair. "You know he has a problem. Why do you keep letting him place bets?"

The man in black shrugs with a lopsided smile that makes me want to punch it right off. "We give people a chance to change. Few in this world are so generous to those who wish to prove themselves."

Generous, my ass.

The man's brows lift as his attention catches on something in the other direction. "Hey there, sweetheart."

Fucking fuck fuck.

CHAPTER 21
A ROMANTIC FLESH WOUND

TED

I told Goldie to go inside, but of course she didn't listen to me.

The man in the snakeskin boots takes a step in her direction, and it's enough to make me want to explode into my bear form. "Hey there sweetheart, you know where I can find Eli? Six foot four, shaved head, matching scowl as this big guy right here?" He gestures to me. "The kid wouldn't be bothering you now, would he? Hanging out in that big house of yours." His beady, hateful eyes scan the shuttered windows.

Something buzzes in the air, and the expression on his thin face intensifies, a hungry gleam sparking in his dark eyes. "I think I better come in and take a look, don't you sugartits?"

Goldie rears back, her face taking on a look of disgust. "Hard pass."

"Go inside," I order again, the words grinding out like gravel between my teeth.

The leader raises his hand without turning to look at me. "No, no, I think I want to talk to doll face here. Get to know her better."

I take one step toward him, when both of his thugs reach into their pants and pull-out guns. They don't point the Glocks at me but having them out in the open is a clear message for me to stay back.

At least their firearms are meant for me and not her.

The air stills around us, and I catch the whites of Goldie's wide eyes even from a distance. I can smell, no, *taste* her fear. It adds a heavy tang to her sweetness, mixing with the metallic of their guns. The fury and fear churning at the pit of my stomach boils upward, swelling and filling my limbs.

The leader closes the distance between him and Goldie. "Hey baby, there is something about you isn't there, sugartits?"

"She's magic, boss," the dracanoid grunts.

Wait. What?

Goldie's eyes fly wide. The tang of her fear intensifies.

"Oh yeah? What kind? He asks his goon without taking his eyes off Goldie.

The dracanoid closes his eyes, inhales deeply, nostrils flaring dramatically wide. "It's weird boss, unlike anything I've smelled before. But I'm picking up *siren*."

The anger, fear, and fury inside me freeze at what the Orc says. Goldie looks as though someone dumped a bucket of ice-cold water on her.

Faefucks. Is she a mage? How did I not know that?

Because mages don't typically live in human cities like Boston. Because mages stink to high heaven as does all of their magic, but she smells. . . gods. . . she smells unlike any sweet thing I've ever known.

But those men at the bar. . . that strange stinging buzz in the air I felt before they all went nuts, fighting over her. It adds up too easily.

No, not easily, but enough that I can't deny what the dracanoid says.

The boss's brows shoot up as a far too pleased smile curls his lips. "Oh I think Eddie needs a girl like you."

"Who's Eddie?" Goldie asks, sounding ballsy but I can tell she is terrified.

His smile turns into a sickening slick curve of bad intent. "I'm Eddie, full name Eddie "Blackjack" McGinty, and why don't we step inside the house so we can get to know each other better?"

Oh hell no.

The rumble that starts in my chest, explodes into a roar as my bones break and creak, resetting into a different form as thick fur sprouts through my skin. Thick claws curl out of my fingertips. My clothes rip loudly as my muscles bulge and swell, bringing me to my full size.

Usually, I keep most of my human brain, but right now it's a whisper as my animal side takes over. And these fuckers are invading my territory. No one touches my mate.

I surge forward and strike the human thug down. The targeted attack gives the dracanoid time to fire a shot.

There's a crack in the air as a searing heat pierces through my right side. An angry roar explodes out of me as I leap onto the scaly skinned man. The dracanoid may possess dragon blood, but his strength is that of a human's.

Eddie reaches for his own weapon, half running toward Goldie, but my fear for her safety puts a supernatural speed on my gallop. My massive paws slam into his back, pushing him to the ground. I hear the wind being knocked out of him as he gasps for air with a strained croak.

Goldie trembles violently, her face a mask of awe and terror. The tang of her terror coats me in its sickening stickiness.

She says something, but I can't understand through the blood rushing in my own ears. My animal senses are in full swing, but I work to focus the human part of my mind.

"Don't kill him," she pleads in a ragged voice.

Stepping off the man who's peed himself, I step around him, until I'm standing between him and Goldie.

I growl a low warning at him, my massive bear form looming over him. The two thugs have already scrambled into the SUV, and the leader staggers to them as quickly as he can, leaving a pair of crushed mini mirrors behind. The men peel out of there with a spray of gravel. I watch them go, but my beast is still restless, still angry, still protective.

But I hate the tanginess of Goldie's terror. I need to change back, to make it go away.

With a deep rumbling sigh, I force myself to shift back to my human form, wincing at the sting of the transformation. I stumble a little, my bare feet finding purchase in the dirt, my torn clothes barely hanging on me.

Goldie rushes forward, her eyes wide, her face a little pale, "You're a were?"

I only grunt in response.

"Are you okay?" She breathes.

I nod, but my eyes are still trained on where I last saw the retreating SUV. They kicked up as much gravel and dust as when they careened in. Unfortunately, I know they'll be back. They always come back until they are paid.

My voice is low and rough, "I'm fine."

Goldie looks up at me, her eyes wide and filled with concern, and then she does something I don't expect. She hugs me, her arms wrapping around my waist, her face buried in my chest. My arms hesitantly close around her, accepting her embrace.

After a few minutes, she pulls back, her eyes flying wide. "You're bleeding!" She exclaims, her fingers lightly touching the wound on the right side of my torso. A bullet wound. It missed any major organs, but it does sting.

"It's nothing, Goldie," I reassure her, but inside, I'm shaken. She was almost hurt because of my brother's debts. And that's something I can't allow to happen again.

The fact the dracanoid scented out magic on her also leaves me deeply unsettled. Does she know? Of course, she knows. Mages are born with their powers and sent to a special school where they are trained to use their magic and classified into a level. But she seemed so shocked, like she was hearing it for the first time too.

Goldie looks up at me, her eyes a storm of emotions. "Thank you, Ted. You saved me, er,again."

I nod, my throat too tight to speak. I gently disentangle myself from her and pull a bit of torn shirt around me for some semblance of decency. "Just stay inside, okay? Lock the doors. I need to make some calls, make sure they don't come back."

I turn and stride toward my cabin, my mind racing. I need to find my brother, need to find out how deep his debts go, and I need to make sure Goldie stays safe. It's the least I can do for the woman who's brought a splash of color into my otherwise gray world.

She shakes her head, grabbing my arm before I get far. "Hell no. We need to get you patched up." She wraps an arm around me, steadying me. I don't know how much I need her help, but I like the feel of her against me too much. "Let's get you inside. I have the best first aid kit in the whole world. I've had to use it for not two, but three broken nails. So I'm practically a nurse now."

How the hell can I refuse that?

A familiar rough voice comes up on my other side. "I'm sorry, I didn't know—"

"Go get me some clothes." I give Eli the command without even looking at him. "And call JJ. Tell him to get his ass over here. Family emergency."

Time to get the damn pack together. I refuse to let this shit spill over onto Goldie, but I fear the damage has been done.

CHAPTER 22
THE FORBIDDEN NAME

TED

Gingerly sitting on the floral couch in Goldie's living room, one of her throw blankets draped across my naked lap, I'm careful not to get blood on anything. By the time she returns from upstairs, I'm already half healed.

"What's wrong?" I ask, sensing it before I even understand why I can sense her distress.

Goldie's eyes have gone wide with fear as she swallows hard. "I found roses on my bed."

"Roses?" Maybe it's the gunshot wound, but I'm not understanding.

Goldie crosses over, drops to her knees in front of me, and I can't help that some of my blood rushes south at the sight of her like that in front of me. But my arousal is stymied by the obvious stress pulling at her eyes and mouth.

She avoids my gaze as she pats disinfectant on my flesh wound. The sting barley registers as I focus on her.

"For the last couple weeks, I thought I'd been moving things around the house in my sleep. After waking up in your house, I came back and found my uh lingerie pulled out and splayed across my bedroom. I told myself I must be getting up and turning lights on and moving things around. But this time—" Her big brown eyes turn up to meet mine as she smooths the bandage over my torso. "Please tell me you have a pink rose bush on your property."

Something icy clenches around my heart, creeping up to my throat. "I don't have any pink rose bushes."

Her face crumples and fear shines out from her eyes. Not even when Eddie advanced on her, did she look this terrified.

I grab her hands, forcing her to focus on me. "What is it?" My question is soft but insistent.

"I don't know," she whispers. "But I'm not so sure I'm sleepwalking anymore. Because there are two dozen pink roses laid out on my bed upstairs."

The cold clamp around my chest turns crushing as I realize what she's saying.

"Someone else has been in your house?"

She nods solemnly even as she gets to her feet, pacing a short distance away before turning back to me. Hands wrap around either bicep as if she is trying to protect herself against an unseen force.

I also stand, fully wrapping the blanket around my hips. The desire to pull her into my chest and tighten my arms around her is strong.

Keep it together Ted. Bring logic and cool rational thinking to the situation, like you always do. "And you don't think it's maybe one of your friends?"

"Maybe," she says weakly, her arms dropping to her sides. I can tell she doesn't believe it which makes something inside of me harden. "No," she goes on, "You are probably right. I gave spares to Red and Cinder. I bet Cinder dropped them off to make me feel better."

There is something in her voice that doesn't have me convinced.

Too many things are crashing into each other. I need to take control of the situation, not only for my brother's sake, but for hers.

Eli saunters in with some clothes for me. He also has my cell phone. I grab the clothes and my phone then text JJ.

I reluctantly introduce them. "Goldie, this is my dumbass youngest brother, Eli. Eli, this is my neighbor, Goldie."

"Hey," he says, with a half wave. Shame and guilt hangs around him like a heavy cloud. Fucking good. He deserves it.

I raised him better than this. But there isn't any use rehashing the same fight we've had for the last several years. It doesn't change his behavior.

Maybe when I kick his ass in private for endangering my neighbor, something will click in that thick skull of his. But the black eye he is sporting probably hasn't knocked any sense into him.

"Hi," she says back, in a far too friendly manner which is more than he deserves.

Eli shuffles awkwardly a second before he says, "JJ said he was in the neighborhood already so I'm gonna wait outside for him." Then he slinks back out the door, leaving us. I'm about to head to another room to pull on the clothes Eli brought.

"Rap figured out you are a were, didn't she? That's why she took you in the back to talk to you?" Goldie stops me with her words.

I nod slowly. "She told me how she lifted the ban from it being a humans-only bar but she made sure I knew in no uncertain terms that if I were to cause any trouble, she would skin me and use my pelt as a rug in her office."

And I believe her. Goldie's boss seems mostly human, but there is something about her that's off. I can't pinpoint what, but I caught a whiff of something. I'd been raised around humans my entire life, and I knew enough to know that Rap isn't quite that. She's more.

Goldie tries and fails to suppress a smile. Then a look of awe overcomes her face, her mouth dropping into an 'O.'

"Wait, so you shift into a bear and your name is Ted. . . "

Oh fuck.

"Blondie, no," I caution her. It's a trigger of mine. Not many things can send me over the edge—other than singing telegrams—but she's about to step onto a landmine.

"A bear, named Ted," she says slowly.

"You better stop right there, or so help me," I advance on her. The clothes Eli brought me slip from my grasp and hit the ground. My heart beats into my throat as my blood heats up uncomfortably.

Then that perfect 'O' of her mouth spreads into a triumphant, brilliant smile and I know I'm seconds away from having to murder her.

"Which means you are—"

"Don't you dare fucking say it, or I will end you," I bellow with every fiber of menace I possess as I stalk toward her.

My threat doesn't register as she looks like she's about to explode with joy.

Her voice slides up to an impossibly feminine octave as she cries out, "You are a Teddy bea—"

The throw blanket I held around my hips falls away as I close the distance and cover her mouth, stopping her from finishing that vile name she's about to call me.

My other hand finds her hip, as I pull her soft, full body against my naked one using her as a makeshift cover. Hand still covering her mouth, I say in a low, dangerous timbre, "I swear blondie, if you say it, I will be forced to show you I am anything but and you will regret *ever* calling me that."

Even though I'm covering almost half her face, her warm brown eyes shine up at me with pure fucking evil delight, and I feel the upward curve of her lips against my palm. Then the dark pupils of her eyes expand into obsidian pools as her body presses a little more into mine.

Different methods of torture filter through my head before the tactics take a more pleasurable turn. My mouth turns dry. How does she have such an effect on me?

Just as I start hardening against her, the front door bursts open. Goldie tries to jerk away, but I grab her hips, keeping her against me to cover my dick from whoever is intruding. JJ strides in, followed closely by Eli. JJ stops short, taking in the scene, Goldie still in her rumpled pink PJ set and me fully nude, plastered to her. My middle brother bites the inside of his cheek as if trying to suppress one of his irritating shit-eating-grins.

Eli lurks by the door, guilt still evident on his face, though his brow has a curious curve to it.

"Looks like we are interrupting," JJ finally gives into the broadest smile, eyes straying to Goldie. "And who is this lovely creature? Oh shit, is this the cream puff you were talking about?"

A growl emits from Goldie's throat. "You seriously have to stop calling me that."

Never.

But I don't say that out loud.

Instead, I shoot JJ a warning glance. "Goldie, this would be my second dumbass brother, JJ."

JJ winks at her and strides past, a cocky swagger in his step, "Now, now, is that a way to talk to your brother who brought all the equipment to make sure this place is looked after better than a bank vault? To keep the creeps out of everyone's house." He fixes Eli with a pointed glare. Eli squirms, looking positively miserable.

Again, *good*.

"What?" Goldie asks, stepping away from me. I take the opportunity to shuck my jeans on under the throw blanket I picked up again.

"Big bro here requested I set up some extra locks and cameras on your house for security purposes." He looks over her head at me. "Lucky for you, I may have already been on the road, but I always keep a stash of equipment in my trunk."

"Security cameras?" Goldie's gaze swings from me to JJ.

"Yeah, you know, little cameras that record everything so if those guys come back, we'll have an eye on them," JJ explains, his eyes never leaving Goldie. He gives her a smile that has probably melted the hearts of countless women. But it's not working on Goldie.

Thank the faelords, because I'd be forced to murder him with what's on hand, which would include a pile of romance novels and the throw blanket. Easy, I'd throw the books in the blanket and pound him until spines broke— his or the books.

I don't bring up that we have more reasons than that to set up surveillance. Partly to figure out if Goldie is actually sleepwalking, but more importantly, to figure out who is leaving flowers for Goldie and touching her underwear. The idea there may be an intruder breaking into her house, touching her underwear, and leaving roses ignites a deep, dark rage I didn't know I possessed. I've seen the way men react to her, so who knows who it could be?

"Weirdly enough," Goldie says with a nervous laugh. "I don't hate the idea of posting up cameras. Are uh, all of you werebears?" Goldie asks, her gaze shifting between us, looking a little dazed.

JJ freezes, alarm crossing his face. Eli stills behind him too, all expression draining away and leaving an implacable mask behind.

"The bear is out of the bag," I tell them before turning to her and speaking softer. "I'll have you know we've managed to keep a low profile for a long time out here."

"That's the reason you want people to stay out of your business," Goldie says, some understanding entering her voice.

"Among other things," I say through gritted teeth. Eli has the decency to look away, but JJ just smiles in that way he thinks charms the pants off any woman.

"Oh my gods, you were the bear I ran into outside your cabin," she exclaims at me. "You scared the crap out of me." She smacks me, her palm connecting with my naked chest.

Before I can respond, someone calls out, "Yoohoo, we're here to help clean this place up."

A slim woman with fire engine colored hair strolls into the house, along with a silver haired man with scars along his sharp face.

The stench of wolf assaults my senses, an overpowering tide of predatory encroachment. It's not just a smell; it's a violation, a trespassing of territory.

My animal instincts surge to the forefront, a primal

force that commandeers my body and thrusts Goldie behind me, safeguarding her from the threat.

Despite my continued attempts to push my feelings for Goldie away, my subconscious plows through all my weak protests and moves straight to protective mode. She's drilled through my defenses, no, more like used a wrecking ball of sugar, smiles, and mischief to blast through my walls. Now I would destroy anyone who even *thinks* of causing her harm.

Every muscle in my body tenses, coils, preparing to unleash a torrent of violence upon the intruder.

A chorus of growls kicks up as my brothers join me as we ready ourselves to tear the wolf apart.

CHAPTER 23

SOUND THE SIREN

GOLDIE

Every single tiny hair on my arms and the back of my neck rise as the four weres growl at each other. My primitive senses kick on with a scream, warning me bloodshed is imminent in a matter of minutes, maybe seconds.

"Whoa," I call out, before sneaking under Ted's arms to jump in the middle with hands raised. "Hey, no one is going to spill a drop of blood in this house. I've cleaned too long and too hard to have my shit ruined. So help me if any of you makes a move to fight in my house, I will murder all of you." I put every bit of steel into my voice. Getting in the middle of a bunch of fanged fae is probably not the smartest move, but I meant what I said.

The growls die off, but the tension is so thick in the room it practically chokes me.

Red joins in the middle of the room, acting as another bodily barrier. "Uh, we came by to help with the house like we promised. I didn't know you'd have company."

"This is my neighbor Ted and his two brothers." I throw out introductions and everyone's names like I'm not in the middle of a territorial pissing match.

Note to self. Buy litter boxes.

Red narrows her eyes at Ted, a hateful gleam sparking in her eye. "Oh, so *this* is the NFH."

That seems to pull Ted out of his defensive stance. "What?"

Red doesn't drop her attitude as she informs Ted, "It stands for Neighbor From Hell."

I shrug at Ted with a 'what did you expect' expression when he blinks at me in surprise.

"Do you need me to get rid of the werebears?" Brexley asks me, eyes flashing gold. I could swear his teeth have elongated to look more like fangs.

"Whoa, no one is getting rid of anyone, Brex," I announce. "We are all friends here."

"Friends?" Red scoffs, crossing her arms, clearly not ready to join Ted's fan club.

Not that I know where I stand with the half-naked bear shifter who bum rushed me out of his house after giving me the best sex of my life, then saved me from a gangster.

Is this the kind of problem one works out through journaling? Or will it take a months' worth of therapy to work through the whiplash I get from my every interaction with Ted?

I notice Brexley's gaze still trained on Ted, and an unspoken understanding seems to form between them. *You don't mess with me, I don't mess with you.*

All four weres slowly but surely begin to relax from their pre-attack poses.

Brexley's scarred, sharp eyes narrow as he sniffs the air, and then they snap to me. "You smell different," he mutters.

"What do you mean, different?" I ask, immediately on the edge of being offended. "Also, I thought your allergies plugged up your nose."

"We got him on some powerful antihistamines," Red explains, crossing back to him and linking her arm through her fiancé's, now that everyone has somewhat relaxed. "No more problems with living with the bun buns."

Brexley's expression is inscrutable as he steps closer to me, sniffing the air around me. "You smell like. . . " He wrinkles his nose before casting a quick look of disgust at Ted.

Oh, for fucks sake, if he outs Ted and I for having sex, I will kill myself. Choke myself on a slop pile of porridge just so I don't have to face this.

"You reek of magic." Brexley finishes. "But in that weird, not so awful way, like Red."

The organ in my chest stalls out.

My friend smacks his chest even as she studies me closer. "Oh witchtits," Red asks in earnest. "Did it happen?"

"Did what happen?" Ted asks, shifting his weight to the other leg, tension setting his shoulders.

The whiplash continues. My brain is going to explode before I can process everything that's happened in the last couple of hours. It's easy to ignore some random loan shark thug I never met, but this. . .

"What did that gangster call me?" My voice is weak, barely audible.

"A siren," Ted answers, his brows furrowing with concern or maybe confusion.

"Wait, what?" Red throws her hands out as if she can slow the room down. "A siren? Like the mages who attract, make others fall in love with them?"

"Aren't sirens fae? Like evil mermaids that call sailors to them and drown them?" Eli asks.

"Good to know you paid some attention in school," Ted grumbles.

"That's what the mages named this power after," Red explains. "Because it does remind them of the siren fae. But no half fish situation."

"No," I protest before cutting my arms in an X shape. Everyone is taking this way too far, and they need to stop. "No way. I did not get mage powers overnight."

"I know I've been busy and we haven't caught up," Red says softly, coming to my side to rub my back. "But I know you texted some weird things have been happening."

I open and close my mouth several times. "But not that. . ." My words falter.

I shake my head in disbelief. This can't be true.

Suddenly, everything that's happened to me recently makes sense. All the strange looks I've received from strangers, the way men always seem to want to be around me. It's all because of this power that I didn't even know I have—the way they hit on me in front of their girlfriends, the overly assertive approach before I've even opened my mouth, the proposals.

"I learned about sirens at the FFA, Goldie," Red explains, her expression becoming drawn and serious. "I can help you."

"The what?" Ted asks. I half expect his head to spin off. Mine will shortly follow.

"Fairy Fine Arts Academy, a school for mages," Red explains, while still rubbing my back in comforting circles.

"Why would they have 'fairy' in the name if the school is for mages? The fairies are a fae race, not mages," JJ comments, slipping his hands in his pockets.

Red waves a hand of dismissal. "Who knows. Either they did it to deliberately piss off the fairy court or they are idiots. But that's not the point. The point is there used to be way more sirens around and now there uh. . . isn't."

"Can someone tell me what's going on?" Ted's anxiety seems to tighten and twist up until he's about to explode. "None of this is making sense."

"Yeah, witches are born not made," Eli says. When the bears are all gathered, I easily spot their familial resemblance. Eli shares the same serious intensity as Ted. JJ has the same nose and set of his lips, but his tall lankiness and limp hair sets him apart.

"We don't say witch or wizard anymore," Brexley says, leaning a shoulder against the wall. "That's outdated and inappropriate, we say mage now." He explains it as if Eli were an idiot child.

He's not wrong. It's just weird hearing the Big Bad give a lesson in political correctness.

"Excuse the fuck out of me." Irritation clips Eli's words, as if he hates submitting the point to a werewolf.

Ted steps in. "Eli is right, though. I don't know much about mages, but I do know they stick to their own cities and are born with varying levels of power. One doesn't just develop powers overnight."

I'm too much in shock to explain, so Red jumps in. "Goldie has eaten some, uh, magic cookies that gave her the potential to develop powers."

JJ snickers. "Magic cookies," he chuckles, until he notices we're not joking. The laughter dies as his eyebrows gather in confusion.

Ted appears to be having a stroke, while I have my own mini meltdown. I slip into one of the rose wingback chairs, clutching the padded arm. Have I gone insane? Am I drunk? Maybe I never woke up? This day started out crazy with Ted inside me, but at least that was a pleasant hallucination.

"The only magic cookies I know about are those Magic Morsels snack cake things made by that company, Grandma's House," JJ says. "They don't work on us fae, but I know from the commercials they give humans super mild, weak powers for like, what? Ten minutes? But this seems more dramatic than the ability to float small objects for a couple minutes at a time." He doesn't know the blue-haired old lady who is a worldwide household brand is Red's literal grandma, and I don't care to illuminate.

Red doesn't share that fact either as she goes on, dropping her hand from my back. "Yeah, well like those, but a million times more potent, so we knew it was possible Goldie might develop powers."

"Why aren't there many sirens left?" Ted asks, coming back to what Red previously said. I'm grateful he asks because I also want to know.

Red's eyes bounce back and forth between him and me as I feel her uneasiness grow.

Or maybe I don't.

She fidgets with her engagement ring. "Sirens enchant others, but sometimes because their power is so firmly rooted in the subconscious, they pull people in too strongly without meaning too. Then those enchanted start to feel they have ownership, feel the siren is an object they must possess. The enchanted can get into such a frenzy they want a piece of the 'thing' they love and will pull out hair, or take a piece of clothing, or uh maybe a finger, until. . . "

"They tear the siren apart?" Eli asks horrified.

My nails dig into the chair arm as my insides quake. A marriage proposal was one thing, but someone trying to tear off a hunk of me?

Oh shit. Do I have to quit my job?

But then my stress doubles down as I think of the

192

money, I need to get this house in order. The idea that I could get stuck with a half-finished house, lose my job at the Poison Apple because of the mess I make, and have to give people a wide berth for protection has my gorge rising.

Too much. It's too fucking much.

That's not even including the dangerous loan sharks that now also may want a piece of me.

"That won't happen," Ted says with authority, coming to stand next to me. His presence and certainty are far too assuring. I remind myself I am capable.

I am enough.

And I don't need a man to fix my problems.

Even if he wanted to, he couldn't.

Red turns to me again. "But it's true? You've developed siren powers?"

"I—I don't know," I stammer. My stomach churns and the lovely breakfast Ted fed me starts to curdle under the stress. "I'm not doing it on purpose. I don't even know how I'm doing it. And if I was, wouldn't it affect everyone? It only seems to affect certain men. Maybe it isn't me." I'm starting to slip toward safe and cozy denial. Yes, that's the ticket.

Red comes to kneel by my seat, her voice soft. "There's probably something in your subconscious running the show, which is why you can't control it. You don't know how to tap into and wrangle it. Mages go to school for years to learn how to control their abilities."

"Oh great," I choke out. "Another major for me to try out." My laugh is wry and bitter.

It's then I notice JJ and Eli slipped out when Ted jerks his head at them, and I'm grateful not to have such a large audience as feelings of vulnerability bloom inside me with uncomfortable force.

"The siren angle makes sense from what I saw," Ted says. "Last night at the bar, I felt something in the air. Like a magnetic or electric field buzzing around. The longer I was there, it seemed to die down, until I left. When I came back, it was so out of control it felt like a hundred bee stings, causing the men to fight each other. It only eased when we got out of there."

Brexley lets out a displeased grunt. "Why didn't you stop it?"

"He tried," I say, rubbing a temple, and trying to ease the hot pressure gathered there. "Everyone was nutso."

"That's not what I mean," Brexley says, pushing off the wall and taking a couple steps toward Ted. "As a were, you can nullify a mage's powers. Why the fuck didn't you shut it down?"

Ted's eyes narrow as he straightens against the underlying accusations Brexley threw at him. "First off, I didn't know she was a mage. How would I? The very few I've crossed paths with stink to high heaven because of their power. And if you are referring to the ability to nullify power, I can't do it explicitly like wolves do."

Red cocks her head to the side.

I reach for Ted's wrist, sensing the rising defensiveness. It's not his fault, or his responsibility to fix my mess.

Ted looks down at me, pain radiating from his gaze. "If I knew what would happen, I wouldn't have left your side. I can't target a person or an area and suck away their power like werewolves."

I start to assure him I wouldn't expect him too, but he goes on. "I emit a null force I can't turn off or on. In hindsight, I believe I dampened your powers the other night, but not entirely. You must be an incredibly powerful mage. The few mages I've come into contact with lost the ability to use their powers rather quickly around me. But when I left to speak to your boss, I came back, and the energy worked the room up into such a frenzy that it would have taken a while for my presence to bring it back down."

Cold shock drips from my neck to my stomach. Because this is too many revelations for one thirty-minute period? Or because I've never heard Ted talk so openly about himself?

"Huh," Brexley says, sitting on the arm of the floral couch across from me. "And here I thought all weres were operated pretty much the same."

A grim curve picks up half of Ted's lips. "What can I say? Unlike you, I can't just turn it off. Bears must be more powerful that wolves."

Brexley's brow arches, but he wears a genuine smirk of acknowledgement. Not necessarily acknowledging that bears are more powerful, but that he underestimated Ted.

Red pulls me up to my feet, making me realize my knees are shaky and weak. "Hey, let's get you cleaned up. You look a bit. . . rumpled." My pink pajamas are dirty, and I can feel the blood has drained from my face.

Red wraps an arm around my shoulders, offering support as she leads me toward the stairs.

I pause to look over my shoulder at Ted. "Are you going to leave?"

He shakes his head. "No. I'll be right here when you get back."

I nod, comforted by that. Warmth spreads from the center of my chest. He wants to stay. I shouldn't be, but I'm not turning my back on him now. Ted grabs his phone from his pocket like he's a bear on a mission.

CHAPTER 24
AN OFFENSIVE AIR-CONDITIONER

GOLDIE

"**O**h honey, you're in trouble, aren't you?"

I look up from where I'm sitting on the bed to find the fairy godmother, Dame Kiki Eleganza, posing in the doorway of my bedroom. The drag queen's large frame and personality fills the space. It's midafternoon, so Kiki isn't yet in drag for her evening performance at the Pumpkin Coach Club. But she's no less striking in her silky, bright floral button-down shirt and black slacks, her platform boots encrusted with black rhinestones.

I've seen Kiki out of drag once before, at the Pumpkin Coach club and heard someone else refer to Kiki as a sir, while yet another called Kiki miss. I asked what pronoun was preferable and Kiki gave a half snort, half laugh as she waved a hand dismissively. "Oh honey, I'll go by whatever gets me what I want."

There was something so wonderfully elevated and

playful about the way she said it, as if she doesn't choose, she simply has it all.

Everyone tells me I'm confident, but the Dame possesses je ne sais quoi. That element of fabulosity that can't be bought or faked.

Red sits with me in my cozy bedroom. Instead of taking the master bedroom, I chose the same one I slept in the summer I stayed with Aunt Astrid.

The faded wallpaper, a tapestry of ivy and roses, covers the walls in patches. I've draped sheer, billowy white curtains over the windows that gently sway when I leave them open. My bed has an aged wooden frame with carved head and footboards, now covered in soft pink sheets and a plush duvet, dotted with mismatched cushions. It's the perfect blend of boho chic.

Kiki sits down on the bed next to me, her massive hand reaching out to touch my arm. "Now, darling, let's talk about your troubles."

"I just found out I developed the powers of a siren, and every dude is acting positively nuts toward me. It's been causing me a lot of stress." I toy with a loose string on my comforter. "So I've been sleepwalking. Breaking into my neighbor's house every night. I know you heal people, and I wondered if this was the kind of thing you could uh... heal?"

I keep it to myself that someone might have been in my bedroom, leaving gifts. I don't want to be greedy with my problems. It still very well could be attributed to my sleep-walking issue.

At the Pumpkin Coach Club, she's known as the Fairy Godmother. Aside from healing powers, she has a talent for granting wishes and making dreams come true.

Or at least that's the backstory for her drag persona. Last we had a girls' night, I was the chosen one pulled on stage. She predicted my forever hunk would be on my doorstep soon but instead I got a call about an inheritance..

I've yet to meet Mr. Right, and even if he did show up, I'm the evil mage, cursing men with my evil enchantments. Again, I rub my hands down my face, wishing I'd gotten any other power.

Kiki stares at me with unerring focus, as if she is staring straight into my soul. It makes me want to squirm, but at the same time I don't want to seem like I lack confidence. I keep her gaze and roll my shoulders back.

Internally I repeat my mantra.

I am capable.

I am enough.

I don't need a ma—

"Is that big hunk of hot man downstairs, your neighbor?" Kiki asks with a not-so-innocent smile.

"Oh yeah," Red waves a hand. "We call him the NFH. The neighbor from hell. He's been super rude to Goldie, which is bullshit cause who the heck can be mean to this ball of sunshine?" She leans over and gives my shoulders a squeeze.

A half smile twists up on my face, as guilt eats at me from the inside. After getting dicked down and then saved from that guy with a gun, it feels wrong to refer to Ted as the NFH any longer. Ted says he wants nothing to do with me, and then he invites me to breakfast, fixes my mirror, comes to warn me about his brother's intentions, and then. . . I let out a breath. I can't shake the way he caught me faking it, before stopping everything, only to wring every last sexual pleasure out of my body. How can someone who is so standoffish and rude have such a piercing insight into me? Something no one else has ever caught onto.

Kiki nods and hums to what Red says before turning

back to me. The way she looks into my eyes, the smile that plays with the corners of her lips, it makes me think she already knows that though she couldn't possibly.

Normally I explode with any new or exciting piece of news, but for some reason I don't feel like correcting Red. Maybe it's because that's not why the Dame is here, and I don't want to waste her time. But I suspect it might be because I actually want to make my mind up about Ted before throwing out information again.

That's... unlike me.

"Well my honey pet," the Dame says, taking one of my hands into hers, before laying her other large, cool palm against my forehead. "Let's see if I can help with this sleep-walking, shall we?"

I close my eyes, ready and willing for her to heal all my bullshit.

I expect to feel tingles, heat, magic, but there is nothing like that before she drops her hand and says, "I hate to tell you this, honey child, but there is nothing physically to heal."

It's like she's popped my balloon with a sharp, merciless needle. Instantly, I deflate.

"But whatever is going on, it might have something to do with that second power of yours."

Red launches off the bed. "What?"

"What?" I echo in a much smaller voice.

Red shakes her head. "Mages can't have more than one type of magic."

"True," Kiki tilts her head before pulling out a gloss from her pocket, reapplying even as she explains. "But one type of talent can have multiple facets. It's rare, but it happens."

I cover my face with both hands, letting out a groan. "I

have one power I don't want or know how to control—why couldn't I get healing, or telekinesis—and now you are saying I have a second one?" Who do I talk to about exchanging powers? I need to speak to a manager, stat.

Kiki shrugs. "Sorry darling, but we don't always get what we want. But I can say with complete and utter sparkling certainty," She leans in. "you always get what you need." With that she taps the tip of my nose.

"What is my second ability?" I ask, already dreading the answer. Does my kiss poison men?

If that were true, Ted would be dead by now.

A little shiver runs through me. I can't decide if it's because I find the thought of him dying dreadful, or because my brain drums up all we did this morning in high definition.

"I can't say," Kiki pouts. "But I would say that if you are a siren, which—" She puts her finger in her mouth then pops it out, as if she is testing for the wind. "I sense that to be true—whatever secondary power will complement the first one somehow. Or perhaps be an opposing force, like the two sides of the same coin."

"I have some resources, I can ask about this," Red suggests helpfully.

"Perfect." The Dame claps her hands.

"There's something else." Red lays a hand on me.

Oh great, what now?

She squeezes my arm. "If what I remember about sirens is true, you need to be careful of your tears."

"I need to what?"

Kiki wags a finger in vehement agreement. "Oh yes, girl, listen to your friend here."

"Are my tears going to turn into monsters that will turn around and eat me?" I ask with a dry laugh. My reality had been all but blown out of the water, so why not?

Red's chin drops as her brows draw in a sympathetic knot. "No," she says carefully, "But they are connected to your power. I didn't want to say it downstairs in front of uh. . . others, but I know they are a way for others to gain power over a siren. I'll do some research and figure out the specifics."

"I'll be sure never to cry again," I assure her even as I near the edge of bursting into tears on the spot.

"Oh, my poor dear," Kiki says, touching the side of my face with affection. "It will be alright. Cannot you see this is the fullest expression of yourself? The way you draw people to you, the expression of your romantic side?"

I bite my lip hard to keep from crying. Because apparently my tears can be used against me. Gods, this is fucked up.

"What use is this power even? Obviously, it was so destructive the siren mages were wiped out."

"There's a lot of helpful aspects of your power," Red assures me, coming to crouch in front of where I sit on the bed. She gathers my hands in hers.

"When people panic in a disaster, natural or otherwise, a siren may use their ability to calmly lead them to safety. Sirens are excellent with conflict resolution, lulling people into feelings of safety and security. Sirens can work with people who struggle to trust or feel safe so the person can open up and work on their emotional traumas in a therapeutic manner. Kind of like how every person already confides in you and trusts you no matter where they came from or what happened. Don't you see? Kiki is absolutely right. This is the fullest expression of your beautiful self."

Staring into Red's pale eyes, I do my best to believe her,

but fear clamps around my heart. My powers manifested, and I'm not doing any of that good stuff. I'm enchanting men, stealing them from other women. My subconscious has an agenda, and as far as I've seen, it's not a benevolent one. I can't take Brexley from Red as he is fae, but the idea she'll soon see me as a selfish man-eating monster feels inevitable. My subconscious is revealing I'm desperate to be admired and loved at any cost.

Just like I was accused of all those years ago...

Dame Kiki taxied here, so she convinced Brexley to drive her back into the city with Red in tow. My friend promised to research sirens more and get back to me. Brexley will be on a private security detail and traveling, but he swears once he comes back he'll hang out at the Poison Apple to keep my powers in check and advised I tell Rap I need some time off until then.

I don't mention I don't have the luxury of money to do that even as I bid them goodbye.

It's only after I've shut the door behind them that a blissful cool breeze hits my body. Tears well in my eyes as I experience an almost angelic sense of relief the cool air gives me from the thick, soupy heat of the house I've been working in for weeks.

Whoa, no tears. We don't know why yet but no crying, Goldie.

Squashing my emotional response down, I follow the source to the front room and find an old, yellowed air conditioning unit whirring and cooling down the space.

Wonder fills me and I barely feel my feet as voices draw me toward the kitchen.

Ted, now wearing a tight white tee shirt, is installing another air conditioning unit into a window while JJ is up on a ladder, installing a camera into a corner of the room.

Eli is on his hands and knees, scrubbing the floor. He'd picked up where I left off and now almost the entire floor is a shale white tile, instead of dirty, caked brown.

"Wh-what have you done?" I croak out.

All three men freeze. After two heartbeats, JJ practically leaps off the ladder. "That one's done, off to install another. Eli, can I get some help?" His words swoop into a higher pitch. The two men are out of there like a shot.

Ted smacks the handle of his screwdriver into the palm of his other hand.

"What do you think you are doing?"

Why am I shaking? Is it because I'm angry? Because I can't stand being around him? Because I'm not used to cold air against my skin anymore? Or because this is the only response I can manage if I can't burst into tears?

Or just maybe it's because I'm not used to men doing something like this, not for me anyway?

How dare he swing back and forth between icy rudeness to carrying me across pine needles when I'm barefoot and fixing shit that is the bane of my existence. How dare he? How dare he confuse me by acting unlike any man I've ever met.

Ted clears his throat and shifts his weight from one foot to the other, unable to look me in the eye. "I had a bunch of old A/C units I was fixing up. I figured it'd be a good opportunity to test out if they work in here."

Tap tap tap. The screwdriver handle continues to thwack against his palm.

"No." I shake my head, my hands balling into fists. "You are trying to fix things again."

The tapping pauses. Ted frowns, a subtle difference from a scowl. I hate that I know that a scowl turns his eyes into a storm, but a frown makes the blue soft and yielding.

It somehow makes him look younger, and a little lost. "No, I'm not."

"Yes, you are," I stalk up to him. Showered, in an oversized white and pink Barbie shirt and black shorts, I'm in my go-to comfy outfit, but now I wish I wore leather and spikes, anything to emit a solid fuck off vibe.

I don't need his help. I've done good enough on my own without him, and now he thinks he can come in here and romance me with his helpful, practical handiness? That my panties would just drop and I'd ask the big bear to save me?

I don't want to want him, or need him. Not someone who could hurt me more deeply than anyone before, crack me down the middle like a porcelain vase before I shatter. That was the old Goldie.

Before, I'd been an exposed vulnerable nerve, and now that I had some of my sense about me again, I hate that I ever left myself so open to caring about him. He overwhelms me.

"It's what you do, isn't it? You fix things. Clean up your brothers' messes, and now you are trying to fix my life too. Well, I've got news for you, I don't need you to fix my life." When I stalk up to him and poke him in the chest, I tell myself it has nothing to do with wanting to feel his solid muscle or breathe in his scent though it instantly comforts me.

His frown deepens as he tilts his chin down to meet my eye. "It's my fault you got mixed up in Eli's bullshit. I'm not going to leave—"

I hold up a hand. "Let me stop you right there. It's exactly what you are going to do. This house is my responsibility, my burden. My man troubles are mine. And sure, I'd appreciate it if you broadcasted that I have nothing to do with your brother's debts, but you can't come in here with your cameras, and your cleaning, and—and—" I realize I'm practically sputtering as my hands wave all about.

My mantra runs hot through me, like a flowing river of lava.

I am capable.

I am enough.

I don't need a man.

He grabs my fingers and pulls me up against his body until our mouths are centimeters away. I can't tell if the heat rolling off him or his stormy eyes is what suddenly has me melting into a puddle.

Searching my eyes, he leaves no place for me to hide. "And what?" he challenges.

There is something else in his gaze, deep in the storm. A question. A question I don't know even though I desperately want to answer it.

"And you brought me air conditioning," I cry out as if he is the devil incarnate.

"And what about you?" he growls, refusing to let me go. "You have to make everyone like you. Dig into their lives, no matter how private they want to keep them. Don't tell me this came on with your siren abilities. You wanted me to like you—"

I cut him off before he goes on. "That's how it started, but then I realized how messed up you are." He slowly shuffles forward until my back hits the refrigerator. His thick tree trunk of a leg pushes up between mine, causing my breath to hiss between my teeth. I fight the urge to close my eyes and grind on his jean-clad thigh. I struggle against the grip he has on my hands, albeit weakly. He's pulled them into his chest, like he's keeping them safe there, thumbs brushing back and forth across my wrists. But the storm is swirling in those scowling blue eyes, sucking the oxygen from my lungs, making me feel like I'm drowning.

"I don't need help," I grind out again, desperately clinging to my point. To the stance I worked so hard to gain ground on.

Ted lowers his head closer still, his drugging warmth surrounding me. His masculine scent of pine and musk makes me lightheaded. My synapses, my lungs, my thighs, all on fire, all ready to ignite.

"I don't need a man," I go on, my voice low and as foreboding as I can make it.

Every cell wrenches me toward him, like he is the world's largest magnet and I'm just a pile of pennies. It's then I notice I'm shaking. His breath puffs against my lips. Goosepimples shoot up across my neck and collarbone with almost painful speed.

My words turn into a ragged whisper even as I quake, trapped between the cool fridge and his hard body. "And I don't need you."

His lips press against mine, silencing me. I shatter into a million pieces. When I jerk my arms, he releases my wrists only to slide his palms over my hips. I claw at his hair, the nape of his neck as I instantly open my mouth to him. Our tongues meet in a heated battle that only drives me into a higher state of desire.

Want. More.

Hate him.

I don't need him.

Some part of my brain convinces me the harder I kiss him, the more I rub against that hard, bulky thigh the more I convince both of us that.

A large hand pushes up my shirt and plucks at my nipple through my lacy bra. My head falls back, mouth open in a gasp as what feels like a dozen sparklers singe me from the inside out before concentrating between my legs, turning into liquid aching heat.

Fingers curl in my hair at the base of my skull as he nuzzles my neck with his nose, the tip of his tongue tracing along my sensitive flesh.

"You are going to keep the air conditioning units." The male-fueled commandment only makes my panties wetter. "You are going to let JJ set up his cameras, and Eli cleaning your floors is only the tip of the punishment I intend on doling out on his dumbass."

I start to shake my head, not sure which part I'm even trying to deny before his fingers tighten, and my head pulls back into that awkward position, sending pleasure down my spine in a waterfall of tingles.

"I don't need you," I grind out again, tilting my head so I can meet his eye with the angriest of scowls. How dare he? How dare he be so rude and pushy and—

"Whoa," JJ exclaims as he practically jumps back from the threshold.

We break apart instantly, both still glowering at each other.

The middle brother looks everywhere but at us, scrubbing a hand along the back of his hair. "Uh, so cameras are set up. We can check out the footage tomorrow and uh yep, that's all, bye." He darts off as fast as he entered, a second set of feet shuffling out the house with him, Eli.

Ted's chest is heaving as he looks away from me as if it's the only way he can keep in control. "My contact information is on the counter. If anything, and I mean *anything*, happens, you will call me, or come to me."

Before I can open my mouth, he grabs his toolbox,

switches on the second air conditioner and walks out of my kitchen and house.

As soon as he's gone, I turn around and bang my head against the fridge in time to my mantra.

I am capable.

I am enough.

I do not need a man.

I do not need Ted.

I do not need Ted.

But oh fuck, I really *really* want him.

CHAPTER 25
SUFFOCATING
SATISFACTION

GOLDIE

That night I tie myself to the bedframe to make sure I fall asleep and wake up in the same place.

There is no fae fucking way I will end up in *his* bed. I am *not* going to sleepwalk tonight. I do *not* want Ted.

I drift off to my new mantra.

Which is probably why big, burly, and scowly invades my dreams again.

That rough beard chafes against my neck in the most delicious manner as he licks and sucks his way up to my mouth. My arms willingly wrap around him, pulling him close. I need him everywhere. I need him deep inside. I need him imprinted into me. I grab his wrist and roughly push it to where I need it most. A growl of satisfaction emanates from his chest and into mine, giving me absolute feminine satisfaction. It doubles down when his hand reaches up my nightgown, and down my panties to stroke up and down my slick entrance. He rubs my swollen clit before spearing a

211

finger between my folds, forcing a strangled cry of pleasure from me.

My senses suddenly clear as my inner muscles pulse around his finger.

I'm awake and I'm in Ted's bed. Again.

I should be ashamed. I should jump up and leave pouring either apologies or rage. Rage at him? I'm the one who broke into his house again. The rage would be because I'm trying so very hard to not want him, and the very universe seems to be conspiring against my efforts.

My legs tighten around his hand, inadvertently driving his digit another inch in me. The thready wail of pleasure that escapes me is equal parts needy and embarrassing.

His mouth parts on a groan as if sympathetically aroused.

Those stormy blue eyes train on me with unerring focus. It's like they are drilling into me, seeing every last part. Including the parts I never intended to share with anyone else.

An insane thought crosses my mind. Is this how it feels when I do it to others? When I try to dig into what makes them tick? Try to claw into their darkest parts to care for their most vulnerable bits?

This feels so invasive, but at least I know I'm doing it with the best intentions.

As Ted slowly, gently strokes me, while watching me like I could save him from dying, I can't say I know what his intentions are. And that makes me incredibly uneasy. For once I don't have the upper hand. I don't have the answers, or the control. Even when I was with other guys, or even Lawrence, I felt I had a hold on the reigns of the crazy train. My focus was on them, but I realize now it had never been on me.

"What is this?" Ted asks, his voice low and rough as his eyes search mine for the answer.

We both still, staring at each other, in yet another battle of wills. Only my fingers curl on his shoulders as I hold my breath.

I don't know what to say. When did we stop being adversaries? Or maybe we still are?

"I don't know," I whisper, my voice barely audible.

Ted cups my face in his free hands, eyes boring into mine.

My heart stutters and trips over the next few beats.

Before I can say anything, he kisses me again. This time it's so tender, it makes my heart ache. Like he's kissing someone who is precious to him, like he never wants anything bad to happen to me.

I must be losing my mind to ascribe so many feelings to the kiss, but I swear when he parts my lips and meets my tongue with his, I blackout a moment. I feel... I feel like I've been waiting my whole life to be kissed by him. Like everyone is a pale ghost compared to Ted, and I can't recall a single face or name of anyone before him.

His finger leaves my body and I let out a whine, wanting it back immediately. But then he is between my legs, hovering over me without crushing me. His hot length presses into me through his boxers. My hips roll against his, seeking friction. I want to feel every part of him.

My hands slide up his white shirt, fingers tracing along his hard abdomen, letting the dusting of hair run through my fingers as I thread them upward. He groans into my mouth. "Fuck, your touch is so sweet, cream puff."

There's that nickname again. A part of me wants to take offense, but every other inch of me is preoccupied with his weight, his delicious scent, the way he touches and talks to me in a way that makes me feel like a fucking queen.

I would have never guessed Ted was a talker in the bedroom. He struck me as one of those guys who pumps into a girl with serious, silent intent until he finishes then rolls over. Faelord knows I'd been with the type enough.

The larger question of what 'this' is and what are we doing disappears when he pulls back to tug his shirt over his head. The expanse of his manly, virile chest is exposed to my greedy gaze.

It hasn't been cultivated in a gym to create a certain aesthetic of abs or shoulder muscle. This body is built on action, on physical labor. It occurs to me I don't even know what Ted does for a living, and a string of guilt snakes through me.

The question scatters from my mind as he leans over my body and undoes one of the buttons on my pajama top with his teeth.

Holy hell.

He does the next and I'm lost in rapt attention to this surprising skill set. His blown pupils stay locked with mine as he gently spreads apart my pajama top. Cold air brushes against my bare flesh and goosebumps rise along my skin. Or maybe it's because I feel vulnerable like this in front of a man I've spent so much time hating, but who is surprising the hell out of me.

A low masculine rumble of appreciation comes from his chest as he cups one of my breasts in his hand. Dark eyebrows knit and he looks almost in pain as he weighs my breast in his hand, brushing a thumb across the aching tip. He covers the other one, giving it similar treatment. I swallow back a moan. Ted drinks me in with his eyes, taking his time looking and feeling.

Somewhere at the back of my mind, a voice reminds me I've sworn off men, but this doesn't count, right?

Not when we've been enemies for so many weeks. This is something else entirely.

And nothing proves that more than when he says, "You have the most gorgeous set of tits I've ever seen, blondie. I have to taste them."

Before I can respond, he dips down and suckles on one. I gasp, my back surging off the bed as liquid heat zings straight from where his hot, wet tongue rolls around my sensitive tip, straight down to my pussy.

The fingers on my other breast begin to increase the pressure until he's plucking at it, playing it like a fucking maestro.

Witchtits, I'm so wet. The anticipation of pleasure builds within me like electricity trapped in a storm cloud. I want to touch myself, push my fingers between my legs and give myself relief. I feel like my body might burst apart from all the tingles coursing through it.

And you say he's a bad guy, my brain whispers.

He's really, really bad, I agree. I should be freaking the hell out right now, but I can't find the strength to freak out. Not with him doing things to my body that I didn't know were even possible.

I can feel the desire coating my thighs fast, as he works me into a frenzy. I throw my head back and forth on the pillow, unable to catch my breath enough to form words. He laves his tongue and plays with my tingling tip like it is his sole mission in life to please me.

Ted's mouth moves to my other breast, giving it the same treatment. If I thought my first breast was pleasured before, I'm wrong. This is a whole other level. A coil in my lower stomach keeps twisting tighter and tighter, until it's almost unbearable.

Unable to wait any longer, I slip a hand down to rub the ache into submission, gasping as I feel how slick I am.

"Oh faelords," I moan.

Ted looks up at me from my chest. "Is it good?" he asks. "Does my good girl need more?"

His good girl? Again, what the fuck is happening? And why am I nodding so enthusiastically with a pathetic little whimper?

Suddenly, he's on his knees, ripping the comforter and sheets off me. He's only wearing a pair of boxers, but the thin gray material doesn't do anything to hide the hard length jutting from his body. Oh faelords, I want that monstrosity in me again.

Ted hooks a finger in my panties and drags the sodden piece of fabric down my body as I lift my hips.

Then he flips us with surprising strength and agility so I'm sitting on his chest. I'm awkwardly balanced, trying not to crush him.

Brain still hazy with the desire he ignites in me, I ask, "What are you doing?"

"*You* are going to sit on my face, cream puff," he rasps. Then his fingers trace the tattoo on my upper thigh. It's a lace garter with a big bow on it. "Faefucking hell," he says in breathy awe before leaning forward to nip at my flesh there. The soft pinch of his teeth causes me to jump.

"Are you nuts?" I ask, rolling away from him as an internal alarm breaks through the spell he's woven. Two strong hands grip my thighs, stopping me.

"No, but I might lose my mind if you don't sit on my face and let me lick that beautiful cunt of yours."

I suck in a breath. Ted has the dirtiest mouth I've ever known, and it just made me wetter than Niagara Falls.

"I'll crush you," I say, wriggling to get off him again.

Instead, he bodily hoists me up his chest with shocking strength, his fingers massaging my hip bones in a way that makes me melt.

"Fucking good. I want you to suffocate me with that pretty pussy. And if I die, I'll go out a happy fucking bear. Now get up here, before I spank that voluptuous ass until it's nice and red. Though knowing you, you'd like the fight." He huffs.

My insides freeze, unable to pick a direction. Both are naughty as sin and get me hotter than I've ever felt before.

I don't get the chance to choose, as he picks me up and sets me over his face with a groan of anticipation. A hot tongue glides along my cleft and I grasp the headboard, looking for any grounding I can get. I also don't fully trust putting all my weight on him.

"Oh fuck yes," he gasps as if he's had his first drink of water after nearly dying of thirst. "Why am I not surprised you have a cunt waxed to perfection. I've wanted this from the moment you stepped onto my porch."

From the second I stepped on his porch? No. He hates me. He has from the beginning. He couldn't possibly have been thinking of doing this when we met.

Another long, wet drag of his tongue and I jolt. Hot tingles riot through my body at his words and unabashed enjoyment of my body. It's unreal. The novelty of the position has set every nerve ending ablaze and his tongue is the fuel turning that fire into an inferno.

My fingers wrap around the headboard as I hang on for dear life.

Fingers dig into my ass as he pulls me more firmly to his

mouth, his tongue ravaging me. I can't help but let myself relax a little more, grinding against him. He suckles and licks at my clit, hitting the mark with shocking accuracy.

More, more. I need more. The twisting, rising sensation inside me strains for more, and I seek it out on Ted's mouth.

He growls, the vibration sending shockwaves through my body. All thoughts scatter from my mind as he takes me to the brink with just his tongue. His fingers bite into the fat of my ass, literally holding me in place for his mouth.

And just when I think I can't take it anymore, he twists his tongue in a way that sends me reeling. Ted clamps on to my clit, furiously sucking it into his mouth. The insistent, hot pull of his mouth hurls over the edge. A muffled cry of pleasure escapes through my clenched teeth. My body spasms and shakes as if it's trying to rip itself apart. My pussy clenches, squeezing out a flood of juices that run down my thighs. Self-consciousness battles with my release, and I start to move away. Ted latches onto my ass, until he is buried in me.

I'm falling, falling, falling into a world of pleasure that I never want to stop. Ocean blue eyes stare up at me with blazing desire. He laps up my juices like a sex-starved beast.

For the past two weeks this man has been driving me insane, and now he's doing it in a completely different way and it's unreal.

And I'm still grinding. Still needing more. It's not enough.

"That's it," he coaxes, his voice husky. "Ride my face, cream puff."

I do as he says, drawing out the orgasm.

A hand smacks my ass with a shocking sharpness. Then I'm gasping for air as he continues licking me, pushing me into another orgasm.

At the peak, I can't hold back any longer. A fresh wave of pleasure crashes over me as I cry out. I convulse, clenching the bedposts, at Ted's mercy.

Finally, I find myself lying next to him, still fighting to breathe. He's perched on one arm, looking down at me like the cat who ate the canary. His lips and beard glisten with my desire, and I come to terms with the fact I've had a full-on mental break.

So I go with it, drawn to his big, erect beast that is out between the slit of his boxers, I get to my knees and wrap my fingers around his length.

Ted freezes and mutters a curse.

My fingers don't meet. A hot shudder washes through me. He brought me off spectacularly, but faefucks if I don't want to be impaled on him again and again.

I lean forward, up on an elbow, and lave my tongue across the large mushroom head.

His hips shoot off the mattress as he sucks in a harsh breath. I lean in even further and circle the head of his dick with my tongue. I'd always been proud of my blowjob skills, taking pleasure in knowing I can give pleasure, but this is different. Another way I've kept my hands on the reigns of any man I've been with. For the first time, I feel I truly have control over Ted and I'm instantly drunk with power and sensation. This is where I excel. My sexiness lies in service to others and it's been too long since I'd been able to rule my role.

I'm going to make him succumb and buckle to me the way I do for him. But as much as I grab for power and note every twitch, gasp, and muttered curse, I lose myself in him. Absorbed in the feel of him, the taste, it becomes more than a show or a service. I want to fucking take all of him into me anyway I can get. I want to take Ted down my throat, feel him as deep as I can.

With a growl he grips my hair, tugging me back a few inches, until my mouth opens wide. I let out a moan of my own and his dick slides between my lips, the tip grazing the back of my throat. Then I'm bundling my hair in one hand, letting him control the pace as I take in as much of him as I can. Even though he dictates the pace, I own him right now and we both know it.

With him gripping my head, I have to put all my weight on the one elbow to stay poised, which is starting to get stiff. I'm barely aware that I'm rocking my hips back and forth, as I suck on his hot, pulsing dick. The taste of him is addictive. Is that because he was so unattainable? Does it make men all the more satisfying when they first deny you?

That's fucked up, but maybe not wrong.

Ted pulls away from me, and the loss of contact leaves me gasping for air. His face is arranged in a concentrated lust-drugged expression.

"If I spend one more second in that hot little mouth, blondie, you'll have to swallow. And I have better plans than that right now."

CHAPTER 26
BREAKING NEWS: SLUT BROTHER GOOD FOR SOMETHING

TED

Witchtittingfuckfaes, I almost blew in her throat. I'd never felt anything so godsdamn good in my life.

But I crave more. I crave her. The way she is splayed on my bed, so inviting, with puffy lips from my thorough kisses, and tousled hair that could get me hard in church on a Tuesday. When her eyes sparked with anger, I was enrapt, but now they are hooded with lust and I'd fucking fall at her feet as long as she kept looking at me like that.

After shucking the boxers off, my fingers instantly seek the soaked petals of her cunt and I moan into her breast, licking and sucking again.

She mewls and I almost come from that sound. I smile around her perfect bud as her fingers clench the sheets and her feet curl up, toes digging into the mattress.

My dick aches for her, aching for all of her. My fingers work in and out of her pussy and she moans, lifting her hips to meet them. I can't imagine a more beautiful sight than her right now, my fucking witch, so willing and open for me.

She cries out when I add a third finger and I'm fighting with my bedsheets to free my hand so I can grip my aching dick. I don't know how much longer I can make this last. Her body winding up, her hips thrusting to meet my merciless pace. I'm going to explode. I've never had so much self-control in my life. I can't remember ever wanting something so badly, but still not being able to have it.

I find the slit of her pussy and rub her clit. A strangled sound comes from her mouth and she lifts her hips even more, like I'm fucking her with my hand instead of just the one finger.

I feel the ripples in her walls. She's going to come for me again. I love getting her so responsive. But I back off, knowing I've got her right where I want her.

I get on my knees and spread her thighs. Goldie blinks up at me with wide eyes.

Gods, she is gorgeous in my bed, sunlight making her tan skin glow. The woman is all soft curves and femininity.

Before I can go forward, I have to make sure she's with me. "You can say no."

She opens her mouth and then closes it. It wasn't a no, but it sure as hell wasn't a yes.

Fuck, Ted. She doesn't want this. She doesn't want you. The poor girl ended up in your bed reluctantly again and you are taking advantage of her.

As I move away, she sits up enough to grab my wrist. "No wait. I want it. I want it so badly I . . . "

Then instead of saying more, she reaches up and pulls my head down to her. There's nothing soft about our kiss. No tongue, no light brushes. Her lips meet mine and we almost clash teeth as we both open our mouths at the same time. She moans this noise and I groan and we meet in the middle with our tongues.

It's only then that I realize I don't have something vital to this situation. Hell if I'm going to make the same mistake twice.

"Give me a second," I say, before I grab my boxers and pull them up. In a heartbeat I'm down the hall in front of JJ's closed door. I knock harder than I intend to, but fuck if I'm not antsy to pick back up where I left off.

The door cracks open and a bleary-eyed JJ blinks at me. I've probably woken Eli up too. I don't give two fucks.

"I need a condom," I announce.

JJ's sleepiness evaporates like water in a boiler. The idiot just stands there, blinking at me in surprise.

"Now," I yell.

That gets him to move. JJ ruffles loudly through a drawer before coming back and sticking a hand out with a long strip of condoms.

I barely mutter a thanks before I'm back in my bedroom, kicking the door shut behind me, shoving off my underwear and opening up a wrapper all at the same time.

"For once, I don't mind his presence in this house," I say. "But fuck, if thinking of you with him didn't make me want to rip his dick right off."

A laugh of disbelief escapes her. "You were jealous? When you thought I was fucking your brother? When I was bombing your house with cakes and singing telegrams?"

She has no fucking clue. Hell, I didn't. But with her gorgeous body splayed out, blonde hair messy and my room smelling of sex, I know now I've never wanted anything else so bad in my life.

"Yes, I was fucking jealous."

My cock throbs and aches, I need to be there so bad. But I'm still reeling from the fact that we are doing this. . . again. She hates me. She can't stand me. She doesn't want a relationship. But I've slipped, so far gone, I can't help myself.

I'm frozen for a second, staring at her, cataloging every detail of her gorgeous body.

I pull her thighs apart and lay my body over hers. I grind against her, trying to make her feel me, to make her understand how much I want her.

I guide my cock to her pussy, moving my hand to spread her. I have to pause when she squeezes so tight, it's hard to go further.

Her pink fingernails dig into my shoulders. "That's it, cream puff, take it all, baby. We'll go slow but in the end you are going to take every inch of this dick."

Slowly but surely, I sink in a little further, gritting my teeth and squeezing my eyes as the sensation of her tight cunt pushes me to the edge of my control.

Fuck why wasn't I on birth control so I could go bareback?

Because you thought the first time would be the last time. Because there was no need to ask the doctor for a quick prick in the shoulder. so you could have sweaty, wild, responsible sex with this blonde goddess. Because it's been years since you've had sex, and you never believed you'd get here with your annoying, pink-obsessed neighbor.

She isn't annoying. Her effect on me is. The way she makes me want her, when I consciously decided to never give in.

Well I'm going in deep now, until we are both panting and shaking, clinging to each other.

She takes my breath away. I want more. I want everything.

I pull out and pound back into her, so hard the headboard bangs against the wall. I can't help myself. I lean forward, wanting to touch her, to get as much of her as possible. We kiss again, tongues and teeth clashing as we both grip at each other, pulling and pushing, dueling for dominance. I don't have the energy to fight, not when my body is already pumping so hard.

The sound of our bodies colliding is loud, our breathing almost as loud. She arches up to meet me in every thrust, her hot pussy squeezing down on me.

I can't stop myself from grinding my hips as I fuck her, wanting to drag out the sensation forever. She's so fucking perfect. The way she curves, the way I fit inside her—she's like a fucking piece of heaven.

I can't—I can't—I can't keep my eyes open as I gaze down at this woman I've wanted from the moment we met. I've always been careful before, but for her I'd do anything. I let her in the goddamn door.

My body tightens with anticipation as the orgasm pushes up through my veins, pounding inside me. A surge of electricity shoots from my core to my fingertips, and I feel my cock twitch inside her, knowing I have maybe moments left.

I buried myself so deep, I'm afraid I'm going to explode. There's nothing I can do about it. There's nothing I can do about the force of my orgasm, about the pleasure that's going to tear me apart. I want to die from the pleasure, to die right here in her arms.

She squeezes me so tight, as I hear her exclaim loudly, her inner muscles fluttering around me as she jerks below me.

We stay there a moment, suspended in time, our breaths evening. I brush a thumb across her jaw, looking into those honey brown eyes.

I want more. I want to have her again, and again, and again. Because this has to be a dream. A dream I never want to wake up from. After all, I keep molesting her while half asleep and waking up to a reality that is too good for me.

Slowly, I pull out, causing us both to groan. I get rid of the condom before I return to sit on the side of the bed, while she sits up, holding my sheets, covering her gorgeous body from me.

The very idea of all this is so ludicrous, I have to struggle to keep from laughing out loud. I'm lying here with a goddess. The woman who hates me more than I can say. Or maybe not so much.

I won't make the same mistake as last time.

"We need to talk," I say, because I have to say something. I have to bank this moment, so it lasts for a little longer.

"I don't think I have any brain cells left," she half jokes.

But I'm not kidding around, I need to know if this is just a one-time thing, if she changes her mind... I need to know what comes next.

"I don't do this," I say, waving my hand back and forth between us, trying to find a way to articulate.

"Do what?" She brushes the hair from her face before tucking it behind an ear. I want to crawl over to her and kiss her again. Kiss her and run my hands down her spine until she falls back asleep in my arms. But if I want to keep my senses, I need a little space.

I'm fully, completely, and utterly addicted to her.

"Where is this going?"

Goldie pales, as if stricken. She pulls the sheets up

higher in a protective mode and I already know I've made another mistake. Something to drive her away when all I want is her close to me.

She laughs, a strained tittering sound that's forced. "It's good sex."

My expression is impossible to suppress. Goldie's fake smile slips from her face. "Okay, maybe the best sex I've ever had. But that's all it is." She starts to dig under the covers until she roots out her panties.

She's about to run again. If I'm not pushing her out the door, she's running out of it. But I'm done with all that.

So I barrel on. "I don't do relationships, Goldie."

Her head pops out of her sleep shirt. Shoulders relax and lower as if I told her the things that will solve all her worries. "Oh, good," she breathes with evident relief.

Oh fuck, I just made things worse. That's not what I meant. She doesn't understand at all. Before I can explain, a loud knock at the door interrupts.

"Since the screams of ecstasy seems to have paused," JJ's voice comes muffled through the door. "I thought you would both like to check the surveillance footage from last night. In case someone needs to cover my virgin eyes from anything indecent that started over there last night."

Goldie jumps to her feet before I can stop her. "See you down there," she says, flashing a smile before disappearing out the door.

Dammit. Goldie is going to be the death of me.

CHAPTER 27

THE MIDNIGHT VISITOR

GOLDIE

I don't do relationships.

Half of me was completely relieved to hear Ted say that. I'd heard it dozens of times before. Even after men promised me engagement rings or a future, they would circle back around to some form of caveman's version of 'ugh, me no do commitment.'

And despite the shitty way I've enchanted men into throwing themselves at me, it has felt good to not give in to the bait. To really convince myself I don't need a man. I haven't envisioned myself in a white dress, or gone over potential baby names the way I used to. More than that, all the energy I've spent trying to soothe another person's ego, or secure a man's feelings has opened up as well. My gods I spent a lot of time doing errands, verbally blowing, or finding all these little ways to be romantic while waiting for some crumb of reciprocation.

It's freed up so much space in my brain. Space I first dedicated to torturing my neighbor and then to working on the house. I now have a serviceable living room, bathroom, one and a half bedrooms and a kitchen in semi-decent condition. With the tips I make at work, the monetary pressure has lifted somewhat, but is this what I want to do? Flip houses? Run a bed and breakfast? I don't know.

While I enjoy learning all kinds of things like tiling, some light plumbing, and other various useful skills. The realization I haven't yet found my 'thing' forces a yawning disappointment to open up in me. Red has accounting, Cinder is an artist, Rap runs the bar, and I flit from thing to thing. A panic follows on the heels of my disappointment. I need to find it. My *thing*.

My gaze shifts to Ted, who is now wearing a pair of worn jeans and a gray tee. His intense stormy blue eyes are trained on JJ's laptop on the breakfast table.

No. Absolutely not. Ted cannot be my thing. I promised myself I would stop letting men jerk me around.

Though the promise of solid ground with Ted seems deeply appealing right now.

What solid ground? He regretted having sex with you the first time, and he just told you he doesn't do relationships. You know exactly how to handle this situation, just like riding a bike. Besides, he's not solid. He's grumpy, bossy, pushy, dominating, sexy, protective, passionate, and he smells so freaking good.

My brain jerks to a halt. *Witchtits.*

I feel caught in a tug-of-war, yanked between the need to remain my own person and the growing, unnerving desire for Ted. But now isn't the time for this whirlpool of thoughts, especially with JJ pulling up the surveillance on the laptop screen.

Eli has slunk into the kitchen where Ted ordered him to make coffee for all of us. Though Eli has himself elbow deep in some bad shit, I feel bad for him. Maybe it's because he looks so despondent, like a kicked puppy. A kicked puppy who distantly resembles Ted, which really makes me want to soothe him and make him feel better. The bear boys all have the same eyes though varying shades of blue.

"Please feel free to direct me away from any footage of my brother boning," JJ jokes before he coughs violently. I only catch the last of the sharp movement of Ted digging his elbow in JJ's side.

"Kidding," JJ wheezes before typing a few things, bringing up a screen. "I set it for motion detection so it should have parsed out any interesting footage, like a certain someone sleepwalking." JJ leans over and winks at me.

All the things Ted warned me about his brother suddenly make sense. The guy does ooze charm even with his lankiness and crooked nose. There is something about him that instantly puts me at ease, but not in a sexual way at all. More in a brotherly way.

Ted straightens, his nostrils flaring. "What is that?"

I force my focus onto the surveillance footage.

The front door swings open in the dead of night.

"I told you to lock your front door," Ted growls, his hands bunched into angry fists.

"I did," I protest, but I am also watching someone break into my house like it's nothing.

No, wait, not someone. . . a shadow? The door swings shut again but there is nothing more than a slight shadow moving in the room.

"What the. . . " Ted trails off. He sees what I see.

"What about the exterior cameras," Eli chimes in.

"On it," JJ says, hitting a button and bringing up scenes of the outside of my house.

JJ starts to mutter as he rewinds then goes through the footage. "There's no car outside, no person outside."

"You must have missed an angle," Ted points out.

"No," JJ's voice elevates in pitch from irritation. "I have all angles. It's just nothing is there." He continues the footage and again the door opens as if all on it's own, a shadow entering my house.

A shudder goes through me. There is a gallery of screens, and I can plainly see I'm sleeping in bed. No idea someone is in my house.

JJ fumbles a bit, managing to zoom in but the figure remains elusive, a specter shifting just beyond clear view. I suddenly wish JJ wasn't sitting between Ted and me. My hands wring at each other.

You don't need a man, Goldie.

Yeah, but I might need a bat and a couple rape whistles.

The figure goes through the house, leafing through my books, sitting in chairs as if making themselves at home.

"Can't you get a better angle?" Ted demands.

JJ shakes his head. "Bro, it's *not* my cameras. I think it doesn't want to be seen and is making a damn good show of it."

"Did somebody hack your cameras and erase their image from the recording?" Eli offers.

"No," JJ growls, and it's the first really bear quality I've noticed from him. "That's dumb." His expressions smooths as he says, "What it does mean is whoever that is or, or whatever that is has some connection to either mage or faekind."

"Like a spell?" Ted asks.

JJ shrugs before rubbing his chin in thought. "A spell, a mage who can prevent their image from being recorded, a shadow fae if there is such a thing? I don't know man; Ma specifically moved up to a human city so we wouldn't have to deal with this kind of bullshit."

"Can't you tell if someone is magic or fae? Like you can smell it?" I ask to keep from drowning in more scary uncertainty.

"Like the wolf said," Ted explains. "We can smell magic."

"It's terrible," Eli interjects, wrinkling his nose in disgust. "Nasty stuff."

"But you are something different which is why I couldn't tell you had powers," Ted explains.

"Bears actually have a keener sense of smell," JJ adds, leaning in. "So much so that we usually taste whatever we smell."

"We haven't come into contact with a lot of fae," says Ted. "So while we instantly scented out the wolf, it's more of a territorial response. We can't do that with every fae creature."

"Trying to sniff out what type of fae creature is on our territory would be like trying to identify an individual flavor in a soup when you've never tasted any of the ingredients before," JJ says, making the screen with the shadow bigger as we watch it move around my house.

"Gross," Eli says, but JJ just shrugs.

Apparently, they are really picky about scents and taste. But I guess I knew that from Brexley.

The shadow creeps up the stairs and my heart lodges in my throat, beating there as I watch my own sleeping form roll over onto my side. My nails dig into my thighs as I bite my lip, watching the figure about to enter my bedroom.

It's like watching a movie where you know the hero is going to come out alive, but you are so wrapped up in the moment, your emotions and brain tell you otherwise. Except the hero is me, and even if I know I'm okay now, I'm not sure I can handle seeing what's about to happen to me on screen.

"I think you both need to go," Ted says to JJ and Eli as he half rises from his chair, voice taut as string about to snap.

Oh faelords, he's thinking the same thing.

If something bad happens to me in my sleep, I don't want them to see either.

Acid rises, stinging my throat as my pulse races. I shove the side of my fist into my mouth to keep from screaming at my own prone form. I don't want to watch but I can't look away.

JJ is half up, but he stops and sits back down. "Did you see that?"

I blink. The bed is empty.

"Did you skip forward? Hit a button?" I ask, my voice shaky. He must have jostled something when he moved.

JJ hits some buttons and rewinds the footage. There I am again. Sleeping in my bedroom. This time I make sure not to blink, not even as the shadow creeps up the stairs toward me a second time.

Then I disappear from the bed. Like a blip, I'm there one second and gone the next. Ted stiffens, his confusion mirroring mine.

"Whoa, no way," JJ breathes, rewinding and playing it a third time. My figure in bed seems to just. . . vanish. A glitch in the matrix.

"What?" Eli asks, crowding in from behind me.

JJ scratches his head. "Did you just. . . teleport?"

A scoff escapes me, my nerves strung tight. "First I'm a siren, now I can teleport? There's no faefreaking way."

But the uneasy glance exchanged between Ted and JJ tells me they are not entirely convinced. The seed of doubt takes root, and suddenly the room is too small, the air too dense.

Dame Kiki's advice returns to me. *"You have a second power."*

That's. . . that's ridiculous.

I surge to my feet and pace back and forth. I need a breather, a moment to sift through the swirling chaos within me. I need to. . . but Ted's hand finds mine, a grounding force, pulling me back from the spiraling path of my thoughts. His touch is both a balm and a trigger, soothing and igniting a fire in me simultaneously. He pulls me toward him, as he stands, towering over me. In his shadow, I feel strangely grounded, safe even.

But I'm not safe. That video proves it.

My gaze collides with Ted's, an unspoken conversation happening in the silent exchange. His eyes are a stormy sea, reflecting turmoil. For a man I thought to be so unfeeling, I realize I couldn't be more wrong. He feels everything far too deeply.

"That's why everything is locked up even after you get in," Ted says finally, his voice steady, yet carrying an undercurrent of concern. "You never use the front door."

"Jeez," JJ says, tipping his chair back. "Seems like your subconscious knew when to get you out of there even when you consciously didn't."

"Two sides of the same coin," I say, the room turning unfocused.

"What?" Ted asks,

He threads his fingers into my hair, forcing me to look at him.

"It's what the Fairy Godmother, er, Dame Kiki said. I have two powers."

Eli snorts. "First humans get powers, and now they can get two?"

"Shut it," Ted snaps at his brother before looking at me, his eyes softening. "What did she say exactly?"

"She said I have a secondary power, and whatever it is, likely complements the first one somehow. Or be an opposing force."

"That makes sense," JJ says with a nod at the computer, arms crossed, chair still tipped back.

"Don't act like you know everything," Eli hisses.

Ted lets me go so he can reach out and smack Eli up the backside of the head. "If you aren't going to be helpful, shut up. This may be your fault after all."

Okay, rounding back to that as soon as I can but first. "How the hell does that make sense?" I ask JJ.

He shrugs. "Zeros and ones, babe."

Ted growls, his body suddenly larger than it was a moment ago. "Don't call her babe."

I set a palm on Ted's chest to appease him and keep the beast at bay so I can get some answers. "Meaning?"

"You're a siren, right?" JJ looks up at me with those eerily familiar eyes. "You attract. Apparently, you can attract too much until your own power becomes a danger to you. So what is the other side of your power? Poof." He explodes his fists like a puff of smoke. "When the enchanted close in on you and you're in danger, you can zappo out of dodge."

"Whoa," I say, taking a moment to digest that. That does make a kind of perfect sense.

"Whoa is right, babe," JJ says with a cocky smile.

Ted kicks one of the back supports on the chair and JJ goes down in a clatter and jumble of limbs. In a second, JJ is back on his feet, brushing the hair back from his face, trying to recover his cool.

"What did I say about calling her babe?" Ted practically roars.

I add a second hand to Ted's chest and turn my attention to him, throwing the other bear brother under the bus to give the first one some slack. "You said this was all Eli's fault. How so?

Ted's face breaks into despair and guilt, and I hear something crack in my chest. Again, his hand gets lost in my hair as he says, "Who do you think would want to hurt you? The only one I know is one of those fuckers Eli led straight here, straight to you."

Oh.

Oh.

Eddie with the gun and the lecherous gleam in his eye flashes to mind.

"You don't know that's him in my house." The words come out barely above a whisper.

"Not for sure, no, but it's likely someone trying to get to Eli," Ted says in an equally low voice. "And it's all my fault."

I push away from him. "How is it your fault?"

JJ clears his throat awkwardly, breaking the charged moment between us. "Did you guys want to see what shadow man does when you're not there, G?" G is preferable to babe since it doesn't set Ted off.

As JJ restarts the video, the room folds in on itself, the atmosphere thick with apprehension. We watch the shadow maneuver, an entity that feels half-there and half-not. It roams with a strange familiarity around the house, touching things with an eerie gentleness, like a lover tracing a beloved's face.

Then, shockingly, it stops at a small nook, a corner

where I keep my dreams and wishes scribbled in the fragile pages of numerous diaries. The shadow leafs through them, pausing at places, as if reading, absorbing the emotions inked across the pages like a sponge. I don't write faithfully, but lately I'd been trying to work out what would make me happy. Many of those pages include plots against Ted, dreams of what I could be, the deep painful shame of being unable to commit to a single fucking avenue.

The intimacy of the act slaps me across the face, a violent tearing open of my deepest sanctums for a stranger to peer in, to judge, to possess.

Beside me, I can feel Ted's fury, a palpable entity, ready to pounce, to protect. But the shadow is gone. It disappeared hours ago, leaving paranoia and anxiety.

This is the moment. I could crumble, run back to Boston, hell, run back to the safety of my Midwest family. A perfect reason to abandon the course, the project, and my other. . . interests. My eyes flit toward Ted.

It's what I do. It's what I've always done.

When things aren't going the way I want them to, I change course.

The shadow finally retreats, but not before leaving something on the kitchen table.

Ted is on his feet in an instant, his frame rigid with anger and resolve. "I'm going over there," he declares, his voice echoing a promise of war, of a looming battle. It takes no time at all to get to my place. Despite being flanked by three bear shifters, I feel fragile.

The token the shadow left is still there. I pick up the three by three frame that encases a preserved butterfly with brilliant yellow wings.

"It's a message," Eli announces.

"Yeah, but what's the message, dingus?" JJ hits him

upside the head with a sound thwack.

"Hey," Eli whines, punching his brother. "I get I fucked up, but lay off."

Ted's head tilts up before he places his nose to the message in question. "I don't detect any scent. None at all in fact."

JJ goes on. "If the person who left this is one of the people after you, Eli, you would know what this means."

"I thought you said this was likely fae or mage related?" I ask, my head spinning as I try to keep up. "Eli crossed human thugs."

"With a dracanoid on their payroll," Ted supplies. "Gangsters don't discriminate when they only care about the color green. Eli has a knack for crossing types that have their hands in black market magic, fae smuggling, or underground fairy court passage."

Eli holds his hands up. "*This* is not something Eddie or any of the others would pull. Ted may be right about the shit they have access to, but I'm telling you they are more a *bash heads in, ask questions later* sort of bunch. Also, why would they go after Goldie like this over money they want from me?"

Tension practically vibrates off Ted from where his palms are set against my kitchen counter, staring at the preserved butterfly like it might bite him. "Because you led them here and they got a look at Goldie. Eddie fell for her siren power, I saw it. If they get that obsessed with collecting money off your broke ass, think of what those degenerates would do to Goldie because they desire her."

Eli's face crumples, making the shadows of his black eye look even worse. "I didn't mean to."

I can't take it anymore. I cross to Eli and touch his arm. "You didn't do this. I have a supernatural power I can't control. So at the very least, we are both to blame here."

A wave of relief sweeps over Eli's face though he still looks pitiful. "You have to believe me, Goldie, I didn't mean to..."

He trails off and I'm not sure if he has the stomach to dig into his sins or how I'm affected by the fallout. Again, the fact he looks like a younger, skinnier, more hopeless version of Ted rakes at my heart more than it should.

"We're going to be okay," I tell Eli, my protective instincts awaken.

Within me, a spark turns my cold fear into vapors. The flame inside me is unwilling to allow this invasion to go unchallenged. I'm a badass bitch and no one bullies me. I refuse to be pushed out of my own home.

As I pick up the butterfly preserved in glass, new resolve steels my spine. I don't know if it's a gift, a threat, or something else entirely, but I'm changing the narrative.

I meet Ted's gaze. "I'm not running away," my voice rings in the room, a testament to my newfound resolve.

CHAPTER 28

THE ALPHA IMPULSE

TED

"You aren't going alone," I tell Goldie for the third time because I'm not sure she heard me the first two times.

"Tedly," she sighs in that way that gets under my skin. I prefer that if she say my name, she scream it. "I have to go to work. You can't guard me every second of the day."

Goldie applies foundation at the vanity in her bedroom, making her already creamy skin a flawless shade. I pace back and forth behind her, but the bedroom is small, leaving me claustrophobic.

"I own my own company and make my own hours, so I can for a while," I argue. "I'm coming, if nothing else, to keep those handsy creeps from proposing to you."

"I can handle them myself," she insists. "I texted my boss and Rap's already looking into some power dampening spells to help me work while we get this under control."

Strange for a woman who owns a humans-only bar to

241

have such connections. But I could easily spot Rap values her secrets as much as I do.

"You never tell these guys no," I point out.

Goldie turns around on her ridiculous little poof seat. It makes her look like some movie star from the 40s the way her hair is curled. But the smoky eye makeup she's half applied and generous cleavage practically spilling out of tonight's corset leaves my nerves battered and my pants way too fucking tight.

"I do too," she shoots back, her pink mouth an outraged 'O' I want to kiss senseless.

"I saw you with those guys. Even the one who followed you home. You never say no. You simply try to put them off, or your last ditch effort of telling them you have a boyfriend so you don't have to straight on tell them you're not interested."

"That's a kind of no," she counters, pointing a makeup brush at me with vindictiveness.

"No, it's not. You are trying to keep your hands clean of being off-putting. But what do you care if these idiots get rejected?"

"Just because I'm not interested, doesn't mean I need to be rude. They are people too, with feelings," she sniffs.

"When men are coming at you like a pack of animals, following you home, and hassling you, rudeness is necessary. If you ever come face to face with the person who has broken into your house, will you try to polite them out of your life?"

She picks up a smaller brush and waves it at me. "That's different, and I'm already working on a solution. There are so many home protection devices one can get off the internet."

"If you think I'm going to let you sleep here, much less alone, you are out of your mind."

Goldie blows a big breath out, her cheeks turning pink. "Tedinator, I am a big girl, both literally and figuratively as you can see."

I rub a hand down my face. "Why do you even feel you need to bring that up? You're beautiful and you know I'm fucking addicted to your body."

She blinks. "I never said I wasn't beautiful. What I am saying is that I've dealt with more than my fair share of bullshit and know I need to take care of things for myself."

"That's not how you liked it this morning," I shoot back, instantly regretting the words as they fall out of my mouth. Faelords, why can I be such a dick?

Because the bullshit you have dealt with has turned you into a bitter old man at an early age. And unlike her, you have zero finesse when it comes to expressing yourself.

Goldie's mouth flops open then snaps shut again as if I struck her.

"Listen," I say already trying to backpedal, holding my hands up, trying to calm the volcano before it erupts.

"No, you listen." She stands and walks over to face me. "Like I told you this morning, I don't need you. While I appreciate your brother's help with the camera surveillance, I will handle things from here out."

"There is a difference between being independent and being stupid," I argue.

Her hands settle on her hips. "Oh, so I'm stupid now."

I pinch the bridge of my nose. "*You* aren't stupid, but what you are about to do is."

"Ted," she says with a finality and resolve I don't like. "I am not one of your brothers. You aren't responsible for my life." She makes her way to the stairs, picking up her satchel along the way. I follow her down. "Though I'd argue you shouldn't make yourself responsible for other grown men either. You may need a lesson in boundaries."

"You first," I shoot back.

She stops at the bottom of the stairs to look up at me. A step higher than her, it forces Goldie to really crane her neck to meet my eye with her cutting glare.

"Please," I say, trying to reason. My fingers curl into tight fists, as if I can keep the fear at bay. But if she doesn't let me be there, I'll go out of my mind. "For my sanity, please let me drive you to work and hang out during your shift. I'll stay out of your way, I promise. I just can't handle the stress of waiting to know if you're okay. It would. . . " I pull at my own hair as if the small pain could overpower my stress. "Drive me crazy if anything happened to you."

"Because you think it's Eli's fault?" she says dryly.

Because I think I love you.

The thought freezes as soon as it forms, petrifying, solidifying. Where I can't move it out of my mouth, I also can't get it off my mind now. It sits there, threatening me with a permanence I didn't see coming.

I don't know what she sees on my face, but Goldie rolls her eyes as she picks her keys up off the entryway table. "Fine. You want to waste your whole evening, knock yourself out."

I've won the battle.

But I just realized I'm in a war for far higher stakes. Goldie's heart. I don't fucking deserve it but when my mind makes itself up, there is nothing I can do to budge it.

CHAPTER 29
BRING YOUR TED TO WORK, DAY

TED

The twinkling glow from the assorted lanterns casts playful shadows around the Poison Apple, creating an atmosphere I never expected to enjoy so much. I'm seated at the far end of the bar, an almost empty glass of beer in front of me, trying not to be obvious as I watch Goldie work her magic—both literally and figuratively—among the patrons. I'm not close enough to hear her, but watching her grace is enough to make my evening worthwhile.

My heart seems to dance in rhythm with her laughter which rings across the bar.

Goldie's enchanting smile lights up the place. She wasn't this genuinely animated when I visited last time, but my presence has effectively helped dampen the over-powering draw of her siren powers which clearly puts her at ease enough to have fun. Men haven't flocked to the bar like they are desperate to breathe the same air as her. Or. . . no one other than me.

"You're the NFH," a voice says beside me.

I turn to meet a pair of olive green eyes through horn-rimmed glasses. The younger guy wears a beanie and a cool expression of boredom. Like nothing has ever interested him in this life and he's waiting for something to happen with a healthy dose of skepticism.

"I typically just go by Ted," I say, taking another sip.

"Why are you here?" the man asks in a monotone voice.

"Why are you?" I shoot back.

He nods his head in Cinder's direction who catches it and shoots him a sly, seductive smile. "We met at BU in a painting studio course," he says, his voice still not giving anything away about how he feels in regard to Cinder.

A silence falls between us as we drink our beers. "She's special," the hipster finally says.

My gaze starts on Cinder but moves to Goldie. "I'll say," I agree though on a different page.

"Makes you wonder what it takes to possess the heart of someone like that."

"It does," I muse.

I feel like we are talking in bro code. He about Cinder and I about Goldie.

"But I do believe it is connected to air conditioning units," I muse more to myself, remembering her rather strong reaction to my installations.

Though I've enjoyed sitting on the sidelines tonight, I feel that may be where I belong. Even without her power running rampant, Goldie enchants and charms whether she is swaying her hips to music or joking with the patrons. Does she have any idea how bright she shines?

Maybe it's the siren ability, but I can literally see it emanate from her, a warm aura she shares with anyone in the vicinity. I possess none of her whimsical nature but being close to it warms me.

I must have said something out loud in dude-speak to that effect because my neighbor answers, "There's something I can unequivocally agree with."

It's then a guy strolls up to the bar, with a swagger I doubt is deserved. The blonde pretty boy heads straight for Goldie. His confident strides have an air of belonging with the place, an intimacy that leaves me feeling suddenly out of place.

Goldie's eyes connect with him and there is familiarity there.

After a minute, I recognize him as the guy who tried to intervene when I was getting Goldie out of harm's way from the bar brawl.

I can't shake off the uneasy knot forming in my stomach as I watch them together. He leans in to speak to her even as her mouth flattens. The way Goldie tilts her head to listen to him, I sense a connection that I cannot read from this distance, but it's there, subtle and yet undeniable.

I catch Cinder's eye, her nose is scrunched in disgust as she watches them too. I lean towards her, needing some information to douse the burning jealousy flaring up within me. "Who is that guy?" My voice is tight, restrained.

Cinder makes a retching sound, "That's Lawrence, her on-again, off-again ex. A real loser."

My eyes return to the two of them, as Goldie slips away so they can talk off side of the bar. "Then why is she talking to him?"

I hear it in my tone. Jealousy. It throbs in me with angry waves that want to push me to my feet and close the distance between me and them.

Her reaction to him isn't like it is to all the other men who belly up to her, wanting her to love them. The familiarity is real, a connection is there, even if it's only a lingering thing.

"Goldie's too nice to turn anyone away outright," Cinder says, disdain evident in her voice.

"Yeah, I got that," I mutter back.

Over by the massive tree, Lawrence leans in closer to Goldie, his hand pressing against the wall behind her, cutting them off from the rest of the bar. His body language screams possession, a clear trespassing into what I have come to consider as my domain.

My bear roars within me, a primal urge to protect what's mine threatening to overtake my calm demeanor.

Calm the hell down, Ted. Everything is fine.

Goldie tries to maintain her composure, but her smile has vanished, replaced by a tense line of restrained frustration.

Nope. I'm up and stalking across the bar in a second. Lawrence doesn't see me coming, too wrapped up in his pathetic attempt to reclaim what he no longer has any right to.

Lawrence's voice rises enough for me to catch snatches of accusations and demands. "This game has gone on long enough. You know how good we are together, baby girl. I can't eat, I can't sleep, I need you. You take such good care of me."

Instantly, I recognize the reason they keep getting back together. Goldie's heart is bigger than she even probably knows. This son of a bitch has been playing on her helpful, loving nature. But what the fuck has she been getting?

Then Lawrence dips down and lays his lips against hers.

I surge torward them, my fingers wrapping around

Lawrence's shoulder and wrenching him away. His eyes bulge in surprise, followed by a scrutinizing icy glare.

"Who are you?" he challenges. Tension crackles through my muscles as the pretty boy stares me down with contempt.

Goldie's eyes widen when she sees me. "Ted?" she asks. "It's okay. Everything is okay."

I reach out for her wrist and pull her out from under the slimeball who kissed *my* girl.

She's not your girl.

She is even if she hasn't admitted it yet.

"Ted?" Lawrence repeats with dry amusement, as if my name is a joke. No part of me is even slightly humorous right now.

"I'm Goldie's boyfriend," I announce to him with a grim, forced cheerfulness. "And if you kiss her again, I will rip the lips right off your weasley face."

"Ted," Goldie urges quietly. She wants me to back off, but a rage pumps through me. A rage I didn't know I possessed. I was the calm one, the reasonable one.

But reason has abandoned me and I'm seeing red.

Lawrence frowns, looking to Goldie for confirmation. "Seriously? This guy?"

"Scratch that. If you even touch her, I'll pull your limbs clear off."

"Ted," Goldie's voice continues to get lower, softer.

"What kind of blue-collar trash are you slumming it with, baby girl?" Lawrence asks, with an incredulous scoff.

My vision turns red as control slips from my grasp.

I'm painfully aware of how I don't fit Goldie's aesthetic, how out of place I am here, though for a moment I started to believe I could be at ease here. But as soon as I step outside, the cold reality of having to deal with Eli's debts, to figure out a way to get enough money to keep him from getting killed, is what's going to keep me up all night. Even if I resell all the appliances I've fixed up, it won't be enough.

And this guy with his expensive shirt and slick demeanor putting me down for honest work makes me so angry I could spit.

Or shift...

Before I can make a move, Goldie steps forward and punches him right in the nose. A crack cuts through the air and blood pours down pretty boy's face, dripping onto his expensive shirt. His hands fly up to his nose with a cry of pain.

Surprise returns my vision back to normal and cools my blood.

"Blue collar trash? Really, Lawrence?" Goldie shouts. The music jerks to a halt as everyone around us takes in the sideshow. "Any blue-collar worker is better than you by virtue of the fact they can get a job and keep it. I'm sick of hearing your woe is me bullshit and making it my problem. I can't even remember the last time you helped me with anything. Ted installed air conditioners in my freaking home without me even asking. He makes me breakfast to keep from eating porridge until it pops out of my eyes. And you know the craziest thing of all? He has a real bed, with a *bedframe*. Not a shoddy mattress on the floor. Grow the fuck up and get over yourself. Faelords knows I have."

With that Goldie turns on her heel and stomps toward the breakroom. Cinder stands a few feet away, her hand held out. Goldie slaps it as she walks by.

Lysander raises his beer glass in her direction as a smattering of applause goes through the room.

Snow appears by Lawrence's side. "Hello sir, I'm new here, but please allow me to show you the exit in case you aren't familiar." Then she grabs him by the arm and drags him along with surprising strength.

"Are you going to just stand there?" Cinder asks me.

"No ma'am," I say, starting after Goldie.

When I enter the small room of pink lockers, Goldie is furiously reapplying lipstick in the mirror.

For a moment, I'm stunned, in absolute awe of her.

She realizes I'm there, and twists toward me. "What?" she practically shouts, as if she is ready to rumble with the next person who messes with her.

"No one's ever. . . " I trail off.

She adjusts her loose curls with a barely restrained violence. "No one's ever what?"

I usher her up across the small space, pushing Goldie against one of the pink lockers and kiss her. My tongue pushes past her lips to sweep in her sweet mouth. We both groan as she clutches and claws at me.

This girl drives me wild. When I break our kiss, our breaths come out in jagged heaves. A dazed, lustful gleam replaces the fiery wrath that was in her eye a moment ago. "What was that for, Tedly?" she asks in a husky voice.

I search her face for any clue that she knows what she's just done. "No one's ever—" the words get stuck in my throat for a moment before I push them out. "No one's ever defended me like that before."

Goldie's expression hardens. "I can't believe I ever went out with such a contemptible douche." Then her fingers trail across my jawline as a smile tugs at her lips. "You have pink all over you."

"That's okay," I say, feeling a dumb smile on my face. "It's my favorite color."

Surprise and skepticism arches her brows. "Oh really?"

"Yeah, didn't I tell you?" I ask before leaning back down

to capture her sweet lips in another kiss. She moans and I find myself harder than a rock. I rub my erection up between her legs only for her hips to buck back.

"How long do you think we can stay back here, unnoticed?" I rasp. I want to be selfish. I want inside her, to rut like a fucking animal until she screams and then finish inside her, marking her as mine. I want her to feel me dribble down the inside of her thigh as she goes about work and feel the ache from me taking her in the backroom like a desperate teenager.

Before Goldie can answer a door rattling knock jerks us away from each other.

Goldie's boss yells through the door. "When you are done *fixing your makeup*, Goldie, I need you back out here mixing potions for the masses."

Rap's words are dry but firm.

Goldie rushes to the mirror to fix the smear of pink on her own face. "Be right out, boss lady," she calls out.

Before I can adjust the hard on in my jeans, Goldie's done, her makeup as flawless as before except for the extra rosy tinge in her cheeks, and her lips are a little puffier.

Faefucks, I want to attack that gorgeous mouth until it's kissed thoroughly, used and abused.

"Coming?" she chirps.

I growl, as an image of coming on those perfect tits invades my brain. Fucking witchtits, what has she done to me? Maybe fae aren't immune to sirens?

Goldie's lashes fly wide when she realizes the effect she has on me.

"I'm going to need a minute."

Her gaze travels down to the evident bulge in my pants. Those sinful lips slip into a pout.

"So help me, Goldie, if you don't leave this room, I will push my dick past those pretty lips until I blow."

The devil girl takes pause at that. She's going to kill me.

Then she nods and is out the door, giving me time to collect myself.

CHAPTER 30
CALL ME PAPA BEAR

GOLDIE

I insist on staying at my house tonight but fighting off Ted's protectiveness is no joke. He's a werebear, and I now recognize the alpha vibes present in his bossiness.

Still, I manage to convince him to go home, though part of me very much wants Ted in my bed.

Okay, more than part of me.

Or rather I in his, because I'm half convinced that mattress is magic. Or is it the things he does to me in it?

One of the only ways I was able to convince him I could spend the night by myself was because Rap sent me home with some warding crystals to place around my doors and windows. Whether the shadow is mage or fae, the crystals will keep them out as long as they are placed at the threshold. She assured me I'd be able to come and go as I pleased without issue.

After washing my face and changing into my lacy nightgown, I slip into bed.

Why pick something so scandalous when I now know the place is under surveillance?

Maybe I'm preparing myself in case I happen to magically relocate in the night. Not that I'm hoping someone breaks into my house, but there is something pulling me toward Ted. It's becoming stronger, more irresistible the more time we spend around each other.

I am beginning to sense when I'm using my powers and some part of me knows I'm drawn to him.

It's a long time before I'm able to fall asleep, but when I do, I dream of a blue storm I would willingly drown in.

Lips that perfectly fit mine push mine apart for a taste. Hands are everywhere and I'm rubbing against Ted—desperate, aching. My skin is sensitive, and I need more friction, more heat, more pressure. Oh faelords, I need him inside me.

Then my panties are dragging down my legs until I feel Ted's hot breath over my lower lips, making me buck and moan. I need it. I need him so very badly.

"Ted," I moan.

"Cream puff," he growls back.

Something about the sound jerks me out of my sleepy haze. I open my eyes, instantly recognizing my neighbor's bedroom and the man crouched by my bent knees. The sky lightens with the dawn, diffusing the room with soft, low light.

Am I sorry I ended up here? Or was I hoping for it? And does that mean I'm learning to control my powers?

When I start to sit up, I'm pushed back down. Ted is there, hovering over me with his shirt off again. His hair is tousled, and his pupils are blown with desire.

"You asked me why I called you that," he says in that same sleep roughened voice from yesterday.

What? Oh, he called me cream puff.

I start to bristle at the nickname, remembering how he studied me eating yesterday. Now I'm starting to worry he's been suppressing some kind of heavy girl fetish that's going to creep me out.

"It's because you're elegant and sweet as a puff pastry, but I also know you have an even sweeter center I want to get to."

Before I can register if I care for his analogy, his finger slips between my folds and it's like being zapped by an electric shock. I gasp for air, unable to find any oxygen as he rubs me from the inside.

"Oh yeah," he croons. "That's the sweetness I'm talking about."

Maybe if anyone else called me cream puff I'd dislike it, but something about Ted saying it makes it scalding hot. Or maybe he's reprogrammed my mind by rubbing out a hypnotic rhythm inside me until I associate the feeling with whatever words he deigns to pair with the motion.

Ted's tone turns brusque. "Blondie, I need more. Please let me have more."

Another pump of his finger has me throwing my head back with a curse. "Yes," I gasp.

I can't fight being in his bed, his touch. I don't want to.

A tongue swipes up my center once before his mouth covers me. With little preamble, he licks and sucks at me like a starving man.

"Gah," I cry out, my fingers digging into his hair as my torso jerks up. I may be lying on my back, but I feel like I'm on a ride. My hips roll, chasing the rhythm of pleasure he is spelling out with his tongue. When his fingers join the party, my breath turns to pants.

"That's it, cream puff. You have all those boys at your

beck and call, but I bet none of them wanted your cum as bad as I do."

What. The. Fuck?

Some part of me feels like this is wrong. I should be proving myself to him by sucking him off. In fact, I find I really enjoy focusing on my partner and amazing them with my enthusiasm. But I don't have even a sliver of a chance to do that.

"You know I want that cream filling, blondie," he says before growling directly into my clit as he sucks it.

"Wh-what?" I stutter. Again, how am I not weirded out more by what he says right now?

He lifts his head, lips and beard glistening with my desire.

"I need you to squirt for daddy."

I couldn't be more shocked if he slapped me in the face and called me a rabid mongoose.

My stutter worsened as my nerves ratcheted up, dullening my desire. "I can't do that."

Heat prickles beneath the surface as his eyes sweep up and down my body, leaving a trail of scorched skin. Licking his lips with deliberate enjoyment, he says, "Oh, I know you can. This body was made to cum hard and often."

A twisting coil jerks tighter in the base of my stomach.

As if to prove a point, he slaps my pussy. Not so hard it's painful, just enough to send a jolt of hot sensation spiraling through me.

"You're an animal," I half sigh, half squeak as he does it a second time.

"Blondie, you have no idea."

Three fingers plunge into my already clenching channel, pumping hard and fast.

I want his dick in me. I want to be fucked, but he wants me to not only orgasm, he expects me to—to squirt?

It's vulgar. It's unthinkable.

I love sex with a compatible partner, but statistically speaking, most of my orgasms are sponsored by a sex toy and none of them did. . . that.

There is absolutely no faefuckingway—

The pressure inside me builds and builds until it's almost unbearable. Sweat pours off me as I clench and keen on his hand.

Slightly curled fingers furiously fuck me as he coaches me. "Tilt your hips up. Yeah, just like that. Feel that, blondie. Feel it building? You're going to come for me. You are going to come so hard, you are going to fountain for me like a goddess."

I could ask what the hell he's talking about, but the pressure leaves me breathless. I'm there. I'm really there. "Oh faelords," I cry out as I feel the first sign of my orgasm.

"You're so damn tight, blondie," he rasps.

As if my body had a mind of its own, I move my ass up and down, meeting his hand, feeling the fiery friction while I build. I start to shake as the sensation burgeons, my eyes clamping tight as I try to hold onto the feeling. Just as I know I'm about to break, he slaps my clit. Hard.

My hips buck up, and I scream. A roaring wave of sensation floods me, ripping apart my control. The orgasm doesn't just wash through me, it pours out of me and I do exactly what he said I would do.

Some part of me is completely self-conscious, another is shocked, and the last part is consumed by the spasms rocking my senses. I shake and rattle until I'm a limp ragdoll.

"Oh fuck," he groans.

I can hardly hear him, barely feel him. I'm completely lost in the waves of pleasure that are still rippling through me. He's still pumping those fingers in my pussy, My ass is still moving in time with his thrusts, as I ride it out.

"That's it, cream puff. You did it *just* right," he says through a groan. "Soaking my bed like a good girl."

The words are tiny electric shocks, singeing my already red hot flesh.

"See?" He pulls back, licking his fingers clean of my juices. "That wasn't so hard, was it?"

I try to answer but all that comes out is a moan full of blissful exhaustion as the tremors of my orgasm slowly fade away. My head is spinning and I'm not sure what to think.

I'm not sure I *can* think. My brain has melted and I'm never going to be able to get up again.

An incoherent sound escapes me.

Then he grins at me. It was the first time I'd ever seen him smile, and it fucking pulls the floor out from under me.

When scowling, he's a rugged, handsome man. When he smiles, it devastates, leaving nothing in its wake.

I'm still fighting to get control of my breathing when the smile slips off his lips and uncertainty flickers in his eyes.

"Are you okay?"

"Am I okay?" I sputter. He has to be completely fucking joking after that.

CHAPTER 31

THREE BABY BEARS

GOLDIE

T push myself back until I can sit up. "Are you seriously asking if I'm okay?"

Concern furrows his brow and pulls his lips into a frown.

"I have never come so hard in my life. What the fuck are you even?" A breath laugh escapes me. My brain is circling somewhere around the explanation of sex god.

There it is again, that fucking grin of devastation. Then he disappears, returning with several water bottles and a towel to clean me up before laying it over the mess I made on his sheets.

I cover my face and groan in embarrassment. Pulling my hands away, he says, "Don't do that. You are the sexiest, most responsive woman I've ever had the pleasure to, well. . . pleasure." He shoves two water bottles at me and commands me to drink them. Considering I'm suddenly dying of thirst, I get through one then start the other before setting it down.

Ted lays back, pulling me to him, though his hard on is still jutting out from his body. When I start to reach for it, he only holds me tighter against him.

"Give yourself a minute," he says.

I lay across his broad chest, a surprisingly comfortable place. Our bodies meld together, and a sense of belonging settles into my bones.

His fingers tangle and twirl in my curls, idly. Again, another surprising thing about him. There is some bit of playfulness under all that gruffness, and I want to tease it out even more.

"Have you always taken care of your brothers?" The question slips out of me before I can stop it. Even in a post sex explosion haze, I can't help but pry.

I've tried to keep myself from getting wrapped up in Ted and focus on my own life, but the man who is so staunchly closed off opened a door for me. It's hard not to walk through and take a peek at what's behind the man. . . other than the bear.

For a minute I don't think he's going to answer. Maybe the door isn't open after all. Despite my thirst for knowing what makes him tick, I don't try to pull the boards off the windows like I do with other people.

"Not always." Ted sighs heavily. Then he forces us to sit up.

"Since when?" I push a little bit. The rush I feel at potentially getting Ted to open up to me sends a unique thrill through my body even though he drained me both literally and physically.

His hand stops toying with my hair and for a heart stopping moment I think he's going to get up and push me away.

Tell me it doesn't matter or talk about something inconse-

quential like the weather, or your favorite sports team. Anything to make this less serious.

Instead, he resumes twirling my hair. "Our dad died in a fight with another pack when we were young. To be honest, I barely remember him or living in Alaska. My mother thought we'd be safe tucked away in a human city, but she couldn't protect us from everything. My mom died when I was eighteen. It was cancer. She got diagnosed when I was thirteen. It was a long, arduous fight with lots of points of false hope that made us believe she was getting better, that she'd get through it. But it kept spreading, cropping up in new places. Sometimes. . . " Ted trails off and I'm almost too scared to speak.

I don't want him to stop talking. The sexual chemistry is already unlike anything I'd ever experienced before, but his raw honesty, feeling him open up to me like this. . . it's more precious than I can say. I want to know everything about him.

Focus on yourself. You don't need to dig for him, it doesn't matter.

"Sometimes what?" I dare to whisper.

My body is still frozen, afraid he'll stop talking. People confide in me all the time, but this feels so different. Ted doesn't angle. This isn't about gaining my sympathy or trying to romance me with a tragic backstory. He is simply raw and honest.

"I managed her medications," he says, breezing past whatever he'd been about to say. "I made sure we had food in the house. She had good insurance that covered us for a while, but eventually it all piled up. She wanted us to stay in school, but I dropped out at sixteen to work a construction job to bring in more money."

He sucks in a deep breath, and I sense he's reliving some

part of his past. My fingers trace through the curled dark hairs across his chest, amazed by how soft they are. I want to soothe the pain he feels, but bite down on my lip to keep from jumping in to comment or ask questions.

He is naturally opening up, and I wouldn't stop it for anything.

"We thought she was going to get better. . . again, the medications were working, she seemed stronger than she had in months and then, she was gone."

I couldn't imagine the pain of having false hope ripped away so violently. If I didn't deliberately put my focus on the silver linings in life, it would be so easy to fall prey to the idea that life is meant to be a cruel journey.

His fingers drop so they skim across my bare back, leaving little trails of fire in their wake. "I was six months away from being eighteen, I wasn't old enough to take custody of my brothers. It was the most terrifying six months of my life. At first, I thought I could hide it. I got away with it for a couple months while madly filling out paperwork, making my mother's arrangements, and working construction. But they still took JJ and Eli. It was only for a couple months, but I don't know if it was my mom dying or their experience in foster care, being uprooted after everything, but when I finally got custody of them, they were different. JJ was fifteen and Eli was only twelve. I'm not sure what point they got fucked up by it all, and I did all I could, but it wasn't enough."

"For witchtits sake." I can't help but whisper the curse as a tear leaks out of my eye and lands on his chest.

I'm not supposed to give anyone my tears. It could be dangerous for some reason, but I can't keep them at bay. The pain. So much pain. So much responsibility and burden on a kid. I would have crumbled like a pecan sandie.

"JJ started seducing girls at too young an age. For as good as his heart, he treats women like temporary fillers for whatever is empty inside him. Probably the spot where our mother was. And Eli. . . I tried to keep money issues out of his line of sight but there were only so many peanut butter sandwiches and meals of ramen I suppose before he figured out how strapped we were. Eli started gambling in middle school. The idiot thought he could help, but as you can see, that's turned out to be a fucking disaster." His other hand raises to scrub over his face.

"And you have dealt with this all by yourself," I say, tilting my head up to look into his face. The storm in his eyes is directed inward, roiling over the past, the present, and every failing he perceives himself to make. My heart jettisons right out of my chest and flops onto his in a bloody beaten heap. I feel every bit of his pain as if it were my own, though it won't make it any better.

"I had some help," he says with a wry smile, crinkles forming around his eyes. "My boss, Gustavo Espada, at the construction site was a good man. Gustavo floated me extra jobs when I needed it, gave me the time off I needed and gave me all sorts of random bonuses to pad my paycheck. In return, I was determined to become the best worker on his crew, and I did. By the time I was twenty, I was heading sites on my own. By twenty-three, he encouraged me to start my contracting company. He helped me set everything up and guided me through it even when I was terrified I was going to end up broke on my ass while trying to take care of my idiot brothers. JJ was in college, and he may be promiscuous, but he got scholarships. Still, I needed to help him through it while bailing Eli out of all the trouble he got into at high school. Idiot kid almost got kicked out. But I love managing my own company.

Recruited some good men I worked with and it's what I'm most proud of."

"I think I'd like to thank this Gustavo," I murmur into his chest.

He sinks his hand back into my hair, his fingers tightening before he drops a kiss on the top of my head. "He passed away last year."

Oh witchtits. I bury my face into his chest. It's too much. It's too much for one person, even as large and strong as Ted is, I can't help but be angry someone has to go through so much.

Ted holds me closer to him, and I smush my face into his warm skin, inhaling his scent.

"Can I tell you a secret?" His voice is rough with emotion.

Don't fall in love, Goldie. Don't you dare do it. Tell him no, because if he gives you one more secret, it's going to happen.

"Since you hate me already and probably can't hate me anymore," he jokes with a wry laugh.

I choke out a similar laugh, realizing my tears are flowing nonstop, covering his sternum, matting his chest hair.

His tone sobers again, and it sounds like there is gravel in his throat. "Sometimes...

This is what he was going to say before but stopped himself.

"Sometimes I wish it had been unexpected and fast." His voice turns raw. "I know that makes me terrible. That I should be grateful for more time with my mother. But she was so sick, and watching her waste away for years was hard on me, on JJ and Eli." I feel him swallow hard against me. "I've never said that out loud before."

I want to jump in with reassurance, but I wait, listening with every fiber of my being.

At that, I push up so I can look down at him. It's only then I realize how soggy my face is from the silent tears I'd been crying for him, for his mom, for his brothers. I wipe my face.

"Don't do that," I say almost angrily.

Ted releases me, arm held out away from me to give me space. His face pales as I react to his emotional confession.

"Don't pile on yourself like that. Of course, you wish your mother didn't suffer that long, that you and your brothers didn't suffer through that. Have you been punishing yourself for secretly thinking that, while enduring and taking care of everyone around you? Well listen here, Tedophelia, you knock it off right now. Because I don't think I've ever met a better person in my life."

It's true.

Ted's face is a mixture of incredulity and surprise, leaving him unresponsive.

Witchitits, has anyone helped him take the load off before? It's just been Ted processing everything on his own, carrying everything on his own.

Like you're not doing that, leaving things out when you talk to your mom and friends these days?

His hands come up to frame my face, thumbs brushing away my tears. Why does it feel like my heart has been squeezed into a bloody pulp?

"Don't cry. I'm sorry, I didn't mean too—"

Again, I should be worried about him touching my tears. Maybe they are a kind of poison? But I can't bring myself to care right now.

"Shut up and take it," I say with an edge of anger. I'm not sure what I want him to take. The reality that his burden is so heavy that it deserves to be witnessed, deeply felt? "You may be able to stuff all of this down, but I can't. Not even if you want me to." I'm sitting next to one of the kindest, most supportive beings, and suddenly I realize how frivolous I am. How stupid all my problems are next to Ted's very real ones.

"I'm not trying to make you feel sorry for me," he says in an almost panic.

I throw up my arms. "Why do people say that? Why do people avoid accepting sympathy, empathy so hard? Like it's something to be avoided? I am sorry for you. I'm sorry you went through something so acutely painful for so long. Not because it's my fault, but because I have empathy and I want better for you. I want a better past for you, I want you to not have suffered. Is that so bad? To accept that someone feels your pain?"

Even I don't know what I'm going on about, as Ted tries to rub his hands along my arms with that panicked look on his face.

But then my nose starts to run. My hand rushes to cover my face. I can't let him see me all sloppy. I start to get off the bed so I can run to the bathroom, clean up my face, and get a hold of myself.

Ted pulls me back to him, sitting up against the bed. To avoid letting him see me, I bury my face in my arm as a buffer between us, so I don't get him anymore damp with my cry juices.

"Where are you going?"

Between sobs, I say, "I'm puffy, and snot's coming out of my nose. I don't want you to see."

Ted grabs a corner of his sheets and pushes it between me and my arm, forcibly wiping my face.

"Stop," I complain. "I'm ruining your sheets."

His body rumbles under me as he lets out a deep, low laugh. "Well, that may have already happened."

I smack him in the chest as my cheeks burn.

"But I have more than enough sheets to wipe your tears, cream puff." Then in a more sincere tone he says, "And you're right. I feel I shouldn't pile my baggage on you, but I'll fucking eat up the sweetness you give me. You are the kindest, loveliest, purest woman I've ever met."

I try to twist away, but he grabs my hips and slides me over on the bed, even closer to him.

"Don't say that." I protest. "I haven't had to go through anything like that. I'm just some ditzy flake who can't figure her shit out and has been so boy crazy for so long because she can't handle her own stuff."

A thundercloud moves in over his face, and I swear I see lightning ignite in his eyes. "Who the hell told you that?"

"What? No one." I am still trying to wriggle away so I can go clean my face, collect myself, keep myself from spilling all my guts out to this perfect, lovely, strong man.

Ted sits up, bringing our faces close together. His fingers frame either side of my jawline to keep me focused on him.

"Someone must have told you that bullshit. I'm guessing one of these fucks with poor self-esteem who thought for one second they were worthy of your sunshine before trying to blot it out because you only illuminated how shitty they truly are."

I lose the ability to move my tongue for a moment. Cinder and Red have been trying to convince me of exactly what Ted just articulated. Why has it been so hard for me to believe them, but hearing it come from Ted's mouth penetrates the core of my being until the words lodge themselves between my ribs.

It either makes me a shitty friend who doesn't value her friends opinion, or only proves the point that I am an empty-headed ditz who needs the validation of a man.

Stinging pierces the backs of my eyes.

"What? What's happening in there? Don't hold back on me now, blondie."

"I—I—"

I don't deserve you.

CHAPTER 32

THE SUMMER OF AUNT ASTRID

GOLDIE

The realization is profound and a first. I usually knew when the men I was with were acting shitty, but from my high horse I believed I could fix them. But Ted is perfect. A million times better than me, and I don't deserve him. It makes something deep inside me ache.

His thumbs stroke the side of my face, still not letting me go. "Who? Who made you feel you weren't enough?"

The second he asks it, a trauma I buried breaches the surface. I'm usually so good about facing the messy parts of life with full acceptance, but I want to push this down and stomp on it until it's dust.

The truth is, this darkness has been rising for weeks. It started with returning to my aunt's house, then the way men have been lusting after me, the way women shoot me blatant looks of disdain. As if I was trying to do all this.

Something lights up in Ted's face and I realize I've given myself away.

271

"Who?" he presses again, before leaning in and laying the sweetest, most tender kiss at the corner of my lips.

I shut my eyes because I may crumble into dust at the sensation. I say it to get it out there quickly. Because it's nothing really. Hardly a thing at all.

"I was twelve and it was my birthday. My parents helped throw a big tea party with fancy dresses and hats for all the girls from my class because I was friendly with everyone and didn't want anyone to feel left out, even though a couple of the girls weren't my favorite. And then as everyone was putting on their coats and leaving. . . "

I WAS HANDING out special bags I made for everyone. The ribbon adorned gifts had special fancy sugar cubes, a teacup I selected for each girl, and different kinds of tea.

My schoolmate Chloe didn't notice me as as she shucked on her bulky purple coat because it was starting to snow. "Madison, I forgot my sleeping bag at home, so my mom is picking me up first and then I'll be over."

"Over where?" I asked Madison, walking up to the two girls. She was going to have a sleepover, and I wasn't invited?

Madison and I had been best friends since first grade, but she'd grown distant lately. She no longer chatted my ear off about Connor, the boy she'd been crushing on for two years. I even tried to engage her in conversation about him because I knew he was her favorite topic, but she repeatedly shut it down before claiming she had to get somewhere.

Chloe's eyes reared up to mine, wild and wide. She didn't realize I was there. Madison's face remained impassive. I never before noticed the calculated, measured coolness about her.

"I'm just having a couple girls over for a sleepover tonight," Madison explained with false modesty. I could tell it was false by the flash of satisfaction in her eyes when I deflated.

"Oh," was all I could say.

Chloe got out of there so fast, but Madison's mom hadn't shown up yet, leaving the two of us waiting by the front door.

"So who's going to your sleepover?" I asked, trying to be polite and show I didn't mind.

Madison leveled a gaze at me that made me feel like she was preparing a death blow of some sorts. I didn't realize how true it was until she said, "Everyone. All the girls."

"Oh right. . . " I tried to recover. "I mean you probably thought I was busy tonight, but I can come over too." Hope filled me up. Ending my birthday with an all-girls sleepover sounded pretty magical.

"No one wanted you to come." My stomach dropped out through my feet.

My voice almost failed me. "What?"

Madison tucked her hair behind one ear as she stepped closer. "Oh, you didn't know?" A sympathetic look crossed her face. "No one likes you. When you're not around, they talk about how fat you are, and how you dress like a slut."

It was like a bucket of ice water had been dumped over my head. The shock of her words pierced my lungs so I couldn't breathe.

A nastiness slipped into her tone, and was directed right at me. "When I found out Connor liked you, I knew there had to be a reason. Because he definitely liked me first and would have asked me out if you didn't grow boobs."

I instantly covered my chest, not understanding yet somehow taking in the horrible things my supposed best friend was saying. As a bigger girl, I had to get a training bra by the time I was ten. It wasn't something I was exactly proud of.

"Oh yeah," she crossed her arms and looked down at me with disgusted superiority. "That's all the boys talk about. Goldie's boobs. And then you dress to show them off and wear makeup at twelve. My mom says only girls who wear makeup before their twenties are sluts."

Madison was my friend. I would have done anything for her, but she stood in front of me, yanking my insides out gut by gut until there was nothing but a bloody mess of me left on the floor.

I spent the rest of the weekend sobbing my eyes out. My parents couldn't find a way to console me other than putting on my favorite movies, covering me in a blanket and letting me silently cry the rest of that day.

When we went to school on Monday, I found out Madison did in fact throw a sleepover and invited every girl in our class except me. Knowing what Madison told me in confidence, I watched everyone so much more carefully. I tried to find the signs of the disdain they felt for me. It was then I noticed the boys watching me, whispering as they ogled my chest. Then the girls started to laugh behind my back. After Connor asked me out to a school dance, which I said no because I knew how much Madison was into him, I thought she'd forgive me and we could be friends again. I told her how I said no because I cared about her.

Bad idea.

∾

I LET OUT A BIG BREATH. Disgusting black tar toxic emotions bubble inside me. I remember exactly how it all felt as if it were yesterday.

"She didn't care about you as a person anymore," Ted growls.

"Yeah, I see that now. She was livid. Claimed the only reason he asked me is because I slept with him, which was absurd. I hadn't even had my first kiss. But the rumors she started caught like wildfire until no one cared what they did or said to my face. Messages were always left in my locker calling me a whore, and they started an online hate group in my honor. Then they invited me to it so I could read all the comments about how I was the worst, and an explicit account of all the sexual favors I'd done for the boys in our school."

Ted's face twists in dark disgust on my behalf. But I don't need saving, not anymore. I roll my shoulders back and tell him the rest, no matter how ugly it was.

"So I started to dress in only baggy clothes and stopped playing with makeup. It didn't stop the bullying though. A year and a half of this made me pull into myself entirely. I became withdrawn, started eating very little, starving myself until I ended up binging late at night. I stopped talking as much. There were a couple times I remember being in front of a mirror, holding my mom's pill bottle of sleeping meds, thinking I could make it all go away." My voice caught. That little girl was in so much pain and still trying so hard to be small, invisible. She believed no one could ever love her.

Ted's hand curves around mine in a tight grip as if bracing himself for what's next.

"Don't worry, Tedford," I say even as my words come out raw and gravelly. "This story has a happy ending." I turn my attention to the window, so I can finish without getting sucked in his stormy gaze.

"But after a lot of prodding and nagging from my loving parents, I eventually cracked under the pressure and told them what was making me so miserable." I crossed my arms over my chest, the need to make myself small cropping up. "When my mom found out what Madison did, she said some of the meanest things I've ever heard her say and that woman *never* curses. Then she and my dad combined efforts to kick ass." A half smile kicks up on my lips. "They pulled me out of school for the rest of that week and forced me to do all things I used to love, clothes and makeup shopping. Though my dad always said shrinks were full of BS trying to scam people out of their hard-earned money, he helped find me a great therapist and took me religiously. They went to the principal and got those girls who made the hate group about me suspended. It was the end of the school year, but I was too scared of running into the girls outside of school, so my parents sent me to live out here with Astrid that summer. I'd only met her a couple times, but it completely changed my life. Astrid. . . " My voice trailed off in awe. "She had so many interests, loved everyone she met and was loved in return."

"Sounds a lot like you," Ted says gruffly.

I dip my head as heat rises to my cheeks. "That summer, I slowly but surely came out of the hole I'd burrowed into. When high school started, everything was different, including me. I found myself again and with the edge Astrid gave me, I was voted homecoming queen and voted most friendly my senior year. And I kept up that reputation ever since. I've been romancing everyone with fashion and killer makeup."

Ted scrubs a hand over his face. "Sweet faelords, sometimes I'm so glad I'm a boy with only brothers. Girls can be so faefucking cruel."

I rear back. "Whoa, raging feminist over here." I point at myself. "Boys can be equally cruel."

Ted drops his chin. "As much as I'm an advocate for equality, let's agree to disagree. I feel teenage girls have a knack for a certain type of psychological warfare most boys are not subtle enough to pull off."

I open my mouth to argue, but Ted grabs my hips and hauls me up onto his lap, so my legs are on either side of his. Instantly, I'm squirming and lifting myself, but he tugs me back down. "You couldn't crush me before, you sure as hell won't now," he says, reading my thoughts.

His hands massage me in a way that almost makes me self-conscious about the folds at my waist, if it didn't feel so good. His gaze bores into mine, keeping me connected mentally.

Then his tone softens, as he asks, "Do you like dressing up the way you do, or do you only pay such close attention to your appearance because you want to be pleasing to others?"

"I like dressing up, putting on makeup, I even love wearing frilly lingerie if no one is there to see it."

A rumbling emanates from Ted's chest as if he likes that idea.

"It makes me feel powerful, feminine, and I feel good about myself." But without all the frills and whistles? I bite my lower lip. "Maybe I do depend on accessories and clothes too much. I should have confidence without those things."

"Don't do that," Ted urges. "Don't feel guilty about the things that make you feel good about yourself. That's like saying you shouldn't love something because others think you shouldn't enjoy it. People naturally like certain television shows, sports activities, or foods, and trying to convince themselves they like the opposite is futile, not to mention a waste of what precious little enjoyment we can scrape together when life is hard. I only ask because I want to know if you like it versus doing it because you think other people will like you better. But it sounds like your parents keyed in on what you love and brought you back to it."

The vibration of what feels like a massive gong being struck tremors into the marrow of my bones before sonorously traveling outward through the rest of my body. It sounds exactly like something Astrid would have told me. Why in the hell does this bear shifter have so much clarity on the world? Oh right, he has really had to live hard.

"You are lucky to have such loving parents." He gives me a small smile.

"Ted." I shake my head, pressing my hands to his chest. "My problems are so ridiculous next to yours."

Suddenly, I'm flat on my back. Ted is hovering above me, holding my hands over my head. "My experience, my life, made me who I am. And your life and experiences made you who you are, and you gorgeous, are a ray of fucking sunshine."

He lowers so he can start planting kisses up my throat. My engines start up with surprising strength, causing my hips to rock up against his.

Lips brushing against my neck, he continues, "Makeup or no makeup, clothes or no clothes." I feel his lips curve up. But then he raises to meet my eye. "Do you have any idea how much I wanted that ridiculous little pink cake? No, wait. That came out wrong. That cake wasn't ridiculous. It was beautiful, lovely, thoughtful."

I arch an eyebrow, more than willing to put him out of his misery. "It was pink, Ted. Rugged werebears like you don't eat little pink cakes in the shape of hearts."

A smirk slides onto his mouth. "Oh yeah? Why not? I already eat cream puffs every chance I get."

CHAPTER 33
A DAY WITHOUT PORRIDGE

GOLDIE

I wake up with two strong arms around me. Something in me purrs as I snuggle deeper into the hard body surrounding me.

After the obscene magic tricks Ted performed on my body, we took care of his hard-on until he was moaning my name like a prayer and losing control.

I feel so safe here with him. Like the core of my being is wrapped in a big fuzzy blanket. Sunlight streaming in through the window warms my face, burning away the softness of my dreams and pulling me into reality.

The one where I know before I even open my eyes that I'm in Ted's room. That it's his arms around me. And I want to stay here. I don't have to make apologies and run out of here though I will have to get up soon. But I want to feel safe a little while longer.

It's a strange phantom pressure that has me opening my eyes. Ted is awake and looking right at me. His scowl is softer than usual, like he's studying me.

He leans in and kisses me. My god, his lips are perfect in a way that is indescribable. We've kissed before but this morning feels different. There is no anxiety or panic, only a relaxed acceptance.

Something at the back of my mind tries to remind me that I've sworn off men, that I should be Ms. Independent and spending every spare minute on getting the house together. I've cut through over half the grime and the house is really starting to shine now. But if I let myself get swept up in Ted, I could lose focus and end up abandoning yet another project and be more in debt than ever.

I melt into the kiss, savoring the feel of his lips on mine. His arms tighten around me. Surrounded by his heat, I want to be wrapped up in him, lost in his embrace forever.

But then, just as quickly as the kiss began, he pulls away, leaving me gasping for air. His eyes are intense, searching mine.

Downstairs, we make coffee, enjoying the post-coital bliss that makes me feel like I'm staring in a romantic movie.

We checked the cameras, and no one broke into my house. Seems like the crystals did their job. Which means, last night I simply blipped over to Ted's because I wanted to be with him.

Red left messages she was on the road with Brexley for one of his jobs, but she did keep hearing about sirens and their tears being important, just like Kiki explained. Though she says finding out the particulars have proven to be more difficult.

It's hard for me to imagine what it could possibly be. As an emotional human, I'd already spilled tears, mainly in front of Ted. I didn't feel anything magical or strange about crying. They didn't crystalize into diamonds or summon monsters but who knew what the hell would crop up next.

As for now, I soak in the blissful pause of events as Ted whips together culinary delights for me in his kitchen. Nutella-stuffed French toast and sausage links.

The cozy intimacy of his sun-filled (yet blissfully air-conditioned) kitchen is broken when a model thin woman with deep, warm brown skin enters the kitchen. She's wearing a man's shirt that has some kind of computer binary joke on it, and her hair looks like someone has been wrapping their hands in it. The bone structure of her face belongs on shop windows to advertise diamonds and expensive perfume.

Ted stiffens as he quickly looks out the front window as if searching for something, then he heaves a sigh.

"I smell coffee," the goddess says. "I figured JJ was down here grabbing some for us, but I got tired of waiting."

The need to cover up comes over me. The supermodel looks stunning, rumpled in a man's shirt, while I'm scantily clad in my lace nightgown. I wasn't expecting anyone else to be here when Ted assured me he sent Eli to work on one of his construction sites today.

"Cute nightie," the girl shoots at me with an impressed smile.

Okay, I feel a little better now.

She returns her expectant gaze to Ted. He pinches the bridge of his nose for a moment, like he's bracing himself. My gaze swings back and forth between him and the supermodel.

"He, uh," Ted checks the front window again as if confirming something. "JJ already went home."

The girl's nose wrinkles in the most adorable way. "But

this is his home," she says with a light laugh as if she is trying to catch up to the joke being played on her.

Except Ted clearly doesn't think this is funny.

"He, uh, lives downtown, but he comes here when, uh. . . " Ted stumbles over his words but comprehension dawns on both me and the supermodel.

"Oh," she says, her tone turning frosty. "I see. Wants to make sure he can make a clean getaway."

Ted goes on, "Please help yourself to some coffee and I'm happy to order a ride to come pick you up if you need—"

I'm caught between feeling this is better than any reality show I've seen and being horrified on the supermodel's behalf. Suddenly the things Ted did to keep me away from JJ, the things he tried to warn me about his brother, it all comes into clear focus.

It's almost insane to think I once believed Ted to be the villain, when he is anything but.

A dry bark that must have been a form of humorless laughter comes out of her. "Oh, so you're his pimp? Sending the clients home after he's done? No, thanks, I can afford my own ride of shame." After that she whirls around and stomps back up the stairs to JJ's room, slamming the door so hard the cabinets rattle.

Ted sinks into the chair next to me. I once thought he was impossible to read, but I now I easily read the tension around his mouth and recognize he's in misery.

"So, that happen often?" I ask, looking at him over the rim of the mug.

Those forlorn eyes find mine. "Only almost every weekend and the occasional surprise weekday."

I set the mug down with a clink. "Yeesh."

More stomping precedes the supermodel now wearing

an appropriately sparkly blue dress that hits her mid-thigh. "You tell that asshole that he's a real class act. And maybe you should rethink being his exit man since it makes you even scummier than him." Another window shaking slam of the front door this time and Ted and I are alone again.

"Whoa," I say quietly.

Ted scrubs a hand down his face. "She's right. I've considered moving and forgetting to give JJ the address, so he has to set up his sin shop elsewhere and leave me the fuck out of it."

I pat his arm and tease, "Yes, but the neighbors are so nice, dear. You mustn't let him drive you out of such a sexy and convenient situation."

Ted lifts his head, meeting my gaze with a perplexed line drawn between his brows. I can't help but burst out laughing. "You poor baby."

After our late breakfast, the day stretches on when we end up back in his bed. One would think we'd had enough kissing, touching, talking, but I'm addicted.

I'm obsessed.

No, that's not right. Obsession for me is one sided and comes with a white knuckled grip around the thing I'm trying to hold on to.

But with Ted there is no anxiety, no question mark about what he'll do next, about what he wants. He simply tells me. And any time I even think of trying to suppress my instincts about what I want to eat, do, or even what I'm thinking, he sees straight through my façade and calls me out. I was convinced that I had been living my life as authentically as possible, until Ted showed me otherwise.

After we've burned far more daylight hours than I intended, I finally insist to Ted I need to go home to change into real clothes and get a little housework done. Despite his rather insistent suggestions that I stay in the silky lace nightgown for the rest of my life, I veto him and flounce off in the direction of my house. He yells after me that he's only giving me a ten-minute start.

Stepping up to the porch, I go to open the door where JJ installed a programmable lock. It's ugly as sin against the beautiful Victorian, but he swore up and down he'll change it back to the lovely original door handle once things get more settled. Though I feel things are already turning around. Or maybe it's because Ted makes me feel so safe and. . . and. . . that word. That word I refuse to bandy about anymore because I totally swore off men, because I don't need a man.

Rationalizing to myself that I don't need Ted but I certainly want him, and certain parts of him in particular. Still, that word, the big one starting with 'L' hovers around my periphery. I'll keep it out there as long as I can, but I don't know how long I'll last before it body slams into me, refusing to leave.

As soon as I close the door behind me, an awareness tickles my senses. I instantly register that I'm not alone. The safety I felt moments ago, shatters into icy shards that slice into me.

"Hey there, sugartits, I haven't been able to get you off my mind."

CHAPTER 34
OBSESSION IN SNAKESKIN BOOTS

TED

The familiar scent of oily snakeskin cologne hits my senses as I reach the landing of Goldie's porch. My head whips around, looking for evidence of *his* presence.

There it is.

The sun catches off the hood of a black Lincoln Continental that's been pulled off the road, so it's mostly hidden in the brush.

Eddie's here.

My fist pounds against the door. "Goldie," I yell, fear wrapping around my throat like a python.

I pull out my phone and text JJ, demanding he tell me how to override the doorknob. Every piece of technology must have some kind of workaround.

When he doesn't respond in point five seconds, I resort to other means. My arm shifts and I release all that panic and fear on the doorknob, smashing it right off with a pathetic beep of protest. Kicking the door in, I start forward, but an invisible barrier knocks me back.

The warding crystals.

I can't pass the threshold as long as they are placed on either side of the door. I can't stick my hand in to move them, though they are so painfully close.

"Goldie," I yell out, my fingers digging in and cracking the wood on the door jamb.

She's fine. She'll be here in a minute to move those witchtitting warded crystals to let me in and assure me everything is okay.

But my gut tells me better. He's here, I can smell him. An oily musky scent mixed with corruption and blood shoots up my nose, floods my mouth.

"Goldie," I yell for what feels like the hundredth time in minutes. I need to hear her voice, see that she's okay.

She steps into the living room, into my line of sight. My body is on the verge of releasing my pent-up tension, but the look on her face keeps me from relaxing just yet.

She's still wearing her nightgown, though she left my place fifteen minutes ago. Her expression is a careful mask with an underlying tension of fear, her body is rigid. I can taste the terror under her sweet scent. It's dark and tangy.

Big brown eyes plead with me. She wants me to get out of here.

The click of a gun being cocked comes from behind her before Eddie's white snakeskin boots step into the room. He takes up a stance behind her and points his gun at me.

"You shouldn't have come," Eddie says. He's wearing all black again, but his tie is loose, his skin appears pale and clammy, and his eyes are bloodshot. Something about him is completely unhinged and a buzzing sensation vibrates off him.

It's Goldie's power. Like a cloud of angry bees, it surrounds him.

I don't know why Goldie didn't teleport back to my place, but I wish she had. My being this close might prevent her from doing so now, but I can't walk away. I won't leave her, I'd never leave her.

"Goldie, are you okay?" I ask in a calm, measured voice.

She nods mutely. Terrified for sure, but as far as I can tell she's unharmed.

"If you touch her—" I growl at Eddie even as he trains his gun on me.

"You'll what?" Eddie interrupts. His mean beady eyes seem a little unfocused, and I wonder if he isn't on something.

"I'll rip your head clean off your body," I promise, meaning every word.

"Goldie doesn't want you, she wants me," Eddie yells at me, his eyes wild. "She needs me as much as I need her." To prove his point, he flails his gun between us. Goldie winces as if expecting it to go off.

Eddie is manic, driven mad by her magic. Eddie looks like he hasn't slept or eaten in a while, judging by the dark shadows on his face and sallow complexion. As if all he could think of was Goldie.

"How did you get in, Eddie?" I ask in a low measured voice.

A smug smile tugs at his wide set lips as he stares at me with superiority and menace. "Man in my position, it pays to always have some black-market magic items on hand." He pulls a necklace out from under his shirt, on the end is a polished piece of black obsidian. "It gets through some of the toughest wards, and really opens doors if you know what I mean."

My eyes narrow. I knew it. He's the stalker. He's the one who's been sneaking into Goldie's place, trying to get to her. I suspected it was my fault, getting involved with her until she was in the crossfire, but now I know for sure.

I've got to find a way to get in or lure them closer so one of them might knock aside a warding crystal.

Eddie slips the obsidian charm back under his shirt, his attention going back to Goldie. A shaking hand reaches out to pet her hair. "You're my girl, aren't you Goldie?"

She winces as he touches her but bites on her lip and nods.

"Say it," he screams at her.

Her voice trembles almost violently, tearing my guts out. "I'm your girl."

"I'm your girl, Eddie," he prods.

After a shaky breath she manages to say, "I'm your girl, Eddie."

He buries his head in her neck, kissing her there. Goldie shuts her eyes tight while I slam at the invisible barrier, my muscles expanding, begging to give into the rage and shift, but it won't get me inside. I have to stay in control if I want to save Goldie before Eddie does something rash.

"So you aren't here to collect on Eli's debt?" I ask, trying to draw Eddie's attention.

Confusion clouds Eddie's beady eyes. "What? Why would I care about that? Not when the only treasure is right here." He goes back to nuzzling her neck and Goldie tries to shrink into herself.

I need to bait him, get him to move over here or give Goldie some space. I need a distraction. "Did you know she's my girlfriend, Eddie?" I ask.

Eddie's head snaps up, to regard me with a gaze full of

fire and rage that goes beyond reasons. I understand, I'm feeling the exact same fucking things.

Eddie snarls, tightening his grip on Goldie. She whimpers in response.

I'm going to fucking rip him limb from limb.

The bear roars inside me, fighting to get to the surface. It takes everything in me to push it back down. It won't help, I have to focus.

Forcing calm into my voice, desperate to keep control of the situation, I go on. "See, I'm a werebear. Were's mate for life. And now that Goldie has chosen me, my bear won't let another male take her without a fight."

"She hasn't chosen you," Eddie screams at me like a wild hyena, bending over at the waist. But in doing so, he's taken several more steps closer to me, to the door. He's dragging Goldie with him too which means she could get a chance to kick the crystal away.

My eyes dart to a crystal before meeting her eye. Understanding registers in her soft brown eyes and she nods almost imperceptibly.

If she gets a chance, she'll take it.

I work to placate the madman with the gun as well as the raging blood thirsty beast inside me. "You're right, you're right, Eddie, I said it wrong. *I* chose her, but now I can't let her go. It's the law of my faekind. Just like how there are rules you enforce for your boss. So if you want her, you'll have to go through me first. Just you and me, man to man. We'll settle this the right way."

I see a flicker of doubt in Eddie's eyes as he takes in my hulking form. For a second, his male ego wars with his fear, tempted by the challenge.

But then his face hardens. "The thing about my line of work is we may enforce rules, but we—" He hits his own chest with the butt of the gun. "Make up the rules. We take what's ours and I don't owe you shit, you filthy animal."

Faefucks.

Backing up several feet, taking Goldie with him, he raises his gun, pointing it at me again.

My muscles swell, fur fighting to sprout from my skin. I have to do something or I'll explode and lose my mind.

Instead, I raise my hands in surrender. They shake as they rise, which likely makes me look afraid.

I am for Goldie but more than that, something dark has woken in me and I can't get it to calm down.

But I have no choice but to back down for now, hoping another opportunity presents itself. Goldie's life is on the line.

Then Goldie's eye catches mine and something akin to an apology flashes on her face. "Eddie, I'm so glad you came for me," she says, her voice still trembling but I can tell she is trying to get it under control. "You know I was waiting for you, right?" she says softly.

He turns his head up to search her eyes with a hungry eagerness. "You were?" He almost seems like a child the way he drinks her attention up.

Goldie sets a hand on his wrist. I'm about ready to swallow my tongue. Any movement or thing could set him off, he's clearly on the edge of sanity preparing to cliff dive off.

Gently, she runs her hands up his arm in a caress. A growl rumbles from my chest.

Mine. She's mine.

I'm not under a spell, but I love her more than anything or anyone ever.

I shut my eyes tight, trying to hold the reins on my animal side.

Don't. You turn, you'll lose her.

Slowly, she rotates Eddie so his back is angled toward me, as she keeps his attention on her eyes. His hands including the one holding the gun hold her now even as her fingers slide up over his shoulders, she gazes up at him and says, "Yes, I was waiting for you and now that you are here, we can be together." Then she pushes up onto her tiptoes and kisses him.

Everything inside me freezes in disbelief.

My bear wants to split me in two to rip him off her, but her eyes are open and looking at me even as he succumbs to the kiss. It's then I notice her fingers working the clasp of his talisman necklace.

She's smart. Too smart. And it may get her hurt.

My weight shifts from foot to foot at the threshold, as I wait for my moment.

Then Eddie yanks his head back too soon. "What are you—"

Goldie grabs the chain on his neck and yanks. It breaks free, and she doesn't waste time, throwing it in my direction. The talisman flies through the air, but from her awkward angle, I'm not sure it will pass the threshold. If it doesn't cross the door, she'll be trapped in there with him, and I won't be able to do a godsdamn thing about it.

At first, I can't tell by the arc of her throw if it's going to make it. My heart lodges in my throat, a meaty, raw organ choking me out.

Eddie presses the gun to Goldie's temple screaming, "How could you? I love you."

The warm obsidian lands in my palm and I unleash.

Eddie whips around as I explode into the house.

A flash of light accompanies the bark of a gun the same time I close on Eddie. And then I make good on my promise and rip his head clear off his body with a window shaking roar. I didn't even shift.

My eyes open—I'm not sure when I closed them—but I'm looking up at Goldie from where I lay on the ground. She's on the phone with someone as she hovers over me.

"Hey, hey," I try to calm her down, though my words come out rough. "Everything's okay."

The acrid scent of gunpowder still lingers in the air as I meet Goldie's wide, frightened eyes. "You were shot, Ted," she says before saying something on the phone that comes in like fuzz to my own ears.

I cover her hand with mine but then realize it's covered in blood and now I've gotten it all over her. Or was her hand already bloody from putting pressure on my chest?

"Yeah, bear Ted can take a hit far better than human Ted. I'll heal, don't worry. Everything's going to be okay, cream puff." My words do nothing to erase the panic in her eyes. Though maybe I've spoken too soon. I cough, tasting copper bubbling up in my mouth.

"Stop trying to fix things, Tedford. You aren't healing fast enough and losing a lot of blood. Now I need you to help me get you into the car." She tries to pull me up but would stand no chance if I was unconscious. I would very much like to close my eyes and rest, but I struggle to my feet, feeling a gush of blood escape the hole in my chest.

"Don't trip over the head," Goldie murmurs as she guides me out toward the car.

CHAPTER 35
HOLE IN THE HEART

TED

The humid night air settles on us as we exit the car by the neon sign of the Pumpkin Coach Club. The placard casts an ethereal glow on the darkened street, breathing life into the otherwise bleak surroundings. We limp down the back alley, where pools of yellow light from the overhead lamps collect on the rain-slicked cobblestones.

A drag queen with cool, brown skin greets us, her sky-high blue wig catching hints of the moonlight. It takes a moment for me to recognize this as the same person who visited Goldie the other day, when the wolf and Red were around.

She ushers us in, her heels clicking rhythmically against the tile as we move through the dimly lit corridor, lined with vibrant posters of past shows, until we reach her private dressing room. It's a space filled with a blend of floral and vanilla scents, a sharp contrast to the scent of hard alcohol and something distinctly in the berry family.

Dame Kiki Eleganza, the Fairy Godmother, approaches me, her hands glowing faintly in the dim room. "This will hurt, but not for long," she warns.

As she places her palms on my gunshot wound, the room blurs out of focus. My body feels as if it's floating between two worlds, and I can't tell if it's from blood loss or the magic coursing through me. The sensation is like cold fire, numbing yet burning at the same time. I want to scream but can barely manage a gasp.

Goldie paces back and forth, clearly unable to remain still. I glimpse her through my clouding vision—her figure distorted like a reflection in turbulent water. She's biting her nails, then pulling at her hair, her movements mirroring the anxiety that seems to engulf her.

Suddenly, my vision snaps back into focus for just a second, and in that moment, I see Goldie's face crumple. It's as if she's teetering on the edge of losing something incredibly precious. Her eyes lock onto mine, a desperate plea for me to hold on. To not leave her alone in a world where her neighbor turned enemy could vanish forever.

But then the blackness encroaches on my vision again, like an ink stain spreading through water. Is Kiki's magic failing?

"Just a bit more," Dame Kiki mutters, her voice tinged with a strain that wasn't there before.

Goldie must have heard it too, because she freezes, her eyes widening. She looks as if she's about to rush over but then hesitates, torn between maintaining her distance and reaching out to touch me. The tension is electric, a stretched wire ready to snap.

Finally, Dame Kiki removes her hands, and like a wave receding, the cold fire inside me wanes. I feel lighter, as if I've been given a second chance at life. Yet my limbs still feel heavy, my head a foggy mess. I'm still teetering on the edge of consciousness.

"You'll be okay," Dame Kiki says, not to me, but to Goldie. "He's stable now. He just needs rest."

Goldie lets out a shaky breath, slumping into a plastic chair as if the strings holding her upright have been cut. Her eyes meet mine again, and I see relief flooding in to chase away the fear. It's like a spell has been broken, but the emotional toll is clearly written in her eyes.

I lay on Kiki's chaise lounge, a deep maroon that contrasts vividly against the chaotic backdrop of a room filled with sequined costumes and a vibrant array of makeup. The woman herself swept out of the room after washing blood off her hands saying she'd be back in ten, after her number.

"How are you feeling, Teddy Bear?" Goldie asks, her fingers twisting a loose strand of hair nervously as she leans forward in her seat. A tan trench coat is the only thing she grabbed to throw over her nightgown when we left her house. I made her stop and slip on some shoes too.

Right now, blondie's expression is unreadable. If she hadn't used my most hated nickname, I would have thought she was distancing herself from me. But she is still trying to yank my chain to see if I'll yank back.

"You'll pay for that," I grit out, attempting to sit up, but a sharp stab of pain halts me.

Across the room, Goldie reaches out instinctively, her hand hanging mid-air, torn between coming to help and staying put. She relaxes when I don't make any further attempts to move. "No, I won't. I saved you," she says, before pausing. "After putting your life in danger."

"Only because you were dragged into *my* family's problems," I point out. I expect her to retort but she goes oddly silent, looking down at her chipped nails.

After I figure out a way to pay Eli's debts, I'm going to take her for a manicure and the one they do for the toes, I don't know what it's called. I bet it's one of those girly things she loves.

"You killed someone," she says. There is no judgement or emotion attached to it. More like she's stating a fact I may or may not know.

"I killed someone," I repeat slowly.

Goldie's hand covers her mouth as if she is processing something internally. She doesn't push the subject though part of me wishes she would.

More words spill out of me. "I should be bothered. I should see the stain of red on my hands and cringe, maybe hate myself, but I don't." In fact, I feel a dark satisfaction at slaying the man who put her in danger.

I go on. "I wonder if this is the fae part of me, the creature that understands kill or be killed and accepts the rule of nature without further contemplation because it is what it is. Or maybe years of fostering my brother's bad habits have chipped away at the humanity inside me until I've become someone who would protect their family no matter the cost."

"That's pack, isn't it?" Goldie asks, her hand making a sweeping gesture as if trying to encompass something immense.

When I give her a questioning look, she goes on, "I learned a lot about were packs from Brexley, how you not only metaphorically rely on each other, but that you'll literally waste away if separated from your pack."

"That's true, but living among humans for so long makes it difficult to revert to were ways of thinking. At least we got your stalker," I say, shooting her a weak apologetic smile. "He won't bother you anymore."

"Do we call the cops?" she asks. From the look on her face, I know she's thinking of the headless body at her house.

I shake my head. "This is pack business. Fae take care of their own." Eli is already over there, cleaning up. She may not be fae, but she's more family than my own brothers right now.

"So that's the end of it," she says in a flat tone I don't like.

"Well, no," I admit though it pains me to do so. "Eddie works for someone else who still wants to collect on Eli's debt. And now that we've sent his people running once and took out one of his top enforcers, he'll be coming for me and Eli." After a moment, I add, "Maybe you."

"That's okay," she lets out a dry, humorless laugh. "He thinks he wants me dead, but when he meets me, I'll just make him fall in love with me."

"That's not funny," I growl. When Eddie dared to lay a finger on her, threaten her safety, he'd ended his own life right then. I thought I was going to lose my mind. Go bear and never come back.

"I'll fix it, Goldie. Don't worry. I've cleaned his mess up before and I'll clean this up too. You have to believe I won't let anything happen to you."

Goldie stands. "I have to get to work. My shift starts soon. I called JJ and he's coming to get you."

She starts to walk by and I reach out, my grip on her arm almost too tight, a fierce, possessive urgency pulsating through me as I pull her close, unable to bear the thought of her walking away into the night, possibly out of my control. I gaze up into those sad brown eyes. "I am so sorry, Goldie."

"I know," she says, her soft smile barely reaching her eyes that shimmers with a mingling of sadness and understanding.

Again I feel some part of her has slipped out of reach from me. Because of how real things had been this morning? It was like being inside a bubble of domestic bliss I aspired to, but always fell so short of it.

Because I killed someone? Because my family put her in danger? I want to pry it out of her.

She bends over and drops a soft kiss on my lips, but I deepen it. My hands tangle in her hair, a desperate need to claim her, to mark her as mine bubbling up from a place dark and fierce within me.

When I let her break away, she says, a little breathless, "I'll check on you in the morning."

I tug on her arm, insistent. "After your shift."

"That's the middle of the night, Tedly, and you need rest," she scolds, her lips quirking into an almost smile.

"I know. And Eddie may be out of the picture, but I won't rest unless you come over and spend the night with me."

Goldie kisses me again and walks out not agreeing or refusing my request.

Maybe it's a side effect of being shot in the chest, but I swear I still feel the hole there.

Dame Kiki sweeps back in, minutes after Goldie has left. "Well, I've met my share of bears, but none so big and burly as you or your brother who is currently out waiting by the stage. If I didn't have a few more performances tonight, I might just climb in one of your beds to see if it's juuust right." She nudges me and winks.

I don't bother telling her there is only one girl I'll ever let into my bed again.

Because whether I mean to or not, I've ensnared Goldie into my dark, tumultuous world. A predatory part of me has woken and refuses to let her go, ready to pull her even deeper into the shadows with me, where the lines between right and wrong blur when it comes to protecting my mate.

CHAPTER 36

A SECRET ADMIRER

GOLDIE

Thankfully I keep clean clothes and makeup in my locker at work, because I only grabbed a trench coat, throwing it over my bloody nightgown when I rushed Ted to see the Dame.

I get to the Poison Apple early enough that I can take my time in the locker room shower, cleaning off the dried red smears from my skin, unsure if they came from Ted or Eddie.

Warm water trails down my skin, rinsing away the lingering scent of blood and fear. I want it to wash away the confusion, the swirl of emotions that have been bubbling up inside me since I saw Ted rip Eddie's head off. Before then maybe, when I discovered Eddie in my house, or maybe when I realized I had a stalker breaking and entering.

But no amount of water can cleanse me from the sight of Eddie's head separating from his body, or the belief that it wasn't my fault.

As I step out of the shower, the quiet surrounds me like a suffocating blanket. I can't shake off the thought that I am becoming a liability, another person for Ted to protect, another source of chaos in his already heavy life.

No wonder he tried to keep me out. He has more than enough to deal with without me showing up and splashing my own problems on top like chocolate syrup on the spectacularly tragic sundae of issues he already has to contend with.

I run my fingers through my hair, wincing at the knots, and the thoughts knot tighter inside me.

Ted's fierce, almost savage need to protect me, his readiness to kill for me. It was terrifying and touching, all at once. But it was also a glaring red sign that things were spiraling far beyond my control.

Is this what love morphs into when mated with a were? I wonder, my heart sinking with the weight of my own questions. *A cycle of violence and protection, one feeding the other endlessly?*

As I apply makeup, my reflection in the mirror seems unfamiliar, but the longer I look the more I recognize the girl there. Someone who was too big, too loud, too much and thought she could find safety in making herself small.

At that realization, I practically dive for the boldest lipstick color in my pack. I refuse to go down that path again. Aunt Astrid's house is where I found myself again, and I don't intend on losing myself there this time around. The answer is not to withdraw into myself, there lies only darkness.

I slip into my work clothes. The fabric feels rough, abrasive against my skin, like a physical manifestation of the turmoil inside me. I need space, time to breathe, to understand who I am in this intertwining world of magic and grim realities.

Cinder and Snow show up while I'm restocking the bar. I deliberately make myself busy to avoid telling them what happened. They smile and say hello but Cinder seems distracted. She doesn't quite meet my eye.

A fear spikes through me. Is she sick of me causing problems at work? I would be if I were her.

The last update I remember her sharing was that she and Lysander were planning a getaway weekend. I was such a selfish friend, I didn't even know what was going on there. He continued to show up night after night at the bar when she worked. Neither of them are forthcoming about their feelings, much less transparent enough for the rest of us to read in on the situation.

And I've had too many of my own issues to dig into hers.

The bar is a whirl of activity, the neon lights casting grotesque shadows that seem to mock the growing darkness in my heart. The clinking glasses sound like warning bells, urging me to reconsider the path I'm on before I get swallowed whole.

"Hey Goldie," Snow says at one point, "Have you heard from your jackass ex since you clocked his sorry ass face?" A glimmer of violent delight shines from her eyes.

I can already see she's come a long way in coming into her own. It's as if there's more substance there than before. Like watching a ghost fill out.

It may be the qualification to be a lost girl. We were all ghosts at one time until we came to the Poison Apple.

I shake my head as I pour out another martini. "Nope. Not a peep. Which is weird." I take in my own words.

"Really weird." Before I can elaborate, someone flags Snow for a cocktail order. But my mind is still churning.

Not only was Lawrence persistent when it came to restarting our on-again, off-again cycle, but I know the effects of my powers only added to his fervor.

Eddie seemed practically infected, or maybe poisoned by my power. I would expect that to happen to Lawrence since we have history. Why would he actually stay away when my power was more volatile than ever?

Before I can think more on it, Geanie begins his midnight intro show for us. He puts on all the bells and whistles per usual until it's my turn to take center stage. The music pops off as we dance and pour drinks into the mouths of excited regulars.

Geanie calls Snow up with us, an introduction that morphs night to night as he works on the material. Since Snow kept her past close to her chest, unwilling to talk about it to give Geanie fodder for his intro, he wanted to make up a background that related to the fairy court. Until Cinder cut him off, saying he shouldn't debase Snow by associating her with the Charming Court. She mentioned she'd met the prince himself once, and he was a real dick. Geanie now rotated through different stories every night to test what landed.

For a moment, I'm not Goldie, the girl caught up in a dangerous world who was stalked and watched a man get decapitated, but just a bartender, serving drinks with her friends. It's a small escape, a momentary reprieve from the harsh realities that wait.

I wouldn't have stepped up for lost girl introductions if I hadn't spotted Brexley sidled up to the bar.

I texted Red and asked if they were in town and if they could come tonight. At least I had the sense to ask for protection against my own powers, as Brexley could drain me of my powers if it got out of hand. Though I spent way too many characters in my text also explaining to Red that I love her too and want her around.

It's more important than ever that she knows how much she means to me and that our friendship is sacred. She laughed it off and told me to relax, but I still need to hear that she understands and believes me.

We pull Red up onto the bar with us, and for a moment, things are as they should be. But then I spot those looks. Some of the women who are regulars' clump into a group that talks amongst themselves even as they shoot nasty glares my way.

My skin turns prickly and way too hot under the spotlight. It's suddenly hard to focus and I'm standing very high up, dancing on a bar, putting myself on display for their judgement.

I struggle to draw air into my lungs.

Catcalls of my name come from the crowd of men at my feet, and I've started to notice the sensation of when my magic is activating. It's subtle like static, but right now it's a constant thrum. The men yell louder, they want more, more Goldie.

"You okay?" Red leans over and asks even as she completes the line dancing steps we do in tandem to the blaring music.

Before I can answer, an empty beer can hits me in the face. The group of women burst into laughter while the rest of the bar bursts into a commotion.

Teetering on the edge of the bar, I fight an invisible war with gravity. One slip and I'll fall in pit of vipers who scream my name, claiming they'll take me home, take care of me.

A hand steadies me and helps me back down the steps to the backside of the bar before I'm led out from behind the bar. Colors and lights blur together as I do my best to fight off the panic attack.

It's only when I'm in the locker room that I see who led me to safety. Lysander.

"Thank you," I gasp, still fighting the hot waves rolling through me, making my stomach roil as my senses drown in overload.

"Here, sit down," Lysander offers, pulling the chair from the vanity. In minutes, I'm seated with a cup of water in my hand while he pats my back.

"There you go, deep breaths," he says.

When the worst of it passes, I'm left feeling shaky and weak. Maybe I should have told Rap I needed the night off after all.

Lysander drops to a knee next to me. "You feeling better?"

I nod and smile in gratitude. "Yes, thank you so much for getting me out of that. I think I'm ready to go back out there."

"You don't have to," he says, adjusting his glasses. "You could stay here, with me."

Then his lips press against mine. The chair screeches back the few inches before it slams into the vanity. We both jump to our feet.

"What the hell, Lysander? What are you doing?" My blood roars in my ears as the panic attack closes back in on me. An iron fist tightens round my chest.

He holds out his hands in an open plea.

"Goldie, I. . . I want you," he says, searching my eyes as if waiting for me to see the perfect sense of it all.

The floor drops out from under me. I think I'm going to

throw up.

"No," I shake my head vehemently. "You want Cinder. You are perfect for each other."

He shakes his head, causing the tip of his gray beanie to flap. "No Goldie, it's you. You are special, unlike anyone else. She's nothing compared to you."

"Don't say that," my words come out in a panicked, half-screech as I back away.

Relentless waves of terror wash over me as I'm overcome by an unshakable dread.

"Why not?" He shakes his head while opening his hands. "It's not like I'm under your spell, Goldie. I know all about your power problems, but I've felt this way about you for a while. I'm not like those other guys. I want you for you," he insists.

A blast of cold shock goes through me. "What?" I ask. This makes everything so much worse.

"Maybe but my power is still affecting you. You can't do this to Cinder," I insist. "She's the best person I know."

He nears, his voice low as if trying to soothe me. "She's great, but she's not *you*. And she knows it. We've been fighting because she knows she's not enough for me. Because she knows you are so much better than she is. Her insecurity, she tries to hide it, but I see it swelling and taking over more and more each day. It started the day I met you."

That was months ago.

My words race to get out, to make him understand. "Cinder is better than me. She's loyal, she's smart, she's creative and has this life wisdom I don't have."

Lysander shakes his head. "Sure, she's all those things, but Goldie, I want you. A categorical list of her positive attributes doesn't compare."

"I can't—" is all I can get out before I practically run out of the room like I've been set on fire.

As soon as I exit, I run smack dab into Cinder. Her violet eyes bounce back and forth between Lysander, who hovers behind me in the locker room, and me. For a girl who often appears unaffected by almost everything, she looks at me with what I can only describe as accusation.

"Guys, a little help," Snow calls out in a strained voice. She's by herself behind the bar and swamped by patrons. The fanclub is restless and I can tell by their faces, they aren't happy with my absence.

Cinder doesn't say a word. She simply turns on her heel and goes to rescue Snow. I follow along, ready to pull Cinder aside and explain though I don't know how the faefucks, I'm going to do that.

I don't get a chance to talk to Cinder.

But I do with Brexley who is still at the bar. "What the hell, Brex? You couldn't drain my power for me?"

His scarred eye studies me in a way I don't love. Like I'm not about to like what he's about to say. "You're too power-ful, Goldie. I can't stop it. Your magic is exploding out of you in sun flares. I've never seen anything like it."

Damn magic cookies. Never again.

Without Ted here, the male fan club reconvenes and there is an edge building to the crowd. Wanting a quick solution, I turn to Red who stands next to him looking equally concerned.

"Take my powers. Eat them with your magic so I don't have them anymore."

Red's expression turns to pity. "I can't do that."

"No, you can," I rush to assure her. "You have my full consent."

She exchanges a glance with Brexley. "Even if I weren't

forbidden from ever doing it again, I wouldn't do that to a friend. Goldie, these powers are a part of you. It'd be like I'm robbing you of your sense of smell or hearing. I can't do that to you."

The levee breaks, and the fan club loses it at not having my attention.

One of the men barrels around the end of the bar and comes straight for me. Seeing one person has broken the boundary, a second, then third guy hop over the sticky bar, knocking drinks over. As they close in, panic strangles me. I'm a trapped animal, trying to avoid their greedy clutches as they reach out for me.

Brexley and Red fight the crowd from their end, but pandemonium has fully broken.

"Hey," Snow yells, getting their attention. She grabs a bottle and breaks it on the edge of the bar, gripping the neck of the makeshift weapon of jagged glass. "Everybody back the faefucks up." She may be tiny, but violence gleams from her bright blue eyes with surprising ferocity.

There is only the slightest pause, but either the men did the math and know they outnumber us, or they don't care.

More of them cross the barrier of the bar, eager to get at me, and there is no way out.

Someone yanks on my hair, while another presses his hot lips against my throat. Hands clutch and painfully squeeze at my breasts. The scream that rips out of me is unrecognizable.

I blink and suddenly I'm released. Cool air surrounds my body instead of the hot press of men trying to tear a piece off me. Something thrums under my skin, like a motor gradually winding down. My hand finds the solid wood of a familiar desk as I steady myself.

It was my power. I teleported into Rap's office. The

closest spot I'd feel safe. Rap is in front of me, she opened the door and is looking out to gauge what the ruckus is about.

"Rap," I say in a strangled voice. She turns and her brows shoot up in surprise when she sees me standing behind her. My clothes are ripped and I'm sure I appear as terrified as I feel.

Assessing the situation almost instantaneously, as she always does, Rap looks at me and says, "Wait five minutes then grab your shit and get out of here, Goldie. Use the back door. Take the next couple days off. In fact, wait for me to call you."

With that, Rap slams the door behind her, and I'm left standing there in shock. I can hear her shouts over the din. The girls and the bouncers are kicking people out of the bar.

I don't know when I start shaking, but my hands violently tremble as I grab my stuff from the locker room. I head out the back door and beeline it for my car. The drive home goes by torturously slow, and ugly thoughts begin to pop up.

Why don't you just jerk the wheel and end all this. Everyone would be better off without you.

The voice inside my head belongs to Madison. It used to talk to me in a constant stream, but I haven't heard it in years.

If I thought things were bad before, my innermost hell had been realized. Not only did I get sent home from work after causing an insane, violent disruption, but I've ruined the happiness of my closest friend.

I already know to my bones that Cinder will never forgive me.

CHAPTER 37
IT'S JUST A BAD DAY

GOLDIE

When I wake, I'm as brittle as a dried leaf and it hurts to look at myself so I don't.

After getting home, I found the door was fixed, lock included. No trace of blood or the body pieces on my living room floor. Like it never happened.

Even though Eddie was out of the picture, it probably wasn't smart to stay home alone. Someone could have followed me from work again.

Still, I dragged my ass up the stairs and crawled under the covers like the lowest creature known to mage, fae, and man. The truth is I don't care. I don't care what happens to me. Maybe I even deserve it.

I'm not capable.

I'm not enough.

And I don't deserve my friends.

Today there will be no makeup, no loud booty shaking music, no pink and pleather. Instead, I lay on the creaky springs occasionally rotating as inky, sucking darkness pulls me down, down, down until it's all I breathe. Each breath is a burden. Life itself is a burden I'm not sure I can bear the weight of.

If being myself hurts people I love, maybe I had it right all those years ago. Maybe I should make myself smaller. Maybe it's plain narcissism to love myself and my need to romance my life is what's ballooning into a dangerous bubble everyone I love keeps getting caught in.

I can't pick up my phone or even bring myself watch one of my favorite reality shows. Instead, I lay there and stew. Stew in how I'm going to tell Cinder. How can I face her? How can I tell her what happened? It hurts me so terribly, which means it will likely spear through her.

Will she hold me responsible? It's magic gone haywire, seducing people against their will. But that didn't matter in middle school, not to Madison, not to the other girls. Did I already mess up by not telling Cinder immediately?

Do I keep it from her because it's magic and it doesn't count, and if I get Ted around, will it take the fervor off Lysander's desire?

With every option I review, I know I've already lost. Cinder has always been cagey about relationships, about being touched, about letting me in. She had such a rough, traumatizing upbringing and if she finds I betrayed her, even by accident, she'll shut me out. Maybe not outright, she won't scream and yell at me. She might not even talk shit about me to other people, but those are possible too. But even if she quickly broke things off, retreating from me, talking with Snow behind closed doors about how I couldn't help but be center of attention. . . I smother myself with a pillow, letting out a long painful groan.

I feel like I'm dying. Like I'll never be happy again.

It's been a long time since depression had sunk its evil claws into my flesh, dragging me down, blotting out any speck of light or joy. But I remember this feeling. It doesn't maim, it drowns, without mercy or reprieve.

There is a knock down at the front door. I ignore it, but it keeps coming until I force myself to get to my feet and walk down the groaning steps with stiff legs. Opening the front door feels like so much pressure, I fear I'll be flattened by it.

"What happened?" Ted asks when he takes me in. I'm sure my makeup-free face is drawn and pale. I can literally feel the bags hanging under my eyes, pulling them down like an undertow. The heather gray pants and shirt have holes in them, but they are soft. Nothing about me is put together.

All I can do is shake my head. I can't bring myself to say words. When I even try, they shrivel and blacken at the base of my throat.

"Is it me? Did I cause this?" he asks, his eyes growing wider with alarm. Large hands grip either side of the doorjamb.

I shake my head, tears welling in my eyes.

Don't do it, Goldie. Don't give him your tears. Red warned you that it could give him power over you. Harshly blinking them back, I turn around and pad into the kitchen, needing something to do to keep the waterworks from switching on. I put the kettle on the stove for tea, though I don't even want any.

The sound of the door creaking and closing comes before Ted fills up my kitchen with his presence. My insides are askew. I have no opinions on his presence or lack of it.

"You're scaring me, Goldie," he says.

All I manage to push past my lips is a couple words and even that takes great effort. "It's just a bad day."

The next thing I know I'm enfolded in a pair of big muscular arms. My eyes shut as I'm smushed against the plaid shirt that smells like fresh pine. Ted doesn't let go. He doesn't ask me what's wrong again. He simply holds me, keeping me together when I'm sure I'd otherwise fly apart like gray ash.

"You don't have to tell me," he says into the top of my head. "But I'm here and everything's going to be okay."

How? How does this feel so good? It's just touch. People can survive without it, but warmth and feelings of safety flood my system as we stand there, him holding me. When the tea kettle starts to whistle, he shuffles our feet so I'm standing on his and he walks the few steps to pull the pot off the burner.

Then that arm surrounds me, and he continues to hold me and whisper how everything is going to be okay and that he knows things are hard right now but I'll get through it. This won't last forever.

Likely things he's told himself in the past when he thought his bones would buckle under all that responsibility.

It's a bunch of nonsense, and yet, his words of comfort and the safety of his arms help raise my meter of well-being, bit by little bit.

"What do you need?" he asks after a while.

Nothing. Everything.

I don't know.

This all filters through my mind before I say, "I miss my mom." And I do. No matter what happens, having someone who loves you so unconditionally that you can say anything to, lessens burdens tremendously.

I miss my dad and my brother too, but it's my mom I'm closest to and she can't be here. And I don't have the strength to go to her. I probably don't have the money either.

"Do you want to call her?" he offers quietly.

Still unable to conjure words, I shake my head no. I can't bring myself to voice what's drowning me. I just know I crave her comfort. I burrow further into Ted's embrace and drink in what he is giving me.

Solid ground to land on. Even though I don't deserve it.

Shouting draws our attention. I follow Ted out to the front door to the porch where we find Eli and JJ wild eyed. "They're coming," Eli yells.

"Three of them," JJ supplies.

"Three of what?" Ted asks, his arm curled protectively around me.

Three black SUVs careen in on the dirt road, and even my numb, depressed brain registers a flicker of fear. The men who want to collect on Eli's debts have returned, and the fight has been brought to my doorstep, again.

CHAPTER 38
PACK ATTACK

TED

Tires spit gravel as the three SUVs roar in. In a heartbeat, I scoop Goldie into my arms and race into her house.

"Stay here no matter what," I yell, my voice urgent. "Use those crystals to lock yourself in."

Outside, the sounds of bones cracking and muscles stretching echo through the night—the grotesque melody of my brothers' transformation.

Goldie glimpses my hands, morphing into claws, fur bursting from my skin as I expand. I meet her eyes one last time before the beast takes over. I slam her front door shut and head into the fray.

Car doors swing open. Sunlight glints off barrels leveled in our direction. The crack of gunfire shreds the night.

We are already in motion.

I barrel toward the shooters, bullets whizzing past. The need to protect my mate drives me. My animal side unleashed, all fury and instinct.

In a blur, Eli zooms into range, drawing their fire. He zigs, zags faster than their eyes can follow. I flank left—JJ right—coordinated and merciless.

Metal shrieks as we slam the SUVs sideways in a cacophony of glass and crushing metal. Cries ring out—surprise morphing into pain.

My fangs find flesh. Copper floods my mouth. I lose myself to the beast, consumed by the primal need to destroy any threat.

Somewhere in the recesses of my mind, I'm vaguely aware of my hide being penetrated and the warmth of my own blood coating my fur.

All I can think is that I must protect my mate, so I do. I follow the part of me born of fang and rage until there isn't a single one of them left standing.

The SUVs lay in ruins, contorted carcasses of steel and fire. I stand amidst it, flanked by my brothers, our breaths syncing in the rhythm of the pack.

I can feel the beast inside me simmering down, retracting its claws and fangs, giving way to the man who is now left to deal with the repercussions of its violence.

The moon bathes us in a cold, remorseless light as his gaze sweeps over the battlefield, a grim canvas of dark stains and unmoving forms. The night air is thick with the acrid scent of blood and gunpowder, a stark contrast to the quiet that has settled around them.

"More are going to come," Eli says, his voice a gravelly whisper, eyes darting to the trees, expecting shadows to jump out at us any minute.

I nod, the gravity of the situation sinking in. We took lives tonight. Blood coats my tongue. How did things go so wrong that it came to this?

It doesn't matter though. This is how it is, and I will handle anything thrown at us.

But there, at the edge of my consciousness, a flicker of light pulls at me. A beacon in the darkness, calling me home.

Goldie.

Fear and concern for her crashes over me in a tidal wave, momentarily drowning the grim responsibility that comes with protecting my own.

"You guys handle this," I give the order while already on the move, "I've got to check on her."

JJ nods. "Go, we got this."

I move with hurried grace, a looming figure swallowed by the shadow as I cross the broken boundary that separates Goldie's haven from the chaotic outside world. My heart pounds a frantic beat.

As the front door creaks open, there stands Goldie. Her face pale from what she witnessed. She looks so out of place amidst this chaos, a vision of vulnerability and softness amidst a backdrop of death and destruction.

When I get to her, she reaches out. Fingertips lightly brush over the scratches and bullet wounds on my skin. The gentle caress sends a shiver down my spine, contrasting starkly with the violence I've just experienced.

"Ted," she whispers, her voice trembling.

She called me Ted. Not Tedly, Tedford, or Tedinator. She said my real name with a resigned finality that instantly makes me desperate to have her call me any of those silly, mocking nicknames. I'd rather she call me Teddy bear, as long as she called me *her* Teddy bear.

But the way she's looking at me. . . dread consumes me without a single word.

I want to wrap her in my arms, tell her it'll be okay, and

promise her that I can keep the danger at bay. But deep down, a nagging thought tells me that promises like these are easier made than kept. "Goldie, it will all be okay."

She stares into my eyes, her gaze searching for something. Maybe for reassurance, maybe for a lie she can believe in, or perhaps she wants me to see the same painful truth she already has in her sights.

I open my mouth, desperate to find the words to convince her, to make her see that she's my anchor, my beacon of hope in a life filled with darkness. I scrounge and dig for those words I've done such a poor job of finding. Everything depends on me finding the right words to make this okay. If I don't, I'll lose her.

"Goldie. I told you, I started to tell you before how I don't do relationships and it's because I've never been able to afford to endanger anyone I care about with this." I wave a hand at the carnage. "I wish I could say I can protect you like that, walk away, and make sure I don't get close enough to you, so you don't get caught in the crossfire of my pack's problems."

Though the fight is over, I am still heaving, my words making me feel like I've been running for miles. "But I can't do that. I'm so sorry, but I can't let you go, not for your own safety because for the first time in my life, I've found something, someone who is just for me, and I want to keep you because I'm a selfish bastard and I just don't care anymore."

"You're fucking this up," JJ mutters off from behind me in a tone only meant for me to hear, but Goldie's eyes flit to him for a moment.

Fuck, he's right, I need to be better. I have to or I'll lose her.

"Ted, we can't do this anymore. I can't do this anymore," she says, her voice barely audible.

I can hear the raggedness in her voice, see the tears welling up in her eyes, and I know she's breaking just as surely as I am. I want to reach out, to draw her to me and shield her from the harsh realities that are tearing us apart.

"Since you waved at me from the porch that first day, I knew. I knew you were going to completely set my world on its ear. I tried to deny how I felt about you and keep you far away, even when you kept leaving little gifts and tried to give me that perfect pink cake. You have to know I regret not taking that little cake every single day because it put days in between me getting to know you, stupid wasted days that you still filled with your sunshine by needling me with singing telegrams. The closer I got to you, the more inside your world I was permitted, the more I was able to confirm your heart was as beautiful as I first thought. It has room for everyone you meet, even me. But if I only get to be near you, my world is brighter, peaceful and full of a joy I have never imagined for myself. I want to make you cakes, take care of you, treat you like you deserve and be there for you."

Goldie's face crumples. I said the wrong thing. I don't know what but it was the exact wrong fucking thing.

"Goldie. . . " I start, but she cuts me off.

"I can't be another burden, another responsibility, another person you have to save." The tears flow freely now, and each one feels like a dagger to my heart. "Look at you, carrying the weight of the world, fixing everything for everyone. I can't. . . I won't be another chain holding you down. You can't fix my life and I can't expect someone else to. I don't want any of that."

She's looking at me with clear, decisive eyes. Her words are a sword cleaving through my already fractured armor.

I can feel something within me breaking, a dam giving

way to a flood of emotions that threaten to drown me. The warrior, the protector, the beast—all of them warring within me for dominance as I grapple with the harsh reality of her words.

The beast within me roars in anguish, a primal sound that echoes the torment ripping through my very soul. But beneath the ferocity, the violence that is my second nature, there's a part of me, a part that has known nothing but solitude and the harsh realities of a world soaked in blood and betrayal, that understands.

"I. . . Goldie, please," I stammer, my voice cracking under the strain of the emotions tearing through me. I want to fight, to claw and scratch my way back to her, to hold onto the sliver of light she has brought into my dark world.

The sensation of blood drying on my hands registers in my brain. What am I thinking? I am the beast asking the beauty to stay with him though he's a murderous monster. As I look at her, really look at her, I see a woman who deserves so much more than a life marred by violence and uncertainty.

With a ragged breath, I nod.

"I understand. I won't bother you anymore."

As she disappears back into the house, a distance between us stretches out, a chasm that threatens to swallow me whole.

I feel like I'm imploding, a black hole sucking in everything good and beautiful that I had dared to dream could be mine. But it's done because that's what she wants, what she needs.

I'm not right for her.

CHAPTER 39
YOU HAVE MY TINY LITTLE KNOB

TED

"I'm sorry, bro," Eli says, setting a hand on my shoulder. The only light in the kitchen is from the hood over the stove. Everything else is draped in darkness which feels fitting as I sit at my kitchen table pouring out another four fingers of bourbon. I've already drained half the bottle, hoping for... what?

To forget? To numb myself?

None of it's working. The only thing I've accomplished is I've cemented I feel like absolute fae shit.

I jerk, shrugging off Eli's hand. "Don't touch me. This is all your fault."

My little brother backs away, rubbing a hand across his shaved head in that patent awe-shucks way. I'd given him leniency before, so many times I can't even count now.

"If I didn't have to clean up your mess, I wouldn't have—"

So many things. Put Goldie in danger, killed people, sacrificed everything I wanted for myself.

"I know," he says quietly, eyes on the tile floor.

"Do you know how close I am to exiling you from this pack," I threaten in a low voice.

"Whoa," comes JJ's placating voice, as he strides in. "Let's not be hasty here. I know emotions are high and we've had a bit to drink." He studies the bottle. "Okay, a lot to drink. But we are still a family."

A humorless laugh escapes me. "Are we?"

"Of course, we are," JJ says, frowning.

I shake my head. "Goldie was right. I spent so much time telling her she needed to stop people-pleasing but that's all I do with you two jokers. I cater to you even if it breaks my back, and you could fucking care less. Just because I people-please two specific people instead of the public at large, it doesn't make me or the situation any better."

Maybe I did find clarity in a bottle. Or it's Goldie's effect on me. She imprinted on me in places I know will forever be branded by her.

"You say we are a family, but do families do this to each other?" I ask. "Do they put all their burdens on one family member every chance they get? Refusing to take an ounce of fucking responsibility for their own actions because hey, who the fuck cares about what Ted wants? He's always done the right thing. He'll always bail you out of a bad situation. Even if it means humiliating women or taking out a second mortgage to pay for a bad hand of cards."

JJ's face contorts in either denial or anger. "Hey, that's not what we do—"

"Stop JJ." Eli sighs. "You know he's right. After Ma died, we took it as an excuse to never grow up because Ted took care of us."

"Well *you* might," JJ protests while crossing his arms over his chest.

"Because dropping women disrespectfully into Ted's lap so you can whore your way around town without any emotional consequences is incredibly mature," Eli shoots back.

Eli's concise way of calling not just himself but JJ out keeps me from reaching for the glass again.

"I don't know about you," Eli says, still speaking to JJ, "But I'm sick of being a fuck up. I'm so sick of my own bull-shit and I'm over it."

JJ's expression is uncharacteristically somber as he takes in what Eli says. Then he side-eyes me. I take that opportunity to lift the glass to my lips again without breaking eye contact.

"Yeah, okay, you may have a point," JJ reluctantly agrees as he shoves his hands in his pockets.

"You want to fix this?" I ask Eli, standing up, but using the table to steady me. "There is a way for you to make this up to me."

When I give him his mission, he shakes his head and says, "I'm not running, Ted. Grimes, the man I owe money too, he's going to come for us."

"You aren't running." I'm sobering up by the minute. "You're making it up to me," I stress again. "As far as Grimes goes, I'll handle him. Eddie went off the rails when Goldie hit him with her powers, but the second Grimes sent those hitmen to our house, the rules changed." I look at JJ, "But I'll need some of your expertise."

JJ gives me a curt nod. "You have my sword."

Eli frowns. "I'm not saying you have my bow, I'm not a nerd like you. I don't get that Lord of the Rings shit no matter how many times you make us watch it."

327

"Then," JJ counters, "You can say 'you have my tiny little knob.'"

Eli jumps up, throwing an arm around JJ's neck, putting him in a headlock. As they wrestle into the living room, I cross over to the sink and pour out the rest of my drink.

I don't know how this road leads to Goldie exactly, but I know it leads to me leading my own life on my terms, and my terms unequivocally include Goldie in it.

CHAPTER 40

SPECIAL DELIVERY

GOLDIE

Days go by. No word from Ted or Rap, and Cinder barely deigns to respond to my texts, simply saying she's busy but she'll call soon.

I know what that means.

The loss of my best friend cuts into me like a knife. Visions of Cinder and Snow going over what I'd done in disgusting detail, maybe even calling Red over to tell her what I'd done.

But Red hasn't treated me like that. When I wouldn't answer her calls, she left messages that her and Brexley were worried about me and trying to find out the thing about a siren's tears because they may be a key to helping me control my power and she'd be in touch.

I wander through the house like a ghost, looking on projects I can't bring myself to pick up again. How many days before Rap gets the time to tell me I'm fired because I'm too much of a disruption at the Poison Apple? Though my stalker is gone, I keep the crystals by the door. I'm not sure if it's to keep people out or a reminder to keep myself in.

My reality shows are on constantly, blaring loudly as if I could get them to drown out my own thoughts and fears that pull me deeper down into the dark place.

Ted's truck has been conspicuously absent the last couple days though I do my best not to notice.

When I finally get up the supreme effort it takes to leave the house and check the mailbox, I'm halfway there when I catch sight of Eli's jeep driving up. But instead of veering over to Ted's driveway, he turns into mine.

I brace myself for whatever new problem might be rolling up to my doorstep now. He unfolds himself from the driver's seat, a hand rubbing over his head in a sheepish manner.

"Hey Goldie, uh, I brought you something. I hope it makes up for the trouble I've caused." As Eli speaks, he rounds the car to the passenger side and opens the door. Someone gets out and I instantly recognize the blonde bob though my brain doesn't believe what I'm seeing.

"What? What is this?" I ask, my mouth flapping like a fish out of water.

Mom walks toward me with her arms stretched out and a wide smile. I practically fall down the steps before I end up in her arms, squeezing the bageezus out of her and inhaling the familiar floral perfume that's her favorite.

I stare at Eli over her shoulder, still not letting her go. "What are you doing here, Mom?"

Eli pulls out her suitcase from the back of his jeep.

She holds me just as tight. "This young man showed up at the house and said his brother sent him on a quest of redemption which involved getting me to you because you were having such a hard time."

"Where should I put these, Mrs. Locke?" Eli asks.

I'm forced to release my mom when she wrenches around to face him. "Eli, as I told you at the fifty mile mark, you don't need to call me Mrs. Locke. I'm just Sabrina."

He blushes and ducks his head before looking at me. "The primary bedroom, please," I say, still in a daze. Eli grabs the bags and heads into the house. The crystals don't bar his entry, since I put them away in a drawer. My stalker is dead, no need to waste magic.

"He's a sweet boy," Mom says to me in a hushed voice. "Doesn't have any parents so he's gone a bit astray, but we've had a good long talk the last two days as we traversed the country. I don't think he realized how much he's been trying to fill those empty parts of himself with gambling. He really misses his mother, poor dear. When he drives me back to Iowa, he's going to stick around. I called your father and he's already set up a job for Eli and talked to Pastor Jim about some counseling with the young man."

Then threading her arm through mine, she leads me up to the porch. "But let's talk about you. I think you've been leaving a lot out of the last couple weekly calls. You have a lot to catch me up on."

Hours later after Eli left, I spilled everything to my mom. Everything from Eddie stalking me to Ted and his brothers being fae.

My mom waved a hand and said she wrenched the bear shifter thing out of Eli by the time they hit Illinois.

Of course, she did.

We round almost every topic, including the horrible repeat of history with Madison, now with Cinder and how she only sends me short, clipped messages claiming she's too busy to talk. And we end on the house and how it's been more than I can handle. That with my obsessive nature, I'm not stable, just like my aunt. Even after so many marriages, she died alone, after abandoning her house to pursue all kinds of ventures that never stuck. I don't want to end up like that, and I'm moments from saying I want to move back home to Iowa. Where life is safe and stable.

"Goldie, baby, I realize I may have spoken poorly of Astrid in a way that affected you poorly. And if I'm being brutally honest with myself, I was always jealous of her. The way she followed her passions with abandon, the way she fell in love so freely. Maybe I did try to temper your admiration for her because I didn't want you to turn out the same way. I viewed her life as fractured and rocky."

A tear slips from her eye that she hurriedly wipes away. "It was the last time we spoke. We were in a screaming match that started over, I don't even know what. I vividly remembering yelling that she was insecure if she had to keep finding people, places, and ventures to fill her up. Astrid became speechless as she looked at me with pity that made me feel so dirty and small." Mom's hands closed into little balls. "She said that she did what she did not because she was empty, but because she was so full of love for herself that she let herself grow and expand in whatever way she needed in whatever time she needed. Then she said a lot of ugly things about me being miserable and jealous of her life because I didn't allow myself to go after my dreams."

That took me aback. "Is that true?" A terrible blanket of guilt fell over me as I thought about that. My parents were. . . my parents. I hadn't given consideration to what their dreams or ambitions were, they just. . . were.

I dug into everyone else for their innermost desires because I wanted to secure their affections, but I knew my parents loved me no matter what, so I didn't have to put as much effort in.

"She was both right and wrong. There are things I did hold myself back from doing at times, but what she couldn't understand is that I was living my dreams. Watching you and Noah grow up, raising a family, being part of my community with your father, those are my dreams. But Astrid and I, our dreams were so completely different we couldn't understand each other. The irony is we desperately wanted to connect with each other, which is why we kept getting so frustrated and ended up in so many knock down drag out fights. We simply didn't have the common ground to love each other the way we wanted." Tears freely flowed. "Maybe. . . " she hiccupped over a sob and I instantly pulled her in for a hug, feeling her pain as if it were my own. "Maybe if our common ground had been that we respected our differences and wanted the best for each other even if it looked different from our own vision of success, we could have built a relationship on that soil."

"Oh Mom," I soothed while squeezing her tight.

She returned the embrace before breaking away but held my arms as if to grab my attention. "You are more like Astrid than you were ever like me. You were meant to seek out new experiences and be admired by people from all over. I agree with your friends that this power is part of you, magic cookies or not."

"Maybe. . . I'm like both of you and Astrid. I love exploring different interests and meeting people, but I also need a solid place to land." Ted springs to mind as soon as I say it.

She pushes curls behind one of my ears. "Then you follow your heart. Try everything you want for as long or as little as you like until this world is just right for you. You want to spend your money on clothes that make you feel like a goddess, you do it. You want to play with makeup, you play away baby. You love working at a bar, talking to people, or starting a new business venture, you do that. You fall for a special man who knows when a girl needs her mother..."

"Mom," I cut off with an embarrassed groan.

Her hands raise in surrender. "I'm just saying, there is all this pressure in your twenties to figure out what you should be."

"You were married at eighteen," I point out.

"Yes, well I'm not blind. I see how this world is coming down on people your age for not having things figured out, and how could you? There is so much more to try and learn. I mean you got powers mere weeks ago, which is still blowing my noodle, but think how long it takes for an infant to walk, to talk. Give yourself grace, baby and remember you have a good heart. The rest is details."

Now I'm crying. "Did I ever tell you that you're the best mom in the whole world?"

We embrace and I forget about Lysander, about my problems with Cinder, and the possibility that gangsters might come down on me.

CHAPTER 41
SECOND CHANCE CAKE

TED

Goldie's mom got in yesterday, Eli assured me. So I sit in my house and wait. Either for Goldie or for the cops to come and get me.

Sitting on my porch, the sky is violent streaks of bright orange from the setting sun. I sip my beer trying to soak in the feeling of a hard day's work at the sites today. But truthfully, I'm about to claw out of my own skin to keep from going to her. To keep from knocking down her door and demanding she take me back.

But Goldie's spending time with her mother. I know she's scared of her powers, and she needs a break, so I'll give her one, even if it's killing me inside.

Eventually, I'll go to her and explain that she's not in danger anymore. Not from Eli's enemies anyway.

I tried to do it the honorable way, walking right into Grimes' own office with his goons, and standing there in good faith. I offered a truce and a payment plan for Eli's debts. When he laughed in my face, and said I had twenty-four hours to turn my brother in before he killed me and everyone I loved, he dug his own grave.

With JJ's technological assistance, I was able to corner Grimes. I shifted and struck him down so fast no one saw it coming. I took out his goons too. When the massacre hit the media, the cops claimed not to know who took out the notorious crime boss. They suspected it was a power play from another family.

That didn't mean they couldn't figure it out. Didn't mean the cops wouldn't show up and put me in cuffs, but it had been two days, and it was seeming less and less likely they would figure it out.

Maybe something hardened in me the day I killed Eddie. But I knew the truth. Goldie is pack. She's my mate and I'll do anything to keep her safe without regret or remorse. Even if she stays in the house, resolute to keep me out of her life, she's close enough that I can work my way into her life over time.

When I walk inside the house, dropping my beer bottle in the recycling bin, Eli passes by. "Hey, there was a package on the porch, I put it on the table."

I confirm with a glance, a white box with no label on it.

"You going somewhere?" I ask, noting Eli is wearing one of my button up shirts. It's a little large on him, but he looks respectable.

He looks down at his shirt and smiles as red tinges his cheeks. "Uh yeah, I was hoping you wouldn't mind. I am taking Mrs. Locke, er, Sabrina to dinner to thank her in advance for setting up some opportunities in Iowa for me. She also had a desire to see a bit of Boston and since Goldie is still under voluntary house arrest, I thought I'd take Sabrina out for a couple hours."

I study my younger brother for a moment. "You look good."

"Thanks," he says. "And uh. . . thank you."

The second one is for everything I've ever done for him. I nod, accepting his gratitude and he's out the door.

Walking over to the box, I lift the lid and find a pink, heart-shaped cake. My heart skips a beat before somersaulting over itself.

This time I won't make the same mistake. Any heart Goldie gives me, I'll gladly take.

CHAPTER 42

THE CAT IN THE HEN HOUSE

GOLDIE

When I regain my senses, I find myself bound, a captive in my own kitchen.

What the hell happened? Last I remember, Mom was heading out for dinner with Eli, while I prepared to pull some wallpaper off one of the many bedrooms.

But now I'm tied to a chair, with a throbbing headache. My heart hammers frantically as I assess the surroundings. I'm in my kitchen. But more surprising and unsettling is Ted sits across from me, tied to a chair. His head hangs forward onto his chest. He's unconscious.

"Ted," I call out in a panic. "Tedly, wake up." It takes a couple more shouts before his head lolls to the side. He lifts his head like it is almost too heavy to do so. Those beautiful stormy eyes are dull and bloodshot.

"Oh good, everyone's awake," someone announces. I

don't want to believe it, but the familiar voice confirms the cold reality before he steps in front of me.

"Lysander?" I choke out, incredulous.

Lysander circles me like a predator toying with prey, his movements smooth and sinister. A cruel smile twists his face. A perverse ecstasy seems to overtake him at the sound of his name from my lips. "Heavenly," he murmurs, his pleasure almost obscene in its intensity.

"What the fuck, Lysander?" My words come out a ragged whisper, but my gut tells me what I already know.

He's the stalker. He's the shadow in my house, leaving presents, touching my underwear, going through my diary and faelords know what else. But how? He's human and it was a shadow in my house.

I thought he'd only had eyes for Cinder. Did I enchant him too? Did I ruin my best friend's chance for romantic happiness? I think I'm going to be sick.

A grotesque desire glints in his eyes as he reaches out to stroke my face. I recoil.

"You can't do this. Not to Cinder. She deserves better."

Lysander drops to his knees at my side, hands sliding up my thighs making my brain explode with panic all over again. I don't want him to touch me. It's not for me. He's for Cinder.

"Cinder is nothing but a dirty smudge in the wake of your blazing glory, Goldie. Your intricacies and depth are like an artist's final masterpiece, a unique blend of colors that I have come to appreciate and desire. Her? She's merely a failed draft, discarded on the path to true brilliance." He whispers in reverent awe, as if I am the most divine piece of art he's ever beheld. It's nonsense, all of it.

"Don't say that," I hiss in a harsh whisper. "She's so much better than me. A true friend who is loyal, she's hardworking, and the toughest girl I know. You can't talk about her like that." Even as I speak it feels like someone has sucked all the air out of my lungs. This can't be happening.

Lysander reaches up to stroke my cheek. I jerk away, but he grabs my chin, forcing me to look at him. "You are more precious than you know. We belong together, Goldie. I can't believe I ever saw anything in your friend when you were standing right there. I'm so sorry it took me so long to see the truth. To see you."

"Let me guess," I hazard. "You've felt this way for three weeks." The exact time my magic manifested. Is it possible my magic had been sinking into his bones, poisoning him against my friend from the marrow outward in a quiet yet deadly way?

The idea of her finding out what I'd done to her makes me wild with fear.

Lysander stands, still holding my chin to make sure my eyes are trained on him. "I've felt this way since I realized you were special."

Ted groans faintly.

"What did you do to him?" I demand.

Lysander lets out a hum of dissatisfaction before releasing my chin and crossing to Ted's side.

Lysander claps a hand on Ted's shoulder. The bear shifter lets out a groan. "I think our werebear friend needed to chill out, so I gave him a little something to make him more. . . subdued. I concocted a perfect little pink heart cake, adding a secret ingredient. Something to make the big bear sleepy."

That sonofabitch.

Lysander flicked Ted's head, causing Ted's head to roll the opposite way with a groan.

"Let him go," I demand. As soon as it's out of my mouth I realize how stupid it sounds. Why would he listen to me?

Lysander tilts his head toward Ted as if considering the question before looking back at me. "No, I don't think I'll be doing that. Though noble to ask for his freedom before your own."

"What do you want, Lysander?" I'm afraid to ask the question, but it may be the only key to getting Ted and me out of here. Or maybe one of us.

He grins. His lips nearly split his face, showing an exaggerated grin that is the stuff of nightmares. My nightmares. It's the smile from the camera. His eyes widen, glowing a luminous green, the pupils shrinking until they are thin vertical slits like a cat's. He shimmers out of view, leaving a dark smudge behind his disembodied eyes and grin.

"What the hell are you?" I whisper, terror rioting up and down my body in a cacophony of icy chills.

The grin disappears and its regular old Lysander again. He pouts at me and tsks. "Never took you for a racist, Goldie. Especially not when you have clearly fucked on the fae side." The last comment accompanies a sneer he sends in Ted's direction.

Ted's head is still trying to raise up as he shifts in the seat. He's fighting for consciousness against whatever Lysander gave him.

Lysander opens his arms. "I'm a cheshire."

Rare feline humanoids.

"So you can turn into shadows and have a killer grin?" I shoot at him.

He shrugs one shoulder. "Cats can slink in darkness better than anyone. Being invisible has its perks." He frowns. "But not in the last month. Not when I've so desperately wanted to be near you. It's like being drawn to

342

the most exquisite piece of art, finding myself ensnared by your complex layers and hues, yearning to delve deeper into the enigma that is you. My pursuits are those of a devoted art connoisseur, relentless in my desire to possess and cherish perfection.

I pause, digesting this new bit of information. Cheshires are a fae race, which means he should be immune to my magic. "So you aren't under my enchantment."

Lysander circles behind me, tangling his fingers in my hair before he drops his nose in and inhales deeply. Revulsion riots inside me, fighting for dominance with pure terror.

"I wouldn't say that," he murmurs, walking past me.

I pretend to listen while testing my restraints, hoping to find a weak point, or see if I can tug any knots free with my fingers. I untangle jewelry all the time. This can't be that different.

"Not with all those idiots panting over you. I knew before any of them that you were special. I always have. It just took me a little longer to realize why. But I watched you." Lysander creeps closer, a glazed look in his eye I recognize as obsession. It makes my stomach roil and panic explode at the front of my mind. I tug harder at the restraints, but they won't give.

"I watched you. The effect you have on men has always been a kind of magic, Goldie, but then I realized the night of the proposal, the fight, I realized you were so much more than I could have guessed. You were literal magic. A siren hiding in plain sight."

I don't bother to correct him. That I was human until very recently.

"Not only am I enraptured by your rare brand of magic, but you achieve what all artists dream of."

Lysander snaps his teeth next to my ear, causing me to flinch.

"I don't understand," I say. "You're fae. I should have no effect on you."

Lysander strokes a finger that is far too soft along my cheek. I squirm but there is no getting away. He could do anything to me like this.

"Oh Goldie," he says in a rough whisper. "You affect me more than you can know." Then he leans over me, and his wet tongue drags up the side of my face. I squirm harder, trying to get away from the wet tongue that is also surprisingly rough. A cat's tongue.

Fury blazes in Ted's eyes when Lysander licks me, his jaw clenching as he struggles against his restraints. "Get the fuck away from her," he growls.

Lysander straightens and turns. Ted's eyes fight to stay open as he focuses that cerulean storm on Lysander. It promises violence and bloodshed, and unlike with Lawrence, I would let him in a heartbeat.

Independence is overrated when tied to a chair.

"Oh, our little Teddy bear has awoken."

It was funny when I said it, but it sickens me to hear Lysander taunt Ted. If I get free I am going to kick his ass.

"Let him go, he has nothing to do with you and me," I plead again. Maybe if I focus on whatever deluded relationship Lysander has created in his mind between us.

Lysander turns toward me, his face somber. "You're right. He doesn't. But he has two excellent purposes for being, I have discovered. The first being that with him near, your powers are dampened and you can't activate that tricky second power that took me a long time to figure out." He raises an eyebrow and smiles as if we are flirting. Ugh.

But he's right. With Ted, I have no way of blipping out of here to safety.

Even in his inebriated state, Ted looks stricken, his jaw tensing and muscles flexing. He's still too weak.

"And the second purpose?"

Lysander taps my nose with his finger. "That will become clear shortly."

"Why didn't you just come to me outright? Why all the sneaking around?"

"Because Goldie, if I'm going to be the last man in your life, I need to know everything about you. I needed to be worthy. I needed to claw up every last one of your hopes and dreams so I could deliver them to you on a golden platter."

"Did you ever even care for Cinder?"

"Sure, I did. At first, she struck me as quite unique. She seemed to carry mystery in those violet eyes. I wanted to possess the stories behind her tattoos, and quite frankly, she's a decent fuck."

I hadn't caught up with Cinder recently. I didn't even know that happened. More proof that she has been deliberately driving a wedge between us.

Lysander adjusts his glasses. "Though in hindsight, I'm not sure how much of that is because of her or because of her... unusual accessories."

I don't comment on his crude description of my friend.

He tucks his hands behind his back and bends over at the waist to smile in my face. "I'm speaking of her pierced cunt of course."

"You're disgusting."

"You're not the first piece of art I've pursued, Goldie. There have been two before you, but they couldn't appreciate the depths of my love, my passion. What good is art if it can't be possessed, adored every day, locked away from the prying eyes of the unworthy? That's what kings and emperors do, they enshrine their treasures, keep them close, a testament to their power and impeccable taste. I, Goldie, am no different, with a keen eye for beauty and an insatiable desire to possess it."

Ted's stare bores into Lysander, promising bloody retribution despite his weakened state. Rage simmers beneath the surface.

"This is some toxic masculinity bullshit, Lysander," I counter.

He ignores my comment. "At first, I thought Cinder would be that for me. The living breathing art I could keep for always, capture on film when I needed to, but then there was you. A siren in the midst. Even before your powers came alive, you've been a celestial beacon of light to the dusty, worthless moths attracted by your flame."

Lysander's eyes glint with a sick and twisted affection as he says, "Remember the butterfly I left for you, Goldie? A cherished specimen from my personal collection, forever captured in its moment of perfection, much like the work of a skilled artist freezing a magnificent moment on canvas. It's a preview, my dear, a glimpse of the grandiose gallery of exquisite art I intend to build, with you as the centerpiece, forever preserved in your youthful grace and beauty, an everlasting expression of art, encased and immortalized under my watchful eye, like a rare, priceless artwork in the hallowed halls of a museum dedicated to the worship of beauty."

Lysander's words fill me with icy dread. My heart hammers frantically against my ribs as the terrifying reality of my situation sinks in. He's insane, legitimately certifiably insane.

"Goldie, if I possessed you, I'd take care of you. I'd worship you. I'd love you, fully commit the way you always wanted those men to in your past."

"You can't possess me. I'm a person with free will."

"That's where you're wrong." His eyes darken, and without knowing why, I feel as if I dropped ten flights. "You're a siren and after some digging, I learned that drinking a siren's tears allows you to possess their heart.

"What?" This is what Red had been driving at.

"I can possess your body and soul, keep you. I'll be the most auspicious collector with a siren, but I don't need to tell anyone. Every time I come home I will admire and adore you like the precious rare beauty you are."

Ted's muscles flex and bunch as he fights the drugged haze, attempting to break free.

"I'm not crying over you, you psychotic douche nozzle. Good fucking luck drinking my tears.

He tilts his head with a soft smile that scares me. A hand drops onto Ted's shoulder. "That's why he's here."

My stomach drops.

"You care about this nobody, and I can use his flesh as a canvas of pain, a grotesque masterpiece born of anguish and suffering, until you cry your sweet compassionate tears for him. Imagine it, Goldie, a live performance of agony and despair, culminating in the creation of the most visceral art, graced by the tears of its muse. A sight for connoisseurs, a testament to my devotion and your radiant compassion." With that he jabs the knife into Ted's gut.

I scream. Or was that Ted?

The motion is violent but the cut is shallow. Confusion and gratitude mix for a brief moment before Lysander begins to cut through Ted's flesh, carving a curved design.

"No, no, no," I chant, struggling against the ropes.

"Come now, Goldie," Lysander coos even as he jerks the knife out and I see he has cut the letter G into Ted's stomach. "No tears for the neighbor from hell? Maybe you really do hate him after all."

Ted groans and squirms in pain as the knife splits his skin.

I continue to chant useless pleas, begging Lysander to stop. Hot needles stab at the backs of my eyes causing them to well with tears.

"Don't do it," Ted commands through gritted teeth. "Don't let him have you, Goldie."

But his words do nothing to keep the tears from slipping over my lashes.

He carves an 'O' in Ted's chest before grabbing a tiny cup and kneeling at my side.

"Goldie," he whispers as he collects my tears with a tiny cup. "You are the most beautiful creature in this world, and I will spend my days in our home gazing upon you in awe and reverence for the rest of our days."

It's some kind of perverse proposal, but I don't want it.

Something builds in me, something I'd been suppressing for far too long. A power I never let myself take control of, but I'd tasted it once.

As Lysander brings the cup to his lips, I say, "No."

He pauses. "What?"

"No," I say it louder this time. I repeat myself, the word coming out clear as a damn bell. I pull something up from inside me, a voice I'd ignored for all my life. The one that puts me first, the one that knows when to tell people to fuck right off because I don't need their negativity in my space. It's what I should have said to Madison and all her friends.

No, I don't accept your treatment, I don't accept your

view of me. I know who the fuck I am and I do not require your approval.

I'd only lived parallel to this doctrine when my parents and Astrid help me come alive again to pursue my interests whether it was fashion, different college majors, or different men trying to find the perfect one for me. But in the background was this gripping fear that I still needed the approval of those around me, that if I didn't work my ass off to earn it someone could come along and wipe me off the face of the earth.

I refuse to put his feelings first. Ted knew, he pointed out how I never could just say no and stand behind that. I've been too busy making everyone more important than the one who matters most, me.

But now that I faced that very thing, I decided I refused to be a slave to Lysander's approval. He would not have my heart because I refuse to give it.

"No, you can't have my heart, you sick fuck. You don't deserve it and I won't allow it."

Lysander holds my gaze a moment before he tips the cup back.

CHAPTER 43
NO MEANS NO

TED

"**N**o," I cry out, but I'm too late. I want to scream, rage, let the darkness inside me off its leash so I can maul him to death. Put her back to rights. But drugs still course through my system, weakening me.

Goldie blinks at Lysander.

I realize I'm holding my breath until a glazed look comes over her face and she smiles at Lysander. Not just a smile, she glows at him in that way she's only ever done for me.

Lysander sighs in contentment.

The beast shreds my hearts with his claws, leaving nothing of me left behind. If there is no Goldie, there is no me.

There's no way Lysander is going to let me go. He's going to get rid of me then lock Goldie in a closet somewhere so he can admire her like a private treasure.

Then Goldie says in a dreamy, far-off voice, "What would make you happy, my everything?"

A strange half giggle, half squeal comes out of Lysander as if he's positively giddy to have gotten what he wanted.

"To gaze upon you is heaven already," he finally says.

"Oh okay, I'll just sit here then," she says, settling into her seat and casting a hundred watt smile at him.

Something vibrates and I realize it's Lysander's phone. He removes it from his back pocket, glancing at it only a moment before shoving it away again. His tone is hurried as he unties her ropes. "No, not here. I want you to come with me." He guides her to her feet, and she obeys like a life-sized doll.

I have to stop him. I have to kill him. He claims to want to keep her as a living art piece but who knows what other depraved things he would do given the chance and complete control of her body and will.

No, I have to fight this. Digging down, I call forth that darkness inside me. Focusing past the fuzzy distracting unwanted warmth of the drugs pumping through my system, I call to the animal within. I used it to kill Eddie, Grimes and his men, and I'd use it to fix this too. I had to save Goldie, if I didn't, no one would.

Lysander grabs the bloody knife and turns toward me. "Thanks for your help, but I need to make this quick." He takes one step toward me when a thunk hits the air.

Lysander's eyes squint before he drops to the ground. Behind him, Goldie flips one of my wrenches in her hands. "Have I mentioned I'm really into having all your tools spread around my house? It's pretty hot."

The vacant glazed look in her eyes has been erased.

"You—you're you," I stutter.

"Excuse you," she says, coming over to untie my ropes. "You may only refer to me as blondie and/or cream puff."

The second I'm free, I pull her into my arms. I don't give a fuck I'm bleeding all over her clothes... again.

I hold her to me so tight I'm probably suffocating her but she doesn't protest. She simply holds me back, just as tight.

I shake my head not understanding. "I couldn't save you. I was going to rip him limb from limb until it released you from the spell."

"But you did save me." she says. "Without you I never would have found that power within me. In loving me, for exactly what I am, you empowered me to be all I can be. Wait... that's an Army slogan."

"I don't understand. How, how did it not work?" I ask, still not quite believing Goldie is okay.

She draws back enough to smile up at me. "I did what you suggested. I said no."

"What?" My brain is still split between panic and the immense relief of holding Goldie.

"Lawrence was my clue. He was the only one I flat out said no too and he dropped off, which normal Lawrence still usually wouldn't take the memo much less enchanted Lawrence. I figured that the power of my no, my boundary made all the difference. These powers have been getting the best of me for a while, but I think I'm finally keying on how to control them."

"Powers or not, you can't get rid of me, Goldie," I say, my voice hoarse. "We sorted Eli's problems out. No one will come for you, I promise you this."

Her hands slip around my neck bringing me down for a kiss. It's full of longing and need as we find solace in each other.

I rest my forehead against hers once we break apart.

"Please say I can have you in my bed again. In my life? Forever. I love you, Goldie. I'll do anything to be with you."

"Like let me call you Teddy Bear in front of other people?" she chirps.

My head falls back as I shut my eyes. "A man has limits, Goldie."

She laughs before it dies off, her gaze boring into mine. "I love you too, Tedford."

I kiss her again, fiercely, possessively and she meets my every bit of fervor with her own.

Lysander groans, so I set a foot on his head in case he manages to fully wake up and gets the urge to get off the ground.

"Don't squish his head," she says into my chest.

"Why not?" I ask, leaning back slightly so I can look in her eyes and she can breathe.

"Cinder," is all she says. I instantly understand. It's not that he doesn't deserve it, it's that he is a key link between her and Cinder and she may need him alive to work things out.

As if on cue, Cinder, Red, and Brexley run into the house, with Snow in tow.

CHAPTER 44

I LOVE YOU, I KNOW

GOLDIE

Taking one look at the scene, Cinder runs to me, throwing her arms around me. "Oh thank the faelords, I thought he might have hurt you. I would never be okay again if something happened to you."

Brexley and Ted make quick work of tying up Lysander and discuss in hushed tones what they plan to do with him. Fae business is not usually settled by police forces, so I don't know what they have planned but I've no doubt it will put my little psycho stalker out of commission.

I am still in shock, wrapped up in Cinder's arms. But I don't miss the opportunity to squeeze her just as tight.

"I thought you hated me," I choke out.

"Oh faefucks, Goldie, no. I could never," she says, pulling back so she can peer at my face.

"You didn't know he was stalking me, you just saw your love interest and me. . . " I trail off when it becomes too painful to speak.

One corner of Cinder's mouth quirks up even as

compassion fills her eyes. "First off," she holds up a finger, "even if I hadn't figured out you were a goner for the sinister brawny man over there, I know you would never do that to me. Number two," she raises another finger, "I was attracted to him, sure, but I wasn't *in love* with him. In an alternate universe without Ted where Lysander isn't a raging psycho—half cat, half douche—if you developed feelings for each other I wouldn't get in the way. I know you staunchly try to adhere to the girl code, but things aren't always that black and white. And thirdly, I have been so worried about you." Her eyes turn serious and intense. "You are a beautiful loving person and having that twisted around on you in such an ugly way is completely unfair. So please tell your subconscious fears to kindly fuck off."

I hug her so tight, Cinder eventually gasps out that she can't breathe. Still, I don't let go.

When she finally wriggles away, she dramatically sucks in deep gulps of air. Getting a hold of that, she says, "He'd been weird the last couple weeks and after I saw him with you, I looked back and thought about our conversations. The way he subtly kept bringing the conversation around to you until I shared things about Ted, about your ex. Goldie, I gave him personal information he used against you, like your address for faefucks sake. But I didn't want to jump to conclusions or panic you, so I slipped away to do my own background work on him with the help of Rap and Brexley. I see now how I must have sent you into an absolute panic spiral, thinking I must have hated you where I thought I was sparing you unnecessary panic."

This wasn't middle school. I didn't lose my best friend. Cinder saw me for me and understood I valued our friendship above everything. Relief spreads through me, nearly bringing me to my knees.

Mom and Eli come in shortly after. My friends explain they found some records on Lysander stalking some girls in his past, and went personally to interview the last one. It was difficult to find her, Brexley explained, because she moved cities and changed her name and number when the restraining order didn't work.

That's when Rap stepped in and used some connections to find out where she lives. Apparently, she doesn't hold any of my power problems against me and was only concerned about my safety and dedicated to helping get me in a safe spot. And when Snow caught onto the whole plot, she insisted to Cinder she come along too.

Snow adamantly claims I saved her from a fate worse than death.

I assure her she probably would have been fine on honey packets for a couple days before some other good luck came her way. Snow stares at me in that icy way before throwing her arms around me and squeezing me until my lungs almost popped. I love it.

Once they explained what they suspected, Lysander's ex spilled everything— how obsessive Lysander was when they were dating until she basically abandoned her old life to get away from him. It was only after talking to her did my friends truly realize how dangerous he was.

As soon as they found out, they headed straight to my house to tell me. When he'd checked his messages, it had been Cinder calling him out for his stalking behavior and warning him to stay away from me.

All through this, Mom forces Ted to sit while she breaks out a first aid kit and fusses over him like he's both the biggest knight in shining armor and the sweetest baby boy she's ever known.

The dazed look on his face tells me he doesn't know

what to do with all this motherly attention, but the curve at the corner of his lips and the blush on his cheeks tells me he absolutely loves it.

Eli seems to get a little jealous after a while, and starts engaging my mom in conversation, but it's really all over when JJ steps in the house. He seduces my mother—not sexually, of course—and soaks up her doting behaviors like a puppy suckling at a teat.

On second thought, that metaphor is disgusting.

Brexley hauls Lysander away, mentioning he knows some fae enforcers who will help him teach Lysander a lesson in a place where he won't bother anyone for a very long time.

I'm about to ask questions when Red stops me. "Yeah, I wouldn't. You probably don't want to know."

After Mom finishes with Ted and lets him up, he crosses over to me.

"I love you, Goldie," he says again.

"Oh Tedford," I say, pinching his cheek. "Who doesn't?"

He growls and nips at my throat in a playful way that makes me laugh. I may have dated a lot and seen romance in all the wrong places, but this bear shifter is just right for me.

EPILOGUE

GOLDIE

My desire to be admired and loved isn't so bad, it turns out. I went back to my old therapist who has some experience in psychology and magic. My fears that being so well loved will only make people hate me turned out to be a self-fulfilling prophecy. In middle school, I learned to subconsciously punish myself for wanting to be liked, when it's a perfectly normal thing to want to be loved and admired. I learned that if I ever got that level of admiration and love, it would destroy my friendships.

So we've been working on building my faith in the present with my new friends who aren't immature or twelve. I'm also learning it's okay to trust myself, though Ted did a lot of groundwork there, encouraging me to set boundaries according to what works for me. Therapy is a whole jumbled mess of complexes where pulling the knot on one string drags out three more.

With guidance from my therapist and Red, I've also

learned how to use my magic to gently weave it around people, so they feel comfortable around me. At the bar, it gives me an opportunity to help people who try to drown their sorrows in booze.

Now I can blip away when I want to, though I only do it if I want to try to scare Ted at his house. It rarely works and he always makes the most of my surprise appearances.

Eli went back with my mom to Iowa and claims to be doing much better. Apparently, a couple months won't hurt their pack bond because it is so strong. He can stay in the Midwest as long as they get together regularly.

Eli goes to meetings about his gambling addiction, and says the fresh scenery already makes a big difference. Ted and JJ agreed to go out there for Thanksgiving. In fact, I think they'd go even if I couldn't. She adores them but probably not as much as they love her.

"So now that it's fixed up, what are you going to do with her?" Ted asks, enclosing his arms around my waist where we stare up at the beautifully revived Victorian. The windows shine, the shutters have a fresh coat of paint and I cleaned her from top to bottom. Ted generously threw in a lot of his time to help with some plumbing issues and install some more A/C units so I could be comfortable.

"Have sex with you in every room," I announce boldly.

Ted squeezes me to him harder, dropping his mouth to my ear. "That's not what I meant, but I sure as fuck aren't opposed." A shiver runs through me as his hot breath fans against my ear, bringing all my nerve endings to attention.

Eight bedrooms, nine and a half baths, a refurbished country kitchen and a detached barn. I even did some gardening in the back. The possibilities for this place are endless. It could make a great bed and breakfast, or maybe some kind of foster home or rehabilitation or retirement home. I could get a bunch of roommates or rent the whole thing out. Artists or writers' retreats could be run from here. I could become a wedding planner and turn this into an event space because of the yard. Ted has already heard all these ideas, and I know he'd understand if I still needed more time to decide.

"I'm going to sell it," I finally say. When I turn in his eyes, I see surprise there.

"Really?" he asks.

I nod. "Yeah, this place is big and beautiful and loved back to health but it's too big for me. It's honestly too big an anchor for me."

"Having commitment issues?" A flash of insecurity goes through his eyes.

"Yes, but not about you," I tease, lifting up to my tiptoes to rub my nose against his. He sneaks in a kiss that turns serious until I moan, feeling my blood heat up. Seems like he might be all about christening each room right now. But I pull away because I'm not done. "I don't know what I want to do. My mom was right, there's so much pressure right now for me to figure out what my thing is. But my aunt didn't listen to any of that, and I'm not going to either. I'm just going to take the next step that interests me and feels right, which in this case is going back to school for business."

"For the business of what?" Ted asks.

I shrug, even as I play with the soft hairs at the nape of his neck. "To be determined. But because I have so many interests, maybe I'll have multiple businesses over the coming years. Like maybe I'll open an all-pink bakery." I waggle my eyebrows at him.

"Funny you should say that, but if you sell this place, where are you going to live?" I can feel the tension in his fingers where he holds me.

"Well Snow lives with Cinder now, and with the funds I could probably afford a new pad downtown, but I'll need my expenses to be reasonable so I can pay for my tuition. I was kind of hoping I could convince this guy I live near to let me move in with him."

Ted's eyes light up as his fingers dig into me more adamantly. He looks like a kid who's discovered Santa just visited his house.

"Of course, I'd pay rent and offer to even redecorate some of the rooms in the house." JJ stopped bringing women over, but remodeling those spaces would further the boundaries Ted has with his pack. Plus, I'd love to put my mark on his home to make it ours.

"I think he would like that very much." Ted nods with a lopsided grin. "That reminds me," he says, breaking away from me to run over to his house. He's only gone a few minutes before he comes back with something in his hands. Something pink.

"Is that—?" I can't believe it. Served on a glass plate is a messy pink cake that sort of resembles a heart if you squint your eyes.

"Since you are moving into the neighborhood, Ms. Locke, was it? I thought I'd officially welcome you to the neighborhood and welcome you with this pink heart cake I made myself."

There is no fighting the smile breaking through.

I am capable.

I am enough.

And I am in love with a man who makes me feel that way every day.

Get the bonus epilogue now to read about when Cinder is invited to a ball!

Head to www.hollyroberds.com and check out the bonuses to read!

LOVE THIS BOOK?

Enjoy more by this author
Vivien woke up with no memories and a terrible thirst for blood.

The Grim Reaper must destroy all blood suckers.

The reaper dogs just want to get pets and loves in between fetching the souls for the Afterlife.

Read this COMPLETE trilogy and you'll laugh, you'll cry, you'll absolutely die.

Vegas Immortals: Death & the Last Vampire

*Available on Audio and Kindle Unlimited

WANT A FREE BOOK?

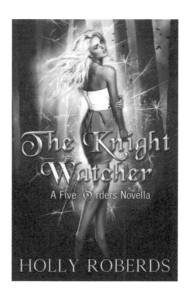

Plus you'll get exclusive sneak peaks, giveaways, fun lil' nuggets, and notifications when new books come out. Woot!

Acknowledgments

First off, a HUGE MASSIVE thank you to my lovely, hell raising assistants Leah Crowell and Tara Volpenhein. For every time, I fired you and you'd say, "See You Next Tuesday" ...for our Tuesday meeting, of course. You are a writer's absolute dream team and I ADORE how we are manifesting big beautiful dreams together! May we keep building our vast empire so we can have more retreats with fancy dinners and raunchy shows! Also, politely...get wrecked.

This has been one of the hardest years of writing for me, so a big thank you to l'husbun who has been unflinching supportive through everything. You solve problems, you don't make them. You love me unconditionally in a way that allows me to grow and expand, and this is a gift I absolutely never take for granted.

Thanks to my online writing group – Ellie Pond, Sarah Urquhart, C.S. Berry, Ivy Nelson, Danielle Romero, Sara Massery, Lucy Smoke, and to all your pets and children that keep me wildly entertained. My gawd, what a bunch of weirdos we are! But boy have we slogged and typed our way through so many books together! I can't imagine working without you guys now. Even with all the disturbing child rearing information you keep pressing upon me...gross.

Thank you to my brainstorming group, Kim Keane, Brooke Davis, and Kimberly Kennedy who are always up to the challenge I pose every month "plot my book, k thanx." You all feed my soul and my creativity in such unexpected amazing ways.

To my author friends Aidy Award, M. Guida, Shannon, Shannon McLaughlin, Nicole Hall, Helen Hardt, and Candice Bundy. You've shared information and support over the years and that has truly turned me into the writer I am today.

To my none writer friends – Nicole, Bree, and my mom Stacy. You deal with my constant fears and worries of 'am I enough,' 'are my stories good enough for the readers I desperately want to make happy and feel good,' and remind me to center myself, that it is all working out for me, and that I am loved no matter what I produce or don't produce.

To my editor Theresa Paolo, goddammit, I hate how you make me a better writer with your notes, though every time I still expect you to return the book with a "it's all perfect, good job!" You are in fact, making me a better writer... against my will. So, thank you.

Thank you, Haley, for your proofing expertise and excellent attention to detail! I feel safe with you. Like a dog wearing a weighted thunderstorm jacket. Keep up the good work. Also...I probably should have had you proof this.

To my reader fans, you are amazing and my appreciation and delight that you keep reading my stories have no depth. I'm keeping you all. No take backs.

Raise Hell.

Read Books.

A Letter from the Author

Dear Reader,

Thank you for reading!

This has been one of the most difficult books I've written because I so wanted Goldie to match Red's energy – mainly the darkness – but Goldie had a different story to tell with a different vibe. No matter how I tried to jerk the wheel to move it in that direction, the story had other plans. I hope you could go with the flow and enjoy this story as well, though Cinder and Rap will not be so light hearted, I'm sure.

Loved this book? Consider leaving a review as it helps other readers discover my books.

And never let it be said I don't listen to my readers. You want Snow, Cinder, or Rap's story? Let me know! And I'm likely to oblige. PBS was right about the dangers of peer pressure.

Want to make sure you never miss a release or any bonus content I have coming down the pipeline?

Make sure to join Holly's Hotspot, my newsletter, and I'll send you a FREE ebook right away!

You can also find me on my website www.hollyroberd s.com and I hang out on social media.

Instagram: http://instagram.com/authorhollyroberds

Facebook: www.facebook.com/hollyroberdsauthorpage/

And closest to my black heart is my reader fan group, Holly's Hellions. Become a Hellion. Raise Hell. www.face book.com/groups/hollyshellions/

Cheers!

Holly Roberds

ABOUT THE AUTHOR

Holly started out writing Buffy the Vampire Slayer and Terminator romantic fanfiction before spinning off into her own fantastic worlds with bitey MCs and heart wrenching climaxes as well as other errr climaxes...

Holly is a Colorado girl to her core but is only outdoorsy in that she likes drinking on patios in Denver.

She lives with her ever-supportive husband and surly house rabbits who supervise this writer, to make sure she doesn't spend all of her time watching Buffy reruns.

For more sample chapters, news, and more, visit www. hollyroberds.com

Made in United States
Troutdale, OR
05/26/2024

20144952R00216